DAVID BALDACCI

Stone Cold

PAN BOOKS

First published 2007 by Hachette Book Group, USA

First published in Great Britain 2007 by Macmillan

This paperback edition published 2011 by Pan Books
an imprint of Pan Macmillan, a division of Macmillan Publishers Limited
Pan Macmillan, 20 New Wharf Road, London N1 9RR
Basingstoke and Oxford
Associated companies throughout the world
www.panmacmillan.com

ISBN 978-1-4472-2835-6

1 3 5 7 9 8 6 4 2

A CIP catalogue record for this book is available from the British Library.

Printed and bound in the UK by CPI Group (UK) Ltd, Croydon, CR0 4YY

Stone Cold

David Baldacci is the internationally acclaimed author of more than 20 bestselling novels. With his books published in at least 45 different languages, and with over 90 million copies in print, he is one of the world's favourite storytellers. His family foundation, the Wish You Well Foundation, a non-profit organization, works to eliminate illiteracy across America. Still a resident of his native Virginia, he invites you to visit him at www.DavidBaldacci.com, and his foundation at www.WishYouWellFoundation.org, and to look into its programme to spread books across America at www.FeedingBodyandMind.com.

Also by David Baldacci

The Camel Club series

The Camel Club
The Collectors
Divine Justice
Hell's Corner

Sean King and Michelle Maxwell series

Split Second
Hour Game
Simple Genius
First Family
The Sixth Man

Shaw series

The Whole Truth
Deliver Us From Evil

Other novels

Absolute Power
Total Control
The Winner
The Simple Truth
Saving Faith
Wish You Well
Last Man Standing
The Christmas Train
True Blue

Critical acclaim for David Baldacci's novels

'Baldacci inhabits the skin of his creations – tripping us up with unexpected empathy and subtle identification'
Sunday Express

'Compelling . . . finely drawn . . . a page-turner worth losing sleep over'
USA Today

'As expertly plotted as all Baldacci's work'
Sunday Times

'Baldacci cuts everyone's grass – Grisham's, Ludlum's, even Patricia Cornwell's – and more than gets away with it'
People

'A plot strong enough to make the bath go cold around you'
Independent on Sunday

'Yet another winner . . . The excitement builds . . . The plot's many planted bombs explode unpredictably'
New York Times

'As usual, Baldacci delivers the goods in fine style, with thrills and spills aplenty'
Independent on Sunday

'Brilliant plotting, heart-grabbing action
and characters to die for'
Daily Mail

'Baldacci excels at making the improbable believable . . . [his] careful plotting and confident depictions of national security procedures make this a thinking man's thriller'
Publishers Weekly

'Another tightly plotted thriller'
Daily Mirror

'Sizzling'
Daily Express

'A compelling, intelligent thriller'
Belfast Telegraph

'I defy you to begin this book
and leave it unfinished'
Sunday Express

'Baldacci's plotting, as ever,
is formidably accomplished'
Sunday Times

To Bernard Mason,
steel true, blade straight

and

To the memory of Frank L. Jennings,
who meant so much to so many

1

Harry Finn rose as usual at six-thirty, made coffee, let the dog out into the fenced backyard for its morning constitutional, showered, shaved, woke the kids for school and oversaw that complicated operation for the next half hour as breakfasts were gulped, backpacks and shoes grabbed and arguments started and settled. His wife joined him, looking sleepy but nonetheless game for another day as a mother/chauffeur of three, including a precocious, independent-minded teenage boy.

Harry Finn was in his thirties with still boyish features and a pair of clear blue eyes that missed nothing. He'd married young and loved his wife and three children and even held sincere affection toward the family dog, a floppy-eared golden Labradoodle named George. Finn was an inch over six feet tall, with a long-limbed, wiry build ideally suited for speed and endurance. He was dressed in his usual faded jeans and shirttail-out clothing. And with round eyeglasses on and his intelligent, introspective expression, he looked like an accountant who enjoyed listening to Aerosmith after a day of crunching numbers. Although he was amazingly athletic, living by his wits was actually how he put bread on the table and iPods in his kids' ears, and he was very good at his work. Indeed, there were very few people who could do what Harry Finn could. And live.

He kissed his wife good-bye, hugged his kids, even the teenager, grabbed a duffel bag that he'd placed near the front door the night before, slid into his Toyota Prius and drove to National Airport on the Potomac River right outside of Washington, D.C. Its official name had been changed to Ronald Reagan Washington National Airport, but to the locals it would be forever simply National. Finn parked in one of the lots near the main terminal building, whose chief architectural feature was a series of connected domes copied from Thomas Jefferson's beloved Monticello. Bag in hand, he trudged across a skywalk into the sleek interior of the airport. Inside a restroom stall he opened his duffel, pulled on a heavy blue jacket with reflective stripes on the sleeves and a pair of blue workpants, slid a pair of orange noise mufflers around his neck and clipped the official-looking ID badge onto his jacket.

Employing a standard turnstile crash maneuver, he inserted himself into a herd of airport employees trekking through a "special" security line. Ironically, this line lacked even the cursory level of scrutiny forced on ordinary passengers. Once on the other side of the barrier he bought a cup of coffee and casually followed another airport worker through a secure door to the tarmac area. The man actually held the door open for him.

"What shift you working?" Finn asked the man, who told him.

"I'm just coming on," Finn said. "Which would be okay if I hadn't stayed up for the damn football game."

"Tell me about it," the man agreed.

Finn skittered down the metal steps and walked over to a 737 that was being prepped for a short-haul flight to Detroit with continuing service to Seattle. He passed several people along the way, including a fuel man, two baggage loaders and a mechanic inspecting the wheels of the Michigan-bound plane. No one confronted him because he looked and acted as though he had every right to be there. He made his way around the aircraft as he finished his coffee.

He next walked over to an Airbus A320 that would be on its way to Florida in about an hour. A baggage train was parked next to it. In one practiced motion, Finn pulled the small package from his jacket and slipped it into a side pocket of one of the bags stacked on the train. Then he knelt next to the plane's rear wheels and pretended to check out its tire tread. Again, people around him took no notice because Harry Finn exuded an air of a man perfectly at home in his surroundings. A minute later he was chatting up one of the ground crew, analyzing the prospects of the Washington Redskins and the deplorable state of employment for those toiling in the aviation industry.

"Everyone except the head honchos," Finn said. "Those bastards are printing money."

"You got that right," the other man said, and the two did a little knuckle smack to seal their solemn agreement on the disgusting greed of the rich and the ruthless who ruled the not-so-friendly skies.

Finn noted that the rear cargo hatch of the Detroit flight was now open. He waited until the handlers left with their train of luggage carts to fetch the bags and then climbed up on the lift parked there. He slipped into the cargo hold and inserted himself into his hiding place. He'd already picked it by studying interior cargo schematics of the 737 series, which were readily available if one knew where to look, and Finn clearly did. He'd also learned from open source research on the Internet that this plane was only going to be half full so his added weight in the rear would not be an issue.

While he lay curled in his hiding place the plane was loaded with fat bags and stressed passengers, and then it was wheels up to Detroit. Finn rode comfortably in the pressurized cargo hold, although it *was* a bit cooler here than in the main cabin and he was glad of the thick jacket he wore. About an hour after takeoff the plane landed and taxied to the gate. The cargo door was opened a few minutes later and the baggage offloaded. Finn patiently waited for a bit after the last bag was removed before he came out of concealment and peered through the open aft door. There were people around, but none looking his way. He climbed off the plane and dropped to the tarmac. A minute later he noticed a pair of security officers heading in his direction, sipping coffee and gabbing. He reached in his pocket, pulled out a lunch bag, took out a ham sandwich and began eating it as he walked away from the plane.

When the two guards passed him he nodded. "You regular coffee drinkers or is that half-caf caramel latte with a twist and four shots of who the hell knows what?" He grinned with his mouth full of ham sandwich. The two cops chuckled at his remark as he walked off.

He entered the terminal, went to a restroom, took off his jacket, ear mufflers and ID badge, made a quick phone call and marched to the airport security office.

"I put a bomb in a bag that was loaded onto an A320 at National Airport this morning," he explained to the officer on duty. "And I just rode in the cargo hold of a 737 from D.C. I could've downed the plane anytime I wanted."

The stunned officer was not wearing his weapon, so he leaped over the desk to tackle him. Finn neatly sidestepped this attack, and the fellow sprawled on the floor screaming for help. Other officers poured out of the back room and advanced on Finn, guns drawn. Yet Finn had pulled out his credentialing letter before the pistols had even appeared.

At that instant the door to the office flew open and three men strode in, their federal badges held high like the scepters of kings.

"Homeland Security," one of the men barked at the guards. He pointed at Harry Finn. "This man works for us. And somebody's in a shitload of trouble."

2

"Great job, Harry, as usual," the head of the Homeland Security team said later, clapping Finn on the back. People had been screamed at and reports filed, e-mails fired off and cell phone batteries sucked dry as the clear lapses in airport security revealed by Harry Finn had been broadcast to all appropriate parties. Ordinarily, Finn would not have been tasked by the Department of Homeland Security, or DHS as it is commonly known, to execute an airport security breach because the FAA kept a stranglehold on that field. Finn suspected it was because the FAA boys were well aware of how many flaws there were in the system and didn't want anyone outside their domain to realize it as well. However, folks at DHS had managed to get authorization to do this one, and picked him to pull the trigger.

Finn wasn't an employee of DHS. The firm he worked for had been retained by the agency to test the security strength of both government and sensitive private facilities around the country. They did this using a hands-on, head-on approach: They tried to breach the places any way they could. DHS did a lot of this type of outsourcing. They had roughly a $40 billion annual budget and had to throw the money somewhere. Finn's firm got a little out of this business, but then even a little slice of billions was a nice revenue stream.

Normally Finn would have left the airport without revealing what he'd done and let the chips fall. However, DHS, obviously fed up with the state of airport security and no doubt wanting to make a robust statement, had instructed him to go in and confess so they could dramatically storm in after him and make a big splash. The media would be salivating and the airline industry reeling, and Homeland Security would look very efficient and heroic. Finn never got in the middle of that. He did not give interviews and his name was never in the newspapers. He just quietly did his job.

He *would* conduct a follow-up briefing for the airport security personnel he'd just run rings around, trying to be both encouraging and diplomatic in assessing their performance or lack thereof and recommending changes in the future. Sometimes the briefing sessions were the most dangerous things he did. People could get very ticked off after finding out they'd been both snookered *and* embarrassed. In the past Finn literally had had to fight his way out of a room.

The DHS man added, "We'll get these people in shape somehow, some way."

"I'm not sure it'll be in my lifetime, sir," Finn said.

"You can wing it back to D.C. with us," the man said. "We have an agency Falcon standing by."

"Thanks, but I have someone here I've been meaning to visit. I'm going back tomorrow."

"Right. Until next time."

Until next time, Finn thought.

The men left and Finn rented a car and drove into the Detroit suburbs, stopping at a strip mall. From his knapsack he pulled out a map and a file with a photo in it. The man in the picture was sixty-three years of age, bald with several distinguishing tattoos, and went by the name Dan Ross.

It wasn't his real name, but then neither was Harry Finn's.

3

Arthritis. And on top of that the damn lupus. They were a lovely duo, perfectly synchronized to make his life a painfully throbbing hell. Every bone creaked, every solitary tendon shrieked. Each movement sent a mule kick right to his gut and yet he kept going, because if you stopped, you stopped for good. He downed a couple of potent pills he wasn't supposed to have and plunked a ball cap on his hairless, pale-skinned head, pulling the brim low over his eyes and then donning sunglasses. He never liked people seeing what he was looking at. And he never wanted people to get a good look at him.

He eased himself into his car and drove to the store. Along the way the meds kicked in and he felt okay, or at least he would for a couple hours.

"Thank you, Mr. Ross," the sales clerk said, glancing at the name on the credit card before handing it back along with his purchases. "You have a good day."

"I don't have good days anymore," Dan Ross replied. "I only have days *left*."

The clerk glanced at the hat covering the hairless head.

"Not cancer," Ross said, reading the man's thoughts. "Might be better if it was. Quicker, you know what I mean?"

The clerk, who was in his early twenties and of course still immortal, didn't look like he knew what Ross meant at all. He gave an awkward nod and turned to help another customer.

Ross left the store and debated what to do next. He had no money worries. Uncle Sam had taken care of him in his old, busted-up age. Pension was first-rate, health care coverage gold-plated; that was one thing the feds did well. One of a *short* list was his opinion. Now he just had time. That was his chief concern. What now? Home to do nothing? Or lunch at the local deli where he could fill his belly, watch ESPN and flirt with the pretty waitresses who wouldn't give him the time of day? Yet he could still dream, couldn't he? Dream of the days when the ladies gave him far more than simply time.

Not much of a life, he had to admit. He thought this as his gaze discreetly eased in all directions. Even to this day he could not overcome the impulse to check whether he was being followed. You got that way when people were always trying to kill you. God, he had loved it, though. Beat the hell out of the deli-or-home bullshit debate every miserable day of this screwed-up dilemma playing out as his "golden" years.

Over three decades ago he'd been in a different country every month. Every month during the busy season anyway. Seen the world on a wing, a prayer and a weapon of choice, he'd always said. He allowed himself a nostalgia-fueled smile. That's all he had now, memories. And the damn lupus. *I guess there is a God after all.* Pretty damn shitty to find out now.

Unfortunately for Ross, while his observation skills were good, they were no longer infallible. Down the block in his rental car Harry Finn sat and studied the inimitable Mr. Ross. *Where to, Danny? Home or the deli? Deli or home? What a long fall it's been for you.*

During the times Finn had observed this internal debate, Dan Ross had picked the deli over home about three-quarters of the time. This ratio held true today as he turned and walked down the street and into the Edsel Deli, going strong since 1954, the sign over the door said, making it far more popular than the dismal car after which it was named.

Ross would be in there eating and watching every move of the cute waitresses for at least an hour. Then it was twenty minutes by car back to his house. After that he would sit out in his backyard, read the newspaper, and then it was time to go in, take a nap, fix a modest dinner, watch TV, play Solitaire by the small table near the front window with the lamp illuminating the cards, and then the man would call it a night. By nine o'clock the lights in the small bungalow would go out, and Dan Ross would fall asleep and wake up the next day to do it all over again. Finn methodically counted off in his head these ticks of the older man's threadbare life.

After Finn had tracked Ross to this town, he'd made several trips here to learn the man's routine. This surveillance had enabled him to concoct the perfect plan to complete his task.

About five minutes before Ross would appear from the Edsel, Finn got out of his car, strode across the street, glanced in the window of the deli, and located Ross at his usual table in the rear, studying the bill he'd just been handed. Finn walked unhurriedly down the street to where Ross' car was parked. In two minutes he was back in his rental. Three minutes after that Ross emerged from the restaurant, slowly edged down the street, climbed in his car and drove off.

Finn left in the opposite direction.

Ross went through his usual litany of triviality that evening, finishing it off with three fingers of Johnnie Walker Black and, ignoring all label warnings, combining it with a potent pop of meds for the pain. He barely made it to his bed before the paralysis set in. At first he assumed it was the drugs, and he actually welcomed the numbing feeling. Yet as he lay on the bed it occurred to him with slight panic that it might be the lupus moving to a higher, more aggressive stage. When he suddenly found it difficult to breathe he knew it was something else altogether. Heart attack? But where was the elephant on the chest, the shooting pain down the left arm? Stroke? He could still think, still talk. He said a few words and none of them constituted a mumble. His face didn't seem lopsided. He had felt no pain beforehand, other than his usual. That was the problem; he could feel nothing in his limbs now, nothing at all. His gaze ran down his arm until it reached his left hand. He tried to rub the fingers together but his mind's command apparently was not reaching the digits.

Yet earlier there *had* been something on his fingers. It had felt slick, like Vaseline. You could rub and rub and never get it to feel dry. He had washed his hands when he got home, and that seemed to do the trick. The fingers didn't feel slick anymore. He didn't know if it was due to the soap and water or to whatever it was having evaporated.

Then the truth hit him like a .50 caliber round. *Or absorbed. As in absorbed into my body.*

Where had his fingers become wet? He strained his mind to think. Not this morning. Not at the store, or the deli. After that? Perhaps. Getting in the car. The car handle! If he could have managed it, Ross would've sat up in a Eureka! moment. But he couldn't manage it. He could now barely breathe. All that emitted from his mouth was a sort of shortened wheeze. The door handle of his car had been slicked with something that was now killing him. He eyed the phone on the nightstand. Two feet away and it might as well have been in China for all the good it would do him now.

In the darkness the figure appeared beside his bed. The man wore no disguise; Ross could make out his features even in the weak light. He was young and normal-looking. Ross had seen thousands of faces just like that and had paid little attention to any of them. His job had not involved normal; it had encompassed extraordinary. He couldn't imagine how someone like this man had managed to kill him.

As Ross' breathing became more labored, the fellow pulled something from his pocket and held it up to him. It was a photo, but Ross couldn't make out who was in the picture. Realizing this, Harry Finn flicked on a small penlight and shone it on the photo. Ross' gaze ran up and down the image. Still recognition didn't come until Finn said the name.

"Now you know," Finn said quietly. "Now you know."

He put the photo away and stood silently looking down at Ross as the paralysis continued to wend its way through. He kept his gaze on the other man until the chest gave one last erratic heave and the pupils turned glassy.

Two minutes later Harry Finn was walking through the woods at the back of Ross' house. The next morning he was on a plane, this time in the main cabin. He landed, drove home, kissed his wife, played with his dog and picked the kids up from school. That night they all went out to dinner to celebrate his youngest child, eight-year-old Susie, being named to portray a talking tree in a school play.

Around midnight, Harry Finn ventured downstairs to the kitchen, where George the faithful Labradoodle rose from his soft bed and greeted him. As he sat at the kitchen table and stroked the dog, Finn mentally crossed Dan Ross off his list.

Now he focused on the next name: *Carter Gray*, the former chief of America's intelligence empire.

4

Annabelle Conroy stretched out her long legs and watched the landscape drift by outside the window of the Amtrak Acela train car. She almost never took the train anywhere; her ride was typically at 39,000 feet where she popped peanuts, sipped watered-down seven-dollar cocktails, and dreamt up the next con. Today she was on the train because her companion, Milton Farb, would not set foot on anything that had the capacity and intent to leave the ground.

"Flying is the safest way to travel, Milton," she'd informed him.

"Not if you're on a plane that's in a death spiral. Then your chances of dying are roughly one hundred percent. And I don't like those odds."

It was hard to argue with geniuses, Annabelle had discovered. Still, Milton, the man with the photographic memory and a budding talent for brilliantly lying to people, had done good work. They had left Boston after a successful job. The item was back where it needed to be and no one had thought to call the cops. In Annabelle's world of high-stakes cons that was equal to perfection.

Thirty minutes later, as Amtrak's only bullet train service wound its way down the East Coast and pulled into a station, Annabelle glanced out the window and involuntarily shuddered when the conductor announced they were arriving in Newark, New Jersey. Jersey was Jerry Bagger land, although thankfully the Acela train didn't stop at Atlantic City where the maniacal casino boss had his empire. If it did Annabelle wouldn't have been on it.

Yet she was smart enough to realize that Jerry Bagger had every motivation to leave Atlantic City and come looking for her wherever she might be. When you ripped a guy like that off for $40 million, assuming that Bagger would do his best to tear thousands of pieces of your flesh off one at a time was hardly irrational thinking.

She glanced over at Milton, who looked about eighteen with his boyish face and longish hair. In reality the man was pushing fifty. He was on his computer, doing something that neither Annabelle nor anyone else below the level of genius would be able to understand.

Bored, Annabelle rose, went to the café car and purchased a beer and a bag of chips. On the way back she spied a *New York Times* lying discarded on one of the café tables. She sat down on a stool, drank her beer and munched her chips as she idly turned the pages looking for that one bit of information that might spark her next adventure. Once she got back to Washington, D.C., she had some decisions to make, chiefly whether to stay put or flee the country. She knew what her answer *should* be. A no-name island in the South Pacific was the safest place for her right now, where she could just wait out the tsunami named Jerry. Bagger was in his mid-sixties and her long con against him had without a doubt considerably raised the man's blood pressure. With a little luck he'd soon croak from a heart attack and she would be scot-free. However, she couldn't count on that. With Jerry you just had to figure that all your luck would turn out to be bad.

It shouldn't have been a difficult decision and yet it was. She had grown close, or as close as someone like her could get, to an oddball collection of men who called themselves the Camel Club. She smiled to herself as she thought about the foursome, one of whom was named Caleb Shaw and worked at the Library of Congress. He reminded her remarkably of the cowardly lion from *The Wizard of Oz*. Then her smile faded. Oliver Stone, the head of this little band of miscreants, was something altogether more. He must've had one hell of a past, Annabelle thought—a history that might even surpass hers in the unusual and extraordinary department, and that was saying something. She didn't know if she could say good-bye to Oliver Stone. She doubted she would ever run across another one like him.

Her gaze flicked up at a young man passing by who did not attempt to hide his admiration for her tall, curvy figure, long blonde hair, and thirty-six-year-old face that, if it didn't actually hit the "wow" level, came awfully close. This was so despite a small, fishhook-shaped scar under her eye; a present from her father, Paddy Conroy, the best short con artist of his generation, and the world's worst father, at least in his only child's estimation.

"Hey," the young man said. With his lean physique, tousled hair and expensive clothes that were designed to appear cheap and grungy, he looked like an Abercrombie & Fitch ad. She quickly sized him up as a privileged college kid with far more money than was healthy and the insufferably cocky attitude to match.

"Hey back at you," she said and returned to her newspaper.

"Where you headed to?" he asked, sitting down next to her.

"Not where you're headed."

"But you don't know where I'm going," he said in a playful tone.

"That's sort of the point, right?"

He either didn't get her point or didn't care. "I go to Harvard."

"Wow, I never would've guessed that."

"But I'm from Philly. The Main Line. My parents have an estate there."

"Wow again. It's nice to have parents who have estates," she said in a clearly uninterested tone.

"It's also nice to have parents who are out of the country half the time. I'm having a little party there tonight. It's going to be a wild ride. You interested?"

Annabelle could feel the guy's gaze running down her. *Okay, here we go again.* She knew she shouldn't, but with guys like this she just couldn't seem to help herself.

She closed the newspaper. "I don't know. When you say wild, how wild do you mean?"

"How wild do you want it to be?" She could see him forming the word "baby," but he apparently thought better of using it, at least so soon in the conversation.

"I hate being disappointed."

He touched her arm. "I don't think you'll be disappointed."

She smiled and patted his hand. "So what are we talking about here? Booze and sex?"

"A given." He squeezed her arm. "Hey, I'm up in first class, why don't you join me?"

"You have anything other than booze and sex going on?"

"You like to get into the details?"

"It's all in the details, uh . . ."

"Steve. Steve Brinkman." He gave a practiced little chuckle. "You know, one of *those* Brinkmans. My father's the vice chairman of one of the biggest banks in the country."

"FYI, Steve, if you've just got coke at this party, and I'm not talking the soft drink, that would definitely disappoint me."

"What are you looking for? I'm sure I can get it. I've got connections."

"Goofballs, Dollies, Hog, with artillery to do it right, and no lemonade, lemonade always pisses me off," she added, referring to crap-quality drugs.

"Wow, you know your stuff," Steve said, nervously looking around at the other people in the café car.

"You ever chased the dragon, Steve?" she asked.

"Uh, no."

"It's a funky way to inhale heroin. It'll give you the greatest pop in the world, if it doesn't kill you."

He removed his hand from her arm. "Doesn't sound very smart."

"How old are you?"

"Twenty. Why?"

"I like my men a little younger than that. I find that when a guy reaches eighteen he's left his best ball-banging behind. So you gonna have any minors at this party?"

He rose. "Maybe this wasn't such a good idea."

"Oh, I'm not picky. It can be guys or girls. I mean, when you're shit-faced on meth, who cares?"

"Okay, I'm leaving now," Steve said hurriedly.

"One more thing." Annabelle took out her wallet and flashed a fake badge at him. She said in a low voice, "You recognize the DEA insignia, Steve? For Drug Enforcement Agency?"

"Omigod!"

"And now that you've told me about mommy and daddy Brinkman's estate on the Main Line, I'm sure my strike team will have no problem finding the place. That is if you're still intending on having a *wild* party."

"Please, I swear to God, I was just . . ." He put a hand out to steady himself. Annabelle seized it and gave his fingers a hard squeeze.

"Go back to Harvard, Stevie, and when you graduate, you can screw up your life however you want to. But in the future just be careful what you say to strange women on trains."

She watched him hurry down the aisle and disappear safely back into first class.

Annabelle finished her beer and idly read the last couple pages of the newspaper. Now it was her turn to have the blood drain from her face.

An American tentatively identified as Anthony Wallace had been found nearly beaten to death at a Portugal seaside estate. Three other people had been found murdered at the home on a remote stretch of shoreline. Robbery was thought to be the motive. Although Wallace was still alive, he was in a coma after suffering extensive brain injuries and doctors were not hopeful for a recovery.

Annabelle tore out the story and walked unsteadily back to her seat.

Jerry Bagger had gotten to Tony, one of her partners in the con. An estate? She'd expressly told Tony to lay low and not flash the cash. He hadn't listened and now he was brain dead. Jerry typically didn't leave any witnesses behind.

But what had Jerry managed to beat out of Tony? She knew the answer to that question. *Everything.*

Milton stopped typing on his computer and gazed up at her. "You okay?"

Annabelle didn't answer. As the train sailed back to D.C. she looked out the window but didn't see the Jersey countryside. Her confidence evaporated, she now only saw graphic details of her coming death, courtesy of Jerry Bagger.

5

Oliver Stone managed to lift the old, mossy tombstone to an upright position and packed dirt around it to keep it there. He sat back on his haunches and wiped his brow. He had a portable radio beside him on the ground turned to the local all-news station. Stone craved information like others needed oxygen. As he listened to the radio he got an unexpected jolt. There would be an awards ceremony at the White House that very afternoon where none other than Carter Gray, recently retired chief of the nation's intelligence agencies, was scheduled to receive the Presidential Medal of Freedom, the nation's highest civilian honor. Gray had served his country with distinction for nearly four decades, the announcer read, and quoted the president as saying that Carter Gray was a man that all of America should be proud of; a true patriot and public servant.

Stone didn't exactly agree with this assessment. In fact, he'd been the reason Carter Gray had abruptly resigned from his post as the nation's intelligence czar.

Stone thought to himself, *If only the president knew*

that the man he's going to be presenting that medal to is the same man who was prepared to put a bullet through his head. The country would never be ready for *that* truth.

He looked at his watch. The dead could certainly exist without him for a little while. An hour later, showered and dressed in his best clothes, which consisted of secondhand issue from Goodwill, he walked out of his cottage, where he was caretaker of Mt. Zion Cemetery, a stop on the Underground Railroad and the final resting place of notable African Americans from the nineteenth century. The trip from the outskirts of Georgetown to the White House was eaten up quickly by the long strides of Stone's lean six-foot-two-inch frame.

At age sixty-one, he had lost very little of his energy and vigor. With his close-cropped white hair, he looked like a retired Marine drill sergeant. He was still a commander of sorts, though his ragtag regiment called the Camel Club was completely unofficial. It consisted of himself and three others: Caleb Shaw, Reuben Rhodes and Milton Farb.

And yet Stone might have to add another name to the roster, Annabelle Conroy. She had nearly died along with the rest of them in their last adventure. The truth was, Annabelle was as nimble, capable and nervy a person as Stone had ever met. Yet his gut told him the woman, who was attending to a piece of unfinished business with Milton Farb's help, would be leaving them soon. Someone was after her, Stone knew, someone Annabelle actually feared. And under those circumstances sometimes the smartest move was to run. Stone understood that concept very well.

The White House was dead ahead. He would never be allowed to enter the hallowed front gates and lacked even the right to stand on that coveted side of Pennsylvania Avenue. What he could do was wait in Lafayette Park across the street. He used to have a tent there until the Secret Service recently made him take it down. Yet freedom of speech was still alive and well in America and thus his banner had remained. Unfurled between two pieces of rebar stuck in the ground, it read, "I want the truth." So did a *few* other people in this town, it was rumored. To date, Stone had never heard of anyone actually finding it within the confines of the world capital of spin and deceit.

He passed the time chatting with a couple of uniformed Secret Service agents he knew. When the White House gates started to open, he broke off his conversation and watched the black sedan coming out. He couldn't see through the tinted glass, but for some reason he knew that Carter Gray was inside the Town Car. Perhaps it was the man's smell.

His hunch proved right when the window came down and he found himself eye to eye with the ex–intelligence chief, new Medal of Freedom winner and major Oliver Stone hater.

As the car slowed to make the turn onto the street, Gray's wide, bespectacled face stared impassively at him. Then, smiling, Gray held up his big, shiny medal so Stone could see it.

Not having a medal of his own, Stone opted for giving Gray the finger. The man's smile turned to a snarl and the window zipped back up.

Stone turned and walked back to his cemetery feeling the trip had been damn well worth it.

When Carter Gray's car turned onto 17th Street, another vehicle followed it. Harry Finn had driven into D.C. that morning. He too had heard of Gray's big day at the White House and like Oliver Stone had come down to see the man. While Stone had ventured here to show defiance to a man he loathed, Finn had come to continue devising a suitable way to kill Gray.

The drive took them out of D.C. and into Maryland, up to the waterfront city of Annapolis situated on the Chesapeake Bay. It was famous for, among other things, its crab cakes and for being home to the U.S. Naval Academy. Gray had recently traded his remote Virginia farm for an isolated place on a cliff overlooking the bay. Since he was no longer with the government his security detail was much smaller than it had been. Yet because he was a former director of Central Intelligence he still received daily briefings. And he had two guards assigned to him because his past work had angered a number of America's enemies, who would love nothing better than to put a slug right between Gray's close-set eyes.

Finn knew killing Gray would be far more difficult than bagging someone like Dan Ross. Because of the complexities, this was one of countless trips he had made reconnoitering Gray. Each time he had used a different vehicle rented under fake names and worn disguises to avoid any profiling. And even if he lost the Town Car in traffic he knew where it was going. He only broke off the tail when the car pulled onto a private gravel road and headed toward Gray's house and the cliffs, where thirty feet down the waters of the bay boomed against solid rock.

Later, using long-range binoculars while perched in a tree, Finn saw the thing in the rear of Gray's house that would enable him to kill the man. He actually smiled as the plan swiftly came together in his mind.

That night he took his daughter, Susie, to swim practice. As he sat in the bleachers and proudly watched her small body glide in perfect form across the pool, he imagined the last few seconds of Carter Gray's life. It all would be worth it.

He drove his daughter home, helped put her and her ten-year-old brother Patrick to bed, had an argument with his teenager and then shot hoops with the boy in the driveway of their home until both were sweating and laughing. Later, he made love to his wife, Amanda, whom everyone called Mandy, and, restless, got up around midnight and packed school lunches for the next day. He also signed a permission slip for his oldest, David, to go on an upcoming field trip to the U.S. Capitol and other downtown sights. David would be attending high school next year and Finn and Mandy had taken him to several school open houses. David liked math and science. He would probably end up being an engineer, Finn thought. Mechanically inclined too, Finn had almost gone that route before his life had taken a bit of a detour. He'd joined the navy, and quickly worked himself to an elite status.

Finn was a former Navy SEAL with special ops experience and combat duty on his résumé. And he possessed unique foreign-language skills from immersion school in California, where he'd spent a chunk of his life learning Arabic, and later acquired the dialects the school hadn't taught him when on the ground in that part of the world. With his current job he traveled a good deal but he was also home a lot. He almost never missed a sporting or major school event. He was there for his children in the hope that they would be there for him later. That's the best a parent could shoot for, he felt.

He finished the lunches, went to his small den, closed the door and began drawing up firm plans for Carter Gray. Out of practicality it would not mirror his confrontation with Dan Ross. Yet Finn had never been one to pound a round peg into a square hole.

Even killers had to be flexible; in fact, perhaps the most flexible of all.

Finn's gaze settled on the pictures of his three kids that sat on his desk front and center. Birth and death. It was the same for everyone. You started breathing on one end and stopped on the other. What you did in between defined who and what you were. Yet Harry Finn realized he would be awfully difficult to categorize. Some days even he didn't truly understand it.

6

The rental car pulled up to the gates of the cemetery as Oliver Stone was finishing some work. As he brushed off his pants and glanced that way, he had a feeling of déjà vu. She had done this to him before, but had eventually come back. Somehow Stone didn't think the lady would let that happen again. He would have to see what he could do about that, because he didn't want to lose her.

Annabelle Conroy got out of the car and walked through the open gates. Her long black coat flapped open in the wind, revealing a brown knee-length skirt and boots; her hair was hidden underneath a wide-brimmed floppy hat. Stone closed the door on the small storage shed near his cottage and padlocked it.

He said, "Milton told me your trip to Boston was a great success. I don't believe I've heard the words 'brilliant,' 'amazing' and 'unflappable' used that many times in describing a person. I hope you recognize yourself."

"Milton would make a great con. Not that I'd recommend that life to anyone I actually cared about."

"He also said you looked troubled on the way back. Did something happen?"

She glanced at his cottage. "Can we talk inside?"

Describing the interior of Stone's cottage as spartan would have been generous indeed. A few chairs, a number of odd tables, sagging shelves of books in multiple languages and an old worm-eaten partner's desk, together with a small kitchen area, bedroom and tiny bath all outlined in roughly six hundred square feet constituted the man's entire domicile footprint.

They sat near the empty fireplace on the two most comfortable chairs, meaning the only ones with padding.

"I came here to tell you I'm leaving. And after everything that's happened, I feel like I owe you an explanation," she said.

"You don't owe me anything, Annabelle."

"Don't say that!" she snapped. "This is hard enough as it is. So hear me out, Oliver."

He sat back, crossed his arms and waited.

She pulled the newspaper article from her jacket pocket and passed it across to him. "Read this first."

"Who is this Anthony Wallace?" he asked after he'd finished.

"Someone I worked with," she said vaguely.

"Someone you worked a *con* with?"

She nodded absently.

"Three people killed?"

Annabelle rose and started pacing. "That's the thing

that's driving me crazy. I told Tony to lay low and not flash the cash. But what did he do? He did the exact opposite and now three innocent people are dead who shouldn't be."

Stone tapped the paper. "Well, from the looks of it your Mr. Wallace will soon be making it a quartet."

"But Tony wasn't innocent. He knew exactly what he was getting into."

"And what exactly was that?"

She stopped pacing. "Oliver, I like you and I respect you, but this is a little . . ."

"Illegal? I hope you realize that comes as no great shock to me."

"And that doesn't bother you?"

"I doubt anything you could have possibly done would surpass what I've seen in life."

She cocked her head. "Seen, or done?"

"Who's after you and why?"

"That's no concern of yours."

"It is if you want me to help you."

"I'm not looking for help. I just wanted you to understand why I have to leave."

"Do you really think you'll be safer on your own?"

"I think you and the others will be a lot safer without me around."

"That's not what I asked you."

"I've been in plenty of jams before and I've always managed to get myself out of them."

"Out of a jam this tight?" He glanced at the paper. "This person doesn't seem to fool around."

"Tony made a mistake, a big one. I don't intend on doing that. I lay low, for as long as it takes, and as far away from here as I can get."

"But you don't know what Tony might have told them. Did he have any information that could be used to track you down?"

Annabelle perched on the edge of the fireplace's raised hearth. "Maybe," she said tersely. "Probably," she corrected.

"Then all the more reason for you not to go this alone. We can help protect you."

"Oliver, I appreciate the sentiment but you have no idea what you're getting into. Not only is this guy the scum of the earth with a lot of money and muscle behind him, but on top of that, what I did was illegal. You'd be harboring a criminal on top of risking your life."

"Not the first time on either count," he replied.

"Who *are* you?" she asked pointedly.

"You know all you need to know about me."

"And I thought *I* was a world-class liar."

"We're wasting time, tell me about him."

She rubbed her long, thin fingers together, drew a deep breath and said, "His name's Jerry Bagger. He owns the Pompeii Casino, the biggest in Atlantic City. He was run out of Vegas years ago because he was a whack job. He would literally rip out your intestines if you tried to steal a five-dollar casino chip."

"And how much did you, um, *relieve* him of?"

"Why do you need to know?"

"It's important to know how much motivation the man has to come after you."

"Forty million dollars. Think that'll motivate him?"

"I'm impressed. It doesn't sound like Bagger is a man easily conned."

Annabelle allowed herself a brief smile. "It was one of my better scams, I have to admit. But Jerry is also very dangerous, and not entirely sane. If he even thinks someone is helping me, that person might as well be me. He'll get the same treatment: death by pain, great pain."

"You have no reason to believe that he's aware you're in D.C.?"

"No. Tony had no idea I'd be coming here. Neither did the others."

"So there are others on the con team? Bagger might get to them."

"He might. But like I said, they don't know I'm here either."

Stone slowly nodded. "Of course, we can't be sure of what Bagger really knows or doesn't know at this point. I'm sure that the public details of our little adventure involving the Library of Congress didn't include your name or picture. However, we can't be absolutely certain there isn't something out there that would help him track you down."

"My original plan was to head to the South Pacific."

Stone shook his head. "Fugitives always head to the South Pacific. That's probably the first place Bagger will check."

"You're kidding me, right?"

"Partly, yes. But only partly."

"So you really think I should stay here?"

"I do. I'm assuming you've covered your tracks well. No trails leading here, names, travel arrangements, phones, friends?"

She shook her head. "Coming here was pretty much a spur-of-the-moment thing. And all under an alias."

"The smart thing to do would be to find out, as quietly as possible, what Bagger knows."

"Oliver, you can't possibly get anywhere near that guy. It would be suicide."

"I know how to look, so let me start looking."

"I've never asked anyone to help me before."

"It took me decades before I could ask anyone to help me."

She looked puzzled. "But you're glad you did?"

"It's the only reason I'm alive right now. Move out of your hotel and into another one. I'm assuming you have money."

"Cash is not a problem." She rose and started to the door but turned back. "Oliver, I appreciate this."

"Let's hope you can say that when it's all over."

7

"Do you think I'm stupid?" screamed Jerry Bagger. The casino chief wedged his arm against the other man's windpipe as he mashed him against the wall in Bagger's luxurious office on the twenty-third floor of the Pompeii Casino. The drapes were closed. Bagger always closed the drapes when he was either going to bang a willing lady on his couch or kick the shit out of somebody who deserved it. These matters should always be kept private, he felt. It was a point of honor with him.

The man didn't answer Bagger's question chiefly because he couldn't breathe. However, Bagger wasn't waiting for a reply. His first blow caught the guy flush on the nose and broke it. The second one knocked a front tooth out. The man fell to the floor weeping. For good measure Bagger kicked him in the gut. That made the beaten fellow vomit on the carpet. As the puke spread across the expensive inlaid wool Bagger's own security force had to pull their furious boss off the fallen man before real damage was done.

The guy was carted away, crying and bleeding and

mumbling that he was sorry. Bagger sat down behind his desk and rubbed his cracked knuckles. Glaring at his security chief, he growled, "Bobby, you bring me any more pissants like that one who say they know something about Annabelle Conroy and end up trying to shake me down while feeding me a sack of shit, I swear to God I will kill your mother. And I like your mother but I will kill her. Do you *hear* me!"

The burly black security chief took a step back and swallowed nervously. "Never again, Mr. Bagger. I'm sorry, sir. Really, really sorry."

"Everybody's sorry but nobody's doing a damn thing to get me the bitch, are they?" Bagger roared.

"We thought we had a lead on her. A good one."

"You thought? You thought? Well, maybe you should stop thinking, then."

Bagger hit a button on his desk and the drapes opened. He jumped up and looked out the window. "Forty million bucks she took from me. This could screw up my whole business, you know that? I don't have enough reserves to meet the state regs. You get a government bean counter in here right now looking at my books he could shut me down. Me! You used to be able to pay those assholes off, but now with all this anticorruption and ethical bullshit going around, you can't do that no more. You mark my word, that full disclosure crap is gonna destroy a great country."

"We'll find her, boss, and get the money back," his security chief assured him.

Bagger didn't appear to be listening. Staring down at the street far below, he said, "I see the bitch everywhere. In my dreams, in my food, when I'm shaving there she is in my mirror. Hell, even when I'm taking a leak, her face is in the toilet bowl staring at me. It's driving me nuts!"

He sat on the couch and calmed down. "What's the latest on our boy Tony Wallace?"

"We got somebody on the inside at the hospital in Portugal. Jerk's still in a coma. But even if he comes out of it, there's nothing there. Our source says the guy's a permanent retard."

"If you ask me he was a retard long before we got to him."

"You know, boss, we probably should've just killed him like we did everybody else."

"I gave him my word. He told me what he knew, he got to live; that was the deal. But in my book brain dead means you're still alive. Lots of people live forty, fifty years like that. It's like being a baby until you're eighty. Get fed through a tube, get your ass wiped every day and you play with blocks. Granted, it's not much of a life, but I didn't go back on my word. People can say I'm violent and I got a bad temper and all that crap but they can never point to one time where I ever went back on my word. You know why?"

The security chief shook his head warily, obviously unsure whether his boss wanted an answer or not.

"Because I got standards, that's why. Now get outta here."

Alone, Bagger sat down behind his desk and put his head in his hands. He would never admit this to anyone, but mixed in with all the hatred he had for Annabelle Conroy was a sincere, if grudging, admiration. "Annabelle," he said aloud. "You are without a doubt the greatest con artist in the world. It would've been a pleasure working with you. And you were probably the best piece of ass I've ever put my hand on. So it's too bad you were so stupid as to take me on because now I gotta kill you. I gotta make an example of you. And it's a waste, but that's just the way it's gotta be."

It wasn't just the loss of the forty million that had enraged Bagger. Ever since word of the successful con had leaked out, cheaters had become far more brazen in his casino. Losses had quickly risen. And his competitors and business associates were also not quite as respectful as they had once been, sensing that Bagger was no longer at the top of his game, that he was vulnerable. Calls weren't immediately returned. Action that he could always count on getting didn't always come through now.

"An example," Bagger said again. "To show these assholes that not only am I still at the top, I'm getting stronger every day. And I will find you, lady. I will find you."

8

The contact Oliver Stone proposed using was an honorary member of the Camel Club named Alex Ford, a Secret Service agent. The two men trusted each other fully and Stone knew it was the one place he could turn to for discreet intelligence.

"Does this have something to do with that woman you were working with? Her name was Susan, right?" Alex asked when Stone called and relayed his request.

"It has nothing to do with her," Stone lied. "She's actually leaving town soon. This has to do with something else I'm involved in."

"For a cemetery worker you get around a lot."

"It keeps me young."

"The Bureau can help out too. After what you did for them last time they owe you. When do you need to know?"

"As soon as you can get something."

"Just so you know, I've heard of this Jerry Bagger guy. The Justice Department has been trying to get something on him for a long time."

"I'm sure the attention is well-deserved. Thanks, Alex."

Later that night, Reuben Rhodes and Caleb Shaw visited Stone at his cottage. Caleb was in a high state of indecision.

"They asked me, but I don't know if I should accept or not. I just don't know," he wailed.

"So the Library of Congress wants you to become the director of the Rare Books Division," Stone said. "That sounds like a great promotion, Caleb. What's to decide?"

Caleb said stiffly, "Well, considering the fact that the position became available *only* because the former director was horribly murdered on the premises and the acting director after him suffered a nervous breakdown from what happened there, it *does* give one pause."

Reuben growled, "Hell, Caleb, go for it. I mean, who's going to mess with a fine young buck like you?"

Caleb, who was in his fifties, of medium height and a bit pudgy, with not a trace of athleticism or personal courage, was not amused by this comment.

"You said it *is* more money," Stone reminded him. "In fact a good deal more."

"Yes, but if that only means I can afford a much nicer funeral, I'm not sure I'm interested."

Reuben added gruffly, "But when you die, you die knowing that you have more to leave to your friends.

Now if that's not true comfort, I don't know what is."

"Why I even bother to ask for your opinion I don't know," Caleb said hotly.

Reuben turned his attention to Stone. "You seen Susan lately?"

Only Stone knew Annabelle's real name.

"She came by the other day, but only for a few minutes. She successfully completed her task with Milton. The item is back where it belongs."

"I have to admit," Caleb said. "She did what she said she was going to do."

Reuben said, "Now if I could just get her to go out with me. She keeps having other plans. I'm not sure if she's trying to brush me off or not. But I don't get it. Look at me. What's not to love?"

Reuben was nearly sixty, with a full beard and dark curly hair mixed with gray down to his shoulders. He was six-five with the build of an NFL left tackle. A highly decorated Vietnam War vet and former military intelligence officer, he had burned many professional bridges and nearly succumbed to pills and the bottle before Oliver Stone had brought him back from the edge. He now worked on a loading dock.

"I saw where your 'friend' Carter Gray received the Medal of Freedom," Caleb said after giving Reuben an incredulous look. "Talk about your ironies. If that man had his way you two would be dead and the rest of us would be getting water-dunked in some CIA-run torture chamber."

Reuben roared, "For the hundredth time it's water-*boarding*, not water-dunking."

"Well, whatever it is, he's a nasty man."

"He's actually a man who believes his way is the right way, and he's certainly not alone in that belief," Stone said. "I went down to the White House and saw him off after he received his award."

"You went down to the White House?" Caleb exclaimed.

"Well, he showed me his medal and I sort of *waved* at him."

"What, you two are now best buds?" Reuben added with a snort. "From a man who tried to kill you a few times?"

"He also saved someone for me," Stone said quietly.

"Care to explain that?" Reuben asked curiously.

"No."

Someone banged on his door. Stone rose to answer it, thinking it might be Milton or perhaps Annabelle.

The man at the door was dressed in a dark suit and had a pistol under his jacket, Stone observed. He handed Stone a piece of paper and walked off. Stone opened the note.

Carter Gray wanted Stone to visit him at his house two days from today. A car would pick him up. There did not seem to be an opportunity to decline the command. When he told the others Caleb said, "Oliver, you're not going."

"Of course I am," Stone said.

9

Harry Finn was currently sucking on oxygen and peering out of his specially designed headgear. They were going so fast there wasn't a lot to see. A storm was raging and those on the deck of the boat were no doubt getting wet and jostled. It wasn't any better where Finn was. Demonstrating once more his affinity for unusual choices in transportation, he was attached to the side of a ship in a very tight ball near the stern using a support device not available to the public. He had discovered a seam in the exterior video and human surveillance perimeters and was now an invisible bump against the gunmetal gray side of the naval ship. The ride was far less comfortable than the plane cargo hold had been. In fact, despite his special device, Finn was nearly jolted off his perch twice. Had he been, his life probably would have ended on impact with the twin screws that were thrusting the ship through the water. His ride had started at what should have been a highly secure military dock at the Norfolk Naval Station. However, the "highly secure" component had broken down completely when confronted by Harry Finn wearing one of his vast array of disguises and his air of belonging perfectly in whatever situation he found himself.

The boat slowed and swung around to the port side of the larger vessel. Finn let it drift to a stop before he slipped underneath the water, kicking away from the boat as he did so. He had a waterproof knapsack slung over his back and an electronic jammer around his waist making him invisible to any tracking gear on board either boat. He dove down farther and headed underneath the other ship, which rode quite low in the water, and for good reason. It weighed over 80,000 tons, carried nearly a hundred aircraft and 6,000 sea and air personnel, housed not one but two nuclear powered generators, and had set the American taxpayer back over $3 billion.

Once he reached the spot, it took him only two minutes to attach the device to the bottom of the ship's hull, and then, keeping well away from the massive screws, he made his way back to the other boat, reattached himself, and rode it back in. He had accepted this mission largely because it would give him some practice for another upcoming task of a more personal nature. He actually thought about the details of that job as the boat he was piggybacking on made its jog back to land. After it docked, he slipped out from his hiding place, swam to a remote part of the pier, clambered out and stripped off his gear. He made his phone call and later reported to the duty officer's chambers with a high-level military escort, the members of which had privately bet there was no way anyone could do what Finn had just done: place a bomb on the hull bottom of the navy's prized Nimitz-class *George Washington* aircraft carrier as it sat off the coast of Virginia. It was a bomb powerful enough to sink the carrier and all hands on board along with a couple billion dollars' worth of aircraft.

This time the admiral of the Atlantic fleet and everyone down his chain of command was given a ten-megaton blast by the chairman of the Joint Chiefs, who happened to be a four-star army general. The man could barely hide his delight at delivering this meltdown to his naval colleague, a dressing-down so loud, it was said the four-star could be heard all the way back at the Pentagon nearly two hundred miles away. This very public whipping was reinforced by the presence of the secretary of defense, who had been standing by in his chopper waiting to see if Harry Finn could actually pull it off. The fact that the man had scored an improbable triumph against massively high odds prompted the secdef immediately to offer Harry Finn a position on his staff.

The secretary of Homeland Security was not amenable to this co-opting of a prized contractor. The two cabinet members went at it like schoolboys on a playground until the president himself interceded by secure video conference call and decreed that Harry Finn would stay right where he was, as an independent contractor to DHS. The defeated and miffed secdef climbed on his private chopper and flew back to Washington.

Harry Finn stayed down in Norfolk to give a briefing to a group of chagrined naval security personnel. While he was always courteous and unfailingly respectful, his comments were not watered down. Failures had happened, here is how I did it, and here is what you need to do to prevent a bona fide terrorist from doing it for real.

What Finn did for a living was often referred to in the field as "red cells." The term had been coined by a former Navy SEAL who'd helped start the program. The red cell project had commenced after the Vietnam War at the request of a vice admiral to test the security of military installations. After 9/11, it had been expanded to test the security of nonmilitary facilities to penetration by terrorists and other criminal organizations.

People with Finn's special skills, almost all of whom were formerly in the military, were tasked to impersonate terrorist cells and attempt to overcome a facility's security. Often the penetrations were conducted in a nontraditional way, something also referred to as humanizing the task. That meant that Finn and his team members would emulate the skill levels of the terrorists they were attacking. Presently, Muslim terrorists were not deemed to have sophisticated skill levels. Even after 9/11 there was disbelief in American intelligence circles that such terror cells could take over a major facility or do what Finn had done that night with the aircraft carrier. They were good at blowing themselves and others up in public or driving planes into skyscrapers, but attacking a nuclear power plant or military installation was a whole different ball game.

However, it had finally occurred to both politicians and higher-ups in the military that Muslims were not the only potential terrorists in the world. China, Russia and other former Soviet bloc countries, as well as several nations in America's own hemisphere, might well want to do harm to the United States. And these countries *did* have the infrastructure, personnel and access to intelligence to make determined and possibly successful attacks on secure American installations. Thus, Finn had been instructed to pull out the stops, use all his skills and cutting-edge equipment to break through the navy's defenses. And he had.

Other men, including several on red cell teams Finn had worked with, might have stayed out all night celebrating this dramatic triumph. However, Finn was not like most people. He had stayed down in the Norfolk area an extra day for one very important reason. His oldest son, David, was on a soccer travel team that had a match in the area. The day after his briefing Finn attended his son's match and then drove the victorious—and in high spirits—David back home that night. Along the way they talked about school, girls, sports. And then David, who at thirteen was nearly as tall as his dad, asked his father, "So what were you doing down there? Was it work-related?"

Finn nodded. "Some people were having problems with a security issue and asked me to come down and help them with it."

"Did you get it figured out?"

"Oh, yeah. Everyone's on the same page now. It actually wasn't that complicated once the problems were identified."

"Security with what?"

"A wide range of things. Nothing too exciting."

"So can you tell me about it?"

"I doubt you'd find it interesting. It's the same stuff lots of people do across the country. The only good thing is I don't have to sit behind a desk every day."

"I asked Mom about it once. She said she wasn't sure what you did."

"I think your mother was just kidding you."

"You're not a spy, are you?"

Finn smiled. "Well, if I were I couldn't tell you."

"Or if you did you'd have to kill me, right?" David said, laughing.

"All I do is help people run things better by pointing out flaws in their systems."

"Like a computer guy does with bugs? So you're like a debugger."

"Exactly. Like I said, pretty boring stuff, but it pays well and keeps food on the table, which, by the way, you seem to be eating about a hundred pounds of a day."

"I'm a growing boy, Pop. Hey, did you know that Barry Waller's dad chased a guy in his police car down an alleyway and wrestled a gun out of his hand after the dude robbed a bank? Barry said the guy almost shot his dad."

"Police work can be very dangerous. Barry's dad is a brave man."

"I'm glad you don't do stuff like that."

"Me too."

"So just keep doing your boring debugging stuff, Pop." David gave his father a playful punch in the arm. "And stay out of trouble, will ya?"

"I will, son. I will," said Harry Finn.

10

Stone and Alex Ford met at a familiar place for both men, Lafayette Park across from the White House. Here the six-foot-three-inch Alex had guarded the occupant of the Oval Office for years and Stone had respectfully protested against this same inhabitant, as he had against the man's predecessors, from across the street. The two men sat on a bench near the statue of a Polish general whom history remembered as a sound ally of the Americans in their war for independence. He was also a man, it was probably safe to say, hardly any American alive today would either know or care about.

"What do you have for me?" Stone said, eyeing the manila folder Alex pulled from a trim black leather briefcase.

"I wasn't sure what you were looking for, so I thought I'd cast a broad net."

"That's perfect, Alex, thanks."

As Stone looked over the file, Alex studied his friend. "Like I told you on the phone, the Justice Department has been interested in Bagger for a long time but can't make anything stick. I talked to Kate about it. She said Justice hasn't given up but if they can't pin something on him soon, they're going to have to move on. Even Uncle Sam has limited resources."

"How is Kate?" Stone asked, referring to Kate Adams, the Justice lawyer Alex had been dating.

"Things didn't work out. She's seeing someone else."

"I'm sorry to hear that. She's a wonderful woman," Stone replied.

"Yes she is, but just not the woman for me or me the man for her. Speaking of women, where's Adelphia?"

Adelphia, a strange woman of undetermined origin and interesting accent, had been the only other protester left in Lafayette Park besides Stone. Alex had long suspected that she had a crush on his friend.

"I haven't seen her for some time," Stone replied. "She even took her sign down."

"She was a strange bird."

"We're all strange birds." He closed the folder and stood. "I appreciate this. It will be a big help."

"Jerry Bagger, Jersey casino operator. So you thinking about doing some gambling?"

"Maybe, just not the way you probably imagine it."

"From what I've heard, Bagger is a real psycho with a mean streak. Not a guy to mess around with."

"I have no intention of doing anything like that."

Alex rose too. "Even so, should I be expecting another eleventh-hour phone call for the cavalry?"

"Let's hope it doesn't come to that."

"Saw our favorite buddy Carter Gray got the Medal of Freedom. It took all my willpower not to call the prick up and tell him to go to hell."

"My willpower's obviously not as strong as yours." Stone then explained what he'd done.

Alex's expression brightened. "You didn't!"

"Yes, I did. And on top of that Gray's asked me to visit him at his house tonight."

"And you're going?"

"I wouldn't miss it."

"Why? What could he possibly have to say that you'd want to hear?"

"I have some questions to ask him about . . . my daughter."

Alex's expression softened and he patted Stone's shoulder. "I'm sorry. I'm really sorry."

"Life is what it is, Alex. You just have to accept it, because you have no other choice."

11

The boat Harry Finn was currently riding on the side of was not quite as fast as the naval vessel he'd piggybacked on previously, but it was more than adequate. Like the military folks, the people he had hitched the ride from tonight had no idea of his presence. He had chosen it because they were heading in the direction he wanted to go. He would have to get home another way, a way he'd already figured out. He had timed out the ride and kept glancing at his illuminated watch in anticipation of when to peel away and swim for shore. A storm was percolating, which was both good and bad for his plan. He'd come prepared; he always did.

As the boat neared where he would be leaving it, Finn reflected on the last conversation he'd had with his wife, Mandy. He'd just finished cutting the grass and gone inside to shower. She stopped him in the bedroom.

"David said he'd talked to you about your work."

"That's right. He said you'd told him you weren't sure what I did for a living."

"I'm not."

"You know once I left the military I started doing contract work for Homeland Security."

"But David can't know that? And I can't know more?"

"It's just better that way. I'm sorry. But you have to trust me on that."

"At least when you were in the navy I knew what I was getting into. What do they ask you to do now?"

He slipped an arm around her waist. "Like I've told you before, I help make us safer. There are lots of holes out there. My job is to patch them up, make us stronger. It's not even remotely dangerous."

The tension was clear on her face. "If it's not even remotely dangerous why can't you tell me?"

"I just can't."

"You never have been much of a talker, have you?'

"I always assumed it was one of the things you loved most about me."

And they had left it at that. Mandy would never know that he illegally flew in the cargo holds of commercial aircraft, and rode without a shred of authorization on the hulls of military ships, because what spouse needed to know such things? And she would never know of the Dan Rosses of the world and the fates that had befallen them. Or of the Carter Grays who once held all the cards, but no longer did.

Yet it was still troubling for Harry Finn; he was a scrupulously honest man, who did not enjoy keeping anything from the woman he'd loved ever since seeing her walk across a college campus nearly fifteen years ago. He'd been on leave then and visiting a friend after rotating back from deployment overseas. He had always been shy and something of an introvert, an attribute that had graded out well for him in his military career. His line of work called for weeks or even months of thoughtful, meticulous preparation followed by seconds of adrenaline-fueled chaos in the midst of which he had to function with a maddening and lethal calm. He had excelled at both ends of that demanding spectrum.

Yet that day seeing the former Amanda Graham walk across that lawn in her jean short-shorts and open-toed sandals, with waist-length blonde hair and a face more lovely than he'd ever seen before, he had walked right up to the young woman and asked her out for that very night. She had declined at first, perhaps offended that he believed she would be free on such short notice. But Finn was nothing if not persistent. He got his date, and his wife. Finn wrangled from the navy a stint stateside and he and Mandy had married right after her graduation. Less than a year later David had arrived, followed by Patrick and Susie. They were a very happy couple. They had raised good kids, children who would make a difference in their world, perhaps only in small ways, but *positive* differences nonetheless.

Finn had no idea why he had some of his deepest

reflections while doing impossibly crazy things, like riding on the sides of boats at high speeds, but he did.

He checked his watch, tightened the strap on the waterproof bag he carried over his shoulder and prepared himself for the next step. This was the tricky part, letting go of his ride at speed and avoiding the screws at the stern. Because when he let go, there was a distinct possibility that if he didn't kick hard enough away from the direction the boat was going and didn't go down deep enough in the water his last memory would be the props savagely cleaving his torso in two.

He coiled his legs and positioned them against the side of the boat. Counting to three, he kicked as hard as he could against the boat's hull and plunged out and then downward even as he felt the force of the screws pulling him toward the stern. He came up to the surface and watched the running lights of the craft disappear. He looked around, quickly gained his bearings and swam hard toward the cliffs.

12

Jerry Bagger never ventured much out of Atlantic City anymore. He had his own Learjet but seldom used it. The last trip on it had been the deadly visit to the unfortunate Tony Wallace in Portugal. He once had a yacht but sold it when he discovered he easily became seasick, an embarrassment for a man who prided himself on toughness. Indeed, he rarely left his casino anymore. It was really the only place he felt comfortable these days.

Ironically, Bagger hadn't been born in Vegas or Jersey. The ballsy, streetwise urban boy had seen his first light in, of all places, Wyoming, on a ranch where his father labored for something less than minimum wage. His mother had lost her life on Bagger's first day from pregnancy complications, complications any hospital could have easily taken care of. But there had been no hospital within three hundred miles, so she'd died. Bagger's father had joined her eighteen months later after an accident involving whiskey and a cantankerous horse.

The Wyoming ranch owner had no interest in

raising a bastard child—Bagger's mother and father had not bothered to marry—and he was shipped off to his mother's family in Brooklyn. It was in the close confines of this New York melting pot, not in the wide-open spaces of Wyoming, that Bagger was meant to be and had thrived.

He had eventually gone back west. After fifteen years of twenty-hour workdays, nonstop hustling and risking and then nearly losing everything he had about a dozen times, he had his own casino. And soon business was so good he started printing money. Then his temper got the best of him and he was eventually run out of Vegas and ordered never to return. He had honored that request, although every time he flew over it he looked out the plane window and ceremoniously flipped off the entire state of Nevada.

Bagger left his penthouse and took the private elevator down to the casino floor. There he walked through a sea of slots, gaming tables and sport betting rooms where gamblers from the novice to the experienced dropped far more money than they would ever get back. Whenever he spotted a kid sitting bored on the floor, with their parents hovering nearby feeding buckets of nickels into the slots—their hands blackened from the process—Bagger would order that food, books and video games be brought to the child, and he would slip a twenty-dollar bill in the kid's hand. Then he would make a call and someone from the Pompeii would immediately confront the parents and remind them that while children were allowed in the casino, they could not be in the playing areas.

Bagger would crush any adult who crossed him, but kids were not to be screwed with. That would change when they hit eighteen—then everyone was fair game—but until then kids were off-limits. It was shitty enough being adults, was his opinion, so let the little punks enjoy the time they had not being grown up. Underlying this philosophy might have been the fact that Jerry Bagger had never had a childhood. Dirt poor, he had run his first racket out of a Brooklyn tenement house at age nine and never looked back. That hard life was a major reason for his success, but the scars ran deep. So deep he didn't even think about them anymore. They were simply what made him what he was.

On his walk Bagger made three such calls for kids left in the playing area by their parents, shaking his head each time. "Losers," he muttered. Jerry Bagger had never bet one dime on anything. That was for suckers. He was many things, but a fool wasn't one of them. These idiots would scream and jump around after winning a hundred bucks, forgetting that they'd thrown away *two* hundred bucks for the privilege. And yet this weird psychological quirk humans possessed had made Bagger rich, so he wasn't complaining.

He stopped at one of the bars and raised an eyebrow at a waitress, who rushed to bring him his usual club soda with a lime. He never drank alcohol on the casino floor, nor did any of his employees. He perched on a bar stool and watched the Pompeii operate at maximum efficiency. All age ranges were represented here. And the whack jobs were aplenty, he knew from decades of experience. There wasn't a single category of nutcase that hadn't at one point strolled into his casino. Truth was, Bagger related to them better than he did the "normal" folks.

He eyed a newlywed couple still in their wedding clothes. The Pompeii offered a cut-rate, tips-not-included deal for those wanting to get hitched, which provided a standard room with a sturdy new mattress, a cheap bouquet of flowers, the services of a properly licensed minister, dinner, drinks and twin massages to work out the kinks from all that screwing. And, most importantly, the deal provided fifty dollars' worth of casino chips. Bagger had no interest in promoting love; he knew from experience that those fifty bucks of free chips typically turned into a two-thousand-dollar profit for the house by the end of a long weekend, even taking into account the freebies.

The couple he was watching seemed to be trying their best to swallow each other's tongues. Bagger grimaced at this public display. "Get a room," he muttered. "It's the cheapest thing you'll find in this town other than the booze. And the sex."

Bagger had never married, chiefly because he had never met a woman who could hold his interest.

Annabelle Conroy *had* captured and held his interest. She was beyond mesmerizing. He'd wanted to spend all his time with her. In fact, before he found out she'd conned him, he had wondered if after all these years he'd finally found a lady he could escort down the aisle. It seemed crazy now, considering what had happened, how she'd screwed him over. And yet with all that Bagger just had to grin. What a picture that would've made. He and Annabelle as husband and wife? What a hoot.

And then, as was often the case, Jerry Bagger had a brilliant idea while he wasn't even trying to.

He finished his club soda and headed back to his office to make some phone calls to find out one thing. When she'd been conning him Annabelle had told him she'd never been married or had children. But what if in reality Annabelle Conroy had been married? Because if she ever had said "I do" it was a golden way to track the lady down.

13

Stone refused Gray's offer of a drink. The two men settled down in Gray's comfortable study, which held as many books in as many languages as there were in Stone's cottage, although here they were kept in much finer style.

Stone looked out the long window that faced the cliffs overlooking the water.

"Tired of Virginia farm country?" he said.

"My ambition as a young man was to be a sailor, see the world from the deck of a ship," Gray said, cradling his Scotch, his wide face strangely offset by a pair of narrowly placed eyes. There was a lot in that head, Stone well knew. Gray was not a man that one could ever reasonably *over*estimate.

"A young man's ambition, can there be a more fleeting prospect?" Stone said idly. The darkness outside the window was complete. No moon, no stars; an approaching storm had hidden the sky.

"I never thought John Carr would be given to lapses into philosophizing."

"Goes to show how little you really knew me. And

I don't go by John Carr anymore. He's dead. I'm sure you were briefed on it years ago."

Unperturbed, Gray continued. "This place used to belong to another former director of CIA, who went on to become vice president. It has everything I need to be comfortable and secure in my old age."

"I'm so happy for you," Stone said.

"I'm actually surprised you came. After your little gesture outside the White House?"

"How is the president, by the way?"

"Fine."

"Did you feel any homicidal impulses when he plunked that medal on you? Or are you over wanting to kill the man?"

"Without directly answering your ridiculous question, circumstances change. It's never personal. You should know that as well as any man alive."

"The point is, I *wouldn't* have been alive if you'd had your way." Before Gray could respond, Stone said, "I have some questions I want to ask you and I'd appreciate answers, truthful ones."

Gray put down his Scotch. "All right."

Stone turned from the window to look at him. "That easy?"

"Why waste what time we have left playing games that don't matter anymore? I take it you want to know about Elizabeth."

"I want to know about *Beth*, my daughter."

"I'll answer what I can."

Stone sat down opposite him and asked question after question for about twenty minutes. His final one was articulated with some trepidation. "Did she ever ask about me, about her father?"

"As you know, Senator Simpson and his wife raised her after they adopted her."

"But you told me you brought them Beth when Simpson was still at CIA. If she had said something, surely—"

Gray put up a hand. "She did. It was actually after Simpson had left CIA and begun his political career. Understand she may have mentioned something about it before, but this was the first I'd heard of such a query. They had told her years before of her adoption. It's not something Beth seemed to dwell on. In fact, I'm not sure she told many people about it."

Stone leaned forward. "What did she say about her real parents?"

"In all fairness, you should know that she asked about her mother first. Girls, you understand, they want to know."

"Of course she should know about her mother."

"They had to be delicate, considering the . . . uh . . . the circumstances of her mother's death."

"Of her *murder*, you mean. By people who were looking to kill me."

"As I told you, I had nothing to do with that. I sincerely liked your wife. And if truth be known, she'd be alive today if you had—"

Stone rose and stared down at him with a look that chilled even Gray, who well knew how many ways John Carr could kill another human being. And no man he'd ever employed had been better at it. "I'm sorry, John—I mean, Oliver. I admit that was not your fault." He paused while Stone slowly sat back down. "They told her a little about her mother, all positive I can assure you, and that she had died in an accident."

"And me?"

"She was told her father was a soldier who was killed in the line of duty. I believe they even took her to your 'grave' at Arlington. To your daughter you died a hero." Gray paused and added, "Does that satisfy you?"

The way he said it made Stone wonder something. "Is this the real truth or the truth Carter Gray style, meaning a load of bullshit to appease me?"

"What possible reason would I have to lie to you now? It doesn't matter anymore, does it? You and me, we don't matter anymore."

"Why did you ask me here tonight?"

In answer Gray went behind his desk and picked up a file. He opened it and held up three color photos of men in their sixties. He placed them one by one in front of Stone. "This first man is Joel Walker, the second Douglas Bennett and the last Dan Ross."

"Those names mean nothing to me, and neither do these pictures."

Gray pulled three more photos from the file, all much older and in black and white. "I think these will look far more familiar to you. And the names as well: Judd Bingham, Bob Cole and Lou Cincetti."

Stone barely heard the names. He was staring at photos of men he'd lived, worked and nearly died beside for over a decade. He looked up at Gray.

"Why are you showing me this?"

"Because in the last two months all three of these former comrades of yours have died."

"Died how?"

"Bingham was found in his bed. He had lupus. The autopsy found nothing unusual. Cole hanged himself. At least it appeared that way, and the police have officially closed that case. Cincetti apparently got drunk, stumbled into his pool and drowned."

"So natural causes for Bingham, suicide for Cole and an accident with Cincetti."

"And you don't believe that any more than I do; three men from the same unit dying within two months of each other?"

"It's a dangerous world out there."

"Something we both know all too well."

"You think they were killed?"

"Of course."

"And you invited me here to what, warn me?"

"It seemed like the most prudent thing to do."

"But like you said, John Carr is dead. Who looks to kill a dead man?"

"These three fellows had excellent cover. Cincetti was particularly deeply buried. If someone could find him, they could find out John Carr isn't really in that box at Arlington. That he's actually a man very much alive who calls himself Oliver Stone."

"And what about you? Carter Gray was the master strategist for our little group. And you've had no cover all these years."

"I have protection. You don't."

"Then you've given me fair warning." Stone rose.

"I'm sorry things ended up as they did. You deserved better."

"You were prepared to sacrifice me and my friends not too long ago, for the good of the country."

"Everything I ever did was for the good of this country."

"At least how *you* defined it, anyway. Not me."

"We can agree to disagree on that."

Stone turned and walked out the door.

14

Carter Gray's mail was screened at an off-site center run by the FBI and then delivered to him in the evening. The courier duly drove up and the mail was given to one of the men assigned to protect Gray. These men lived in a cottage about a hundred yards from the main house. Gray would not agree to anyone living with him in the house, which was protected by a latest-generation security system.

Gray opened the letters and packages, not really focusing on any of them until he reached one item. The envelope was red and had been postmarked from Washington, D.C. There was only one thing in it, a photo. He looked at the picture and then over at the file on his desk. His time had come, it seemed.

He turned out the lights in his study and went to his bedroom. He kissed the pictures of his wife and daughter that had places of honor on the fireplace mantel. In a grotesque twist of fate, both women had perished at the Pentagon on 9/11. He knelt, said his customary prayers and then turned off the light.

Outside, about five hundred yards away from the

house, Harry Finn lowered his long-range nightscope. He'd seen Gray open the red envelope. He'd gotten a good look at the man's face as he stared at the photo. Gray knew. The climb up the sheer rock cliff had been a challenge, even for Finn. But it had allowed him to get this far. And he only had a little farther to go.

Finn waited another hour to allow Gray to fall asleep and then slid over to the gas regulator post. A natural gas line had been placed here specifically because Carter Gray preferred gas heat and cooking. Ten minutes later the gas pressure going into Gray's home blew out all the pilot lights and overwhelmed the built-in safety systems. In seconds the house was full of the deadly gas. If he were still awake Gray would be able to smell it, because the utility company added an odor to the naturally odorless gas as a warning. Yes, Gray could smell it if he were awake, but that would be all he could do.

Finn loaded one bullet into his rifle. It looked rather ordinary except its nose was green-colored. He took aim and fired at the long window in the back of the house. It was not a difficult shot. The slug cracked the glass and the small amount of flame-creating powder in the incendiary bullet he'd chambered ignited. The roof was blown ten feet into the air while the walls were knocked outward a dozen feet on all sides. What was left of the roof came back down, landing squarely on a raging fire. Within seconds it was hard to believe a house had actually been there at all.

Finn had turned to flee on his planned escape route when he heard a scream and looked back. One of the guards had come out of the guesthouse, been hit with a chunk of flaming debris and was on fire. There was no sign of the other guard. Without really thinking about it, Finn ran forward, tackled the man, who was flailing around, and rolled him on the ground, putting out the flames. Then he leapt up and ran full tilt back to his gear near the gas regulator post. He'd already turned the pressure setting back to normal and relocked the access door. He grabbed his bag and gun, sprinted to the cliffs and flung his rifle and other equipment over the edge. The tide would soon carry them far out to sea.

Finn took a few steps back and sprinted toward the cliff. He flew out into space and plummeted down, his body unfolding into classic high-dive form. He hit the water cleanly, went under, and then resurfaced. He struck out with a strong, practiced stroke and made it to shore about a half mile down. In a small wooded area here he had covered under a layer of leaves a small motorcycle. He cut through myriad back trails to a main road, then finally pulled off on a small side street where a van was parked. He rolled the bike into the rear of the van, hopped into the driver's seat and sped off. The van and motorcycle were left at a private garage Finn maintained about ten miles from his house. He drove home in his Prius, and changed in the garage before coming into the house, putting his dirty clothes into the washer and turning on the machine.

A few minutes later he headed quietly upstairs, looking in on his kids. Mandy was asleep; a book she'd been reading was still lying across her chest. He closed the book, put it away and turned off the lamp on her nightstand before slipping into bed. Finn mentally crossed Carter Gray off his list and moved on to the next name.

He looked down at his hands. Even though he'd worn gloves they were slightly singed from putting out the fire on the man. He'd put ice on them and then some salve in the kitchen before coming upstairs. "Don't do that again, Harry," he whispered to himself, but still causing his wife to moan and roll a bit in her sleep. He put a hand on her head and started rubbing her hair. His reddened hand and his wife's beautiful blonde hair; the odd pairing suddenly made Finn want to run as fast as he could, as if he could outrun any of it. His lovely wife and their three wonderful children. A nice house, a job he enjoyed and was very good at. His life was filled with things he had always wanted to have. And with one thing he had never wanted to face. It didn't seem fair really. Yet how in the world could he stop? It had been beaten into his head ever since he could remember. It had become more a part of him than anything else, even more than his role as husband and father. And that was the only thing in all of this that truly scared him.

Finn hid his hands under the covers and tried to sleep.

15

"Bagger got to Tony," Annabelle said. She hadn't slept all night and had called her former partner Leo Richter at the crack of dawn. She had no idea what time zone he was even in and didn't really care.

On the other end of the phone Leo sat up straight and felt his last meal start to come up on him. "What the hell are you talking about?"

"Tony screwed up. Flashed the cash and Bagger tracked him down. Bagger killed three people and left Tony for dead after turning his brains to mush."

"Well you can bet the little weasel ratted us out, then. Why can't somebody just kill Bagger? Is it that hard?"

Annabelle said, "What if Tony found out my last name? You told Freddy, maybe Freddy told Tony. Or the kid might've overheard."

"I don't know what to tell you, Annabelle. We both might be screwed regardless. There are only so many Annabelles and Leos in the con world who operate at that level."

"If you know where Freddy is you might want to warn him."

"I'll do my best. Look, you want me to hook up with you? Try to get us out of this mess?"

"And make it easier for Jerry to bag two for the price of one? Just stay where you are, Leo, and dig as deep as you can." She clicked off the phone and sat back on her bed. Maybe she should put her millions to work for her right now. Just use it to run like hell. Private plane, private island, plenty of guards. It sounded tempting, but her gut told her this would be like waving a flag in front of a bull. She was still pondering what to do when her phone rang. It was Oliver Stone.

"I hope I didn't wake you," he said.

"I'm an early riser," she lied.

"I have news. We can meet at my cottage later," he said.

"Why don't you come my way, Oliver," she said. "We can have some breakfast. There's a place around the corner from where I'm staying." She gave him the address. Thirty minutes later they took a corner table in the back away from the other customers. After they ordered, he told Annabelle what he'd found out.

"I'm not sure how that helps," she said, spooning sugar into her coffee.

"The best defense is a good offense. The government would love to nail him to a wall. If we can help them do that, I doubt he'd have time for you. Actually, if we can simply distract Bagger with a government investigation, that may be enough to keep you safe."

Annabelle looked uncertain. "You don't know Jerry. He has forty million reasons to devote every second of the remainder of his life to killing me."

Stone nodded knowingly. "I do know Jerry, at least men like him. It's not just about the money, of course. It's about loss of face, of respect. He has to seem invincible to everyone. Otherwise he's not Jerry Bagger."

"You sized him up right away."

"As I said, I've known many men like Bagger, even worked for some."

She said cautiously, "So if we *were* going to go after Jerry how would we do it?"

"We have to find where he's vulnerable. There's the point of least resistance, of course. He killed three people in Portugal and put a fourth in a coma. If we can pin that on him he goes away forever."

"I know he did it, but I have no proof. And if I go to the cops, I'll have to explain everything, and then I don't think they'll be waiting to hand me a medal."

"Or you could give your share of the money back to Bagger and hope that's enough."

"I earned that money, every last cent of it. And like you said, it's not about the money. He'd still want to kill me."

"But if we can tie Bagger to these crimes without

you having to give testimony or being involved at all?"

"Well, that would just solve all my problems, wouldn't it? Only I don't quite see how that can work."

"That's for us to figure out." Stone was about to say something else when his cell phone rang. It was Alex Ford and his voice was strained.

"Oliver, did you see Carter Gray last night?"

"Yes, I did."

"What time did you get there and what time did you leave?"

Stone told him. "I'm sure the driver can verify that. What's this all about?"

"I can't believe you haven't heard."

"Heard what?"

"Somebody blew up Carter Gray's house last night, with him in it. I know this is going to be awkward, but I think the FBI will want to talk to you about your meeting with Gray."

Stone clicked off. *The FBI will want to talk to me. About Gray.*

Annabelle said sharply, "Trouble?"

"A little," he said slowly as his thoughts raced ahead. "Maybe more than a little, actually."

She tapped her coffee cup against his. "Welcome to the club."

16

Oliver Stone stared at the wall opposite him while the two thirty-something men in shirtsleeves with their guns and badges hanging on their black belts hovered around like vultures over roadkill. His voluntary appearance at the FBI's Washington Field Office had not earned him any brownie points, even with Alex Ford of the Secret Service accompanying him to the interview. Alex had told the agents in charge of Carter Gray's homicide investigation about Stone's recent heroics in foiling an espionage ring. However, the agents had brushed that off.

One of them said to Alex, "I deal with murder and I got a big one hanging around my neck and a lot of pressure from upstairs to get results." He plopped down in front of Stone at the small table.

"Now let's try the name thing one more time. What's yours?"

"Oliver Stone, like I told you the last four times you asked."

"Let me see some ID."

"And as I told you four times before, I don't have any."

The other agent said incredulously, "How does anybody in the twenty-first century not have ID?"

Stone looked at him, bemused. "I know who I am. And I don't really care if no one else does."

"So you came all the way down here to tell us what—nothing other than the fact that you're apparently a famous film director who dresses like a bum?"

"Actually, I came down here to tell you that I visited Carter Gray at his home last night at *his* request. I arrived around nine and left about forty-five minutes later. He sent his driver for me. The man can certainly vouch for the fact that when I left, the house was still standing and the man inside that house was still alive."

Alex interjected, "Have you talked to the driver?"

The two agents glanced at each other. One said to Stone, "What'd you two talk about?"

"It was private. I'm certain it had nothing to do with what happened to Mr. Gray." Stone of course had every reason to believe that what Gray had told him about the other three men dying was very much tied to Gray's death.

"I sense uncooperative behavior," the same agent said.

His partner added, "And I sense an obstruction charge coming. You like to sit in a jail cell, Mr. Stone, while we run down who you really are?"

Stone said calmly, "If you believe you have enough to charge me then charge me. If you don't I'm late for another appointment."

"You're a busy man are you, *Mr.* Stone?" one of the agents remarked sarcastically.

"I try to stay productive. But I'll make a deal with you."

"We don't do deals."

"I'll go with you to the crime scene. If I see anything that strikes me funny, I'll let you know."

"Strikes you funny? What the hell is that supposed to mean?" the first agent said.

"Just what it sounds like."

"No way in hell are we taking you to the crime scene."

"If you killed the guy you might be looking to screw up some evidence," the other agent said.

Stone sighed. "Call the director of the FBI, please."

"Excuse me?" one agent snapped, looking incredulously at him.

"Call the head of the FBI. He sent me a commendation letter recently. By coincidence I brought a copy of it with me. I called his office before coming down here. I told him if I had any trouble, I'd give him a call."

Stone handed the letter across to the agent. With his partner looking over his shoulder they read it word for word, then glanced at Alex, who merely shrugged.

Stone said, "Do you call or do we choose not to bother the director and just go to the crime scene? I don't have all day."

"No reason to bother the director," one of the agents said finally.

Stone rose. "Delighted to hear it."

17

Stone walked near the wreckage of Carter Gray's house with one of the FBI agents and Alex Ford.

"Gas explosion?" Alex asked the agent.

"That's what it looks like, although I'm not sure how it was possible. The place wasn't that old. And it had all the latest safety features."

Stone was staring at what was left of the house he'd been sitting in only last night. "Where was his body found?"

"Sorry, can't say. The *remains* of a body were found in the bedroom."

"Positive ID?"

"Suffice it to say that we consider this a homicide investigation regarding the owner of the property."

"Did you find the driver to confirm Oliver's story?"

The agent shook his head. "The man's gone missing. He was with the CIA. Not sure what the story was there. Of course, that means we just have your word for it that he drove you home," he added, eye-balling Stone.

"If I were going to blow up the man I wouldn't have told anyone I was meeting with him, especially a United States Secret Service agent. And I certainly wouldn't have done the deed on the very night I did meet with him."

"The fact that the house blew up right after he met with you *is* the reason you're a suspect," the agent countered.

"And it's also the reason I'm out here," Stone said. "Because the faster you find the real killer, the sooner I'm off that list."

"Anyone else around?" Alex asked.

The agent nodded, his gaze still on Stone. "A guard. He came out of the guesthouse over there and got hit by some debris and was actually on fire. He says he remembers somebody knocking him down and putting out the flames. He passed out and the next thing he remembers is being put in the back of an ambulance. He's in the burn unit at a hospital in Annapolis. He'll be okay."

Alex said, "So there *was* somebody else out here last night."

The agent was still staring at Stone, who raised his hands and said, "You can check me for burns, if you'd like."

"It wasn't the other guy, the driver?" Alex said quickly while giving Stone a "knock it off" look.

"The guard was in so much pain he could only see

it was a guy," the agent admitted. "But if it *was* the driver why should he have run off?"

"He would if he had something to do with the explosion," Stone noted. "And the fact that he's gone missing now? Not to tell you how to run your investigation, but it is something to think about."

"We have thought about it," the agent said gruffly.

"Find anything useful in the house?" Stone asked.

"If we did, you would not be on the list of people we would inform."

Stone smiled, turned away and saw it. He said slowly, "Well, since I'm not in the loop you won't mind if I just take a walk along the cliffs. Be sure to keep me in your line of sight in case I make a run for it."

As he walked away the agent said to Alex, "Okay, fed to fed, who the hell is that guy?"

"Someone I'd trust my life with. Someone I *have* trusted my life with."

"Care to share?"

"No, it's national security stuff and you'd never believe me anyway."

The agent stared at the rumpled Stone. "National security! The guy looks borderline homeless."

"Actually, he works in a cemetery," Alex said helpfully.

The agent just shook his head and then followed Stone, who was over near the cliffs.

What had caught Stone's eye was the gas regulator post. As he headed toward it the same agent called out, "We've checked that out already. Obvious point."

"And?"

"And it was working fine and no forced entry."

"There wouldn't be any sign of forced entry if the person knew what he was doing. But the gas pressure can be manipulated from here?"

"Presumably. But we checked the box and the pressure hadn't been changed."

Stone recalled the long window of Gray's house looking out onto the cliffs. There was something gnawing at his memory. He turned back to the agent.

"Well, if you can change the pressure, you can change it back."

"Okay, anything else strike you funny?" the man asked.

"Let's say you greatly increase the gas pressure going into the house, which blows out the safety overrides. In seconds the place is filled with gas."

"But you need something to ignite that gas."

"Turning on a light would create enough of a spark to do it."

"True. We've got some bomb-sniffing dogs coming out. Unless they turn up some dynamite or C4, we might have to look at the gas angle more closely."

Stone suddenly remembered what he needed to. He left the agent and rejoined Alex.

"Anything occur to you?" Alex asked.

"You fill the house with gas by manipulating the pressure. A light spark will ignite the gas, but if Gray is asleep you can't count on that. And you don't want him to smell the gas and escape. So you have a man standing about two hundred yards from the back of the house, near the cliffs over there. He fires an incendiary bullet through the window. The bullet passes through the glass, igniting on impact and triggering the gas explosion. If they find a colored bit of metal in there it may be from the bullet's nose. Incendiary rounds are typically colored so people don't mix them up."

Alex nodded thoughtfully. "But how would he get away? The front was blocked. Unless the guard who got burned passed out and didn't see the guy get by him."

Stone and Alex walked back over to the agent. "Any evidence of the person leaving through the woods over there?" Stone asked the FBI man.

The agent shook his head. "We've been all over it. No trace, and there would have been. And there's no easy way to get back to the main road from there."

"But the person could have left directly by the main road, then?"

"Don't think so. I forgot to mention that the guard who got burned said the guy who helped him ran back this way, not toward the road."

Stone walked over to the cliffs with the agent tagging along. "Then he went out this way. Probably came in the same way."

The agent looked down. "That's sheer rock, a good thirty feet."

"It's not sheer. There're plenty of handholds if you know where to look."

"Okay, you climb up. But what about the going down part?"

"Well, since I don't see anything around here you could attach a rope to, I'm assuming he jumped."

The agent gazed at the swirling water far below. "That's impossible."

"Not really." Stone thought, *Actually, I did the same thing thirty years ago. Only it was fifty feet up and there were people shooting at me.*

Stone drove back to D.C. with Alex.

"Not a bad morning's work," Alex said appreciatively.

"Knowing how it was done and finding out who did it are two very different things. Carter Gray had a lot of enemies."

"Granted, but don't you have any guesses? I mean he had to have some reason to want to meet with you."

Stone hesitated. He didn't like keeping things back from Alex, but sometimes honest disclosure, even for good reasons, turned out to be a bad decision. "I don't believe it's connected."

He could tell Alex didn't buy this statement, but he chose not to add to it.

As they drove on Stone stared out the window. Three men he'd worked with decades ago were suddenly all dead. Carter Gray had met to warn him about this strange chain of events. The very night of that warning he had been blown up. Whoever had done this had found three deeply covered, highly skilled former assassins and murdered them. And then he had succeeded in killing Carter Gray, a man who had few peers when it came to outwitting the competition.

A person smart enough to do all that could conceivably discover who Oliver Stone really was. And come and kill him too.

And maybe I would deserve it, Stone thought. Because the only thing he had in common with the dead men was that they were all former killers themselves.

18

Annabelle stood outside the gates of the cemetery where Stone was caretaker. After her talk with Leo and her conversation with Stone, she had made up her mind. This was not Oliver Stone's fight. Friend or not, she could not allow him to get involved. If Bagger somehow killed him, Annabelle knew she could not live with that guilt.

The gates were locked, but with a tension tool and lock pick two minutes later they were open and she was on the front porch of the cottage. She slipped the note she had taken nearly an hour to compose, despite its brevity, under the door. A minute later she was back in her car. Three hours later she was riding into the sky inside a United Airlines jet. As the plane tracked the Potomac River on the climb out, Annabelle glanced out the window. Georgetown was directly below them. She thought she could see the little well-tended cemetery, *his* cemetery. Perhaps he was down there amid the hallowed ground working away at his tombstones, attending to the dead and buried, atoning for past sins.

"So long, Oliver Stone," she said to herself. *Goodbye, John Carr.*

"I love this Internet crap," Bagger bellowed as he stared at the papers one of his IT guys had just handed to him.

"It is quite amazing, Mr. Bagger," the young bespectacled man began in an immodest tone. "And frankly—"

"Get the hell outta here," Bagger roared and the terrified man fled.

Bagger sat down behind his desk and studied the papers again. He'd retained an Internet search organization. He didn't know what their sources were and he didn't really care. They had delivered, that's all that mattered. Annabelle Conroy had walked down the aisle, over fifteen years ago, with a guy named Jonathan DeHaven. They had been married, ironically Bagger thought, in Vegas. The downside was there were no pictures of the happy couple, only the names. It had to be the same Annabelle Conroy, how many people getting married in Sin City would have that name? But he had to be sure. So Bagger picked up his phone and called a PI firm he had used in the past. These folks worked right on the edge of the envelope and occasionally skirted past that barrier. He loved them for it, and also because they got results. He would have put them onto Annabelle before now, but he wanted a piece of information for them to start with, and now he had it. When people got married they signed lots of documents. And they had to live somewhere and get things like insurance, and utilities and maybe wills and cars in both the names.

He chuckled. Annabelle had posed as a CIA operative when running her scam on him. Well, he would show the lady what real intelligence was.

He said into the phone, "Hey, Joe, it's Jerry Bagger, got a job for you. A really, really important job. I need to find an old friend. And I need to do it fast because I want to wrap my arms around her and give the lady a nice big squeeze."

19

When Stone arrived back home he saw the note. Instinctively knowing what it was before he even opened it, he still took his time reading through it. When he was done he sat back and sighed deeply. Then he got angry. He called Reuben, Milton and Caleb. He told them there would be a meeting of the Camel Club that night at his cottage. Though Caleb whined about having to work late to finish a project, Stone insisted that he be there. "It's important, Caleb. It has to do with our friend."

"Which friend?" he'd said suspiciously.

"Susan."

"Is she in trouble?"

"Yes."

"Then I'll be there," Caleb said without hesitation.

Stone spent the next few hours working in the cemetery, shoring up old tombstones that always seemed to lose their grip on the earth after a rainstorm no matter how many times he straightened and reinforced them. He was not merely doing busy work. He wanted to get something that had been buried for a long time, both in the ground and also in his mind.

The old tombstone had a statue of an eagle perched on top. Pretending to be trying to straighten the headstone in case anyone was watching, Stone let it fall to the ground as though by accident. Revealed underneath was a small hole in the dirt. In this hole was a rectangular-shaped airtight metal box. Stone lifted the box out and placed it in the trash bag he was using to collect weeds. He left the tombstone on its side, dusted off his hands and went inside the cottage with the bag.

At his desk he opened the box with a key he kept taped behind the light switch panel in his tiny bathroom. He spread the box's contents out in front of him. This was his insurance policy, in case anyone ever came looking to do him harm. Stone had been smart enough to know that what he was being asked to do for his country could be seen, from another perspective, as simply crimes done under the flimsy banner of counterintelligence. He had been told on countless occasions that if he or his team members were ever caught during one of their missions, they couldn't rely on Uncle Sam to bail them out. They were on their own. To young men possessing special skills and insane levels of confidence that had seemed like a challenge they couldn't refuse.

He and men like Lou Cincetti and Bob Cole had often joked, in sessions of gallows humor, that if their capture seemed imminent they would each simply shoot the other, fittingly leaving the world together, as a team. Yet as the years passed and the killings went on, Stone had started collecting information and documentation from these "tasks." Uncle Sam could say he wouldn't be there for him, but it was another thing altogether if Stone could hold his agency accountable. In the end none of it had mattered, though. His wife had died, his daughter was lost to him and the people who'd ordered his destruction, simply because he didn't want to kill anymore, had never suffered a single minute for it.

Stone stared at one photo for a long time. It was from Vietnam when he'd still been a soldier, albeit one with highly specialized skills. He had been given the assignment of assassinating a North Vietnamese politician, a man the enemy had been rallying around. Normally, long-range sniping was done by a team. You had lookouts and spotters and people to check the wind and other weather conditions. However, Stone had been sent in alone, charged with a task that even for him seemed impossible. He would be dropped by chopper into a jungle crawling with Viet Cong. He was to travel five miles by foot over dangerous terrain and kill the man at a rally that would be attended by over ten thousand people, with massive military security. He was then to reverse his tracks and travel miles back to an assigned spot that would be difficult to find in the daylight, much less at night.

The chopper would be there precisely four hours after dropping him off. It would make one pass. If he wasn't back in time, Stone was target practice for the Viet Cong.

Ostensibly he'd been chosen for what amounted to a suicide mission because he was the best they had; the finest shooter and the most tireless in the field, it was generally acknowledged. Back then Stone was a machine. He could run all day and night. He had been dropped into the South China Sea from a chopper once, and swam miles through rough water to kill someone deemed hostile to the United States. From half a mile away he'd placed a shot through the man's head while he sat at his kitchen table reading the newspaper and smoking a cigarette. Then he'd swum back out and been picked up by a sub.

Yet with the assignment in Vietnam Stone had suspected his superiors were making a statement about his increasingly reluctant attitude about the war. Some of them were no doubt praying he would fail. And die. He hadn't accommodated them that night. He had killed the politician from a challenging distance even for a top sniper using a scope that expert marksmen today would have laughed at. Stone had made it back to the clearing to find the chopper about to turn off after its single pass. He knew the pilots had seen him but apparently couldn't be bothered to come back to get him. He put a heavy-caliber round right through the open cargo doors to show them the error of their ways.

They had landed, only momentarily, but enough to allow him to jump on the skids. As the chopper flew off, shots poured at them from the jungle below. Stone had run that night like never before in his life. Yet, still, he hadn't been that far ahead of a battalion of angry North Vietnamese. It had been that successful assignment that had garnered the attention of the CIA, and resulted in his induction into the "esteemed group" of government assassins known as the Triple Six Division.

The Triple Six was a component that even most people at the Agency didn't realize existed. They probably slept better for not knowing. Yet every "civilized" country had its assassins who did things to protect their national interests, and America was certainly entitled to hers. At least that was the company line.

Stone turned to another piece of paper with some names on it and a photo attached. They were Stone, Bob Cole, Lou Cincetti, Roger Simpson, Judd Bingham and Carter Gray. This was the only photo he knew of that had all six men in it. And it had only been possible because, after a particularly difficult mission, they had all gone out and gotten drunk as soon as the plane touched back down on American soil. As Stone looked into his mostly unlined face from decades ago, a killer's confident face that had no idea of the personal hardship and loss to come, he felt a heaviness in his chest.

He squinted at the picture of the tall, elegant man that Roger Simpson had been back then. Simpson had never been a field agent; instead, like Carter Gray, he'd orchestrated the activities of Stone and the others from a relatively safe distance. He had gone on to the political arena where he was still tall, still handsome. However, the ambitious streak he possessed that had seemed a very positive attribute when he was younger had turned him over three decades later into a devious plotter and a man who never forgot a slight no matter how trivial. Not content merely to be one of a hundred senators, he desperately wanted the presidency, and had worked long and hard to win it. And when the term of the current president ended, it seemed that Simpson was indeed a front-runner to take his place. His wife, a former Miss Alabama, gave him a glamour quotient that the somewhat stiff Simpson could never have inspired himself. It was discreetly and anonymously bandied about that Mrs. Simpson didn't really enjoy her husband's company all that much. Yet apparently she wanted to be First Lady badly enough to play along.

Stone had always considered Simpson a weak-willed, backstabbing prick. That such a man was in position to capture the top office in the land in a few short years merely reinforced Stone's already low opinion of American politics.

He put the items back in the box and returned it to the hole, setting the monument back in place. While he waited for someone to possibly come and kill him, he would focus on ensuring that Annabelle Conroy stayed among the living, even if she said she didn't want his help.

He had lost his daughter. He was not going to lose Annabelle.

20

The Camel Club met that night at eight o'clock at Stone's cottage. As usual, Milton brought his laptop and pecked on the keys, while Caleb sat anxiously in a rickety chair and Reuben leaned against a wall.

Stone told them about Susan's dilemma and also that she had left town.

"Well, damn," Reuben said. "We never even got to go out for a drink."

Stone explained, "Jerry Bagger probably killed those people in Portugal and left her partner for dead. She needs our help, but feels it would put us in too much danger."

Caleb squared his shoulders. "She obviously doesn't know that this group absolutely *revels* in danger."

Stone cleared his throat. "Yes, well, my original plan had been to investigate this Jerry Bagger and see if we could work to have him put in prison."

"A good plan in *theory*, but how do we do it for real?" Reuben said.

"I thought it might be worthwhile to go up to Atlantic City and check him out."

Milton said, "Here's a picture of him. The Pompeii Casino has its own Web site."

Caleb looked at Bagger smiling up from the computer screen and moaned fearfully. "Good God, look at that face; those eyes. He's clearly a mobster, Oliver. You don't go and *check out* mobsters."

Reuben eyed Stone. "It might be a little dicey going to his home turf."

"It's only for information gathering," Stone said. "No confrontations at all. Just observing and perhaps talking to a few people who might be helpful."

"But if this Bagger person finds out? He might come after us!" Caleb said.

"What happened to you *reveling* in danger, Caleb?" Reuben reminded him.

Caleb retorted, "This man kills people, probably for jollies."

"The good news is you don't have to go, Caleb," Stone said. He turned to the other two. "I thought Milton and Reuben could do the first recon; that is if Reuben can get some time off from the dock."

"I can always find an excuse not to go lug big shit off big trucks for not-so-big bucks."

Milton said simply, "Sounds good."

"Sounds good?" Caleb exclaimed. "Milton, this man is dangerous. He's a *casino* operator, for God sakes," he added in a hiss. "He makes money off people's addictions. I bet he's involved in drugs too. And prostitution!" He ended with a dramatic flourish.

"You need to be careful," Stone warned. "No unnecessary risks."

"Understood," Reuben said. "I can pick Milton up in the truck tomorrow morning."

"And while you're doing that, I'm going to track down Susan. She's checked out of her hotel, but I have some ideas."

"So what am I supposed to do while the three of you are out gallivanting around?" Caleb asked.

"Just the usual stuff, Superman," Reuben said. "Keeping the nation's capital safe for truth, justice and the American way."

Stone said, "Oh, Caleb, I need to borrow your car. I doubt Susan's still in the city so I'll have to travel."

Caleb stared at him in alarm. "You want to borrow my car? My car! That's impossible." Caleb's ride was an ancient pewter gray Nova with an eternally rattling tailpipe. It had more rust than metal, more springs than upholstery, no working heat or AC, and the man treated it as though the wreck were a vintage Bentley.

"Just give him the keys," Reuben growled.

"Then how will I get home tonight?"

"I'll drive you on my motorcycle."

"I refuse to ride in that death trap."

Reuben gave him such a ferocious look that Caleb hastily pulled out his car keys and handed them to Stone. "Then again, there's nothing wrong with trying new things."

Caleb said suddenly, "Oliver, do you even have a driver's license?"

"Yes, but unfortunately it's been expired for over twenty years."

Caleb paled. "But that means you can't drive legally."

"That's right. But given the seriousness of what we're doing I knew you'd understand."

Stone left Caleb standing there openmouthed and moved over to Reuben, who was motioning to him from the front door.

Reuben spoke in a low voice. "Carter Gray's house was blown up with him in it."

"I was aware of it."

"I hope not *too* aware."

"The FBI has already spent time with me. I went out to Gray's house or what's left of it with a pair of agents and Alex Ford and gave them the benefit of my thoughts."

"Murder?"

"Undoubtedly."

Reuben said, "This doesn't have anything to do with, you know, your past?" He was the only member of the Camel Club who remotely had any knowledge of what Stone had done decades ago.

"I hope not. I'll see you when you get back from Atlantic City. Remember, keep a low profile."

"While I'm there, you want me to lay down a bet for you at the craps table?"

"I never gamble, Reuben."

"How come?"

"One, I don't have any money, and two, I hate to lose."

21

The next morning Bagger met with Joe, from the PI firm. The man was trim, with calm gray eyes. Though soft-spoken, Joe was not intimidated in the least by the casino king. It was one of the things Bagger loved about him. He sat down across from Bagger and opened a file.

"We got some quick results on this one, Mr. Bagger." He scanned the pages and then looked up. "I've got a written report for you, but let me just give you the essentials." He handed a photo across. "We had an associate of ours in Vegas check out the wedding chapel where Conroy and DeHaven were married. It's a typical mom-and-pop; the same couple run it today, in fact. After a little financial encouragement they let us take a peek at their records, and that's where we got a copy of that photo. Apparently they take pictures of all the people they marry and put them up on the wall. I'm assuming from the look on your face, Mr. Bagger, that that's our girl."

Bagger was smiling and nodding as he stared down at a photo of a much younger Annabelle Conroy and her brand-new husband, Jonathan DeHaven. "That's my little friend. Good work, Joe. What else you got?"

"Well, this has the potential to make our job easier. I'm just not sure yet."

Bagger looked up from the photo. "What has the potential?"

In answer, Joe handed Bagger a newspaper clipping. "The name DeHaven rang a bell for me, but I didn't know why at the time. Then I did some digging. And bingo!"

"He was murdered!" Bagger exclaimed, reading the headline.

"Very recently. Found in some vault at the Library of Congress in D.C. It was all tied into some spy ring going down in Washington."

"Are we sure it's the same DeHaven?"

Joe handed Bagger another photo of DeHaven from a newspaper article detailing his death. "You can see it's the same guy, only older."

"So Annabelle's hubby was a spy and got whacked?"

"Her ex-husband. We also found out that the marriage was annulled a year later."

"Annulled? Doesn't that mean they didn't have sex or something? For a whole freaking year?" Bagger stared down at Annabelle's wedding picture. The lady was a stunner. Bagger of course hated the woman for ripping him off, but how in God's name did her husband keep from jumping her the minute the "I do's" were said? "Was this DeHaven guy secretly gay or something?"

"I don't know the details of why the annulment took place, but it did and was made a matter of record in Washington, D.C., where the couple presumably came back to live. And DeHaven wasn't part of the spy ring. Details are still coming out and some of it's being buried because of national security interests, but it looks like he was an innocent guy who got killed because he stumbled onto something he shouldn't have."

A pensive Bagger sat back. Annabelle had conned him into thinking she was with CIA and that the money he had given her was a way for the government to launder cash overseas. But what if she really was with CIA? What if it had been the government that had screwed him? You couldn't sue the government. You couldn't kill Uncle Sam.

He stared across at Joe. "Good work, Joe. Keep digging and see what you come up with."

Joe rose. "Already on it, Mr. Bagger."

After Joe left, Bagger stared down at the picture of the youthful Annabelle. She looked happy although her new hubby looked like, well, like a librarian.

Bagger rose and looked out the window, onto his empire that occupied nearly an entire block on the Boardwalk. Making up his mind, he picked up his phone and called his chief of security. "Warm up the jet, we're heading out."

"Where to, Mr. Bagger?"

"My favorite city. Washington, D.C."

22

The next morning, while Reuben and Milton drove to Atlantic City, Harry Finn was also busy. He and two team members were surveying a parcel of land near the United States Capitol. Their uniforms were perfect, their equipment spot-on. Most importantly, they exuded the confident air of people who had every right to be where they were. When two Capitol police officers approached them, Finn calmly pulled a piece of paper from his pocket and showed the pair his official-looking orders.

"I just go where they send me, guys," he said apologetically. "We won't be here much longer. It's the damn visitor center project."

"You mean that taxpayer hell pit?" one of the cops growled. The project had become D.C.'s version of the Big Dig fiasco in Boston.

Finn nodded. "You know in this town everybody thinks somebody else has jurisdiction. So we have to do the same thing ten times because somebody's panties got in a wad."

"Tell me about it," the other cop said. "Just make it quick."

"Roger that," Finn said, turning back to his work.

The surveyor's apparatus they were using was actually a video camera currently filming two entrances to the Capitol building and detailing the rotation of security guards and other essential elements for a successful penetration later. Ever since a man had broken through the Capitol security perimeter with comparative ease, several high-ranking pols had been livid. They had secretly retained Finn's company to test whether the "enhanced" security measures put in place were the real fix or not. From what Finn had seen so far, they clearly weren't.

Back at the office, Finn spent the next two hours "phone freaking." This was a complex exercise involving phoning one person after another and building on the intelligence with each call to elicit more specific information from each new person called. Finn had used this technique to learn the central location in the United States of the vaccine for a nasty bioterrorism bug by pretending to be a marketing student doing a term paper on commercial distribution techniques. He talked to eight different people, finishing with a vice president of the company that manufactured the vaccine, who unknowingly confirmed the location while answering what he obviously thought was a totally unrelated series of questions.

Today Finn was gathering info on two upcoming

projects: the hit on the Capitol and a far more involved crashing of the Pentagon. While it had been unfortunately proved beyond doubt that one could fly a large plane into the headquarters of the U.S. military and damage it, there were far subtler ways of breaching the facility's security and perhaps doing more harm than the doomed jumbo jet had. Among other possible scenarios, one could booby-trap the military's command and control system, or sabotage its air filtration system, killing or sickening tens of thousands of key government personnel, or even blow up the building from the inside out.

As Finn went about his work, he kept an eye on the Internet for news of Carter Gray's death. As expected, the authorities were keeping a tight lid on all of it. There had been no leaks and most stories were confined to telling and retelling the glorious career and public service of the dead man, Carter Robert Gray. Finally, Finn couldn't take it anymore. He went for a walk.

And then he decided, on impulse, to visit his mother. He would catch a flight that very night, after the kids were in bed. He could see her the next day and be back home that same night. After the navy gig, he had some downtime coming anyway. His was not a nine-to-five occupation. And with several jobs percolating in the prep stage before the field operations would begin, now was actually a good time to go.

He both loved and hated to see his mother. The

routine never varied; it couldn't, actually. Yet since it had all begun with her, Finn had to return to that touchstone from time to time. It wasn't like he was reporting in, but in a way that's exactly what he was doing.

He booked the flight online and called Mandy and told her. He left work early, drove his two youngest to swimming and baseball practice respectively, and then picked them up later. After they were asleep he left for the airport, for the short ride to one of the longest days of his life.

23

Stone punched in Annabelle's phone number. Four rings went by and he assumed she wasn't going to answer when her voice said, "Hello?"

"Where are you?" he said.

"Oliver, I left a note."

"The note is bullshit. Where are you?"

"I don't want you involved in this, so just forget me."

"I've sent Milton and Reuben up to Atlantic City to do a recon on Bagger."

"You did what?" she screamed into the phone. "Are you insane!"

"Now there's the Annabelle I've come to know and admire."

"That's suicide, sending them to Bagger's turf."

"They know how to take care of themselves."

"Oliver, I left town so you *wouldn't* get involved."

"Then come back, because we *are* involved."

"I can't come back. I won't come back."

"Then just answer one question for me."

"What?" she said warily.

"What did Jerry Bagger do to you to make you rip him off for millions?"

"I ripped him off because that's what I do. I'm a con."

"If you keep lying to me I'm going to get really upset."

"Why do you care?"

"You helped us, now it's our turn to help you."

"I helped myself. You guys were just in the way."

"So be it, but you still need us. And we're wasting time. If Bagger's as good as you say he is, you may not have much time left."

"Thanks for your vote of confidence."

"I'm just being practical. Where are you?"

"Forget it."

"Then let me guess. But if I guess correctly you have to tell me where you are. Deal?"

"Whatever makes you happy."

"I said deal?"

"Fine. Deal."

"Okay, you've taken my advice and you're trying to pin something on Bagger. And what you're trying to pin on him is the reason you ripped him off. And that's where you are right now, at a place where he did something so bad to you or yours that you had to come back at him. And do it damn hard. Am I right?"

Annabelle was dead silent.

He said, "Now, since I won the bet you have to tell me where you are."

"You didn't give me a specific location."

"I didn't say I'd give you a specific location. In fact, what I told you was far more than just naming a town. But if you want to welch on a bet."

"I never go back on a bet."

"Then tell me."

There was a very long pause. "I'm in Maine."

"Where in Maine?"

"A little south of Kennebunk on the coast."

"Is that where it happened?"

Stone waited through another long pause.

"Yes."

"And what was it that did happen?"

"It's my business," she snapped.

"I think I've proved that you can trust me."

"I'm not sure anyone can prove that to me."

"Okay, have it your way. I'll head up to Atlantic City and have a go at old Jerry myself."

"Oliver, you can't do that. He will kill you. Don't you understand that?"

"Then my blood will be on your hands," he said in a joking tone.

"Don't screw with me. I don't need this shit right now."

"Exactly," Stone said in a tight voice. "You don't need stupid wisecracks from me; you need a plan to get you out of Bagger's gunsights. And then you need to execute on that plan."

"And you think you can do that?"

"I used to do it for a living. And I'm sure Jerry Bagger is one bad SOB, but my old playground wasn't exactly Disneyland." There was silence on the phone. Stone thought she had hung up.

"Annabelle?"

"He killed my mother. There, now you know."

"What'd your mother do to Bagger?"

"Nothing. It was my father, Paddy. He ripped Jerry off for ten thousand bucks and it cost my mother her life."

"Did he kill your father too?"

"No, somehow my old man slipped away and forgot to tell my mother that homicidal Bagger was coming to town."

Stone let out a long breath. "That's a lot of baggage to have to carry around. I'm sorry, Annabelle."

"I don't need sympathy, Oliver. I just need a way to take this animal down once and for all, because, to tell the truth, stealing forty million bucks from him didn't even come close to squaring things with that bastard."

"Tell me exactly where you are. I can be there tonight."

"How are you going to get here? Fly?"

"I don't have the money to fly."

"I can get you the plane ticket."

"Unfortunately, I don't have any ID, and without that I can't get on an aircraft."

"I wish you'd told me, I could get you stuff so

good the FBI couldn't spot it as fake, much less TSA grunts."

"I may take you up on that one day. For now, I'm driving."

She told him where she was. "You're sure about this? You can still walk, no questions asked. I'm used to going it alone."

"No friend of the Camel Club goes it alone. I'll see you in Maine, Annabelle."

24

Milton was standing behind some players at a blackjack table watching the action, his gaze roving like a laser beam over the cards coming out of the chute.

Reuben appeared beside him. "How's it going?"

Milton smiled. "This looks like fun."

"Well, it's our job to blend in, so play a few hands. Just don't lose your shirt. We need gas money to get back home."

Reuben strolled along, his gaze wandering here and there, looking for anything or anyone that might be useful. After being in combat in Vietnam he had toiled for years with the Defense Intelligence Agency, or DIA, the military equivalent of CIA. Though he'd been out of the game for a long time now, it wasn't hard to remember how to do it well. And for Reuben, that meant heading to a bar for a drink.

He parked his butt on a stool and ordered a gin and tonic, checked his watch and ran his gaze over the bartender, an attractive middle-aged woman but with the pasty, beaten-down look of someone who'd spent too many years on the casino clock and under casino lights.

"So what action looks good these days?" he asked her as he munched on peanuts and idly sipped his cocktail.

She wiped the bar with a rag and said, "Depends on what you're looking for."

"Something besides slots and dice and other things that cost money."

"Then you came to the wrong place."

He laughed. "Story of my life. I'm Roy." He put out a hand.

She shook it. "Angie. Where you from?"

"Someplace a little south of here. You a native?"

"I started life in Minnesota, if you can believe that. Been here long enough I guess I qualify for native status. Once the casinos moved in how many people can say they're from Atlantic City? I mean, it's a place you go to, not come from, at least not anymore."

Reuben raised his glass. "I toast your eloquence." He stared around at the expensively decorated interior. "Must be some big-ass corporation that owns this place. It makes the Bellagio or Mandalay Bay look cheap."

Angie shook her head. "No corporation. One man."

"Get out of here, Angie. I thought all casinos were run by fat-cat companies."

"Not this one. It's owned by Jerry Bagger."

"Bagger? Name sounds familiar."

"He's pretty memorable. You meet him once, you don't forget it."

"From the way you say it I take it he's not your basic, loving humanitarian."

"You don't build a place like this being a human anything." She suddenly eyed Reuben with suspicion. "This isn't some trick, is it? You don't work for Mr. Bagger, do you? I'm not saying anything against him. He's a good boss."

"Angie, relax. I am what I look like, a poor sucker from out of town who blew his wad early at craps and decided to spend his last evening here having some real fun before hitting the road with my tail tucked between my legs." He looked behind him. "But thanks for the info. I don't want to run into this guy and say something I shouldn't. He sounds pretty tough."

"Not to worry, he's out of town. Saw him leave with his boys yesterday."

"Oh, he travels a lot?"

"Not really, even though he has his own jet."

"Then he's probably going to Vegas to check out the competition."

"He was run out of Vegas a long time ago. I actually know where he went, because my best girlfriend is dating Mr. Bagger's pilot."

"So where's the big honcho off to, then?" Reuben said in a bored tone as he swallowed a handful of nuts.

"Washington, D.C."

Reuben gagged so badly Angie had to pound him on the back.

Recovered, he said, "Damn reflux. It's closed my throat down to almost nothing."

"Jeez, you gave me a scare. Never had anyone die on me yet, though." She looked around and lowered her voice. "Can't say the same about everybody else in this place."

Reuben said slowly, "You have somebody kick the bucket here recently?"

"Let's just say we had a couple top-level employees in the hospital. We were told they had the flu. I got a friend who works over at the hospital they were taken to. Since when does the flu cause cuts and bruises? Tell me that."

"But they're still alive."

"They are, but we had another guy here, a computer whiz type. He disappeared. They said he left to take another job. Well, he didn't tell his family and he forgot to clean out his apartment."

"Damn, what could have happened to him?"

Angie eyed Reuben's big frame appreciatively. "I get off work at nine, Roy. You buy me dinner and I'll tell you some more. Okay?"

After he left the bar Reuben called Stone on his cell phone and told him about Bagger being in D.C.

"Good work, Reuben," Stone said. "I'm on my way to see Susan now."

"I thought you said she was gone."

"Let's just say I convinced her to give us another chance. You didn't find out why Bagger's in Washington?"

"Figured I'd try and get that out of her tonight. Didn't want to push too hard. You know what I mean?"

"Absolutely. Keep me informed."

"And tell Susan I still want a date."

25

Reuben continued walking around the casino, trying to memorize as many key details as he could. He didn't know exactly what sort of intelligence Stone wanted so he decided to be over- rather than under-inclusive. In any event it beat the hell out of working on the loading dock.

He finally decided to hook back up with Milton at the blackjack table. When he got there his jaw dropped. Milton had huge columns of chips stacked neatly in front of him.

Reuben said, "Milton, what the hell happened?"

"What happened," the bettor next to Milton said, "is that your buddy's up about four thousand bucks."

Reuben stared at the man and then at the beefy pit boss glaring at Milton and his winnings.

"Holy hell, Batman," Reuben exclaimed. "Four grand!"

The pit boss leaned down into Milton's face. "You're cheating."

"No I'm not," Milton said indignantly.

"You're counting cards, you little slimeball. Is that

how you get your kicks? What, the ladies a problem for you? You have to come here and cheat? And then you go home and jack off. Is that it?"

Milton flushed red. "This is the first time I've ever been in a casino."

The pit boss roared, "Do you really think I'm buying that bullshit?"

Reuben said politely, "Look, I'm sure it's nothing really—"

Milton cut in. "And so what if I am counting cards? Is that illegal in New Jersey? I don't think so, because I looked it up. And you can employ countermeasures against me, but only if I'm a 'skilled player,' which I'm not, and by law the countermeasures you can use are limited. Now, in Vegas you can claim I'm trespassing, read me the Trespass Act and ban me from the casinos for a year, but this isn't Vegas, now is it?"

"You know all this stuff and you say this is the first time you've been in a casino," the pit boss scoffed.

"I looked all that up last night online. Gee, what a concept. So back off and let me play my cards."

The thick-necked boss looked like he was going to come over the table at Milton, but Reuben stepped between them. "I think my friend will cash out now."

"But Reuben," Milton protested. "I'm on a roll."

"He'll cash out now," Reuben said very firmly.

Later, Milton said to Reuben, "Why wouldn't you let me keep playing?"

"How about that whole living thing, Milton, you still interested in that?"

"Oh come on, this is the twenty-first century. They don't do that stuff anymore."

"You think so? Forget the laws, a casino can pretty much kick you out for any reason they want. You're lucky the pit boss was probably slow to get to the table. Dollars to donuts we gotta couple goons tailing us right now."

Milton whipped his head around. "Where?"

"You can't see them!" Reuben paused. "So how'd you win all that money?"

Milton said in a low voice, "I started out employing a multilevel Hi-Lo scheme with a side count add-on based on the Zen Count system. Of course I was utilizing an overall true count methodology to take into account the multiple decks being played. Later, I took it up a peg to the Uston Advanced Point Count method and paid particular attention to strategically optimizing my bets using the three-color chip scenario to disguise my wager."

Reuben gaped. "Milton, how the hell do you know all this stuff?"

"I read twelve Internet articles on the subject last night. It was very interesting. And once I read something—"

"You never forget it, I know, I know." Reuben sighed. There seemed no limit to his friend's intellectual gifts. "So the pit boss was right, you were counting cards. Luckily you were doing it without a computer, that's a big no-no."

"I've got a computer, it's called my brain."

"Okay, Mr. Brain, just so you know, it's a rule on recon missions that the team splits everything right down the middle."

"Down the middle?"

"Yep. So I'm two grand ahead. Now fork it over."

Milton handed over the cash. "Remember, you have to pay taxes on that."

"I don't pay taxes."

"Reuben, you have to pay your taxes."

"Uncle Sam can get his pound of flesh off somebody else. And while you were cleaning out the casino I was doing some real intelligence gathering." He told Milton about Angie.

"That's sounds really promising, Reuben, good work."

"The way Angie was eyeballing me, the price might be pretty damn steep."

"Well, that shouldn't be a problem, you've got two thousand dollars."

Reuben gazed at his friend and just shook his head.

26

Carter Gray walked slowly down the long corridor that was for some reason painted a salmon color, perhaps to induce calmness, he thought. However, this was not a building that inspired calm, only crisis. At the end of the underground hall was a solitary room housed behind a bank-vault-class door. He entered his security codes and let the biometric readers sweep over him. The door noiselessly swung open. This James Bond style of security had set the taxpayers back millions. Yet what else were taxpayers good for, he thought. They consumed far too much, paid too much in taxes and their government spent far more than it should, usually on stupid things. If that wasn't balance, he didn't know what was.

Gray walked over to the wall of locked miniature vaults and slid his electronic key in one while he simultaneously rubbed his thumb across a fingerprint reader. The door slid open and he took the file out, sat down in a chair and began to read.

A half hour later Gray had finished perusing the file. Next, he took out the photo he'd received in the mail, comparing it with the one in the file. It was the same man, of course. He'd known him very well. In many ways he'd been Gray's closest confidant. For decades he'd feared that the unfortunate matter of Rayfield Solomon would come back to haunt him. Now it had.

Cole, Cincetti, Bingham, all dead. And Carter Gray had almost joined them. And he would have except for the safe room built underneath the house by the former CIA director and VP who had lived there before him; an underground room that was both fire- and bombproof. When Gray had explained to Oliver Stone that he was both comfortable and *secure* in his new home, he was being quite literal. And his home included a fortified tunnel that had carried him safely off the property and to the other side of the main road, where a car driven by one of his guards had picked him up. Gray had been gone from the house for over an hour when it exploded. He'd left minutes after receiving the photo. Still, it had been a relatively close call. The FBI had initiated a homicide investigation, publicly acknowledging that a body had been found in the wreckage. Gray had put this in motion behind the scenes. He *wanted* people to think he was dead.

He would've been dead except for the fact that his would-be killer had sent him this photo. What a risk that had been. What a tactical error. And yet it must have been important for the person that Gray clearly understood why he was being killed; that fortunately revealed much about his potential murderer. It was undoubtedly someone who cared very much about Rayfield Solomon. And for Gray, that evidenced a familial relationship or something close to it.

The other targets were now obvious, Gray mused as he sat in his chair a hundred feet underneath the headquarters of the CIA in Langley, Virginia, a juggernaut he had once commanded. Only the current and former directors of the CIA were allowed in this room. Here there were files that contained secrets the American public would never know. Indeed, there were stories here of which American presidents were ignorant. When one said "files," of course, one meant more than mere paper. It included flesh and blood. Certainly that had been the case with Ray Solomon. Gray hadn't known about the order to kill Solomon. If he had he would've prevented it from being executed. He had regretted his friend's death all these years. Yet in this case regret was a very cheap emotion to have. You felt bad, but the other person was dead.

Gray put the files back and locked the vault. There were many important folks who would not want the matter of Ray Solomon ever to resurface. They would use all their resources to hunt down whoever tried to kill Gray before the person struck again. And now Gray was fully on their side. His friend had been dead for decades. No good could come from rekindling those fires.

And he had played fair by warning John Carr. The man would get no more help from him. And if he died, he died.

27

As Jerry Bagger was being driven through Washington he passed by the Justice Department building. On noticing this, he immediately gave the finger to the entire federal agency.

"Talk about a great place for a nuclear strike. And maybe they could take out the FBI at the same time. I mean lawyers and cops, who needs 'em? Not me." He looked at one of his men. "Mike, you need 'em?"

"No, sir, Mr. Bagger."

"Good thinking."

Bagger had received a more detailed report from his PI after arriving in D.C.; that's why he was now climbing out of the car and walking into a library. It wasn't any library; it was, for many erudite folks, *the* library: the Library of Congress.

His men made some inquiries, and two minutes later Bagger and his entourage walked into the rare book reading room where the late Jonathan DeHaven, who was also Annabelle's ex-husband, had once been director. It was also where Caleb Shaw currently worked. The man himself came out of the vaults as Bagger walked in.

To his credit Caleb did not start vomiting on recognizing Bagger from the picture Milton had shown him, although his gurgling stomach made that a clear possibility. Instead, he simply stood there as a smile spread across his face. He had no idea why he was smiling. With a sudden pang of horror he thought it might actually be a first step in his becoming hysterical. He had to do something and fast.

"Can I help you?" he said, walking over to the group of big young men in dark suits surrounding the very fit, sixty-six-year-old, broad-shouldered, white-haired and deeply tanned Bagger, with his broken nose and hideous scar running down one cheek.

He looked like a pirate, Caleb thought.

"I hope so," Bagger began politely. "This is the rare book thing here?" He looked around.

"The rare book reading room, yes."

"So how rare are the books in this place?"

"Very, and it's not just books, we have codex manuscripts, incunabula, broadsheets, a Gutenberg Bible, a copy of the Declaration of Independence, Jefferson's personal library and many other fine works. Some of them the only one of their kind in the world. Literally one of one."

"Yeah?" Bagger said, clearly not impressed. "Well, I got something even rarer than that."

"Really, what is it?" Caleb inquired.

"The book that *I* read," Bagger said. "Because that's zero of zero." He laughed and so did his men. Caleb chuckled politely even as he clutched the back of a chair to steady himself.

Bagger put an arm around Caleb's shoulders. "You look like a guy who can help me. What's your name?"

Caleb desperately tried to think of an alias, but all that came out was, "Caleb Shaw."

"Caleb? Whoa, you don't hear that one every day. You Amish or something?"

"No, I'm a Republican," Caleb said in a small voice as Bagger's muscular arm cinched tighter around him. *Is this the same arm that killed all those people?*

"Okay, Mr. Republican, is there someplace we can talk in private? I mean, this is a big building. Must be someplace we can do a little mano a mano."

Caleb had feared something like this. At least in the reading room there were potential witnesses around, if only to see him being hacked to death by the mobster.

"I, uh, I'm quite busy right now." Bagger's arm instantly tightened even more around him. "But I can certainly spare you a few minutes."

Caleb led them to a small office down the hall from the reading room.

"Sit," Bagger ordered Caleb, and he quickly sat in the only chair in the room. "Okay, now, I understand that the guy who used to run this place got whacked."

"The director of the Rare Book and Special Collections Division was killed, that's correct."

"Jonathan DeHaven?"

"That's right." Caleb added in a low voice, "He was murdered. Right in this very building."

"Wow," Bagger said as he eyed his men. "In a freaking library. I mean, is this world we live in violent or what?" He turned back to Caleb. "Thing is, I got a friend who knew this DeHaven character. She was actually married to him at some point."

"Really? I never knew Jonathan was married." Caleb managed to tell this lie quite capably.

"Well he was. Kind of short-lived, though. I mean he was a book geek. No offense. And the woman, well, the woman wasn't. She was sort of like a, how do you say—"

"A tornado and a hurricane all wrapped into one?" Caleb offered.

Bagger shot him a suspicious glance. "Yeah, what makes you say that?"

Realizing he had come dangerously close to giving Bagger adequate reason to torture him for further information, Caleb said smoothly, "I was married once too, and my wife left me after only four months. She was a hurricane and a tornado and, like you said, I'm a book geek." It was stunning how easily lying came to him.

"Right, right, you get the picture. Anyway, I haven't seen the woman in a long time and wanted to catch up with her. So it occurred to me that she might have heard about her ex's death and come for the funeral." He looked expectantly at Caleb.

"Well, I went to the service but I didn't notice anyone I didn't know. What does this woman look like and what's her name?"

"Tall, nice curves, a real looker. Little scar under her right eye. Hair color and style depends on the day of the week, you know what I mean? Her name is Annabelle Conroy, but that also depends on the day of the week."

"Doesn't ring a bell at all." The name clearly didn't, since Caleb only knew Annabelle by the name Susan Hunter, but the physical description was certainly dead-on. "I'm sure I would have noticed someone like that. Most of the people at the funeral were pretty average-looking. You know, like me."

"Yeah, I bet," Bagger grumbled. He snapped his fingers and one of his men produced a card that Bagger handed to Caleb. "You remember something useful, call me. I pay well. I mean really well. Five figures."

Caleb's eyes widened as he clutched the card. "You must really want to find her."

"Oh, you got no idea how bad, Mr. Republican."

28

Harry Finn quietly entered the room, sat down in the chair and stared at her. The woman looked back at him, or through him, Finn was never sure. She had once spoken fluent English without a trace of any accent. But the multilingual lady had, perhaps out of growing paranoia, decided to mash four languages into one, creating a confusing amalgam of chaotic communication. He didn't quite know how, but Finn managed to understand it. She would have accepted nothing less from him.

She muttered in his direction and he answered her blunt greeting in a few words. This seemed to please her, because she nodded appreciatively, a smile edging across her fallen cheeks. Actually she had known that he was here before Finn had even entered the room. She had explained this before as having felt his *presence*. He had a particular aura, she'd told him; a pleasant one, but distinctive. As a man who did not like to leave any trace of himself anywhere, this bothered Finn greatly. Yet how did one wipe away his aura?

As a child he remembered his mother's tall, strong

body with the hands of a pianist. Now she was shrunken, withered. He studied her face. It had once held a rare, fragile beauty, a loveliness that growing up he had always associated with the most beautiful of daylilies. This was because when he was a child, at night, the beauty receded and she became moody and sometimes violent; never against him, but against herself. And then Finn would have to step in and take charge. As early as age seven he had done this. The experience had made him grow up quickly, faster than he should have. Now the beauty was gone from her face, the body collapsed, the once lovely hands scarred and wrinkled in her lap. She was only in her early seventies and yet looked more than ready for the grave.

But she still could dominate him with her indignation, with her demand that a wrong be righted. Despite her physical disintegration her words had retained the power to make him feel the grief, the injustice she'd endured.

"I have heard the news," she said in her strange talk. "It is done and it is good. You are good."

He stood and looked out the window at the grounds of this place that he thought they still called a sanatorium. Stacked neatly on the windowsill were the four newspapers that she read every day, cover to cover, word for word. When the papers were done she listened to the radio, or watched the TV, until she fell asleep late at night. The morning would bring more news that she would devour. There was nothing in the world that she seemed to miss.

"And now you move on to the next," she said, in a higher voice as though she feared her words might not reach him from across the room.

He nodded and said, "Yes."

"You are a good *son.*"

Harry resumed his seat. "How's your health?"

"What health?" she said, smiling and swaying her head. She had always done that, he remembered. Always, as though she heard a song no one else did. As a child he had loved that about her, that mysterious quality all children sought out in their parents. Now he didn't like it as much.

"I have no health. You know what they did to me. You cannot believe this is natural. I am not that old. I sit here and I rot a little more each day."

They had poisoned her, years ago, she had told him. They had gotten to her somehow, she wasn't quite sure how. The poison was meant to kill, but she had survived it. Yet it was eating away at her, from the inside out, laying claim to organs one by one until there would be none left. She probably believed that one day she would simply vanish from the earth.

"You can leave. You're not like the others here."

"And where would I go, tell me that? Where would I go? I am safe here. So here I will stay until they take me away in the bag and burn me. Those are my wishes."

Finn held up his hands in mock surrender. They had this same discussion during each of his visits, with the same result. She was rotting and afraid and here she would die. He could have articulated both parts of this conversation, so well did he know them.

"And how is your wife, and those beautiful children?"

"They're fine. I'm sure they miss seeing you."

"There's not much left to see. Your little one, Susie. She still has the bear I gave her?"

"It's her favorite. She's never without it."

"You tell her never to let it go. It represents my love for her. She must never let it go. I have not been a proper grandmother to them. I know this. But it would kill me if she ever let go of the bear. Kill me."

"I know. And she knows. Like I said, she loves it."

She rose on shaky legs, went to a drawer and pulled out a photo. In twisted fingers she clutched the item before handing it across to him. "Take it," she said. "You've earned it."

He slipped the photograph out of her hands and held it up. It was the same picture that Judd Bingham, Bob Cole and Lou Cincetti had seen before they died. Carter Gray, too, had gazed on this image before he was blown to the next world.

Finn traced the delicate line of Rayfield Solomon's cheek with his index finger. In a flash the past came racing back to him: the separation, the news of his father's death, the erasing of the past and meticulous creation of a new one, and over the years the devastating revelations of a wife and mother telling her son what had happened.

"And now Roger Simpson," she said.

"Yes. The last one," Finn replied, a hint of relief in his voice.

It had taken him years to track down Bingham, Cincetti and Cole. Yet he had finally located all of them, and that's when the killing had started a few months ago. He had known the whereabouts of Gray and Senator Roger Simpson since they were public figures. But they were also harder targets. He had gone for the points of least resistance first. It made it more likely that Gray and Simpson would be forewarned, but he had built that into his equation. And when Gray had left the government, he had also left most of his protection behind. And even forewarned, Finn had managed to kill him. Simpson was next in line. Senators had protection too, but Finn was confident he would eventually get to the man.

When Finn looked on the life he had now as part of a family of five in a quite ordinary Virginia suburb complete with a lovable dog, music lessons, soccer matches, baseball games and swim meets, and compared it to the life he had as a child, the juxtaposition was close to apocalyptic in its effect on him. That's why he rarely thought of these things together. That's why he was Harry Finn, King of Compartmentalization. He could build walls in his mind nothing could pierce.

Then his mother said, "Let me tell you a story, Harry."

He sat back in his chair and listened, though he had heard it all before—in fact, could have told it as well as she could now. And yet he listened as she spoke in her fractured, discordant collage of words that still managed to radiate a visceral power; her memories carved out an eloquent factual case that only truth could arouse. It was both wonderful and terrifying—her ability to conjure a world from decades ago with such force that it appeared to be occupying the room they were in with the agonized heartbreak surrounding a flaming pyre. And when she was finished and her energy spent, he would kiss her goodbye and continue his journey, a journey he carried on for her. And maybe for him too.

29

"Calm down, Caleb," Stone said. "And tell me exactly what happened." Stone had pulled off the road on the way to Maine when he'd received Caleb's frantic call. He listened for ten minutes to his friend's breathless recounting of his face-to-face with Jerry Bagger.

"Caleb, are you sure he didn't know you were lying? Really sure?"

"I was good, Oliver, you would've been proud of me. He gave me his card. Said to call if I had any other information. He offered to pay five figures." Caleb paused. "And I found out her real name is Annabelle Conroy."

"Don't tell that to anyone!"

"What do you want me to do now?"

"Nothing. Do not contact Bagger. I'll give you a call later."

Stone clicked off and then phoned Reuben in Atlantic City, relaying what Caleb had told him. "Well, your information was correct, Reuben, Bagger *is* in D.C."

"Hopefully this Angie gal will be even more

informative tonight. By the way, where are you, Oliver?"

"I'm on my way to Maine."

"Maine? Is that where she is?"

"Yes."

"Why Maine?"

"Let's just say our friend has some unfinished business up there."

"Having to do with this Bagger dude?"

"Yes."

Stone put his phone down and continued driving. Caleb's car, though old and rotting, had performed well enough, though on no occasion had he been able to coax it past sixty. Hours later, the night well established, Stone crossed from New Hampshire into Maine. Checking his map, he exited off the interstate and headed east, toward the Atlantic Ocean. Twenty minutes later he slowed and drove through the downtown area of the place Annabelle was staying. It was quaint and filled with shops offering everything from touristy items to nautical gear, as many coastal New England towns did. This was the off-season though, and most of the visitors were long gone, having no desire to expose themselves to the coming Maine winter.

Stone found the B&B where Annabelle was staying, parked in the small lot, grabbed his duffel bag and went in.

She was waiting in the parlor for him, standing in

front of the fire that flickered pleasantly behind her. The floors and doors here creaked; the smell was of a recently served dinner mixed with the aroma of centuries-old wood and the heavy bite of the ocean's salt air.

"I got the owner to save us some supper," Annabelle said. They ate in the small dining room, and a hungry Stone wolfed down the chowder, thick buttered bread and crispy cod while Annabelle merely picked at hers.

Finished, he said, "Where can we talk?"

"I got you a room next to mine."

"Um, I'm a bit short of funds right now."

"Oliver, don't even go there. Come on."

She got a carafe of coffee and two cups from the kitchen and led him upstairs, first to his room to drop off his small bag and then to hers, which had a tiny sitting room off the bedroom. There was also a fire crackling in the fireplace. They sat and drank the hot coffee.

Annabelle reached in her bag, pulled out an ID, a credit card and a wad of cash and tossed them to Stone. The ID had his picture on it and other pertinent information making him a citizen of the District of Columbia.

"Quick job from a guy I found. I used a picture of you I had with me. The credit card's legit."

"Thank you. But why'd you do it?"

"Again, don't go there."

Annabelle just stared into the flames while Stone studied her, debating whether to tell her or not.

"Annabelle, put your cup down."

"What?"

"I have something to tell you and I don't want you to spill hot coffee."

A rare look of fear crossed her features as she slowly put down the cup. "Reuben? Milton? Dammit, I told you not to send them to Atlantic City!"

"They're fine. This has to do with Caleb and he's fine too. But he had an unexpected visitor today at the library."

Annabelle seemed to stare right through him as she said, "Jerry?"

Stone nodded. "Caleb apparently played his part well. Bagger offered a lot of money for information on you."

"How did he know to come to the library?"

"He found out you were married to DeHaven. It was a public record and these days that information is easily available on the Internet if you know where to look."

Annabelle slumped back against the small sofa. "I should have just followed my damn exit plan. God, I'm so stupid."

"No, you're human. You came to pay your respects to a man you were married to and cared for. It's normal."

"Not when you've ripped off a homicidal nutcase

like Jerry Bagger for forty million bucks it's not. Then it's just stupid," she added bitterly.

"Okay, but you didn't go to your island, your partner screwed up and Bagger is on your tail and he's narrowed the gap decisively. Those are the facts we have to deal with. You can't run now, because no matter how well you run, you will leave some sort of trail. And he's too close to miss it. If you go to your island, all that guarantees is that when Bagger shows up at your door, you'll be all alone when he kills you."

"Thanks, Oliver. That really makes me feel better."

"It should. Because here you have people willing to risk their lives to help you!"

Her expression softened. "I know that. I didn't mean what it sounded like."

Stone looked toward the window. "This is quite the sleepy town. It's hard to believe someone could be murdered here. Where did it happen?"

"Right on the outskirts. I was planning to go there tomorrow morning."

"Do you want to talk about it tonight?"

"You had a long drive and you must be tired. And, no, I don't want to talk about it tonight. If I'm going to face this tomorrow I need to get some sleep. Good night."

Stone watched her bedroom door close, then he rose and headed to his room, unsure of what the morning would bring.

30

Reuben dropped over a hundred bucks for drinks and dinner with Angie, but he figured it was a good return on his investment for he learned some interesting things. The two guys who'd ended up in the hospital and the one who'd disappeared completely had evidently displeased their boss, Jerry Bagger. How, Angie was not quite sure, but it seemed to come down to money. Unfortunately, Angie didn't know why Bagger had gone to Washington, only that it had happened all of a sudden.

I bet, thought Reuben.

Over her third "Dark and Stormy," a rum and ginger beer concoction that Reuben tried a sip of and almost retched as a result, Angie said, "Funny stuff going on around here lately. Got a buddy in finance for the casino. He told me he was under strict instructions to do everything he could to delay a routine Control Commission inspection of the casino's books."

"This Bagger guy in money trouble?"

She shook her head. "Don't see how. The Pompeii

Casino is like the Bureau of Engraving and Printing. It's a gold mine, and Mr. Bagger is the smartest operator in town. Tough with a nickel, and he knows how to make a buck."

"Something must have happened, then," Reuben said. "Maybe the guys who got hurt and the one who disappeared screwed up somehow with some of the casino's cash. Maybe they were ripping him off, and Bagger found out and brought the hammer down."

"Mr. Bagger ain't dumb. You don't break knees anymore; you just sic the cops or lawyers on cheaters. So this must've been something really big, and he took it personally."

"Cops looking into it?"

She looked incredulous. "Mr. Bagger knows what palms to grease. And do you know how much tax revenue the Pompeii generates for New Jersey?"

Reuben nodded thoughtfully. "He probably paid off the pair in the hospital. And the other guy's not gonna be squealing to the police."

"Dead men don't talk, you're right." Angie had scooted closer to Reuben in the booth they were sharing. She patted his thigh with her hand and then kept it there. "So enough shop talk, tell me about yourself. Did you use to play pro football? You look big enough." She squeezed his leg and leaned into him.

"Played some in college. Did a couple tours in Nam. Won some medals, collected some shrapnel."

"Really? Where? Here?" She playfully poked a finger into his chest.

"Let's just say I won't be having any more children." Reuben couldn't believe he was telling this lie to a woman who obviously wanted to go to bed with him, but he had other things on his mind.

Angie's jaw fell so far, it was in jeopardy of smacking the table.

"Check, please," Reuben called out to the waiter as he passed by.

31

While Reuben was disappointing Angie, Milton was trying out a system he'd read about for the craps table. So far he wasn't doing as well as he'd hoped. Granted, he had gone up eight thousand dollars fairly early on in his run; however, he had higher standards than most people. Still, fellow gamblers were lined up around the rail, telling him he was hot, he was on fire. Over two dozen players were riding bets on his coattails desperately hoping he would lead them all to riches, or at least allow them to recoup some of the cash they'd lost thus far to Jerry Bagger.

Women with their boobs falling out of their halter tops and sipping cocktails crowded around him, pushing their bosoms into his shoulders and splashing liquor on his shirt. They also pestered him with silly questions as to his technique. Milton didn't know they were casino ringers whose job it was to break the concentration and hopefully the streak of any hot roller. Yet it didn't matter. It would take far more than multiple pairs of inflatable breasts and inane queries to interfere with Milton Farb's focus.

The two croupiers and the stickman running the table scrutinized the action, accounting for bets and keeping an eye on all that was going on, including those hovering around the rails and players looking to get in on the action. At this point there was little room at the rail, but if someone caught the eye of one of the croupiers and flashed enough chips, he might get in. And this was a table everyone wanted to join.

The stone-faced pit boss hovered in the back taking this all in too. He was the court of last resort in case there were any problems, and it was his job to see to the casino's well-being at all times while putting on a front of being fair to players. The casino world was not a touchy-feely one; there was only one god here and his name was money. And at the end of the day the casino had to keep more of it than it paid out. Yet this pit boss was worried, because he'd been doing this long enough to know a truly hot shooter when he saw one. The Pompeii was going to take one on the chin; he just had a bad feeling.

The table had a $50 minimum bet and a ten grand maximum, and Milton was laying his bets with surgical precision. He'd long since figured out all the statistical probabilities and was putting that knowledge to good use. He'd rolled a seven on his very first throw, the only time that number could be a winner. He'd won $500 on that fling of the dice with an aggressive initial bet and never looked back. He was leveraging his behind-the-pass-line bets, maxing out the fives, sixes and eights up top, then the nines and fives and the most lucrative, but least likely odds-wise, tens and fours, with the finesse of a decades-long craps impresario. He'd nailed a hard four twice and hit a hard eight and ten once each. He'd rolled his points six times now and the heat just kept building.

Finally, the nervous pit boss ordered a change in the table crew. The croupiers and the stickman were more than a little upset about this and their sour expressions showed it. Tips were laid on the house at the end of a shooter's run, so these folks wouldn't be seeing a dime of Milton's winnings. Yet the pit boss's command was law. He'd done it to cool down Milton and the table. But such a move, while allowable under the gaming rules, was always unpopular, and howls of protest erupted from around the rail.

Two security gents drifted over to the table after receiving a call from the pit boss over his headset. After seeing the hulking figures approach, the crowd quickly calmed down.

The pit boss' ploy didn't work because Milton hit his points three more times over an array of intricate bets. He was now up over twenty-five grand. Unless he rolled the dice off the table, the croupier couldn't change them on him, so the nervous pit boss really had few tricks left to pull. He just stood and watched as Milton continued to mow down the Pompeii Casino.

A stunned quiet hit the table when Milton laid

$500 down on a one-time horn bet that he would roll a three. When the one-two combo flashed up the bet paid off with fifteen-to-one odds, turning his $500 into $7,500. He was now up $35,000.

The sweating pit boss was forced to play his final card, subtly nodding his head at a ringer stationed at the table. The man immediately laid down a bet on number seven. This, in effect, was betting against Milton, for if he rolled a seven now, or craps, he was done as shooter and all bets on the table lost. In the gambling world it was generally believed that betting against the shooter generated bad karma, siphoning the energy off the table and causing the shooter to lose his steam. The crowd immediately started growling at the ringer betting craps. One man at the rail even bumped him, but the security stepped in and quelled this mini-riot.

Milton was unfazed by the casino's obvious move to derail him. With the stunned crowd looking on, he calmly laid a thousand dollars' worth of chips on boxcars, or the combination of six and six. This, along with betting snake eyes, was the most aggressive move one could make on a craps table, for it paid off thirty-to-one. However, because it was a one-time bet only, if he didn't roll double sixes on the next throw, Milton lost the cash. Thus, betting a thousand bucks on boxcars was considered insane.

Absolute silence prevailed at the table. There wasn't one square inch of free space at the rail and the onlookers were packed six deep behind the players, straining to see the action. Nothing spread faster through a casino than word of a craps shooter on absolute fire.

Milton glanced over at the pit boss and said, "Do you feel lucky? Because I do."

Before the stunned man could reply Milton let the dice fly. The two cubes rolled down the felt, neatly missing all stacked chips on the table and bouncing off the far rail.

There was a moment of intense calm and then a collective scream audible around the casino erupted as the double sixes came to rest face up. Milton Farb had just won thirty grand and nearly doubled his take to $65,000. The guy beside him was whooping and pounding him on the back. The next words out of Milton's mouth caused the cheers to be replaced with groans of disbelief.

"I'm cashing out," he said to his croupier.

The sea of faces around the rail would have looked far more appropriate at a funeral or plane crash site.

"Let it ride," one man screamed. "You are smoking hot. Let it ride."

"This is paying off my kids' college tuition," yelled another.

Milton said, "I'm smarter than I am lucky. I know when to stop."

This bit of truth never goes over well in a casino.

"Screw you," a big man exclaimed as he strode up

to Milton and put a meaty paw on his shoulder. "You keep rolling that dice, you hear me, you little prick? I've been losing all night until you came along. Keep rolling, you hear me!"

"He heard you," a voice said as a far bigger hand was placed on the man's shoulder, jerking him backward.

"What the hell," the man spat out, whirling around with fists balled. He stared up into the face of the towering Reuben Rhodes, who snatched the stick off the table and held it up.

Reuben said, "The man's done playing, so I suggest you let him collect his chips and go on his way, before I take this stick and ram it right up your fat ass."

32

Later, over a drink in a bar, Reuben scolded Milton. "Dammit, first blackjack and now craps. I told you to blend in, Milton, not stick out. You're making our job a lot harder by turning into a casino shark."

Milton looked chastened. "I'm sorry, Reuben, you're right, of course. I guess I got carried away. It won't happen again."

"And exactly how are you going to get your cash without revealing who you are? When you win big in a casino you have to fill out tax paperwork with your name, address and Social Security number. You want Bagger to have that info?"

"I read about that requirement, Reuben. I'm going to use a fake ID. They won't know the difference."

"What if they run the ID from here on some database?"

"My ID shows me to be a citizen of Great Britain; the U.S. has no taxing authority over me. And I highly doubt the casino is linked to any database in England."

Sufficiently mollified, Reuben explained to Milton what he had learned from Angie.

"So if we can pin those crimes on Bagger, Susan will be home free," Milton said.

"Easier said than done. A guy like Bagger knows how to cover his tracks."

"Well, maybe I can start uncovering them."

"How?"

"Oliver told us about this Anthony Wallace. Bagger found out about him and nearly killed him. Well, *how* did he find out about him?"

"I don't know."

"I know it's late but call Oliver and Susan. Ask her for any information about Wallace that she can think of. Where he was staying, doing, that sort of thing."

Reuben made the call and then turned back to his friend.

"Oliver woke her up and asked her. Wallace was staying in the hotel right across the street from the Pompeii. He was using an alias, Robby Thomas, from Michigan. Five-eight, slender, dark hair, a real cute-boy type. He was staying in a room with a direct sight line onto Bagger's office."

"That's what I needed to know." Milton rose.

"Where are you going?" Reuben asked.

"Across the street. Because the probabilities are that Bagger figured out Wallace was spying on him. If so, he'd want to check it out. So that's what I'm going to do."

"How?"

"I haven't been hanging around Susan for nothing. Sit tight."

Milton's nimble mind worked out the details on the way across the street.

At the front desk of the hotel he said, "I'm looking for a Mr. Robert Thomas. He goes by Robby. He's supposed to be staying at this hotel. Could you ring his room for me?"

After a quick check on the computer the clerk shook his head. "We don't have a guest by that name."

Milton displayed a confused look. "That's very odd. He and my son went to Michigan together. We were supposed to have dinner together."

"I'm sorry, sir."

"Could I have gotten the date wrong? My secretary made the arrangements and she's been known to mess up in the past. I'd feel just terrible if I stood him up."

The clerk clicked a few keys. "We did have a Robert Thomas from Michigan staying with us, but that was some time back."

"Oh my God, I am going to fire my secretary the minute I get back home. I wonder why Robby didn't call me."

"Who gave him your contact information?"

Milton let out a gasp. "My secretary! That idiot!

Wrong date, probably wrong phone number if she bothered to give him one at all."

The clerk gave him a sympathetic look.

"Well, I hope Robby had a good time while he was here."

The clerk glanced at the screen. "Records show he had a massage. So if you missed dinner with him, at least he was relaxed."

Milton laughed. "God, a massage, I haven't had one of those in years."

"We have a great staff."

"Do you have to be a guest here?"

"Oh no, I can make an appointment for you right now if you'd like."

"I tell you what, let me have the same masseuse Robby did. She and I can swap Robby stories. He's quite a character and I'm sure the masseuse will remember him."

The clerk smiled. "Right you are, sir. Let me make the call."

The clerk dialed the spa, spoke for a couple minutes and then his face clouded. "Oh, right, I didn't realize it was her. Okay, I'll get back to you." He hung up and turned to Milton.

"I'm afraid you can't have the same masseuse, sir."

"Oh, she no longer works here?"

"It's not that." The clerk dropped his voice. "She, well, she died."

"Oh my God. Accident?"

"I really can't say, sir."

"I completely understand. So sad. Was she young?"

"Yes. And Cindy was a really nice person."

"Well, that's just awful."

"Would you still like a massage with someone else? We actually have an opening for you now."

"Yes, yes, I believe I will. Cindy, you said her name was?"

"That's right. Cindy Johnson."

"I'll have to let Robby know."

An hour later Milton had received a vigorous massage by a very enthusiastic woman named Helen. However, when he casually raised the issue of Cindy's death, Helen became somber.

"It was awful. Here today, gone tomorrow sort of thing."

"Accident, I heard," Milton said as he sat in the lounge wrapped in a robe and sipping a cup of spring water.

Helen snorted. "Accident?"

"You don't think it was?"

"I'm not saying one way or another. None of my business really. But her poor mom's busted up over it, I can tell you that."

"Her mother? Poor woman? Did she have to come to town to ID the body?"

"What? No, Dolores lives right here. Works a craps table at the Pompeii."

"Well, goodness gracious, I was just there."

"Small world," Helen said.

"Poor Mrs. Johnson," Milton said. "To lose one's daughter like that."

"I know. And it's Mrs. Radnor now, she remarried. Cin liked her stepdad all right, so she said."

Milton finished his water. "Well, thank you for a great massage. I feel like a new man."

"Anytime, sir, anytime."

33

Once back at the Pompeii, Milton filled Reuben in on what he'd discovered.

His friend looked impressed. "Damn, Milton, Susan *has* rubbed off on you."

A few well-placed twenties later, the two men were directed to Dolores Radnor's craps table. Milton bet on a hot shooter while he sized up the woman. She was thin and wrinkle-faced with a perpetually sad air about her. An hour later she took a break and Milton followed her to a table outside the bar area where she sipped on a cup of coffee, an unlit cigarette dangling in her free hand.

Milton said, "Mrs. Radnor?"

Startled, the woman looked at him warily. "How do you know my name? Is there a problem?"

"This is very awkward," Milton began as Dolores looked at him expectantly. "I was in town a few months ago and your daughter gave me the best massage I ever had."

The woman's lips began to quiver. "My Cindy was

damn good at giving massages. She went to school for it, had a certificate and everything."

"I know, I know. She was great. And I promised her the next time I was in town I'd look her up. I was just over there and they told me what happened. And they were kind enough to give me your name and where you worked."

"Why did you want to know that?" she asked, though her look was now more sad than suspicious.

"She was so nice to me that I told Cindy that the next time I was in town I was going to place a bet for her on the craps table."

Dolores looked at him more closely. "Hey, aren't you the shooter who burned up Table No. 7? I popped over there on a break because people were all talking about it."

"I am the very one." He took out his wallet. "And I wanted to deliver Cindy's share to you."

"Sir, you don't have to do that."

"A promise is a promise." Milton handed her twenty one-hundred-dollar bills.

"Oh my God," Dolores said. She tried to give it back but Milton insisted until she put it away in her pocket.

"You coming over and giving me this money is the only good thing that's happened to me in a long time." She suddenly broke down in tears.

Milton handed her some napkins from the holder

on the table. She wiped her eyes and blew her nose. "Thank you," she said.

"Is there anything I can do to help, Mrs. Radnor?"

"You can just call me Dolores. And you just did something wonderful."

"Helen over at the spa told me she died in an accident. Was it a car accident?"

The woman's face hardened. "*Accidental* overdose, they said. That's crap. Cindy never took drugs in her life. And I'd know, because I did drugs, in my time. A druggie knows another druggie, and she wasn't one."

"So why did they think that's what killed her?"

"Stuff in her body. And a container of stuff by her bed, and bam, she's a crackhead. But I know my Cindy. She saw what the stuff did to me. I finally got myself straightened out, got a good job, and now this. Now my baby's gone." She started snuffling again.

"Again, I'm very sorry." Milton left and rejoined Reuben.

Milton said, "Okay, Cindy gives Tony Wallace a.k.a. Robby Thomas a massage. Wallace gets nearly beaten to death by Bagger. And Cindy dies of an accidental drug overdose even though it appears she didn't use drugs."

"Can't be a coincidence," Reuben said.

"The probabilities are Bagger had her killed. I can do some poking around on the Pompeii Web site. There might be a back door there I can exploit."

They walked off without noticing the man in the suit who'd been watching Milton talk to Dolores. He spoke into a walkie-talkie. "We might have a big problem. Get hold of Mr. Bagger."

34

It was a late-stage probe and penetration mission, which was the only reason Harry Finn was standing in a queue early in the morning after having flown in the night before from visiting his mother. While he listened to the man in the front of the group drone on, Finn's thoughts kept going back to his frail mother with the resolute spirit. The story she had told him, as she had hundreds of times before, concerned Rayfield Solomon, who was Harry Finn's father. Solomon had been a man of inexhaustible intellectual curiosity and possessed an unassailable integrity. He had labored on behalf of his country for decades, building a reputation as not only a true patriot but a man who could fix things with his ideas, who could see the answer when no one else could. Then, later in life, he'd fallen in love with Harry Finn's mother and married her. Finn was born and then things began to change, or, more accurately, implode.

And then his father was dead, by his own hand it was claimed, in a fit of guilt. Yet Finn's mother knew better.

"It was all lies," she had told him over and over. "None of it was true. Not about me or him. They killed him for their own reasons."

Finn knew what these reasons were because his mother had drilled them into him. Rayfield Solomon's career as a servant of his country had been forgotten, his good name besmirched. It wasn't the unjust shame that hurt Finn's mother so much. It was the fact that she had lost the man she loved far sooner than she should have.

"He deserved none of this," she had told Finn. "And now there must be retribution."

Finn remembered hearing this story for the first time when he was just seven years old, soon after his father's death. It had astounded him then, assaulting his still developing sense of justice. Today it still stunned him, how one man could be destroyed so unfairly, so completely.

He broke free from these thoughts and concentrated on the task ahead. In the crowd with him were three other members of his team. Two were college students pulled out of his office for a little adventure in the field. The third was a woman who was nearly as accomplished at her work as him.

With some wrangling and sleight of hand they had garnered tickets for a VIP tour of the almost completed U.S. Capitol Visitor Center. The nearly 600,000-square-foot three-level complex was located beneath the east Capitol grounds. This was because its footprint was larger than the Capitol building and the planners didn't want it to detract from the historic structure. The visitor center included orientation theaters, gift shops, food services, a great hall, exhibition space, an auditorium and other attributes both functional and ceremonial, including much-needed space for the operations of the House and Senate. Once open, it would host millions of visitors a year from all around the world. And in keeping with Washington's stellar reputation for efficiency and integrity, the project was only years behind schedule and only several hundred million dollars over budget.

Finn was most intrigued by two elements: first, the connecting tunnel from the visitor center to the Capitol itself, and second, a service tunnel for truck deliveries. The delivery he had in mind was one that no member of Congress ever would have wanted.

Each member of the team carried a buttonhole digital camera and surreptitiously snapped byte after byte of the underground site. Unfinished tunnels and hallways veered off in interesting directions that would come in very handy to Finn and his people later.

Finn asked several questions of the guide, innocent enough on the surface. Yet just as he did with phone freaking, these queries were subtly designed to elicit information that the guide would never have knowingly revealed. On cue, other members of Finn's team asked tagalong questions that revealed even more. Once all was put together, the unsuspecting tour guide had given them nearly enough information to take down the Capitol and everyone in it.

You're a terrorist's best friend and you don't even know it, Finn thought to himself about the affable guide.

Outside, Finn studied the bronze Statue of Freedom that crowned the dome of the Capitol. It was a nice image, he thought. Yet he didn't know if the people who worked inside the building deserved such a nice topper to their digs. It seemed to him that concepts like freedom, truth and honor were the last things on people's minds here.

He and his team strolled through the Capitol's nearly sixty acres of grounds, compiling still more useful data. They congregated at an empty deli off Independence Avenue to go over their results and form new additions to their planned assault on the Capitol.

"I guess congressmen like to keep safe," said one of the team. "Because the operation we're putting together is costing Uncle Sam a bundle."

"Just another drop in the federal budget," the woman said. "We're heading back to the office now, Harry. I've got some phone freaking to do on the Pentagon assignment."

"You can go back," Finn said. "I've got something else to do."

He left them at the deli and headed to the Hart Senate Office Building, the newest and biggest of the three complexes devoted to taking care of America's one hundred senators and their enormous staffs. It amazed Finn sometimes that a hundred people couldn't manage to fit their operations inside something less than the over *two million* square feet the Hart, Russell and Dirksen Senate office buildings collectively provided. After all, this equaled over twenty thousand square feet per senator. And still the politicians were clamoring for ever more expansive digs and more tax dollars with which to build them.

The Hart Senate Building was located at Second and Constitution and was named after Philip Aloysius Hart, a Michigan senator who died in 1976. The deceased Hart, as the inscription above the main entrance to the building said, "Was a man of incorruptible integrity."

The gent would feel quite alone in the Capitol these days, Finn thought.

He strolled around the interior of the building admiring the ninety-foot-high central atrium and its major feature, a mobile-stabile entitled *Mountains and Clouds*, sculpted by the renowned Alexander Calder. The sculptor had come to D.C. in 1976 to make the final adjustments to the piece, which was enormous—the tallest peak in the mountain rose fifty-one feet high—and then had promptly died that same night back in New York. This was a stark testament to the old saying that "Washington can be downright deadly to your health."

While there were over fifty senators in the Hart

Building, Finn was only interested in one: Roger Simpson of the great state of Alabama.

The security in the building, even post-9/11, was a joke. Once you passed through a metal detector, you could pretty much go wherever you wanted. Finn took the elevator up to the floor where Simpson's office was located. It was hard to miss. The Alabama state flag was standing at attention next to the man's portal. As Finn waited near the glass door he took several shots of the office's interior with his buttonhole camera, focusing on the young female receptionist. He noted all other details on this floor and was about to leave when the door opened again and the man himself came out, accompanied by a considerable entourage.

Roger Simpson was tall, nearly six-five and fit, with blondish hair that had white infringing all over, and the calm, aloof air of a man used to having his personal boundaries respected and his commands followed.

The elevator door down the hall opened and a tall blonde woman stepped out. When he saw her Simpson smiled and stepped forward, giving her a quick embrace. She in turn favored him with a peck on the cheek that to Finn's eye was all show and no substance. This was Mrs. Simpson, a former Miss Alabama, with an MBA from an Ivy League school. It was an unusual résumé for a potential First Lady.

Finn noted the two men next to Simpson. They

had earpieces and were armed, maybe Secret Service. Simpson had no doubt taken extra precautions, particularly since the three former Triple Sixes and Carter Gray had died. Finn's plan did not involve a direct attack on Simpson. The only problematic piece might be the picture of Rayfield Solomon. Simpson needed to know why his life was ending. Yet Finn would think of a way; he always did.

He quietly left the building.

35

Stone rose early but Annabelle was already downstairs having hot tea in front of the fireplace. He nodded to her as he came into the room, and then looked for others about.

"We're it," she said bluntly. "You want some breakfast?"

They ate in a chilly room off the small kitchen. Annabelle barely looked at her food while Stone chewed his eggs and toast and shot her glances.

"Did you hear back from Milton and Reuben after they called you?" she asked. "Did they find out anything else?"

"Not yet but I'm sure they'll let us know."

As soon as he finished his cup of coffee she rose. "You ready?"

"Are we going to see the house?"

"We can't. They knocked it down and put up a monster in its place. But we can still check out the area."

Her cheeks were flushed and her eyes looked unfocused. Stone wondered if she was ill.

As though in answer to his thoughts she said, "I'm fine. I just didn't sleep much."

A half hour later they were standing in front of the plot of land where Annabelle's mother had been murdered.

Annabelle said, "That's it. Or at least where it was. My mom's place was just a little cottage."

The current house wasn't a little anything. It was a ten-thousand-square-foot shingled and turreted *Architectural Digest* cover home wannabe right on the ocean.

"How long ago was the cottage knocked down?" Stone asked.

"Six years. Not too long after she was killed. Ocean views trump brutal murder every time."

"Okay, how do you want to do this?" he asked.

"I suggest we're a father and daughter, no offense, looking for someplace for you to retire. We grab a local Realtor and start asking questions."

Later that afternoon Annabelle and Stone followed a short dark-haired woman built like a keg of beer around the exterior of a large house for sale. It was four lots down from where Annabelle's mother had gotten a bullet fired into her brain courtesy of Jerry Bagger.

"It's adorable, Dad," Annabelle cooed as they surveyed the tumbledown place. "I can't understand why no one has snatched it up."

"First of all, it's not little. And second, it obviously needs some work," Stone said firmly.

"Come on, Dad," Annabelle said. "It's oceanfront. You've been looking a long time and never found anything worth writing home about. Can't you see yourself retiring here? Just look at those views."

He turned to the Realtor. "The place at the end of the street on the right is a real beaut and in great condition. Know whether they're interested in selling?"

"The MacIntoshes? No, I don't think they want to sell."

Annabelle said, "MacIntoshes? That doesn't sound familiar. But I did know some folks that used to live up here. Well, I didn't really know them, friend of a friend thing. Visited them once; that's why we're up here looking, actually. I remember it being so pretty."

"I've been here a long time, do you remember their names?"

Annabelle pretended to think. "Connor, or Conway. No, Conroy, that's right, Conroy."

"Not Tammy Conroy?" the Realtor said sharply.

"I think so, yes. Now I remember. A tall, thin woman with red hair."

The Realtor looked flustered. "Tammy Conroy, oh dear. You're sure?"

"Why, is something wrong?" Annabelle said.

"How well did you know her?"

"Like I said, friend of a friend. Why?"

"Well, I guess you'll find out sooner or later. Some

years ago Tammy Conroy was killed in a little cottage that used to be on the site of the MacIntosh house."

"Killed!" Annabelle clutched Stone's arm.

Stone said, "When you say killed, do you mean by accident?"

"Actually no, she was, well, she was murdered." The woman added quickly, "But we've never had another murder since. This is really a very safe place."

"Did they catch whoever did it?" Annabelle asked.

The Realtor looked even more uncomfortable. "Actually, no, they never caught the person."

Stone said, "Hell, he could still be out there waiting to kill again. Maybe he has a fixation on this neighborhood. Stranger things have happened."

"I don't think that was the case," the Realtor said. "Before the woman who was killed owned it, an elderly widow lived there. She died of old age and her son sold the place to Mrs. Conroy. In fact, I represented the seller in the transaction."

"Maybe her husband did it," Annabelle suggested. "I mean, if she was married. So many murders are domestic in nature. It's awful!"

"There *was* a husband, can't recall his name offhand. But he was gone by the time she was killed, I believe. Leastways, the police never named him a suspect. I always thought some stranger did it. Tammy kept to herself. I don't even think she had any children. But that was years ago, and, like I said, this is actually a very safe area. Now, would you like to see the inside of this house?"

After a quick tour of the house they took the woman's card and said they would get back to her.

As they drove off Annabelle pulled out a brown scarf from her pocket and rubbed it gently.

"What's that?"

"A scarf my mother gave to me. It was for my birthday. It's the last thing she ever had a chance to give me."

"I'm sorry, Annabelle."

She sat back against the car seat and closed her eyes. "I couldn't even attend the funeral. I'd heard rumors in the con world that Bagger was involved and that my father had gotten off scot-free as usual. I knew Bagger would be watching. I've never even been to her grave."

"And you think your father is dead?"

"Let's put it this way, if my dream came true he is."

As they were driving down the street, the light changed and Stone stopped. Annabelle idly glanced at a tall, thin man coming out of a bar and her face froze.

Stone noted her look and said, "What is it?"

"The man coming out of that bar across the street," she whispered as she stared.

Stone glanced over. "What about him?"

"He's my father, Paddy Conroy."

36

"Pull over, Oliver," Annabelle barked.

"What are you going to do?"

"Right now, I'm trying hard not to throw up." She rested her chin on the dashboard, but kept her gaze on her father. "God, it's like I'm seeing a damn ghost."

She slowly sat back up and wiped clammy sweat from her forehead.

"What do you want to do?" he asked.

"I don't know. My mind pretty much just shut down on me."

"Okay, I'll make the call. We follow him. It might lead to something useful."

"That bastard let my mother die." Stone could see that Annabelle was clenching the armrest so tightly her fingers were turning white. He put a calming hand on her shoulder.

"I understand, Annabelle. I understand completely about how and why people get to live and die all for the wrong reasons. And I know it's been a shock finding out that your father is, one, alive, and, two, right here. But we need to keep our wits about us. I can't believe it's a coincidence he's here. Can you?"

She shook her head.

"So we're going to follow him," he said again. "You up for that? Or do you want me to drop you off? I can do it alone."

"No, I want in on this," she said sharply. Then she added more calmly, "I'm good now, Oliver. Thanks." She gave his hand a grateful squeeze.

They both looked out the window where Paddy Conroy was climbing into a beat-up pickup truck parked on the street.

The drive only took ten minutes. By that time they were well away from the small downtown area and out in the country. When the truck turned in through the wrought-iron gates, Annabelle snatched a breath.

Stone waited a few moments and then pulled through the gates into Mt. Holy Cemetery. A few minutes later they were out of the car and slipping stealthily toward a stand of trees. They watched from this concealment while Paddy shuffled along until he came to a flat grave marker on the ground. He produced a few flowers from inside his shabby overcoat, knelt down and placed them on the sunken earth.

He took off his hat, revealing thick white hair, put his hands together and seemed to be praying. Once they heard a long, loud moan come from the man. He reached in his pocket, pulled out a handkerchief and wiped his face.

"Your mother's grave?" Stone asked.

She nodded curtly. "Like I said, I've never been to see it, but I looked up the location."

"He seems to be grieving."

"He's only doing it to make him feel better about what he did, the asshole. He's never changed."

"People do change," Stone said.

"Not him, not ever." She grabbed him as he stepped past her. "Oliver, what are you doing?"

"Putting your theory to the test."

Before she could stop him he walked out into the open and headed toward Paddy. Stone slowed and seemed to be reading the grave markers before stopping at one two down from where Paddy was kneeling and crying.

Stone said softly, "I don't mean to intrude on your privacy. I haven't been by to see my aunt's grave in a few years. I wanted to pay my respects."

Paddy looked up, rubbed his wide face with the cloth. "It's a public cemetery, friend."

Stone knelt down in front of the grave marker he'd picked out, though he was also keeping Paddy in his peripheral vision. "Graveyards just seem to take all the energy out of you, don't they?" he said quietly.

Paddy nodded. "It's penance, you know, for the living. And a warning to us all."

"A warning?" Stone turned to look at him. And now he knew. Paddy Conroy was terminal. He could see it in the gray tinges around the white sunken face, the emaciated body and the trembling hands.

Paddy nodded. "Look at all these graves." He held up a shaky arm. "All these dead people waiting for the Almighty to come down and tell them where they're headed. Waiting in the dirt or in Purgatory if you believe that way. Waiting for the Man to come down and tell them. For all eternity."

"Heaven or hell," Stone said, nodding.

"You a betting man?"

Stone shook his head.

"I spent all my life betting on one thing or another. But if you were a betting man, how many of 'em you reckon are going up and how many going down?"

"Hopefully far more going up than down," Stone said.

"You'd lose your money, you would."

"More people evil than not, is that it?"

"Take me. I might as well pick out a nice sunny spot in the pit of hell right now. Ain't no question where this old boy's headed."

"You have things you regret?"

"Regrets? Mister, if regrets were dollars, I'd be Mr. Bill Gates himself."

Paddy bent forward and kissed the grave marker. "Good-bye, me darling Tammy. You rest easy now, girl." He rose to his feet on rubbery legs and put his hat back on.

He turned to Stone. "Now this one here, she'll be getting into heaven. You know why?" Stone shook his head. "Because she's a saint. She's a saint because she put up with the likes of me. And for that reason alone, come Judgment Day, old Saint Peter will welcome her with open arms. Only wish I could be there to see it."

37

It was early morning. Jerry Bagger was sitting in his suite at his posh hotel seriously thinking that he should up the room rate at the Pompeii. For him a view of the White House was not worth a grand a night. As he was gazing out the window at the president's house one member of his security team, Mike, came into the room. "We just got a call from the casino late last night but we didn't want to wake you. There was a guy talking to Dolores."

Bagger turned around. "Talking to Dolores about *what?*"

"From the little he overheard, the daughter's name came up a couple times."

"Old Cindy," Bagger said slowly. "I guess Dolores is still pining away for her kid. Who's the guy? Cop? Fed?"

"We're running that down right now. And he's got a big guy with him. We've got a tail on them. They're staying at a dump outside the Boardwalk area."

"Well, run it down fast."

"And if it is a cop?"

"You let me know. Then we'll see. Killing a cop is a whole other ball of wax. You kill one, a bunch pop up, same with feds. Keep on top of it. Check around to see where else this guy's been." Bagger sat down as Mike headed out. "Wait a minute, Mike, did that Republican Amish jerk-off call?"

"No sir."

"You know, his story sounded legit, so why do I think he was lying his ass off?"

"You got the best instincts of anybody I know, Mr. Bagger."

Not good enough, Bagger thought. *Annabelle Conroy took me right by the balls and squeezed me dry.*

"You want us to have a chat with the guy?"

Bagger shook his head. "Not right now. But follow him. I wanta see where rare book boy goes at night."

"So we gonna be in town for a while?"

Bagger looked through the window. "Why not? Place is starting to grow on me." He pointed at the White House. "Look there, Mike. That's the home of the president, the most powerful son of a bitch in the world. One nod of his head an entire country gets nuked. He farts funny, the stock market drops a thousand points. He's got a freaking army surrounding him. Anything he wants, he gets it." Bagger snapped his fingers. "Like that. Blow job in the Oval Office, tax breaks for the rich, invading other countries, pinching some queen's ass, anything. Cause he's the man. I respect that. The guy only makes four hundred thousand bucks a year, but the perks are sweet and he gets a free ride on a jet a lot bigger than mine. But with all that, you know what, Mike?"

"What, Mr. Bagger?"

"Once he's out of office, he's nothing. But I'm still Jerry Bagger."

38

Harry Finn watched his youngest son, Patrick, swing and miss on a ball that was at eye level. Parents in the stands next to Finn groaned, the third strike was called and the game was over. Patrick had left the tying run on second and the winning run was standing in the boy's cleats at home plate. The ten-year-old walked dejectedly back to his dugout, bat dragging, while the other team started celebrating. Patrick's coach gave them all a little pep talk, the boys had their after-game snack, which for many was the highlight of the entire evening, and parents started rounding up their future all-stars for the ride home.

Patrick was still sitting in the dugout, his helmet and batting gloves on as though he were just waiting for another shot to put the ball over the fence. Finn grabbed a snack for him and sat down next to him in the dugout.

"You played a great game, Pat," he said, handing the boy a bag of Doritos and an orange Gatorade. "I'm proud of you."

"I struck out, Dad. I *lost* the game for my team."

"You also got on base twice, scored both times and drove in three more. And playing center field you caught a ball that was actually over the fence with two men on and two outs. That saved three runs right there." He rubbed his son's shoulder. "You played a good game. But you can't win them all."

"Is this where you tell me losing builds character?"

"Yeah, it is. Just don't make a habit out of it. Everybody really hates a loser." He playfully slapped his son's helmet. "And if you're not going to eat those chips I'll take 'em." He grabbed the bag.

"Hey, those are mine. I earned them."

"I thought you lost the game for your team."

"The game wouldn't have been close except for me."

"Finally figured that out, did you? I knew you had the Finns' brains in there somewhere." He rapped his knuckles on the helmet. "And take this thing off, you're hardheaded enough already."

"Gee, Dad, thanks for all your support."

"How about we grab some dinner on the way home?"

Patrick looked pleasantly surprised. "Just you and me?"

"Just you and me."

"Won't David be mad?"

"Your brother is thirteen. He doesn't really like having his old man around all that much right now. I'm just not that cool or smart. That'll change in about ten years when he's in debt from college, can't find a job and I'm suddenly brilliant again."

"I think you're smart. And cool."

"That's what I love about you." As they walked back to the car, Finn lifted Patrick on his shoulders and took off running. As they arrived at the parking lot, a breathless Finn put his son down.

Laughing, Patrick said, "Dad, why do you keep carrying me around on your shoulders?"

Finn's smile eased off his face and his eyes grew a little moist. "Because pretty soon I won't be able to do it anymore, son. You'll be too big. And even if you weren't you wouldn't want me to anyway."

"Is it that big of a deal?" Patrick said as he munched on his chips.

Finn unlocked the car and threw his son's bag inside. "Yeah, it is. You'll understand really well when you're a dad."

They ate at a local burger place about a mile from their house.

Patrick said, "I love this food; nothing but grease."

"Enjoy it while you can. When you get to be my age, it's not that easy on the body."

Patrick stuffed a french fry in his mouth and said, "How's Grandma?" Finn stiffened just a bit. "Mom said you went to visit her. How's she doing?"

"Okay. Well, actually not too great."

"How come we never visit her anymore?"

"I'm not sure she'd want you to see her like she is now."

"I don't care about stuff like that. She was fun even if she talked a little funny."

"Yeah, she was," Finn said, staring down at his half-eaten cheeseburger, his appetite suddenly gone. "Maybe we'll go see her soon."

"You know, Dad, she doesn't look very Irish."

Finn thought of the tall, broad-shouldered woman with the sharply chiseled, near-gaunt features so many Eastern Europeans from that generation possessed. He could barely reconcile that image with the shrunken mass his mother had become. His son was right, she didn't look very Irish, because she wasn't. Still, Finn looked far more like his mother than his father. He said quickly, "She's not. Your grandfather was Irish." He didn't enjoy lying to his son, but he knew the truth was not possible on this subject. Yes, his father, the Irish Jew.

"You said he was a cool guy."

"Very cool."

"I wish I could've known him."

Me too, thought Finn. *For a lot longer than I did.*

"So where's Grandma from, then?"

"Your grandmother was really from all over," he answered vaguely.

★

When they got home Mandy met them at the door. After sending Patrick to get changed for bed she said, "Harry, you're supposed to go into Susie's class tomorrow. It's parents' career day."

"Mandy, I told you I really don't feel comfortable doing that."

"All the other kids' parents are doing it. We can't leave Susie out. I'd go but I'm not sure cooking, cleaning and driving qualifies as a career."

He gave her a kiss. "It does with me. You work harder than anybody I know."

"You have to go, Harry. Susie will be so disappointed if you don't."

"Honey, come on. Give me a break."

"Fine, but if you're copping out, you go and tell her. She's waiting up in bed."

Mandy walked off, leaving Finn standing by the door. Groaning, he trudged up the stairs.

Susie was sitting up in bed, surrounded by her stuffed animals. She had eleven of them she kept on her bed; she couldn't go to sleep without them. She called them her guardian angels. Around the foot of the bed were ten more stuffed animals. These were her "Knights of the Round Table."

Her big blue eyes looked up at him as she got right to the point. "Are you coming tomorrow, Daddy?"

"I was just talking to Mom about that."

"Jimmy Potts' mom came in today. She's a marine biologist." Susie formed the words slowly while she scratched her cheek. "I don't know what that is, but, Daddy, she brought live fish."

"That sounds really cool."

"I know you'll be cool too. I've been telling everybody about you."

"What have you been telling them?" Susie had no idea what he did for a living.

"That you were a soldier."

"Oh, that's right, I was."

"I've been telling everybody that you were in the navy. And that you were a *walrus*," she added importantly.

Finn tried hard not to laugh as he patiently explained that he had been a Navy *SEAL*, not a walrus. "Remember, sweetie, up in this area there are a lot of people who used to be in the military. It's not that special."

"But you'll be the best, Daddy, I know you will. Please come, please." She tugged on his sleeve and then wrapped her arms around him.

In the face of this, what father could say no? "Okay, honey, I'll be there."

As he turned out the light and was leaving, Susie said, "Daddy, can I ask you something?"

"Sure, what is it?"

"When you were a soldier, did you ever kill anybody?"

Finn leaned back against the door. This was not the question he'd been expecting.

Susie added, "'Cause Joey Menkel said his dad killed lots of bad people in Iraq. And he's a soldier too. So did you?"

Finn sat back down next to her, took his daughter's hand and said slowly, "When people fight, people get hurt, sweetie. It's never a good thing to hurt someone else. And soldiers only do it to protect themselves and their country, where their families live."

"So did you?" she persisted.

"I'll see you at school tomorrow, baby. Hope you sleep well." He kissed her on the forehead and nearly sprinted from the room.

A minute later he was in the garage. He kept his gun safe here. It weighed nearly a thousand pounds and had a key, combo and biometric lock system that only he could open. He unlocked the heavy door and took out another, smaller box that also was key and combo protected. Opening that, he carried the file over to his workbench and started looking through it. The photos, the reports, were both now faded, yet they never failed to incite in him a nearly uncontrollable rage. He read the words aloud to himself: "Rayfield Solomon, Alleged Traitor, Commits Suicide in South America." He looked at the photo of Rayfield Solomon, his father, a dead man with a hole in his right temple, and the legacy of having betrayed his country.

Finn still felt rage tonight, but it was not the same as all the other times he had looked at the final wreckage of his father's past, and that was due to a little girl's question: *Did you ever kill anybody, Daddy?*

Yes, honey, Daddy *has*.

He locked the items back up and turned out the garage light. He didn't return to the house. He went for a walk. He walked until it was midnight. When he got back to the house, everyone was long since asleep. His wife was used to his late-night ramblings around the neighborhood. He slipped into Susie's room, sat on her bed and watched her chest rise and fall as she clutched one of her precious guardian angels.

When dawn came, Finn left his daughter, showered, dressed and got ready to go to school, to talk about being a soldier. Of course, he would not talk to them about being a killer. Though a killer he was.

As he walked through the hall to his daughter's third grade class, a tiny crack appeared in the wall of his mind that separated Harry Finn from the other man he had to be. It was doubtful he even knew it had happened. He opened the door to the class and was nearly knocked down by his daughter, who flew across the room to give him a hug.

"This is my daddy," she announced proudly to her classmates. "And he's a seal, not a walrus. And he's a good guy."

Am I? thought Harry Finn.

39

Stone filled Annabelle in on his conversation with her father at the grave site. "He looks like he's dying."

"I'm delighted to hear it."

"And he seems sincerely guilty about what happened to your mother."

"I highly doubt that."

"Do you want to follow him?"

"No, I want to kill him."

"Okay, what now? More sleuthing around town?"

"No. Let's just go back to the inn. I need to drink and I want to do it in the privacy of my own room."

Stone dropped her off at the inn and headed back out. He drove through the town's few streets until he saw Paddy's truck parked at the curb. Father and daughter had had the same idea. He parked and went inside.

The bar was dirty and dark. At this time of the afternoon there was only one man at the bar, a pitcher in front of him. Stone sat down next to Paddy, who barely looked up.

"I guess cemeteries make people thirsty," Stone said.

Paddy gave him a sideways glance and took a sip of his beer. His eyelids were droopy, his skin grayer inside the bar than it had been in the sunshine.

"Never needed a reason to have a pint or two," Paddy replied, his speech a little slurred.

"My name's Oliver," Stone said, extending his hand.

Paddy didn't take it; he studied Stone warily.

"You run into a man once, no problem. You run into a man twice in the span of an hour, it makes a body wonder."

"Town's not that big."

"Big enough to let a man have his space."

"I can move."

Paddy's gaze burned into him for another second or two. "Forget it. What are you having? I'm buying."

"No need to do that."

"There's never a need to buy another man a drink. It's a privilege. And don't turn it down. I'm Irish. I'd have to slit your bloody throat for refusing."

Two hours later, Stone and Paddy left the bar, Stone holding Paddy up.

"You're a good bloke, you are," Paddy blubbered. "A good frien'."

"Glad you feel that way. I don't think you're in any shape to drive. Tell me where you live and I'll drop you off."

Paddy fell asleep in Stone's car. It was for the best because Stone was taking father to see daughter.

Annabelle had stared at the bottle of gin for at least an hour without touching a drop. She only drank when a con demanded that she do so. She had enough memories of her drunken father saying and doing incredibly stupid things to swear her off the stuff forever. The knock on the door barely made her look up.

"Yeah?"

"It's Oliver."

"Door's unlocked."

It opened. Annabelle didn't glance over until she realized she was hearing the sounds of four feet instead of two.

"What the hell are you doing?" she screamed.

Stone half carried Paddy over to a sofa and let him drop onto it.

However, the sounds of his daughter's voice had managed to pierce right through the wall of booze. Paddy half sat up. "Annabelle?"

Annabelle moved so fast that Stone had no chance to stop her. She lunged at Paddy, hit him right in the gut with her shoulder and they both toppled to the floor. She pinned the old man to the floor and started slapping his face.

Stone wrenched her away, holding her off the floor as she tried to kick and punch her father.

Stone pushed Annabelle up against the wall, holding her there. When she wouldn't stop thrashing he slapped her. She froze, stunned. Then she looked over at her father lying there on the floor in time to see his face turn white, and he threw up.

In the next instant she had ripped free from Stone and had fled the room.

Two hours later Paddy opened his eyes and stared around. Then he sat up and immediately felt Stone's hand on his shoulder.

"Just take it easy," Stone said. "You had a nasty shock."

"Annie? Annie?" Paddy scanned the room.

"She'll be back," Stone said. "She had to, uh, step out for a minute." He'd already cleaned up Paddy's sick and had waited for the man to awaken.

"Was it really Annie?" Paddy asked, a shaky hand gripping Stone's arm.

"Yeah, it was really Annie."

When Stone heard Annabelle's footsteps on the stairs he put himself between Paddy and his daughter. The door opened and she stood there, her face white, her expression, well, expressionless. For a terrifying moment Stone wondered if she'd gone out and bought a gun.

She closed the door behind her, pulled a chair out from the small dinette set in one corner and sat down facing the two men.

She stared between Stone and her father before settling her gaze on Paddy. "You done puking?"

He nodded dumbly. "Annie?"

She held up a hand. "Just shut up. I didn't say you could talk, did I?"

He shook his head and sat back against the sofa, a hand over his flat stomach.

She turned her attention to Stone. "Why the hell did you bring him here?"

"I figured it was time the two of you talked."

"You figured wrong."

"I didn't get a chance to tell you before you stormed out. When your mother was killed, your father was in a federal holding cell in Boston on a counterfeit check kiting charge."

Stone sat back next to Paddy and studied Annabelle. The woman *was* the greatest con of her generation, he felt, because her face didn't betray the slightest hint of emotion at the stunning news.

"How do you know that?" she finally said, her gaze never leaving his.

"I checked with my friend Alex on the way over here. The stuff's all computerized now."

"How did you even know to check?" she asked dully.

"Because the bloke asked me about your mother's death when we were sitting at the bar," Paddy broke in. "I told him. I was in that damn cell for nearly a month. They didn't have enough to convict me, but

I couldn't afford a lawyer. By the time I got out your mother was long since buried."

"That doesn't change the fact that you're the reason she died in the first place."

"I never said it did. Not a minute goes by that I don't wish it was me in the ground instead of her."

Annabelle stared over at Stone. "And you bought that sob story? That's Con 101."

"No, it's the truth, and I don't give a damn if you believe it or not," Paddy exclaimed, rising unsteadily to his feet.

"He comes all the time to see her grave," Stone added.

"Who cares?" Annabelle snapped. "But for a lousy ten thousand bucks that this scum ripped off Bagger, she'd be alive today."

"I never thought he'd come after your mum. I don't know who tipped Bagger off where she was. If I did know, I'd have killed the bastard."

"Save it for someone who cares."

"And not a day goes by that I don't think about having my hands around Jerry Bagger's neck."

"Really? So why haven't you? It's not like you don't know where the guy lives."

"He's got a damn army around him."

"Tell me something I don't know."

Paddy stared at her curiously. "I heard Bagger ran into some trouble recently. Scuttlebutt around the con world. Was that you?"

Annabelle rose and opened the door. "Get out."

"Annie—"

"Get out!"

Paddy left, stumbling against the wall as he did so. Annabelle looked at Stone. "I'll never forgive you for this."

"I'm not looking for forgiveness." He stood.

"So why did you really bring him here?"

"Why don't you think about it and see if you can come up with the answer on your own. It might mean more to you that way."

Stone walked out the door and Annabelle kicked it shut.

40

Two of Bagger's men discovered that Milton had been to the hotel across the street from the Pompeii. They talked to the clerk on duty and also to Helen, the masseuse who'd worked on Milton. Confronted with Bagger's grim foot soldiers, neither held back anything. And Milton clearly was not a cop or a fed. The call was made later that morning to Bagger with this information.

"Pick him and his friend up, find out what they're up to and then kill them," was Bagger's response. "Then make sure Dolores knows about it. If that doesn't shut her up for good, I know something else that will."

The men drove to Milton and Reuben's motel on the outskirts of the casino strip, where Bagger's surveillance team had told them the men were staying.

They pulled to a stop in front of the motel and got out. Milton and Reuben were on the second floor, room 214.

They went in hard and fast. Milton was on the bed packing his bag.

One of Bagger's men said, "Okay, you sorry sack of—" That was all he could manage because his jaw was cracked by Reuben's hammer fist. He dropped to the carpet, out cold. Reuben grabbed the other fellow, lifted him up and slammed him against the wall, laid a massive elbow into the back of his head and then let him fall limp to the floor.

Reuben quickly rifled through their pockets, taking the ammo from their pistols and their car keys. He flipped through their IDs. Pompeii Casino. They were Bagger's goons. He had watched them drive up in the Hummer, slipped into the bathroom and pounced when they'd burst in.

"How'd you know they were coming here?" Milton asked as he gazed at the two unconscious men.

"I figured if they killed that Cindy chick, they'd probably be keeping a close eye on the mother. They must've spotted you last night talking to her, spent the time in between retracing your steps, found out you were interested in this Robby Thomas guy and Bagger ordered a little visit."

"Pretty good deduction."

"Ten years in military intelligence wasn't entirely wasted on me. Let's go."

They loaded their bags in Reuben's truck. Five minutes later they were heading south as fast as Reuben's decade-old ride could carry them.

"Reuben, I'm scared," Milton said as they hit the interstate.

"You should be scared, because *I'm* shitting in my pants."

41

Carter Gray was briefing the current CIA director on the matter of Rayfield Solomon. "I think it's someone close to Solomon," Gray told the director. "The picture that was sent, they wanted me to know why I was being killed."

"Did Solomon have any family?" the director asked. "I know about the case, of course, but it was before my time here."

"Solomon was involved with a Russian. That's what started the whole thing. We only knew her first name, Lesya."

"And after Solomon died, what happened?"

"She disappeared. Actually, she disappeared *before* he died. We believed it was prearranged. They knew we were closing in. We got him, but not her."

"And this was how long ago?"

Gray said, "Over thirty years."

"Well, that means if she's still alive I doubt it's her running around killing people."

"I don't believe that it is. But that doesn't mean

she's not involved. She was always very good at manipulation."

"You know that much about her, but not her surname?"

"Actually, since she's Russian, she would have *three* names: her given name or *imia*, a patronymic name or *otchestvo*, and a surname or *familia*." By Gray's condescending expression, he could've finished this mini-lecture off with the words "you idiot," but he wisely refrained.

"Cold War baggage," the director replied. "Not really our focus anymore."

"You might want to rethink your priorities. While you're placing all your bets on Muhammad, Putin, Chávez and Hu are eating this country's lunch. And they make Al Qaeda look like kindergarteners as far as their potential for destruction on a large scale."

The director cleared his throat. "Yes, well, how come you didn't try to find this Lesya back then?"

"We had other priorities. Solomon had been eliminated. Lesya had gone deep underground. We made a tactical decision that using additional assets to pursue her was not worth the cost. We did believe that we had for all intents and purposes put her out of commission. And for over three decades she has been."

"Until now, at least you believe. So any associates of this Lesya we have to account for?"

"We have to find that out."

"What specifically *do* you know about the woman?"

"She was one of the best counterintelligence agents the Soviet Union ever produced. I've never seen her in person, only photo images. Tall and beautiful, she hardly fit the model of a spy because she tended to stick out. But she proved that stereotype wrong. She had more sheer nerve than just about anyone in the field. Indeed, she was aptly named, as Lesya means 'bravery' in Russian. She didn't work directly for the KGB. She was a cut above that. We always believed that her chain of command went right to the Soviet leadership. She worked in this country for a time, then England, France, Japan, China and all the other typical high-level assignments. She did her best turning others. She recruited Solomon, secretly married him and turned him against his country. His treachery cost America dearly."

"How do you know they were married?"

"Let me correct that. We *believe* that they were married. It was based on facts uncovered at the time. Largely circumstantial, but taken together, it looks like they walked down the aisle."

"And he killed himself?"

"That's what the file says, yes. I believe it was both from guilt at what he'd done to hurt his homeland and also the fact that we were closing in on him."

"But you said before that 'we' got him. So did we

kill him and the suicide was window dressing? Or did he really commit suicide?"

"Whether we did it or he killed himself, it doesn't really matter; he would have been executed for treason in any event." From Gray's tone it was clear he was not going to say any more on that particular subject, even to the director of CIA.

"I looked at the file. There seem to be some gaps in it."

"We didn't have reliable computers back then. And paper files are notoriously incomplete from that era," Gray replied smoothly.

The director apparently gave up on this line of inquiry. He had actually worked under Gray years ago and wasn't nearly as smart as the man, and he knew it. "Fine, Carter. And you've alerted Senator Simpson?"

"Of course. He's well-prepared."

"Anyone else?"

"There was another man who was part of the team, a John Carr, but he's long dead."

The meeting ended there. It was obvious that Gray hadn't told the entire truth. He had astutely gauged that that was for the best because no one wanted to hear the entire truth anyway. The country had too many current problems than to bother with what really occurred over thirty years ago to a man remembered only as a traitor.

Gray personally loathed what had happened to

Solomon, but he could do nothing to change it. He had to look ahead, not to the past. And that meant finding a killer before he struck again. And Lesya, too, finally had to be run to ground.

The result of Gray's meeting with the director was that a regiment of agents in the field were officially now "looking into the matter." Though innocent-sounding, it actually meant that they were doing their best to find whoever was killing ex–CIA agents. And their orders were to terminate the person or persons responsible. No one wanted a trial on this. They simply wanted a body.

42

Harry Finn escaped the third graders relatively unscathed. They'd asked a lot of questions, though, and once or twice Finn actually wished he *had* been a walrus instead of a SEAL.

When he'd finished Susie had given him a hug and said, "You have a really great rest of the day, Daddy."

She sounded so grown-up, for a moment he felt like his heart would burst. His former SEAL team members would have been astonished to learn that beneath Finn's stainless steel skin was a heart as vulnerable and susceptible to emotion as one could find. His only defense, his only way of keeping going, was to block it out. He led two lives and never let either of them mix. What he did for his mother would never wash over into his own family. And what he did with his family would never become part of his other life. At least he prayed to God it wouldn't.

He drove to the office and met with his team to go over the hit on the Capitol. The session lasted for several hours as they carefully mapped out their strategy and then did more prep work. Toward the end of this meeting, Finn, whose mind worked best when multi-tasking, had reason to smile. He had just thought of a way to kill Simpson.

He grabbed some lunch and headed to his storage unit. He had a bomb to build.

Jerry Bagger screamed into the phone, "Nice going! That's just great. Why don't I come back to town and kick your asses too." He calmed down when he heard the next bit of news. With a little more digging they'd ascertained that the little guy had won a ton of cash. And in a casino that meant one thing that was as certain as death: In order to get your money you had to fill out what amounted to a 1099 so Uncle Sam would know you'd won the money in case you forgot to pay tax on it.

Bagger took down this information and said, "Wait a minute, the guy's from England?"

"That's what it says."

"Did he sound British?"

"I don't know."

"You don't know! Does anybody know?"

"I'll have to check," the man said nervously.

"Yeah, well after you *check* and then find out the ID's total bullshit, why don't you *check* back with me so I can strangle you." Bagger slammed down the phone.

43

When Stone walked outside the next day, a bleary-eyed Annabelle was sitting on the front steps of the B&B.

"What do you want from me?" she said bitterly.

"Nothing. What do you want from yourself?"

"Don't play shrink with me."

"Your father was in jail when your mother was murdered."

"He was still the reason she was killed."

"All right. But what's wrong with giving him the benefit of the doubt and believing that he never intended your mother to be hurt by Bagger?"

"What's wrong with that? What's wrong with that is that my father is a liar who has never cared about anyone except himself."

"So he was really bad to your mother? Beat her, starved her?"

"Don't make this into a joke!"

"I'm just trying to understand the situation."

"No, he never abused her."

"So he might have loved her."

"Why are you doing this to me? Why are you taking his side?"

"I'm not taking sides, Annabelle. The man is dying. He was at your mother's grave paying his respects. You thought he'd set your mom up but he didn't." Stone spread his hands. "All I'm saying is you might want to reconsider the situation. Life is short. Family is not forever. I know that as well as anyone."

Annabelle slouched against the car, hands tucked into her armpits.

"It took me two years to plan my hit on Bagger. Two shorts and then the long. I put nearly every dime I had into it. Took more risks than I ever had before. One little mistake in front of Jerry and I'd be dead. And I loved every minute of it. Do you know why?"

Stone shook his head. "Tell me."

"Because I was finally getting back at the son of a bitch who killed my mother. After all those years he was finally going to pay. And I did it, I won. I conned more money from him than anybody ever had. Enough to really hurt him."

"And?"

"And after I did it I realized it was all for nothing. Jerry was just being Jerry when he killed my mother. Jerry took his pound of flesh; that's the law of the street we all live on. Don't get me wrong, I'll always hate the bastard for what he did. But the man I hated most of all was my father."

"And today you found out he was innocent, at least of that."

She pointed to the scar under her eye. "Some innocent. He gave me this when I was just a teenager, for blowing a claim in a casino. He said it was the only way to learn. And he's the reason my mother's dead. And what's happened to him? Not a damn thing. Everything just bounces off the son of a bitch. He just goes along like the bullet in her brain never even happened."

"I'm not seeing it that way, Annabelle. It doesn't look like life has been kind to him. And he was here grieving over your mother. Doesn't sound like a guy who got off scot-free."

"I can never forget it, Oliver. I can never forget what he did."

"I'm not asking you to forget. I'm just asking you to maybe think about forgiving. People do bad things all the time. It doesn't necessarily make them bad people."

"So what do you want me to do? Run and give him a hug?"

"This is something you need to deal with inside yourself. Before it destroys you. Because if we manage to nail Bagger you still won't be satisfied because you have all this hate inside for Paddy. If you really want to get on with your life, you need to deal with that."

Annabelle pulled her car keys out of her pocket. "Well, you know what? I don't want to."

She drove off in a spit of gravel.

As soon as she was out of sight Stone's phone buzzed. It was Reuben recounting everything that had happened to them when they were in Atlantic City, including Milton's big winnings and them being attacked by Bagger's men. Stone told Reuben to not take Milton home, but to go to Reuben's house instead.

"He didn't use his real ID there when he collected his winnings, Oliver," Reuben pointed out.

"It doesn't matter. I don't want to take a chance. You recently moved. Your house doesn't even have an address. It'd be very hard for Bagger to track you down."

"How's it going with Susan?"

"Couldn't be better." Stone clicked off and stared after the fleeing Annabelle.

Family. It just doesn't get any more complicated than that.

44

Gray was on a secure phone in a bunker the CIA had arranged for him to use. The president had been briefed on the matter and had used his executive powers to give Gray, even in an unofficial capacity, any and all resources of the United States government that he required to set the situation right. Gray of course had only communicated his version of the truth to the president and his top people, but it had been enough to allow him the carte blanche he needed to carry out the required mission.

Though set fifty feet in the dirt, the bunker had all the amenities of a five-star hotel in downtown Manhattan, including its own valet and a chef. Gray had always been treated like a rock star by the intelligence community.

Into the phone he said, "If Lesya and Rayfield Solomon were married there has to be a record of it somewhere. I know we couldn't find it back then, but times have changed. The Russians are, at least in public, our ally. Run down every lead you can on that angle. There are some old codgers still running around the reincarnation of the KGB that may be able to help us. Bring euros, they prefer them to dollars, at least these days." He nodded as the man on the other end said something. "The former Russian ambassador to this country, Gregori Tupikov, is an old friend of mine. It might just be worth a phone call to him. Tell him you're doing it in connection with the investigation of my murder. Vodka by the barrel, two-pound lobsters and a natural redhead, that's all you ever needed to corrupt old Gregori."

Gray clicked off and continued to study the file while his four-course dinner was being finalized. Though computers and servers dominated his business these days, the old Cold Warrior loved the feel of paper between his fingers. He ate his sumptuous meal alone in front of a gas fire that gave the room an enchanting glow even this far underground. Gray never did things like others. Even dead he was fifty feet under the earth instead of the normal six and his "coffin" was far more luxurious than the rank and file got.

Taking a snifter of brandy into a wood-paneled library, he sat behind an ornate desk and continued to ponder the matter. He loved this part of the game. It was a battle of the minds, a perpetual chess match; one side trying to outmaneuver, outthink the other. And the United States had never had a man who could perform those tasks better than Carter Gray. His actions had saved so many Americans that he had long since lost count. The Medal of Freedom was the least his country could do. If he was a Brit he'd already have been knighted. And yet he'd been forced to resign, long before he was ready. Because John Carr had forced his hand.

The more Gray thought about this, the angrier he became. Yet from within that anger a cold-blooded idea took form. Whoever was killing Gray's old assassination team one by one probably believed John Carr to be dead. Yet why should Carr be spared the thrill of being a target? And the man had given him the finger!

Gray picked up his secure phone and hit a button. "I want to get some information out using the normal channels. It has to do with the alleged death of a man named John Carr. I think the time has come to set the record straight."

45

Finn held up the device. Barely the size of his palm, combined with a few seemingly innocuous elements it could easily kill anyone within thirty feet. But it would only kill one man; Finn would make sure of that.

He tried on his disguise and thought through all the steps he would take to enter the Hart Building and penetrate where he needed to go.

Once Finn had gotten on Roger Simpson's trail and dug deeply, he'd learned that the distinguished senior senator from Alabama had been a hellion early in life, with little regard for anyone or anything other than himself. Though the man was still like that, this flaw had been buried under layers of PR once his political career had begun. This was done with the full though invisible support of the CIA, where he had worked in a very special though undisclosed capacity. His c.v. was filled with accolades from the Agency and very little in the way of hard facts. Yet to his country he was a hero. And he was poised to make a run for the White House, Finn had heard.

I don't think so.

Simpson had never forgotten his former employer's support. As head of the powerful Senate Select Committee on Intelligence he'd let the CIA get away with whatever it wanted. There did not seem to be any action too extreme that Simpson did not find necessary for national security reasons. He had been Carter Gray's champion or lapdog, depending on how one looked at it, for years. Finn considered it perfect justice to send them to the same place, and in the same manner.

He drove home late that night, but Mandy was still up waiting for him. Over a couple slices of pumpkin pie and some hot tea she said, "You were a big hit today at school. Susie waited up to tell you but she couldn't stay awake."

"I'm sorry I'm late, but something came up."

"Are you sure everything's okay? You haven't really seemed yourself lately."

"Just work. Lot to think about."

"How's Lily?"

Lily was Finn's mother. Like Finn it wasn't her real name. Harry Finn wouldn't have known what it was like to use a real name for anything.

"The same. Actually, a little worse." Finn didn't use his mother's word, "rotting."

"I know we have a lot going on, but if you want your mother to come and live with us, I'm okay with that. We'll make it work somehow."

"Not a good idea, Mandy. She's fine right where she is."

"Okay, Harry, but there might come a time when we need to make that decision."

"Maybe, but that time isn't now. So let's not worry about it. We have enough on our plates."

"You're sure there's nothing bothering you?"

He shook his head, but didn't look at his wife.

She touched his hand. "Harry, you seem to be drifting away from us."

His response was delivered with a harshness that surprised even him. "I went to Susie's school. I almost never miss a ball game or soccer match. The yard doesn't have a weed in it. I help with all the homework and housework. I play chauffeur as much as you do. What more do you want from me, Mandy?"

She withdrew her hand slowly. "Nothing, I guess."

They finished their pie in silence. Mandy slowly headed upstairs but Finn remained sitting in the kitchen staring at nothing.

"Not coming?" she said.

"Got a few things to do."

"Don't go out, Harry, not tonight."

"Maybe just a walk. You know."

"Yes, I know," Mandy said to herself as she climbed the stairs.

"Mandy?"

She turned back around.

"Things will get better. I promise. They'll get better soon." *I'm almost there.*

"Sure, Harry, sure."

46

There was really only one place for Annabelle to go: the graveyard. She had never had the opportunity to pay her respects to her mother. She was going to take care of that tonight.

She parked her rental, slipped through the gate and walked along the darkened pathways. The location of her mother's grave was seared into her head. However, when she arrived there, she found that her mother already had a visitor. She ducked behind an evergreen and watched.

He was stretched out on the ground next to the grave. As Annabelle listened she could hear the words floating to her from the prone figure. He was singing an Irish ditty to the dead woman. It was a song that Annabelle had heard him sing to her mother when Annabelle was a little girl. The lyrics had to do with dreams and a green, lush land and a man and a woman very much in love. As she continued to listen tears started sliding down her cheeks, though she didn't want them to. The sounds grew fainter and she finally realized her father had fallen asleep next to the grave of his wife—her mother.

Annabelle stepped out from behind the tree, strode quietly over to the burial plot and knelt down on the other side of the grave from where her father lay quietly snoring. Then she did something she hadn't done since attending mass as a little girl. She crossed herself and prayed over her mother. More tears poured down her face as she spoke to God and tried to talk to her mother, telling her how much she missed her, how much she wanted her to be alive.

She prayed and spoke until her heart was nearly bursting. Then she rose, crossed herself again and, staring down at her slumbering father, made up her mind.

He was painfully light as she gripped him under the armpits, lifting him to his feet. He awakened slightly. She half carried him to her car, put him in, drove back to the inn and got him to bed in her room. She sat outside on the couch until she heard a tap on her door.

It was Stone. He looked worried. He filled her in on what had happened with Milton and Reuben. Then he glanced toward her bedroom door, from which loud snores were now pouring forth.

Stone didn't say anything about that because the look on Annabelle's face told him quite clearly that any questions would not be welcome.

"Do you want to go back home tomorrow?" he asked instead.

"I don't have a home," she replied. "But we can go back to *your* home tomorrow."

The next morning Annabelle had breakfast sent up to the room. When her father came out of the bedroom hot coffee was poured and eggs and bacon were on the plate.

"You look like you could use some food," she said.

He looked around. "How the hell did I get here?"

"You were at the grave last night. So was I."

He nodded slowly, rubbing his tangled hair down with one hand. "I see."

"Come and eat."

"You don't have to do this, Annie."

"I know that. Eat."

He sat and managed to down a few bites and drink a bit of the coffee.

"How bad is it?" she asked, studying his gaunt, gray face.

"Bad enough. Six months without treatment. A year with. But who wants to go out sick all the time?"

"Do you need anything? Money? A place to live?"

He sat back and wiped the napkin across his lips. "You owe me nothing, Annie. And I ain't taking nothing from you."

"There's no reason you have to be in pain or sleeping in the back of a truck. I have money."

"I've got whiskey for the pain and that old truck of mine is what they call a low-end recreational vehicle. I'm fine."

"You're obviously not fine."

His expression darkened as he pushed away from the table. "I don't want your pity, Annie, okay? I can deal with your hatred a lot easier."

"Is that why you never found me and told me you were in jail when Bagger killed Mom?"

"Would it have made a difference to you?"

"Probably not," she admitted.

"So there you go. Would've been a bloody waste of time."

He rose and fumbled in his pocket, fishing out a cigarette pack and a lighter. "Do you mind, seeing as how it's already killed me?" She shook her head and he stepped to the window, opened it and blew the smoke out that way.

"So did you hit Jerry up in Atlantic City?"

"I did."

"Did you hit the bastard hard?"

"Millions."

"Well, then you're a lock for heaven, 'cause there ain't no man what deserves it more than that bloke."

"But it wasn't enough," Annabelle said in a low voice.

Paddy stared moodily out the window. "Course it wasn't. One thing Jerry has is lots of money. You can take all you want and he'll make it all back off the sorry types tramping through his casino every bloody minute."

"So how do I hurt him enough?"

He swung around to look at her. "You take away one of two things: either his life or his freedom. Only way."

"There's no statute of limitations on killing someone."

"You got proof he murdered your mum?"

"Nothing that will stand up in court. But I know he did it."

"I do too."

Father and daughter stared at each other for a long time.

He finally said, "There're only two people in the whole world who've conned that bastard and lived to tell about it. And they're both in this room."

"So you want to con Jerry, together?"

"I want him to pay for what he did to your mum."

"You think I don't?"

"I know you do. You went after the bastard. I never had the balls to do it. Sure, I'm a good con, maybe one of the best. I've got nerve, more than most."

"And things have changed?"

"I'm dying already. So what the hell does it matter to me? Better to get a bullet in the brain courtesy of Jerry than watch my insides dissolve on me."

"And how exactly do you propose doing that?"

"I've been thinking about it a lot actually. Probably the only thing I've been thinking about. But your conning Jerry gives us a way to nail him."

"Because he's coming after me?"

"Right. You had a crew of course."

"Two people you know, or know of, one you don't."

Paddy flicked his cigarette out the window and sat back down at the table. "Jerry hit any of them?"

"One. He's a veg."

"And maybe ratted you out?"

"No maybe about it, he did. In fact, Jerry is in D.C. trying to find me right now."

"That tall, older bloke with you, can you trust him?"

"He's never let me down."

"Good friend to have." Paddy fell silent, staring down at his unfinished breakfast.

"You think you're in shape to run a con on Jerry? I got away from him last time because I worked it to perfection. I'm not looking to walk in and get my head blown off because you fall on your face."

"Always admired your bluntness."

"Guess who taught me?" she shot back.

"I *am* ready for this. In fact, it's the only thing keeping me alive. And I've got the plan."

"What is it?"

"Basically to get Jerry to confess to killing your mum."

"Oh, really, is that all? Hell, I wish I would've thought of that one."

"You have a problem with the concept?"

"No, with the execution, as in yours and mine. Because correct me if I'm wrong, but getting someone to confess to a murder, wouldn't that involve getting up close and personal?"

"Absolutely. The closest possible proximity."

"Well why don't we stop right there then. I've done my face time with Jerry. I have no desire to do it again."

"With my plan the risk will be minimal to you."

"Define minimal."

"Just trust me, Annie."

"You must be insane."

"No, I'm just a dying man who's got to make peace with his God. And to do that, I have to make this right. I have to."

This remark came so out of left field that Annabelle could only stare at him.

"But there is a small problem with the plan," he said.

"How small?'

"We need access to the good guys, the cops. Not exactly my specialty." He glanced at her. "Any ideas on that score?"

Annabelle sat back, not looking very confident. "You know this is suicide, don't you?"

"I will never let you come to harm at the hands of Jerry. But I have to do this. I swear that to you on your mother's grave."

This last remark did something to Annabelle she never thought any words could ever do. She actually started feeling something for her father. She wasn't sure if it was sympathy, pity, or maybe even something more.

"Then maybe I can find the good guys to help us," she said quietly.

47

Annabelle left her father and walked to Stone's room.

"He wants to team with me to con Jerry into confessing to my mother's murder," she said bluntly and then collapsed on the small couch next to Stone's bed.

"You think you can trust him?"

"Damn it, Oliver, you just spent all that time telling me to forgive the man."

"Forgive him, yes, not trust him."

"I have no reason to trust him at all."

Stone looked at her warily. "I sense a but coming."

"But with all that I *do* trust him. I don't know why, just call it my gut."

"But you need the cavalry?"

"That's what he says."

"I might be able to help."

"I thought so. I mean, they owe you after the last time."

"They never owe you, Annabelle. Or at least they never think they do. But let me see what I can work.

So what do you do with your father in the meantime?"

"I was sort of hoping he could come back to D.C. with us."

"And stay with you? That might be a little dicey with Bagger in the same town."

"Any help there would be appreciated."

"Tell your father to get his things together."

Paddy didn't have anything *to* get together. Everything he owned was already in his battered truck. He insisted on following them down. "Truck's all I've got left. I ain't letting it go."

With Paddy behind them, Stone and Annabelle drove south to Reuben's house in one of the few remaining rural areas of northern Virginia. It was very late when they arrived there, but Stone had called ahead.

They pulled down a gravel drive that was more path than road and bracketed by thick woods. They passed leaning shacks and rotting cars as the wilderness and poverty grew with each click of the odometer. A few minutes later the Nova's headlights flicked across a weed-filled yard and spotlighted a garage with its single overhead door open. The interior was bursting with tools and car parts. Parked beside the garage were six cars, two trucks, three motorcycles and what looked to be a dune buggy, all in various states of being rebuilt. Next to the garage was a mobile trailer that was no longer mobile, being set firmly on cinder blocks.

"Reuben just moved here recently," Stone remarked.

Annabelle gazed back at the garage. "Does he run a chop shop on the side?"

"No, the man's a mechanical genius. I think he's closer to his machines than he is to most people. That's why he loves his motorcycle so much. He says it's far more reliable than any of his three wives ever were."

"Oliver, do you have any *normal* friends?"

"Well, there's you."

"Oh, God, are you in serious trouble."

Stone noted Reuben's truck in the yard and a light on in the trailer.

"They're waiting for us," he said.

Reuben met them at the door and then stared over at the pickup truck, Paddy at the wheel.

"Who's that?"

"A friend," Annabelle answered quickly.

"I thought he might be able to stay here, at least for tonight," Stone said.

"What the hell's one more? He can have the presidential suite. It's right next to the bathroom."

"Where's Milton?" Stone asked.

"Crashed. Apparently winning a shitload of money at a casino and then nearly getting whacked is really exhausting."

"We're going to return Caleb's car now," Stone said. "And then tomorrow I want to meet at my cottage, put all our facts together and see where we go from there. And I'm going to call in Alex to help us." He shot a glance at Annabelle. "With a new angle."

Reuben looked from one to the other. "Okay," he said slowly.

"Thanks, Reuben."

An hour later Stone and Annabelle pulled into the parking lot of Caleb's condo building in D.C. and rode the elevator to the man's apartment. Stone knocked and they heard footsteps approaching the door. It opened. Unfortunately, it wasn't Caleb standing there.

48

"This really is intolerable, Carter," Senator Roger Simpson said.

The two men were in the CIA bunker, seated in leather armchairs and nursing glasses of cabernet.

Simpson continued, "For something like this to raise its ugly head now. When in a few years I'll be sitting in the White House if things go according to plan."

"Roger, if this comes out, you won't be in the running. You might actually be in prison."

Simpson flushed at Gray's stinger but only stared moodily into his wineglass before saying, "Ray Solomon. Who would've thought that would come back to haunt us?"

"It was always a possibility. It was a calculated risk. Sometimes they work, sometimes they don't. I'm sure you did what you thought was right at the time."

"You sound like you weren't involved at all. You were up to your neck in it, same as me."

Gray snapped, "*I* didn't order Ray's death. He was my friend. *You* are the reason he's dead."

"The man committed suicide, in Brazil."

"No, you sent John Carr and his team to kill the man because you were afraid if he found out the truth, he'd expose you."

Simpson stared at Gray over the lip of his glass. "Expose *us*, Carter. Don't ever forget that."

"Ray Solomon was a good man, and a top agent. And now he's called a traitor. His memory has been besmirched."

"Sacrifices are necessary all the time, for the greater good."

"Funny, why do I think you'd never be willing to sacrifice your life for the greater good?"

"Fate has a way of preserving those who can truly make a difference, Carter. The great men always persevere."

"Well, you should call upon the fates now, because someone clearly wants you dead."

"And you too. Don't forget that."

"The fact that the killer thinks I'm already dead gives me a certain latitude with which to operate. Yet in one sense you can't blame the person. Indeed, what you did was inexcusable."

Simpson flushed angrily. "I did what I did for the right reasons. And it was a long time ago. The world was very different. I was very different."

"None of us are *that* different. And it wasn't really that long ago. In fact, it's not past, it's now the present.

It's a lesson in never burning bridges or doing stupid things."

Simpson said nervously, "Donna will go ballistic if any of this comes out."

"And can you blame your wife? Your action could be seen as abominable."

"My action! You had people killed, Carter. Killed."

"We were running the Triple Six Division, Roger, not a preschool for wannabe spies. Every target we were given was duly authorized, often right from 1600 Pennsylvania Avenue. It was our duty to execute on those orders, because the other side was playing the game for all it was worth. Anything less on our part would have been akin to treason."

"Not every killing was authorized, Carter, you know that."

Gray stared pointedly at the senator. "Sometimes it's better that the politicians don't know everything. But Ray Solomon should not have been one of those times, Roger. You shouldn't have done it."

"Easy to say in hindsight. And it was the only time I did such a thing."

"Really? What about John Carr?"

"He was the worst of the lot. Tried to resign from Triple Six. I mean, come on."

"As usual your judgment is simply *stellar*. Carr was actually the *best* of them all."

"That's your opinion."

"And that's why you ordered his death? Because he wanted to stop being an assassin?"

Simpson stiffened. "I don't know what you're talking about. Kill one of our own men? Preposterous."

"You're a very bad liar, Roger. If you really want to make a run for the White House you're going to have to improve your poker face."

"I did not have the man killed."

"About four years ago I had a long chat with Judd Bingham. He told me. It was he, Cole and Cincetti that did it. Carr's own team went after him on *your* orders."

"That is an outrageous comment. I didn't have the authority to order that."

"Authority? Back then? We ran a group of killers. Most of them, except for Carr, enjoyed their work immensely. Bingham said he and the other two were glad to do it for you. They were very upset that Carr wanted to quit the club. They took it as a personal affront."

"Well, since Bingham and the other two are dead there's really no proof of that, is there?"

"And Carr too. He's currently residing at Arlington National Cemetery."

Simpson took a sip of his wine. "I know that."

"At least that's what the official record says."

Simpson glanced at him sharply. "What are you talking about?"

"Carr isn't dead."

Simpson sputtered, "But Bingham said—" He caught himself a second too late.

"Thank you for confirming what I already knew to be true. Bingham was always a liar. He didn't want to admit that Carr got away that night. And Carr managed to kill three of our operatives in the process. Bingham, Cole and Cincetti barely got out alive, though apparently Carr didn't know it was them. Carr was in a class by himself when it came to killing. It was a costly mission, Roger. And one that you should have been taken to task for. You're lucky that Bingham and the other two kept their mouths shut all these years. But they would've been in just as much trouble as you if the truth had come out."

"Again, I don't know what you're talking about."

Gray waited until Simpson had swallowed a mouthful of wine before saying, "Jackie was Carr's daughter; did I ever tell you that? You adopted his daughter."

Simpson slowly set down his glass. Gray noted that the man's hand was trembling.

"No, you failed to mention that," Simpson said in a strained voice. "You said she'd been orphaned but you didn't say who the parents were. I didn't even know Carr had a daughter."

"You'd think when you tried to kill a man that you'd know those details."

"If you suspected my involvement, why did you give the child to us?"

"Something had to be done with the little girl. And you and Donna couldn't have any children. Despite what some people think, I do have a conscience, Roger. It wasn't her fault what happened. And it wasn't mine. It was yours, Bingham's, Cincetti's and Cole's. Do you sense a pattern?"

Simpson jerked straight up. "You think Carr killed them?"

"And tried to kill me. He must've thought, understandably, that I had something to do with his family's death."

"But why would he wait all this time to do it?"

"There, I can only speculate. But he must be considered a suspect."

"If he's still alive."

"Men like Carr are awfully difficult to kill, as you must surely admit now. A team of Triple Sixes couldn't get the job done."

"But I don't understand, how does this tie into Solomon?"

"It may not. Carr may be operating alone and using the Solomon angle as a cover. That's for us to find out. But if Carr is working with someone connected to Solomon's past then we need to track those people down. I have the resources to do so. The current director certainly sees things my way. He should; I trained him."

"And you'll get whoever's doing this?"

"Yes, hopefully before he gets *you*. Since you are most assuredly on the hit list—and quite the easy target actually."

"That's not funny."

"I didn't mean it as a joke. Three men who were far more skilled and far more deeply buried than you are dead. Practically speaking, you're a much softer target."

"I'm getting out of the country for a while, starting tomorrow morning," Simpson snapped. "I'm not going to wait around here to be murdered by some psychopath."

"I'm sure the American taxpayers will understand your shirking your duties in the Congress."

"I don't like your tone, Carter."

In response Gray picked up his Medal of Freedom off the table next to his chair and held it up. "They gave me a lump of metal in return for nearly forty years of service to my country. I was surprised to get it, actually. After all, I had resigned my post as director of National Intelligence, leaving the administration in the lurch."

"I often wondered why you did that."

"You can keep wondering, Roger. That bit of intelligence is mine alone."

Simpson gazed contemptuously around the bunker's interior. "Feels a bit like a rat in a hole down here."

"A person that can kill three former Triple Sixes and nearly me as well is not someone to underestimate. I'll take being in my cozy bunker, for now."

"Wonderful, while I'm exposed on the surface," Simpson said angrily.

"Don't worry, Roger, I understand that they award the Freedom Medal posthumously."

49

Harry Finn had worked hard the next day and, that night, visited an apartment complex in Arlington. The parking spaces were all numbered so it was simple for him to locate the right one. He pulled his van into an empty space, walked over to the jet black Lincoln Navigator and pressed a device against the left rear fender. The blinking red alarm light on the SUV's dashboard instantly died. Finn slid the lock buster out of his jacket pocket and in seconds the truck's door lock cylinder was in his hand. He slid the special ID badge off the rearview mirror where the moron who owned the Lincoln always kept it, replacing it with an identical one, although it wouldn't work like it was supposed to. It didn't have the encryption codes burned into it—codes that were impossible for Finn to duplicate, hence the theft tonight. The owner would just believe it to be defective and have a new one issued. Yet this particular federal agency was notorious for failing to cancel old ID badges. Old badge, new badge, it didn't seem to matter to many bloated bureaucracies. Yet it mattered very much to Finn.

He put the cylinder back, relocked the door, pressed his device against the fender and the alarm system came back to life. There was no sign he'd ever been there. If only the public knew what was out there to rip them off. Yet better they remain oblivious in the belief that they were actually secure.

On the way home Finn glanced at the stolen badge. Good thing he wasn't really a bad guy, because with a little doctoring of the plastic he could topple the entire legislative branch of government single-handed, all 535 members. But there was only one he wanted. Just one.

Stone, Annabelle and Caleb were in the back of a van. Mike Manson, one of Bagger's men, sat next to them. Mike had been the one to open Caleb's door, gun pointed straight at them. Stone hadn't thought they would be following Caleb; it was a miscalculation that apparently was going to lead to their deaths.

"So how's Jerry?" Annabelle asked casually. "Run into any good scams lately?"

Mike said, "Don't know what you're talking about."

"I doubt we're going to the hotel where he's staying," Stone said. "A little too public."

To this Mike said nothing.

An anguished Caleb had his face pressed to the window and seemed focused on not passing out.

"I guess a bribe wouldn't do any good, would it?" Annabelle asked.

Caleb wrenched his face away from the window. "Are you aware that you could go to prison for this!"

Mike pointed his pistol at Caleb's head. "Shut the hell up!"

The van swerved to the side as another vehicle suddenly cut it off. As the driver fought the wheel, Mike took his gaze off Stone for only an instant, but that was enough.

"What the–" Mike began before he slumped hard against the door. His gun clattered to the floorboard. Stone snagged the weapon and leveled it at his head.

Mike's left side was in spasms after Stone had pressed his finger against a spot near the man's rib cage. "Come on, *old man*, give me the pistol before you hurt yourself," Mike said, grimacing in pain.

Stone cranked off a round, blowing away a tip of Mike's ear before the bullet shattered the window. Then he pointed the gun at the driver's head. "Pull it over *now*, before I put the next one in your brain."

The van jerked to a stop on the dirt shoulder.

Stone stared at the stunned and bleeding Mike. "Next time you kidnap someone, *sonny*, tie them up. That way, you won't look like an idiot again."

"Who the hell are you?" Mike cried out.

"Just hope you never really find out."

They bound Mike and the driver using straps and rope they found in the van, and then laid them in a ditch next to the road. They searched them for ID but found none.

Stone climbed in the driver's seat and the three drove off.

Annabelle looked over at Caleb. "Are you all right?"

He turned to her, his face a delicate shade of rage. "I'm fine. Why shouldn't I be? In less than an hour's time I've had my home broken into, been kidnapped and then nearly killed. And now this Bagger monster knows that I lied to him. And he also knows where I live and where I work. Oh joy, joy for me."

"Well, we're not dead, that's something," Stone pointed out.

"Not dead *yet*!" Caleb shot back.

Stone handed Caleb his phone. "Call Alex Ford at home. His number's on my speed dial. Tell him what happened and where he can pick up Bagger's men." He looked at Annabelle. "Jerry made a big mistake. And now we have something to hang him with that doesn't require you and Paddy going after him."

Caleb made the call and they continued on down the road. When they passed a curve a truck shot out from a side road and blocked their way. Stone tried to swerve around it but Annabelle cried out, "It's my father. And Reuben."

It was indeed Paddy Conroy driving and Reuben in the passenger seat. Paddy pulled the truck up next to the van and rolled his window down.

Annabelle leaned across Stone. "What the hell are you two doing here?"

Reuben said, "Got to thinking after you two left that Bagger had visited Caleb at work and maybe he had his guys follow him home. So me and Paddy decided to play a little backup."

Paddy added, "We drove to your friend's place in time to see them come out with you. From what Reuben told me, you"—he pointed at Stone—"just needed a bit of a distraction to take over the situation. And I guess he was right, as it turns out." He glanced over at Annabelle. "I can see why my daughter trusts you so much."

Stone shot a look at Reuben.

"Paddy and me had a nice chat on the way over." He clapped the Irishman on the back. "And let me tell you, the dude can drive."

"Started my career as a wheelman." Paddy added hastily, "For the army, of course."

Stone drove off in the van with Paddy and Reuben following. All were in high spirits at having nailed Bagger and his men. Yet it was not to be.

After Alex sent agents to get Bagger's men, they reported back that the pair had disappeared. After that the news didn't get any better. The pistol Stone had taken from Mike was sterilized; the van stolen. Their kidnappers had not mentioned Bagger's name, so there was nothing to connect any of it to the casino chief. They didn't even have enough to bring him in for questioning. The authorities were not happy about coming up empty. In the future it was made very clear that the cavalry would not come running when called.

It seemed to put them back at square one in their war with Bagger.

Yet it was Oliver Stone who was the most worried. Sterilized weapon, stolen van, no IDs, bound people disappearing in the night with no trace? What if it hadn't been Bagger's men who'd kidnapped them? What if instead of being after Annabelle they were after him?

50

When Mike and his prisoners didn't show up at the pre-arranged spot, Bagger didn't shout or throw objects. He was far more introspective than most people realized. You didn't get to his level without thinking things through from every angle.

The casino boss knew that losing Mike was not a good thing. Worse than that, he didn't know who he'd lost Mike to, or what Mike might be saying to them. The town was crawling with feds. You could spit on any street corner and hit five of them, easy. Bagger's instincts had allowed him to survive many dangerous moments. He could sense this was one of them. He could hop on his jet and make a run for it. Yet that cut against everything he'd built his career on. Jerry Bagger never ran from trouble.

He made some calls. The first one was to bring down some reinforcements from Atlantic City. Bagger then called Joe, his PI guy, and instructed him to dig up some more information that Bagger felt he would need as this whole thing unfolded. The last call was to his lawyer, who knew more of Bagger's secrets than anyone. The man immediately began constructing alibis and legal strategies in case the feds knocked on his client's door.

With that business finished, Bagger decided to take a stroll alone. Unlike Atlantic City, D.C. closed shop early. On a weeknight there were few restaurants, bars or clubs open this late. Yet after about a ten-block jaunt, Jerry found a neon-lighted dive, went inside, grabbed a stool at the bar and ordered a whiskey sour with a chaser from a bartender whose features clearly showed that life had come down on him like a sledgehammer. The fat guy seated next to him gazed droopily into his beer while an Elvis Costello song drifted from the dented jukebox that was coated with decades' worth of beers and tears.

Bagger had grown up in places just like this, hustling for scraps. Nearly sixty years later he was still hustling, only the scraps were now valued in the millions. Yet sometimes he wished he were again that dirty-faced kid with the infectious smile and mile-a-minute mouth ripping people off for dollars with tried-and-true scams, the marks never knowing what had hit them until he was long gone and on to the next scheme.

"So what do people do for fun in this town?" he asked the bartender.

The man started mopping the bar and said, "It's not a town built for fun, least that's my opinion."

"Serious business here, you mean?"

The man grinned. "Only place that can nuke you *and* tax you."

"Some people think we'd all be a lot better off if somebody nuked *this* place."

"Hey, just give me twenty-four hours' warning."

"I'm from Atlantic City."

"Cool place. Afraid I dropped enough of my retirement dollars there, though."

"Ever been to the Pompeii?"

"Oh yeah. Neat casino. Guy who runs it is bad news, so I've heard. Real hardass. But I guess you gotta be to make money in that racket. So more power to the man."

"You been tending bar long?"

"Too long. I wanted to be a Major League pitcher, but my stuff wasn't quite good enough. By the time I realized it, pouring drinks was all I knew how to do. But with three kids to feed, you do what you gotta do."

"What about your wife?"

"Cancer, three years ago. Just when things were looking good, life kicks you right in the gut. Know what I mean?"

"Yeah, I do." Bagger laid ten Franklins down for a tip and rose to leave.

The stunned bartender said, "Mister, what the hell's this for?"

"Just a reminder that even assholes aren't all bad."

Bagger walked back to his hotel. His cell phone

was buzzing, no doubt his security detail checking up on him. He had a lot of enemies and his boys didn't like him being out alone. It wasn't because they loved him, Bagger knew. If he went down, their jobs went away. In Bagger's world you got loyalty either at the end of a gun barrel or by waving enough dollars in front of someone. He didn't bother to answer the call.

He passed by the Washington Monument and stopped. The 555-foot-tall obelisk wasn't capturing his attention, it was the man and woman walking hand in hand along the path near the monument.

Bagger had never had a serious relationship with any woman; he'd been too busy hustling for his fortune. All the women he'd been involved with had either been paid for or looking to get some action from old Jerry in return for giving in. He knew they didn't really care for him and so he never cared about them.

That was his life until Annabelle Conroy had come along and turned him upside down. There had been something about her right from the get-go that had hit him in a place he didn't think he even had anymore. He'd allowed himself to believe that she actually cared for him and not because he could do anything for her.

And then the bottom had dropped out and here he was in the city he hated almost as much as Vegas, looking to kill a woman he could've loved forever. The loss of the forty million hadn't destroyed him. He could always make more money when it came down to it. Yet Annabelle Conroy had stolen the unthinkable from him: his heart.

So enraged was Bagger by this sense of betrayal that if he'd had a gun, he would have shot the couple passing just a few feet away from him. It was all he could do to keep himself from running over and pounding both of them into the dirt.

He turned and walked quickly back to his hotel. When he got there he was in for another surprise. Mike Manson and his sidekick had just returned looking bloody and disheveled.

Before Bagger said anything to them he motioned to one of his other men and mouthed the word, "Clean?"

"We searched 'em," the man said. "No surveillance devices."

Bagger looked at Mike. "What the hell happened?"

"We blew it, Mr. Bagger," Mike admitted. "We had 'em in the van, then the old guy got the gun away from me and tied us up. Took us all this time to get free and back here."

"We had to walk five miles," the other man said.

"I don't give a shit if you had to crawl using your tongues," Bagger roared. "You let a woman and a damn librarian get the drop on you?"

"It wasn't the librarian," Mike said. "He was an older guy, but he was one serious dude. He stuck a finger against my ribs and my whole body went numb." He pointed to his wounded ear. "Then he took a chunk of my ear off with a round from my gun like it was nothing. He was a pro, Mr. Bagger. We weren't expecting that kind of trouble."

"Mike, if I didn't know you're not a screw-up, I'd put a round right through your head."

Mike said nervously, "Yes sir, Mr. Bagger. I know. We crawled behind some trees, and Joe found a chunk of glass we used to cut the ropes off. Right as we were taking off the cops showed up. They must've called them. They didn't see us, though."

"You're sure?"

"Yes sir."

"The guy who nicked you was a pro, huh? What'd he look like?"

Mike told him.

"Maybe a fed?"

"He wasn't dressed like a fed. And he was a little old for that. But the guy was still a pro. And he and Conroy were tight."

Bagger slowly sat down in a chair. Who the hell was Annabelle hooked up with?

51

The senator was not in today, having departed on a sudden fact-finding trip, taking many of his staff with him and leaving only a skeleton crew behind. Finn had found this helpful information out on Simpson's Web site, where the senator touted the trip as one that would benefit all Alabamans and Americans. How a first-class trek to the Grand Cayman Islands was going to accomplish that, Finn didn't know. What he did think was that Simpson had been warned about the other killings and had decided to get out of town. That was all right, he had to come back to D.C. at some point. After all, he was a U.S. senator. They couldn't avoid their duties forever, though some had made valiant efforts to do so over the years.

Finn was dressed in government-standard work clothes, his badge dangling from his neck, his case of tools swinging in one hand. His assured demeanor, dead-on photo ID and polished story of work to be done here resulted in his being quickly allowed on his way.

Getting off the elevator, Finn eyed the glass door

of Roger Simpson's office, the Alabama state flag next to it. The banner was a crimson Saint Andrew's Cross on a white field patterned after the Confederate battle flag. As it had over 150 years ago for the Union Blue, the flag represented a perfect target for Harry Finn. He walked up to the door and through the glass saw the young receptionist sitting at the front desk.

He'd enlarged the photos he'd taken of the office and the woman on his previous visit here. They had clearly shown her nameplate on the desk.

He poked his head in the door and held up his phony work order. "Hey, Cheryl, Bobby from building maintenance. I was called about your front door lock a few days ago. Sorry I'm just getting to it, but we've had a backlog. Do you know what's wrong with the darn thing? We've had complaints from other offices about theirs too."

The harried young woman, who was fielding phone calls in rapid succession, cupped her hand over the phone receiver. "No idea."

"I'll just take a quick look at it, then. Just sit tight," Finn said. The receptionist smiled gratefully before turning back to her work.

Finn knelt down, examined the lock and slid a tiny piece of metal into the keyhole. He spent a couple more minutes pretending to fuss with the door and said, "You're good to go now, Cheryl."

She gave him a wave. As Finn packed up his tools he glanced inside the office. He had already learned there was no alarm panel and no motion sensors, but it never hurt to check again.

Out in the hall there was a surveillance camera set up on the ceiling at the juncture of two halls. Finn had already timed it. It changed positions every two minutes so it could sweep both corridors. He walked down the hall and watched the camera while checking his watch. It was still on the two-minute sweeps. That would be all he needed. Guards patrolled the halls at night, but he had learned that they did the even floors on odd hours and the odd floors on even hours. He waited until the hall was clear of people and the camera pointed away from him. Then he quickly jimmied the lock of a room he knew was used to store holiday decorations, and slipped inside. He wedged himself in the back, lay on the floor and went to sleep.

At two minutes after midnight, Finn slipped a video wire under the door of the storage room and did a quick look-see up and down the hall. It was clear. The camera was sweeping the other corridor.

He hustled to Simpson's office door. The piece of metal he'd inserted in the lock earlier performed only one function, but did it flawlessly. It made the door seem to be locked when it actually wasn't if you had one special piece of equipment, which Finn did. He inserted the magnetized end of his tool in the lock, pulled out the metal piece and the door clicked open.

Finn immediately went to work. He jogged

through the anterooms and into Simpson's spacious office. He knelt down by the desk's kneehole and flipped the computer CPU around, revealing the back. He unscrewed the cover, slipped his device inside and connected it to other components inside the computer.

Finn had been able to get his device past security because it didn't have any explosive materials in it. Instead, the device had been designed to ignite a chemical reaction inside the components in the CPU. It was a reaction that would make the otherwise harmless CPU a bomb, a possibility no one in the computer industry would want you to know. The device had attached to it a wireless receiver with a range of about fifteen hundred yards, more than enough, Finn had calculated. He replaced the CPU's cover and put the unit back under the desk.

Next, he sat down at the computer and turned it on. The screen powered up but a password was needed. Busy senators didn't have time to recall elaborate or obscure passwords, so Finn started simply typing in names. The third one did the trick: "Montgomery," the capital of Alabama.

He typed in the commands he needed and then shut the computer down. The last thing he did was place a miniature battery-powered surveillance device near a flowerpot on a high shelf by the senator's couch. The vines of the plant provided an ideal cover for the tiny camera. Now Finn had a direct video and audio link to Simpson's office. He would put it to good use.

He went back to the glass door and checked his watch, waiting for the surveillance camera to click to the other hall. As soon as it did, he was out the door and back into the storage room. He retrieved from his tool bag and powered up a small receiving unit that looked like a BlackBerry, and stared at the picture on the screen. He had chosen the location of his miniature camera well; he could see all of Simpson's office clearly. He turned off the unit, lay on the floor and went back to sleep.

The next morning he slipped out of the storage room and spent some time going up and down elevators, pretending to be heading to assignments. Then he walked out of the building with a group of other people, caught the Metro out to Virginia, picked up his car and drove to the office.

Now all he had to do was wait for Roger Simpson to return. And what a homecoming it would be for the man who'd helped kill his father.

Yet even more than that, Simpson's death would mean the end of Harry Finn's journey. No more killing, no more hearing the story from his mother. Something told him that his mother was only alive because she was waiting for that to happen. As soon as Simpson was dead, Finn suspected that his mother's life would also end. Revenge was a powerful force, and could keep even death at bay. And when his mother passed, Finn would mourn her, grieve for her, but also be immensely relieved at finally being free.

After doing some work at the office and going over still more details on the plan of attack against the Capitol, he left and picked the kids up from school. He spent an hour of batting-cage time with Patrick, helped Susie with her homework and went over high school choices with David. When Mandy got back from the grocery store, he helped her make dinner.

"You seem to be in a good mood," she commented as he scraped potatoes in the kitchen sink.

"I had a great day yesterday," he said.

"I wish you hadn't had to pull an all-nighter. You must be exhausted."

"No, I'm actually pretty full of energy." He finished with the last potato, wiped off his hands and slipped his arms around her. "I was thinking we all could take a trip somewhere, maybe out of the country. The kids have never been to Europe."

"That would be great, Harry, but it's expensive."

"We've had a good year. I've got some money socked away. Next summer might be a good time to do it. I've sort of got things mapped out."

"How come I'm always the last to know about these things?"

"Just wanted to have my ducks in a row before I presented it to the commander in chief for approval, ma'am. That's how the navy trains you." He gave her a kiss.

"You really do have mood swings, mister," she said.

"Like I said before, I see light at the end of the tunnel."

She laughed. "Let's just hope the light isn't a train heading your way."

As she turned back to the stove, Finn's jovial manner disappeared.

A train heading my way, he thought. He hoped his wife didn't turn out to be prophetic.

52

After the spoiled kidnapping attempt Caleb and Paddy had stayed at Stone's cottage, while Annabelle had gone back to her hotel, checked out and moved into another one in a different part of the city. She called Stone with the new address.

Early in the morning Stone received a call from an upset Reuben.

"Milton's driving me nuts, Oliver," Reuben complained. "He's cleaned up my whole house. I can't find a damn thing. And Delta Dawn's afraid to even come inside because the damn vacuum's been running nonstop for hours." Delta Dawn was Reuben's hound of no pedigree whatsoever.

His voice dropped to a near whisper. "And you're not going to believe what he's done in the bathroom. It looks like something out of a women's magazine. I'm too damn embarrassed to even take a crap in there."

Stone said wearily, "I don't have room for him here, I'm pretty full at the moment, Reuben."

"I know, that's why I called. I thought Paddy could

come and stay with me while Milton bunked with you. I mean, Paddy's more my kind of roommate."

"Finding you the ideal companion is not a priority right now; staying alive is," Stone said bluntly. "And the less Paddy's out in public the better."

Reuben let out a deep sigh. "Okay, I guess I can hang with Mr. OCD for a little while longer. But we better nail this Bagger creep soon. Milton's already started to talk about taking me clothes shopping. And I draw the line at that shit."

Several hours later Stone watched as a very irritable and wrinkled-looking Caleb came out of the bathroom dressed in his clothes from the night before.

"Caleb, when the men grabbed you last night, did they say anything?"

Caleb scowled. "Oh, yes. They said if I made a sound they'd kill me! And to think that when I was putting the key in my door, all I was contemplating was having a nice glass of sherry and rereading the opening to *Don Quixote*."

"I meant did they mention that they were working for Jerry Bagger?"

"No, they didn't. Actually, they didn't really say anything. They didn't have to, they had guns."

"Did they mention Annabelle?"

"No, nothing like that. Why?"

"Did they mention someone named John Carr?"

"Who's he?"

"Never mind. Did they say that name?"

"No."

Stone really had no way of knowing if the kidnappers were after Annabelle or John Carr. They could have tracked him down through Caleb, Stone reasoned. He had been to the library before to visit his friend. They had all just assumed that the men were with Bagger. But what if they were part of the team that had been killing Triple Sixes? That had killed Carter Gray? Yet if they were after him, surely they could have discovered his alter ego and also where he lived.

"So what do I do now?" Caleb asked, breaking in on Stone's musings. "I should've left for work ten minutes ago. I've got no clothes, no toiletries, nothing."

Stone, annoyed at being interrupted, said curtly, "Call in sick."

"That takes care of today. What about tomorrow and the day after that?"

"Do you have vacation time?"

"Yes, but I work for the federal government. You can't just up and take vacation time. You have to plan, you have to give notice."

"We'll worry about that tomorrow. For now, just stay here and relax."

"Relax! After being kidnapped and almost being killed? After being shut out of my home and job because some maniac is after me? You expect me to relax?"

"Well, it's either that or slit your wrists. I'll let you make the decision," Stone snapped as he headed out the door.

"Where are you going?"

"To see our friend."

"Great. You can tell *Annabelle* that I need more friends like her like I need a colonoscopy without anesthesia."

Paddy emerged from the bathroom, his hair wet from the shower. "What's going on?"

Stone said, "Caleb here was just about to make you some breakfast, right, Caleb?"

"What?"

Paddy looked from Stone to Caleb and smiled. "Well, that's damn nice of you."

For an instant Caleb looked like he might start screaming, but he calmed just as quickly. While Paddy had been sleeping, Stone had told Caleb all about the man, including the fact that he was dying.

Caleb said graciously, "I am a *public* servant after all."

"I'll leave you to it then," Stone replied.

As Stone walked quickly out of the graveyard part of him was afraid that Annabelle would have fled again, after the close call the night before. Yet half an hour later he found her in her room at the new hotel. She'd just finished breakfast. She poured him a cup of coffee and perched on the edge of the bed in her hotel robe, looking tired and anxious.

"How's Paddy?"

"He actually seems better this morning. More of a spring in his step."

"It's because of the action last night. He thrives on that. Always has."

"We're lucky he was there last night. He saved our lives."

"I know," Annabelle said in a not-so-pleased tone. "It pisses me off. Now I sort of owe him."

Choosing his words carefully, Stone said, "Did you recognize the men last night? I mean as definitely being with Bagger?"

"No, but who else could it be?"

"You remember that little problem of mine I mentioned?"

"Yes."

"Well, it might be possible that the men last night were after *me*, not you."

"What? Who would be after you?"

"Get dressed. We're going to take a little ride. There's something you need to know about me."

"Where are we going?"

"Arlington National Cemetery. There's something I have to show you."

53

"Oliver, don't you get tired of graveyards? I mean, it seems a little obsessive," Annabelle commented as they trudged along the asphalt at Arlington, the nation's most exalted burial ground for its military dead. Most of the graves were represented by a simple white marker, although some of the statuary over the tombs of the famous, or else the very rich, were extraordinarily ostentatious, and often in rather poor taste. To Stone it seemed the less grandiose the grave marker the more the departed had actually done for his country.

He said, "Come on. It's not much farther."

He led her down the familiar path, counting off the rows in his head. This was a quiet section of the cemetery, one that he had often visited just to have some peace.

An instant later, he felt himself stagger, his balance suddenly gone. The area was not so quiet and peaceful today. At the thirty-ninth grave marker in the fourth row of this section of dead there was a great deal of activity in fact. Men were digging. As Stone and

Annabelle watched, the coffin was raised out of the earth and carried past them to a waiting van that had been driven onto the path.

"Oliver?" Annabelle said. "What is it? What's wrong?" She put a hand on his shoulder as he steadied himself against a tree.

Stone finally found his voice. "Do not follow me out of here. I'll meet you back at the cottage."

"But—"

"Just go." He set off in the direction of the departing van.

As the cemetery workers started to fill the hole back in, Annabelle strolled casually by the grave.

"I thought they were supposed to put coffins *in* the graves, not take them *out*," she said.

One worker glanced up at her, but said nothing. He went back to his shoveling.

She moved a bit closer, squinting to read the name on the marker.

"Uh, can you tell me where they do the changing of the guard here?" she asked as she edged closer.

As the worker told her she glanced over his shoulder and finally made out the name chiseled on the marker.

"John Carr," she said to herself.

On foot, Stone followed the van until it hit the main road and then shot out of sight, after passing around the traffic circle leading away from the cemetery. It didn't cross over Memorial Bridge into Washington. Instead the van headed west, farther into Virginia. Stone had a good idea where it and the coffin were going: Langley, home of the CIA.

He called Reuben on his cell phone.

"I want you to contact every friend you have at DIA and find out why a grave was exhumed at Arlington National Cemetery today."

"Whose grave?" Reuben asked.

"A man by the name of John Carr."

"Did you know the guy?"

"As well as I know myself. Hurry, Reuben, it's important."

Stone clicked off and made another phone call, this time to Alex Ford, the only living person other than Annabelle Conroy who knew that Stone's real name was John Carr.

"You saw them dig it up?" Alex said.

"Yes. Please find out what you can."

Stone walked back to his cottage, certain that Annabelle, who'd driven them both over to Arlington National, would beat him there.

She was standing by his desk when he walked in. "You look good for a dead man."

He said, "Where are Paddy and Caleb?"

"They went to the grocery store. You apparently don't keep much food here. Caleb told me to tell you he was appalled." She motioned to the papers on

Stone's desk. "You've got quite a file going on Jerry here."

"Jerry and you," he said, startling her.

"You dug up stuff on me?"

"No, my friend only pulled Bagger's file. The stuff on you is just conjecture."

He sat down behind his desk.

"So the cemetery piece is bad, I take it."

Stone said, "Let's put it this way—when they open that coffin, they'll be surprised what they don't find in it, namely me."

"Is there another body in the coffin?"

He shrugged. "I didn't have any input in the decision. I was too busy avoiding *being* the body in the coffin."

"Why would they be digging it up now?"

"I don't know."

"So what was the problem you mentioned earlier?"

"It's not something I can really talk about."

Her face flushed angrily. "You're telling *me* that? After I spilled my guts to you? And I've never done that with anybody. Ever! Now I want the truth."

Inwardly, Stone winced. For years he'd kept a sign in Lafayette Park that had read, "I want the truth."

"Annabelle, it's not something I can talk—"

"Don't. Don't try to make bullshit excuses. I took bullshit to an art form."

Stone simply sat there, while Annabelle tapped the heel of her shoe on the plank flooring. "Look,

Oliver, or John, or whatever the hell your real name is."

"I told you my real name before. It's John Carr."

"Good, that's a start. Keep going."

He rose. "No. I won't. And I can't help you now with Jerry Bagger. In fact, the faster you can get away from me the better. Take your father and use all your money to run as far and as fast as you can. I'm sorry, Annabelle. I'm sorry. If you're anywhere near me, you'll die. I can't have that on my conscience too."

He gripped her arm, walked her to the front door and closed it behind her.

54

Harry Finn's mother rose early. The pain, the gnawing at her bones, always made her rise before dawn.

She used the bathroom, shuffled back to her bed and read through her newspapers with the discipline of a lifetime. The radio and TV news shows followed in her ritual of endless fact-finding. And that's when she found herself staring at his face up there on the screen. She clawed at the remote control, and his grinning, smug countenance disappeared.

Her breaths coming in gasps, she looked down at the cell phone her son had given her. She had never called him on it; it was only reserved for emergencies, he'd told her. She kept it tied to a string that she wore around her neck. She only took it off to bathe. She needed to call him. She needed to know about the man. The face on the TV. Was it true? Could it be true?

She heard someone coming and quickly slipped back on the bed. The door opened and the attendant came in, whistling.

"How are we today, Miss Queenie?" the attendant

said. The nickname had come from her patient's imperious manner.

The old woman's face had assumed a vacant expression. She muttered a few words in the odd language she spoke. To anyone else it would sound like mindless ramblings, which was exactly what she intended. The attendant was very familiar with this speech.

"Okay, you just go right on jabbering while I get your dirty clothes and clean up the bathroom. Whatever makes you happy, Miss Queenie." The attendant glanced over at the well-thumbed newspapers and smiled. Miss Queenie wasn't nearly as out of it as she wanted people to think.

The woman performed her duties and left. Only then did she sit up and look at the phone again. It was odd that when one grew old decisions that were made quickly when young now required extensive internal deliberation. To call or not to call?

Before she had actually made up her mind her fingers punched in the numbers.

It was answered before the first ring was even finished. He had obviously recognized the number on the caller ID.

Finn's voice was low but clear. "What's happened? Are you hurt?' he asked firmly.

"No. I am fine."

"Then why did you call?"

"I saw on the news that he left the country. The

man is going on vacation. This man can take a holiday? Is this true? Tell me!"

"I'll take care of it. Hang up, now."

"But he must—"

"Don't say it. Hang up. Now."

"No one can understand what we're saying."

"Now!"

She clicked off and put the phone back around her neck. Harry was angry with her. She should not have called. But she could not help herself. All day and all night she sat here, in this place, in this hell, rotting, and thinking only of it. And then to see the man on the TV.

She scuttled over to the window and looked out. It was a beautiful day and it didn't matter to her. She did not belong to this world anymore. She belonged to the past and that was nearly gone as well. Her family, her friends, her husband, all dead. Only Harry was left. And now he was angry at her. Yet he would get over it. He always got over it. He was a good son; a mother could have no better son than she did. She opened the drawer and pulled out the single remaining photo she had of her husband.

She lay back on her bed, the photo over her heart, and dreamed of the death of Roger Simpson.

Harry Finn slowly put the phone back in his pocket and returned to the kitchen, where Mandy and the children stared anxiously at him. When his phone had rung and he saw the number come up, he'd forgotten that he even had a family. He had raced from the room, certain that his mother was calling to tell him they had found her. That she was about to die.

Susie had a bit of oatmeal dangling from her mouth. Patrick had dropped his fork on the floor, where George the Labradoodle was licking the egg off it. David had stopped stuffing his backpack with schoolbooks and was staring worriedly at his dad. Mandy was standing by the stove, spatula in hand, the pancake in the pan turning black.

She said anxiously, "Harry, is everything okay?"

He tried to smile, but his mouth couldn't manage it. "False alarm. Thought something weird was happening, my mistake."

Susie, perhaps because of the look on her dad's face, or the unnatural tremor in his voice, started to cry. He picked her up and pressed her face against his. "Hey, baby, it's okay. Daddy just made a mistake. That's all."

She cupped his face with her soft hands and gave him the kind of penetrating stare that only little kids seemed able to muster. "You promise?" she said in a tiny voice. The undercurrents of fear in her question cut right through Finn's soul.

He kissed her on the cheek, partly so he wouldn't have to look into those pleading, piercing eyes. "I promise. Even daddies make mistakes." He looked over at his wife, who had recovered a bit from her own terror. "But mommies don't, right?" He gave Susie a tickle and with his other hand squeezed Patrick's slender shoulder. "Right?"

"Right, Daddy," Susie said.

"Right," Patrick agreed.

Finn drove the kids to school and dropped them off. David was the last out of the car. He leaned back in, pretending to fiddle with his shoelaces while his siblings headed into the building.

"Hey, Pop, you sure everything's cool?"

"Absolutely, buddy, no worries."

"You can talk to me, you know, about anything."

Finn smiled. "I thought that was my line."

"I'm serious, Pop. I know sometimes it's hard to talk to Mom about stuff. Sometimes you need another guy to kick stuff around."

Finn reached out and shook his son's hand. "I appreciate that, Dave. More than you'll ever know." *I wish I could tell you everything, son, but I can't. I will never be able to. I'm sorry.* He thought this even as his immensely strong fingers tightened around his son's. He didn't want to let go.

"Have a good one, Pop." David closed the door and followed Susie and Patrick inside.

Finn slowly drove off, passing the cars of other parents, who, he was reasonably certain, would never knowingly trade their lives for his.

He looked in the rearview mirror as David disappeared into the school building.

If I fail, son, just remember me for the father I was, not the man I had to become.

Down the hall from Finn's mother's room a man named Herb Daschle yawned and stretched as he sat in front of a bed where another man lay unconscious. Daschle had been here since midnight and his shift did not end for another four hours. He nodded to an attendant as she came in to check the patient. It was at that instant that the man in the bed started moaning and a few words rolled from his mouth. Daschle jumped up, grabbed the attendant by the arm and pushed her out the door, slamming it shut behind her. He bent down to the man's face and listened intently. When he fell silent, Daschle whipped out a telephone and made a call, repeating exactly what he had said. Then he went to the door and called out. The attendant came back in, looking a little flustered. But this had happened before.

"Sorry about that," Daschle said politely as he resumed his seat.

"You people are going to give me a heart attack," the woman said under her breath. She didn't dare say it out loud. No, she didn't dare. Not with people like that.

55

"I'm grateful that Gregori was so helpful," Carter Gray said to the CIA director.

The men were sitting in the study in the bunker. Gray was actually growing quite fond of his current billet. There was something to be said for living underground. The weather was never a problem, no traffic jams, and he rarely enjoyed anyone's company as much as his own.

The former Soviet ambassador to the U.S. during the final years of the Cold War, Gregori Tupikov, was no longer serving the Russian people; he was doing quite well serving himself. He was now a fat and happy capitalist and a recent export from his homeland. He had joined an investment group that had taken over the formerly state-controlled coal industry and then sold it to another group of fellow Russians. Gregori had been wise enough to flee the country before the government hammer came down on the country's newly minted rich. He lived most of the year in Switzerland but owned apartments in Paris and New York, his millions carefully managed by Goldman Sachs.

Gray finished reading over the file report obtained from the meeting with Tupikov. "So Lesya and Rayfield Solomon *were* married in Volgograd; then the newlyweds managed to get out of the Soviet Union."

The director nodded. "According to what Gregori remembered and found out from old colleagues, they apparently made their way first to Poland, then to France and from there to Greenland. Was Lesya Jewish, by the way?"

"I don't know. Solomon was, although he wasn't a practicing Jew. The spy business oftentimes put a cramp in one's religious obligations."

"I make it to the Presbyterian church every Sunday," the director said.

"Congratulations. If Gregori knew that much back then, why didn't he do something about it?" Gray answered his own question. "He assumed she was still working for the Soviets."

"Well, wasn't she?" the director said in a puzzled tone.

"Of course," Gray said casually. "And after Greenland?"

"Unfortunately, there the trail turns cold. And it might well remain cold. It was a long time ago, after all."

"It *can't* remain cold," Gray snapped.

"Where exactly was Solomon found dead? That part of the file is missing too."

Gray looked up from the documents he was studying, pretending to recall the details. They were actually seared into his mind. "Brazil. São Paulo."

"What was he doing in São Paulo?"

"Not sure. He wasn't working for us then, of course. Lesya had turned him."

"And he died there?"

Gray nodded. "We were alerted by our contacts in South America. We did an investigation. But it was clear he'd killed himself."

The director looked at Gray and Gray looked at the director.

"Of course," the director said. "And Lesya was left on her own?"

"Looks that way. Anything else?"

"Perhaps."

Gray glanced up to see the director smiling smugly. He recalled that as a young case agent the current CIA director had possessed the worst poker face of any man he'd ever trained, and also a vastly annoying air of superiority, most of it undeserved. Gray believed he had shamed these weaknesses out of the man. Yet as head of the CIA it was clear his insufferable qualities had risen once more.

"Tell me."

"Gregori must've been in a good mood. As you suggested when our man met him in Paris, he fed him lobsters by the ton."

"And Moskovskaya vodka? That's his favorite."

"By the gallon. And we scrounged up a redhead or two."

"And?"

"And he said that he recalled a rumor that Lesya *had* to get married."

"*Had* to get married?" Gray said, looking puzzled.

The director made a motion with his hand in front of his stomach.

"She was pregnant?" Gray said immediately.

"That's evidently what Gregori believes."

Gray sat back. *It's the son out there murdering people.* "So based on the rough timeline we're working with, the child would be in his or her mid-thirties today?"

The director nodded. "But I highly doubt that the kid's last name is Solomon."

"But if Lesya and Solomon married in Russia while she was pregnant, and showing, where was the child born? If they left Russia immediately after the wedding the birth could have been in Poland, France, Greenland, or of course Canada."

"Canada? The last known stop of theirs was in Greenland. Where does Canada come in?"

Gray studied the man who headed up the nation's premier intelligence agency. He had started out at the CIA, then gone into politics, and there he had stayed until a president of dubious judgment had tossed his friend a political bone and made him CIA director. *God help this country.*

"Why does one go westward to Greenland except on the way to Canada? Even back then there were numerous direct flights to the U.S. And it was a favorite stopping place for spies. When I was in the field I often stopped in Greenland before coming home. You could always spot someone following you in Greenland. Humanity damn well stuck out in the frozen tundra!"

"Okay, but maybe they came to *this* country to have the child? That would make him a U.S. citizen. It'd be easier."

"I don't think so, not for the birth. And less complicated for her to sneak into Canada and have the baby there than in the U.S. The records could always be falsified later."

"Even with all that, it doesn't leave us much to go on."

"I disagree. From Greenland to Canada the ports of entry are limited, and were even more so back then. Montreal? Toronto? Ottawa? Perhaps Nova Scotia and Newfoundland? We can start there."

"Start there doing what exactly?"

"We'll limit it to a single twelve-month period." Gray named the year. "And we will search the records of births in those places. Just boys for now."

"Why not girls too?"

"Just boys for now," Gray repeated.

"That's still an enormous search. And we have that disaster readiness drill on Capitol Hill coming up that

DHS demanded and left us to do the lion's share of the work. It's requiring an inordinate amount of our time."

"The birth records should be computerized now. That should simplify things greatly."

"Yes, but still. The resources required to—"

Gray leaned forward and silenced the man with one of his most intimidating stares. "The consequences of *not* doing so are potentially catastrophic to this country."

56

Annabelle waited outside until her father returned from the nearby grocery store with Caleb. Without a word of explanation she told Paddy to follow her back to her hotel in his truck. When they got there she led her father up to her room.

Annabelle's mind was racing. She'd been counting on Stone to help her. And now the man had simply abandoned her, literally closing the door in her face. She should never have trusted him. She should've learned by now that you could only count on yourself.

"Annie?" Paddy finally said. "Talk to me, girl, what the hell's going on?"

She looked over at her father as though she'd forgotten he was even there. "What's going on is we just got screwed. The help I thought we were going to get with Bagger isn't coming."

"No cavalry?"

"No cavalry."

"The guy named Oliver. Reuben told me a bit about him. Is he the guy who was going to help us do it?"

"Yes, but he's not going to anymore. He apparently has more pressing business."

He slapped the arm of his chair. "Now what?"

"Now we run. Bagger will have the airports and train station watched, but he doesn't have enough manpower to cover the roads. We'll need to dump your truck. Then we'll be on our way."

"On our way where?"

"Does it matter? So long as it's not here?"

"And we just let Jerry walk away?"

"Better than him *carrying* us away, don't you think? We live to fight another day." As soon as she said the words she glanced at her father. "I'm sorry, I didn't mean . . ."

"I don't have another day. I either do it now, or I don't do it at all."

"I told you, we don't have the cavalry."

"Then I'll think of something else."

"You can't take on Jerry by yourself."

"I've got you, don't I?"

She looked out the window, shaking her head. "Do you know how long it took me to plan my hit on Jerry?"

"Probably longer than I've got left. But I'm not walking away from this. I *can't* walk away from this."

"Yesterday you weren't doing anything to go after Jerry. What's changed?"

He rose and gripped her arm. "What's changed is *you*. Now you know I was in jail when your mum got killed. I'm still a son of a bitch, but not as big of a one as you thought."

"What are you saying, that you're doing this for me?"

"No, I mean, not just you. I'm doing it for Tammy, because she didn't deserve to die like that. And I'm doing it for me, because Bagger took the only person I ever really loved from me."

Annabelle pulled her arm free and looked away.

"I didn't mean it that way, Annabelle."

She pointed to the scar on her face. "Let's just say I never had any delusions that you actually loved me."

Paddy reached his hand out to touch her face but she jerked back.

"I had no right to do that," he said. "But I was teaching you a lesson I never wanted you to forget. You blew that claim at the casino. Sure, you were young, and the young make mistakes. But I'll wager you never made that mistake again, did you?"

"No."

"I never gave a shit about any of the crews I worked with. Hell, I never bothered giving any of 'em a scar. If they made a mistake I let 'em know it, sure. But I didn't give a damn if they screwed up down the road with somebody else and got their knees broken for the trouble."

"So, my scar was what, tough love?"

"Your mum never wanted you to get into the con.

But we were shorthanded that summer and it was my idea to use you. You caught on fast, faster than I did at your age. Ten years later you were better than I ever was. Moved on to the long cons while I was still doing my three-card monte on street corners. For chump change."

"That was your choice."

"No, not really. Plain fact was I wasn't good enough to do the long. They say you're either born to it or not. I wasn't."

"Okay, where does that leave things? You can't do the long and the long is what it'll take to get to Jerry."

"I can't do it without you, Annabelle. But if you won't help me, I'm going to try anyway."

"If you do, he'll kill you."

"I'm dead anyway. And I doubt even Jerry could come up with a more painful way to die than what I've got ahead of me."

"You are really complicating my life."

"Will you help me?"

Annabelle didn't answer him.

"Look, can't you talk to your friend again? Maybe he'll reconsider."

Annabelle was about to say no, but hesitated. What she was thinking was she might go back to Stone's cottage. If he was there she could make another pitch for help. But if he wasn't there, which she suspected was the case, Annabelle would just take all of the "files" that Stone had compiled on her and her problems with Jerry. She didn't want any of that just lying around for someone, cops or bad guys, to find.

"I'll give it another shot."

As she walked down to her car she realized she couldn't just leave her father to deal with Jerry alone. Which meant they would both end up dying.

Some choice.

57

After Annabelle and Paddy had left, Stone put Caleb in a taxi with some old clothes of his and gave the driver the address of a hotel nearby.

"Oliver, why can't I stay here?" Caleb said, obviously frightened.

"That would not be smart. I'll call you later."

It was only when the cab had driven away and he was finally alone that Stone started thinking about what he'd done to Annabelle.

"I abandoned her," he said. "After I promised to help. After I told her to stay." Yet what could he do? And anyway, she'd probably be on a flight within a few hours, on her way to that South Pacific island. She'd be safe there.

But what if she didn't run? What if she stubbornly decided to go after Bagger anyway? With no support? She'd said she needed the cavalry. Could he still deliver that to her?

The next instant the phone rang. It was Reuben. He said, "Nothing from my contacts at DIA, Oliver. They didn't know about the cemetery thing. But

Milton did find something on the Net. Here, I'll put him on."

Milton's voice came over the phone. "It wasn't much, Oliver, but there was breaking news about a grave being dug up at Arlington. No one from the government would comment."

"Did it mention the name on the grave marker?"

"Someone named John Carr," Milton said. "Is that a problem?"

Stone didn't bother to answer. He clicked off.

After all these years John Carr had suddenly come back to life. Ironically, Stone had never felt more dead than he did right now.

Why now? What had happened? The truth struck him as he slowly walked back through the cemetery gates and sat down on his front porch.

He'd been set up.

If John Carr was no longer dead, then the person killing old members of Triple Six would now add him back onto his list of targets.

I'm bait, Stone said to himself. *They're going to use me to flush the killer. And if he murders me before they catch him, who cares. And even if I do manage to survive? It won't be for very long.* All John Carr would be now was an embarrassment to the government. His own country would have many reasons to want him dead and not a single one that Stone could think of to keep him alive. It was absolutely brilliant in its simplicity. His death warrant had been signed.

And there was only one man who would've been capable of thinking it all up, Stone knew.

Carter Gray! He is alive.

He packed a small bag, locked up the cottage and fled through the woods behind the cemetery.

Harry Finn was carefully balancing a butter knife on a table where he was sitting so the knife was standing up on edge. It was harder than it looked, yet Finn could accomplish it every time and within a few seconds. He did this whenever he was unsure of something. He was seeking balance. If he could do it with the knife, he could do it with his life. At least that was his thinking. It was never that easy in reality.

"Harry?"

He looked up into the face of one of his team members. They had been discussing the Capitol building project over lunch at their office.

"Did you get a chance to review the ventilation plans?" the woman asked.

He nodded. They'd gotten the documentation through an ingenious tactical combination that involved breaking into the van of the architect hired to work on the Capitol Visitor Center. From that they copied necessary information and then used that to phone freak their way to many details of the new construction.

"The plans indicated that it will hook into the

Capitol building, but I need to confirm that. We're going tonight, in fact, to do it. And it should be accessible from the delivery tunnel, but I'm going to verify that too." He looked at the man sitting next to him, who was going over a set of drawings and specs. "How about the transport?"

"All done." The man laid out the details to Finn.

Finn glanced down at the ID badge he'd earlier stolen from the SUV. This one badge had gotten him a lot of mileage. With the embedded encryption he could simply change out the surface information—photo, name, etcetera—and the badge would get him into myriad places, none of which he should have access to. He'd heard the government was beginning to discover this flaw in their security system, but Congress moved with glacial speed when it came to things like that. Finn figured they'd have the problem worked out by the time he was drawing Social Security. And even that might be optimistic.

The meeting adjourned and he went to his office and worked for the rest of the day. Later, he changed into a Capitol police uniform, doctored his badge and headed to D.C. that night, where he met up with a buddy, similarly dressed. There were sixteen hundred officers on the Capitol police force to guard roughly one square mile of land. It was a ratio any other city would have killed for. Congress liked to feel safe, and it did control the purse strings.

And yet all that money had not made the folks

much safer, thought Finn as he and his colleague strolled around the grounds of the Capitol that night. In fact, he was going to prove the truth of that statement tonight.

They made their way to the construction site of the visitor center and went in, pretending to make rounds. Work here went on 24/7, so he and his buddy jawed with some of the construction workers and then moved along. They passed a fellow officer, whom they exchanged both pleasantries and gripes with. Finn informed the cop that he'd just transferred over from the U.S. Park Police, where he'd been assigned to the San Francisco area.

"Housing is cheaper here," Finn said. "San Fran is off the charts. I actually bought a town house for what I paid for a condo out there."

"You're lucky," said the other cop. "I was a postal cop down in *Arkansas* before I moved here about five years ago. I'm still living in a three-bedroom apartment in Manassas that I can barely afford, and I've got four kids."

Finn and his friend headed on and finally arrived at the spot that was the only reason they'd come here tonight.

It was right where the plans indicated it would be. Ready access from the tunnel, and by the look of things it was already operational. That would make their task easier. Finn picked the lock of one door and they slipped inside it. He studied the instrument boxes on the wall and then snapped several pictures of the flow schematic. Next he drew a diagram of the area on a notepad, listing all access doors, halls and checkpoints they'd passed. Then they made their way through a series of hallways and into a small HVAC room. The ventilation return was in the ceiling. The opening was too narrow for Finn to get through, but his partner was smaller. Finn gave him a boost and the fellow disappeared into the ductwork. Thirty minutes later he was back.

"Like we thought, Harry, goes right into the Capitol." The man gave Finn a detailed description of the route he'd just taken, and Finn drew it out on paper.

They slipped back outside, walked away from the Capitol and turned down a street toward the Hart Senate Building. His partner went to the right and Finn to the left. He passed alongside the building, where nine stories up sat Roger Simpson's office. As Finn counted across the windows to the one he knew was the Alabama senator's digs, he pointed his finger at the window and said, "Boom."

He couldn't wait.

He reached his car and drove off. Turning on the radio to the local news station, he heard the announcer talking about a grave being dug up at Arlington National Cemetery that morning. As yet no one knew why.

"John Carr," the radio said. "That's the name of the soldier whose grave was dug up."

"John Carr," Finn repeated in a voice brimming with disbelief. Surely his omniscient mother would have heard this news by now.

And he started to wonder if his nightmare would ever end.

58

Alex Ford sat at home worrying. He had been trying to reach Stone but the man wasn't answering his phone. The story about the grave being dug up at Arlington was not front-page news but it had people talking. Alex didn't know what had been found in that coffin. He knew, however, that it wasn't the body of John Carr. He had learned much about Stone's past when they both had nearly died at a place called Murder Mountain not too far from Washington. And yet Alex felt that there was a part of Oliver Stone/John Carr that neither he nor anyone else would ever know.

He tried to reach Stone by phone one more time, and then his own phone started ringing. He answered. It was the man himself.

"Oliver, what the hell is going on?"

"Not a lot of time to talk, Alex. You heard about the grave?"

"Yes."

"It was Carter Gray's doing."

"But he's—"

"No, he's not. He's alive and trying to set me up for a series of murders related to my past."

"Oliver, what the—"

"Just listen! I can take care of myself. Reuben and Milton are laying low. So is Caleb. But I need you to do me a favor."

"What is it?"

"My friend, Susan Hunter. You remember her?"

"Tall, leggy, with a fast mouth."

"She's in trouble and I offered to help her, but I can't now. Will you step in for me?"

"Is she the reason we got called out last night?"

"That was my fault, not hers. But if you do help her you have to promise me something."

"What?" Alex said warily.

"Her past is not exactly perfect. But she's a good person with good motives. Don't dig too deep there."

"Oliver, if she's a criminal—"

"Alex, you and I have been through a lot together. I would trust this woman with my life. I hope that means something to you."

Alex sat back and let out a deep breath. "What do you want me to do?"

"Go to my cottage. On the desk are some notes. They will help you to understand the situation better. I'll give you Susan's phone number. You can contact her and tell her that I asked you to help."

"This is really important to you, isn't it?"

"I wouldn't be asking this big of a favor if it weren't."

"Okay, Oliver, I'll do it."

"I appreciate it, Alex, more than you'll ever know."

"Are you sure I can't help *you*?"

"No. This is something I have to handle on my own."

Alex drove to Stone's cottage. It looked empty, yet he still pulled his gun before unlocking the door, using a key Stone had once given him. It didn't take long for him to see that no one was there. Following Stone's instructions, he sat down at the desk and started going over the papers there, all in Stone's precise handwriting.

There were names: Jerry Bagger, Annabelle Conroy with a circle around it, Paddy Conroy, Tammy Conroy and someone named Anthony Wallace. There were notes about Stone's recent trip to Maine, along with some lines detailing conversations with Reuben, Milton and Caleb. And apparently Milton and Reuben had been to Atlantic City, to the Pompeii Casino.

Bagger's place.

Alex stuffed the notes in his pocket, rose and stretched out his lean six-foot-three-inch frame, massaging the muscles in his neck with his hand. He'd broken his neck in an accident years ago while on presidential protection detail and the surgically installed metal there sometimes gave him fits. Next step was to contact this Susan Hunter, if that was really her name, which, after seeing these notes, he was pretty certain wasn't the case.

The next instant he froze. Someone was coming. He slid over next to the bathroom door and waited.

The intruder came in, went immediately over to the desk and seemed to be very upset that nothing was there.

Alex stepped out and put his gun against the person's head.

True to her unflappable nature, Annabelle Conroy didn't scream, but she did say, "I hope to hell you have the safety on."

He lowered his gun and stepped back. Annabelle was dressed in a short skirt, sandals and a jean jacket; her long blonde hair was tied back in a ponytail and partially covered under a ball cap. She took off her sunglasses and stared up at the tall federal agent.

"You're Secret Service, right?"

He nodded. "Alex Ford. And I know you, you're—"

"Unemployed." She looked around. "He's not here?"

Alex was staring at the small hook-shaped scar under Annabelle's right eye. He caught himself and said, "No, he's not."

"Any idea where he might be?"

"Not really."

"Good-bye then."

As she headed to the door, Alex said sharply, "Annabelle!"

She jerked around.

Alex smiled. "Annabelle Conroy, pleased to meet you. Let me guess, father is Paddy, mother or maybe sister's name is Tammy?" He pulled out the notes from his pocket. "And it seemed you might have been looking for these."

She eyed the papers and said, "I thought Oliver was more discreet than that."

"He is. I figured it out on my own."

"Good for you. Well, I guess I'll be leaving."

"You want me to tell Oliver anything in case I see him?" Alex asked.

"No. I don't think I have anything to say to him. Not anymore, anyway."

"But you came to see him?"

"So? Why are *you* here?" she said.

"Because I'm his friend and I'm worried about him."

"He can take care of himself."

"Any idea why he disappeared?" Alex asked, though he knew the answer.

"It's because they dug up a grave at Arlington Cemetery. *His* grave, apparently." She watched Alex closely, presumably to see how he would react to this. "Did I pass your little test?"

He nodded. "Oliver must really trust you if he told you about that."

"Let's put it this way: I thought he did trust me, but it turns out he didn't."

"I heard Bagger can be pretty ruthless."

If she was startled by this Annabelle didn't show it. "What's a Bagger? You mean like at a grocery store?"

He handed her one of his cards. "Oliver called me and told me to help you while he was otherwise engaged."

This news did startle her. "He asked you to help me?"

"He insisted on it, in fact."

"And you do what he tells you to?" she said.

"He said he'd trust you with his life. There aren't many people he says that about. I happen to be one of them. We tend to look out for each other."

She hesitated, before slipping the card in her purse. "Thanks."

Alex watched in silence as she walked back to her car.

59

Camp David, though it was often used as a working retreat, was also a place that allowed the president of the United States to get away from the stresses of the most impossible job on earth. The White House Press Office had issued a notice to journalists covering the president that this weekend was only for the president and his family. That was a lie, or at least a subterfuge, as statements issued by the press office sometimes were. The president was receiving a visitor, a very special visitor, and complete secrecy was necessary.

"Thank you, Mr. President, for seeing me so swiftly," Carter Gray said as he sat down across from the man in his private office at the camp. As much as Gray had come to enjoy his bunker life, there was something to be said for venturing aboveground every once in a while.

"I'm just glad you're all right," the president said. "A very narrow escape for you."

"Well, I can't say it was the first time, but I hope it is the last. And I appreciate the latitude you've given me, on an unofficial basis of course, to pursue this matter."

"I could sense its urgency when we spoke by phone. But I'd like a fuller understanding."

"Of course." Gray gave the president a thumbnail history of Lesya, the treachery of Rayfield Solomon and the recent murders of the Triple Sixes. "And now we come to the last member of that unit, John Carr."

"The fellow who they dug up at Arlington? I've been briefed on that."

"Yes, well, that coffin did not hold the remains of John Carr."

"Who was it, then?"

"Not important, sir. What is critical is that John Carr escaped thirty years ago."

"Escaped? Was he a prisoner?"

"No, a traitor. He worked for us, but we had cause to terminate his association with CIA because of his actions."

"Terminate? Why not just prosecute him?"

"There were extenuating circumstances, sir. A public trial would not have been in the best interests of this country. So we had to take matters in our hands. Duly authorized of course by your predecessor."

The president sat back and fingered his teacup. "Different times back then, I suppose. Dirty business."

"Yes sir. That sort of thing is no longer done, of

course," Gray said quickly. "However, the termination attempt failed. And now I think it's come back to haunt us."

"How so?"

"It seems clear that the man behind the deaths of the three former CIA agents is Carr."

"Why do you think that?"

"They were the ones who turned him in. And now he's exacting his revenge."

"Why would he wait three decades for that?"

"I can only speculate there, and that would hardly be a good use of your time, sir. However, there's only one man who had grievances against all three, and that's John Carr."

"And he tried to kill you? Why?"

"I managed his unit. I was the one who brought him up on *internal* charges, in fact."

"You ordered him terminated?"

"My superiors did with, as I said, all appropriate authorization." Gray told this lie as though it was perfectly true. Perhaps he had convinced himself it was.

"Are these superiors still around?"

"No, all dead. As is, as you know, the president in office at the time."

"How does this tie into Solomon and this Lesya person?"

"That was the reason Carr was terminated. We believed he'd been turned by Solomon and Lesya."

"But Solomon died. Suicide, I think the report said."

"Yes, but presumably Lesya is still out there. And I recall that Carr and Lesya had grown especially close. They could be working together now."

"Why would this Lesya help Carr kill the CIA's former Triple Sixes?"

Inwardly Gray sighed. This president was not as stupid as others he'd served under. "Let's put it this way, sir. Rayfield Solomon officially committed suicide. But that's only the official version. It could be that he had help."

"Help? From us?"

"He was a traitor, sir. He cost many Americans their lives. He would've been executed in any event. He's on the 'Wall of Shame' at Langley next to Aldrich Ames and other spies. The lives he cost this country, incalculable. A venomous traitor if ever there was one." It pained even Gray's hardened conscience to say these things about his deceased friend, but Solomon was dead. Gray wanted to remain alive.

"So we terminated *him*, too!"

"It was, as you said, a different world then. I for one applaud the more open and public face of the CIA and the government in general that we have today. But back then we were fighting against the possible annihilation of the world."

"So Carr and Lesya may be out there. Anyone else on their target list?"

"Only one—Roger Simpson."

"That's right, he was with the CIA way back. So Roger was involved with this?"

"Only tangentially. We've taken appropriate precautions to ensure his safety."

"I certainly hope so. We don't have much of a majority in the senate. Every vote counts."

Gray's features remained inscrutable, but his mind did reflect for a moment on the president's concern for maintaining a majority in the Senate over the life of an individual senator. "Certainly," he said. "I can see why that's important to you."

The president said quickly, "Of course a man's life has to take priority."

"I never doubted that," Gray said. He suddenly wondered if there were recorders in the room and the commander in chief was making that statement for posterity.

"So what do you propose? John Carr's name has been all over the news. The man must've heard about it by now. I don't think I would have done it that way, Carter. I would've kept it on the QT while I hunted for him."

The president didn't know that Gray knew exactly where John Carr lived and that he was now known as Oliver Stone. Stone certainly would have found out by now that his grave had been dug up and his secret exposed. He was no doubt now on the run. As quick-witted as the man was, he'd also probably deduced that Gray was alive and actually plotting against him. Gray *could* have kept it on the QT, and then simply gone to Stone's cottage and arrested him. Or killed him. But he couldn't do that, because Stone had a piece of incriminating evidence against him. And Gray wanted it back. Now he had something to bargain with: the evidence in exchange for letting John Carr live. He had wanted Carr to know. He had wanted Carr to go on the run, with Gray's men keeping him on a long leash. It would make him more amenable to negotiating.

Gray said, "In hindsight that would probably be the best strategy. But we have to keep in mind that we need to avoid dredging up a lot of Cold War history with Solomon, Lesya and the others. Russia is in a fragile state right now, and the last thing we want is for accounts of our old skirmishes to surface. Frankly, sir, both sides played dirty back then, and public sentiment needs to be kept in check here and in Russia. Contact has been made with the Russians and they understand what is at stake. They've pledged their support to eliminating the problem."

"Of course. Well, you can count on my full support too, Carter. Good to have you back in the saddle. Never understood why you resigned in the first place."

"Perhaps neither did I." *And I never would have if it hadn't been for John Carr.*

Gray was taken by chopper back to his bunker. He

looked out the window of the helicopter as it soared along over the Maryland countryside. Down there Carr was running hard, with Gray's men right behind. And Lesya's son was probably planning his next attack: on that same John Carr. Which was why Gray had wanted this to become public; he *wanted* Carr to become a target.

Now all he had to do was get to Carr first, pretend to give him back his life in exchange for the evidence, and then Lesya's son could have him. And then they would kill the son and Lesya and finally put an end to this once and for all. As for Roger Simpson, he didn't care whether the man survived or not.

Admittedly, it was a complicated plan. Yet in Gray's world, nothing seemed to be simple.

60

When Annabelle returned to the hotel, Paddy was waiting for her in her room.

She sniffed the air. "You haven't been smoking."

"I tossed them in the trash can."

"Why?"

"I need to be in fighting shape when we go up against Bagger."

He looked so determined and yet so frail, like a stubborn little boy hell-bent on standing up to a bully, that for an instant Annabelle's heart went out to him. She felt her hand reach out and touch him on the shoulder. And then the moment passed and she withdrew her fingers.

Yes, he was dying. Yes, he hadn't technically let her mother die. But he was not suddenly the greatest father on earth. And he would be dead in six months. She was not going to let herself go down that road. She had grieved long and painfully for her mother's passing. She would not do the same for him.

"Any luck with getting us some help?" he asked.

"Maybe."

"Tell me about it."

"Secret Service agent, Alex Ford. Oliver asked him to step in."

"This bloke Oliver has some damn fine connections. Who the hell is he? I mean, living at a graveyard and all."

"I'm not really sure who he is," Annabelle said truthfully.

"But you said you could trust him."

"I do trust him."

Paddy looked hopeful. "Secret Service, that's good stuff. Maybe they can pull in the FBI."

She slipped off her sandals and sat down in a chair across from him. "I never thought I'd hear you sound so enthusiastic about having feds around."

"Circumstances change. Right now, I'd take every bloody cop in the country marching in lockstep with us."

"With Bagger, it might take that. So if I can get the cavalry how do we do it? I need details now, not generalities. How do we get him to confess?"

"You ran a long con on Jerry."

"Right, so?"

"So you must have his telephone number."

"I do. And again, so?"

"I'm going to call him and make him a deal he can't refuse. I'm going to sell you down the river, Annabelle. He'll offer cash, a ton of it. But I'll tell him that's not what I want."

"So what *is* your motivation?"

"You bad-mouthed me to the con world after your mum died. Haven't had a decent gig in years."

"You'd have to sell that line one hundred percent."

He stared across at her. "Not a problem, since it happens to be the truth."

"So you ship me down the river, then what?"

"That's where the cavalry comes in." He added, "Obviously that's a critical part of the plan."

She stared at him suspiciously. "Obviously."

"I've got the delivery all worked out."

Annabelle hunched forward. "Tell me every detail of it so I can tell you it'll never work."

"Don't forget, I've run a con or two in my day."

When he'd finished, she sat back, impressed. It had holes, like all initial plans did, but nothing that couldn't be sufficiently tweaked. It was actually pretty good.

"I've got some ideas we can add to it," she said. "But the underlying concept is sound."

"I'm flattered."

"Jerry will do everything in his power to make sure once they leave the pickup spot they won't be followed."

"I realize that."

"Well, since I'm the bait I have a heightened reason for making sure that we *will* be able to follow him."

"He'll send his boys to do the pickup. He won't be there, just in case it's a setup," Paddy pointed out.

"I know that. And that's our way in, actually."

"How do you figure?"

The answer that had shot into Annabelle's head made her smile. "We get to Jerry first."

"How are we supposed to do that?"

"You're going to do it."

"I am?" Paddy snapped his fingers. "On the phone call?"

"On the phone call."

"But we still need the cavalry or none of it does us a damn bit of good," he added.

She put her sandals back on and grabbed her car keys. "Then I'll go get it."

61

They sat at a table in a coffee shop near M Street and Wisconsin Avenue, barely a mile from Stone's empty cottage. Annabelle gazed out the window while Alex kept his eyes on her. He was trained to read people's expressions and body cues. This lady was tough to decipher, but it was clear she was under considerable stress.

"So why the sudden call?" he asked. "I didn't figure I'd be seeing you again."

"What can I say, I'm a sucker for tall cops."

"Does that translate as a cry for help?"

"How much do you know?"

"Oliver asked me to dig up stuff on this Bagger guy and I did. It seems Milton and Reuben went to Atlantic City, presumably to the Pompeii Casino. Oliver said they were laying low now. They're friends of mine too, so if they're in trouble I'd like to know about it so I can help them while I'm helping you."

"Is that what you do, run around helping people?"

"That's what it says in my job description. So tell

me about you and Bagger. And why did Oliver go to Maine?"

"You already seem to know everything."

"Everything and nothing. But if you really want my help you're going to have to trust me." He cocked his head as she stared moodily off. "I take it trusting people is not something you do well."

"That's a philosophy that's served me incredibly well over the years."

"I don't doubt it. But just so you know, I've covered Oliver's back, more than once. And I'd trust him with my life."

"I know, he told me. He said he'd go to war with you any day."

Alex sat back. "There you go. So maybe I *can* help you, if you can bring yourself to trust me."

Annabelle took a deep breath. Enlisting Alex's aid was critical to her father's plan to get Bagger. Yet even with that goal in mind this was so damn hard for her. She was sitting across from a cop—no, not just a cop, a federal cop! Someone who could bust her in a second if she misspoke. On the drive over it had seemed so simple. Now it appeared impossible.

Come on, Annabelle, you can do this.

With one more deep breath, she decided to do something she almost never did. She swallowed her principles and decided to tell the truth. At least part of it.

She quickly went through the main points. Bagger killing her mother. The fact that he was now in town.

That she had teamed with her father to bring him down. Alex already knew that they'd been kidnapped and almost killed by Bagger's men. She added, "I don't have evidence of any of this. Nothing that would stand up in court. But it's the truth."

"I believe you. But my cop friends were a little pissed when they showed up to arrest the guys and found no one home."

"No less pissed than I was."

"Why is Bagger after you now?"

Annabelle went automatically to lie mode. "He knows I'm trying to nail him for my mom's murder. He found out I went up to Maine where it happened. He doesn't want me to find something that could put him away for good."

Alex sipped his coffee and studied her some more. Either she was the best bullshitter he'd ever run across or what she said was legit. "And so you're teaming with your old man? How exactly do you propose sticking it to Bagger?"

"My dad's going to pretend to double-cross me with Bagger. Bagger gets me, I get him to confess, and the cops are there to nail him."

"That's your plan?"

"Yeah, why?"

"Because it has about a million holes in it, that's why. And all of them end up with you dead."

"That's just the broad concept. It's all in the details. It's always in the details."

"You really think you can make this work?"

"I sort of have a knack for it. My old man's not that bad either."

"Uh-huh. I'm going to need a little bit more than that if I'm going to be able to get you the backup you need."

"I tell you what. We'll get everything in place, you can take it to your people with a big nice bow, and then you can decide? Then if you say no, I die. That do it for you, big fella?"

"Hey, I'm just trying to be realistic here."

"No, you're being a classic bureaucrat. You look at how you *can't* do something instead of how you can."

Alex managed a tight smile. "Actually, the Secret Service is pretty can-do."

"Good. Show me."

"Give me a break here. I'm doing you the favor. I'm going out on a really big limb and it's a long way down."

Annabelle nervously balled her napkin up. "I know, I'm sorry. It's just . . ."

"The good news is the Justice Department really wants something to stick on Bagger. If I can dangle a big enough carrot in front of them, we should be able to get some FBI support. Bagger's been involved in a lot of questionable stuff. Several murders in fact, but the evidence just wasn't there."

"I know of a few more, but without his tripping himself up, nothing you can use."

"Just so you understand, I've only believed about half of what you've told me."

She started to say something but Alex said, "But I'm not going to press it."

Annabelle eyed him curiously. "Why not?"

"Because Oliver told me not to ask too many questions. He said you were a good person with an imperfect past."

Annabelle studied him closely. "So who was John Carr?"

"He worked for the U.S. government doing some highly specialized work."

"He killed people, didn't he?"

Alex looked around but the place was empty and the girl at the counter was too busy reading about Britney Spears' latest comeback in *People* to waste time eavesdropping on them.

"He doesn't do it anymore. Not unless he has to. Not unless someone's trying to kill him, or his friends."

"I saw him kill a man," Annabelle said. "He did it with a knife. Just a flick of his wrist and the man was dead. But the guy was trying to kill us." She fiddled with her coffee cup. "Do you have any idea what's really going on with him?"

"Did you hear about Carter Gray's house blowing up the other night?"

"Yeah, I read about it."

"Well, Oliver and Gray go way back, and not in a

good way. Oliver was at his house, at Gray's request, shortly before it blew up. And it was no accident. Oliver had nothing to do with it, but somebody else did. Somebody else who might just have Oliver on his target list."

"So he's got someone looking to kill him too?"

"Looks that way. And that's why he didn't want to hang around any of us."

"And I was really upset that he abandoned me."

"Hey, he called me in. I might only be the JV, but I've been known to get a few good punches in from time to time."

"That stuff I said before about you being a bureaucrat."

"I believe the exact phrase was *classic* bureaucrat."

"Yeah, well, I take it back. I appreciate your help."

"I need to make a few calls. And then I can help you fill in some of the details now that we have the *concept* nailed down."

She returned his grin. "I've never met a fed like you before, Alex Ford."

"That's okay, you're a new one in my book too."

62

As the night settled in Oliver Stone knew he was still being followed. Well, now was the time to say goodbye to the shadows. He ran for a cab and gave the driver an address in Alexandria. With deadly men in pursuit of him he was heading to a rare book store.

The taxi dropped him off in front of the shop on Union Street a block from the Potomac River. With the hunters behind him Stone hurried inside, nodding at the owner of the place, Douglas. The man had used to be called simply Doug, and had once sold pornographic comic books out of the trunk of his Cadillac. Yet he harbored a secret passion for rare books and a desire to be rich. That dream had gone unfulfilled until Stone had hooked him up with Caleb. Now *Douglas* ran a successful high-end rare book store. As part of the bargain Stone was given access to the place at all times, and had a room in the cellar area that he used to store some of his most important possessions. And it also provided something else that Stone was going to use right now.

Stone reached the cellar, unlocked a door and

entered the room where an old fireplace sat, long unused. He reached inside the fireplace opening, where next to the damper switch was a small pull cord. He tugged and a door on an old priest's hole-like chamber swung open. The room was filled with boxes stacked neatly on shelves, well above the flood line.

Stone opened a box and pulled out a journal that he stuffed in his bag. From another box he drew out a set of clothes, including a floppy hat, and changed into them. From a small metal box he took out an object that was more precious to him than all the gold in the world. It was a cell phone. A cell phone with a very special message carefully preserved on the built-in recording device.

When he left he did not reverse his path and go upstairs. He walked down a different passage-way, toward the river. He unlocked one more door, passed through, knelt down, pulled on an iron ring that was seated into the floor, yanking hard, and a square of floor came up on hinges. He dropped through, traversed a dark tunnel that smelled of river, dead fish and mold, clambered up a set of rickety stairs, unlocked another door and came out behind a clump of trees. He passed along a footwalk by the river and plopped into a small boat owned by Douglas that was docked at one of the slips.

He engaged the Merc outboard and headed south, his white stern light the only sign of him in the darkness. He ran the boat up on the shore about two miles north of Mount Vernon, George Washington's home, tying its bow line to a tree. He hoofed it to a gas station and called a cab from a pay phone.

On the ride back to town, Stone read through the journal. These records represented a significant part of his distant past. He had started keeping them almost immediately after he was recruited into the CIA's Triple Six Division. He had no idea if the CIA still had the division operational and didn't know if the men who'd attempted to follow him tonight were part of that element. However, he assumed that if they were ordered to kill him they would carry out the task with suitable skill.

Page after page of the journal was turned as Stone took a painful walk through his past work for the U.S. government. Then he focused on several photographs he'd pasted on one page along with his handwritten notes and some bits of the "unofficial" record he'd managed to snag.

He was staring at the photos of his three Triple Six comrades, all now dead: Judd Bingham, Bob Cole and Lou Cincetti. And then he looked at the older bespectacled man in the picture at the bottom of the page.

"Rayfield Solomon," he said to himself. The hit had been quick and efficient but still one of the most unusual of Stone's career. It had been in São Paulo. The orders had been clear. Solomon was a spy, turned by the legendary Russian operative Lesya, last name unknown. There was to be no arrest and no trial; it would be too embarrassing for the American public to endure; not that lengthy explanations were ever given to the Triple Six teams.

Stone remembered the man's expression as they burst in the door. It was not fear, he recalled. At best it was mild surprise, and then his features hardened. He politely asked who had ordered him to be terminated. Bingham laughed, but as the leader Stone stepped forward and told Solomon. There was no official requirement to do this. Stone simply felt every doomed man had a right to know.

Rayfield Solomon was a man of average height and build, more professor than secret operative in appearance. But to this day Stone remembered those wondrous eyes that burned into him as he raised his pistol. It was a gaze that bespoke a brilliant mind behind it, and a man who was unafraid of the death knocking on his door. He was no traitor, Solomon said. "You will kill me, of course, but understand that you kill an innocent man." Stone was impressed at how calmly the man spoke while four armed men encircled him.

"You will have been told to make it look like a suicide of course," Solomon said. This too stunned Stone because those had been his exact orders. "I am right-handed. As you can see, the hand is larger, stronger, so I'm not lying to you. Thus, place the shot in the right temple. If you wish I will also hold the gun and place my finger on the trigger so that my prints are on the weapon." Then he turned to Stone with a gaze that froze even the veteran killer. "But I will not pull the trigger. You will have to do the killing. Innocent men do *not* commit suicide."

After it was over, the men left as quietly as they had come. An overnight ride on an American cargo plane operated by a shell company of the CIA carried them back to Miami the next day. Bingham, Cincetti and Cole went out partying that night because the team had been given a few days off, as a reward for a job well done. Stone did not join them. He never did. He had a wife now and a young child. He stayed alone in his hotel room that night. He stayed up all night, in fact. The image of Rayfield Solomon would not leave his mind. Every time he tried to close his eyes, all he saw was the man's gaze ripping into him, the words eating away his soul.

I am an innocent man.

Stone hadn't wanted to admit it then, but all these years later, he could. Solomon had been telling the truth. Stone *had* killed an innocent man. Somehow he had known that this death would come back to haunt him. In fact, the Solomon case was one of the reasons Stone decided to leave Triple Six. It was a decision that ultimately destroyed his family.

They had called him a traitor, just like they had Solomon. And just like Solomon he'd been innocent. How many more Rayfield Solomons might have wrongly died by his hand?

He closed the journal and the cab dropped him off a few minutes later. He called Reuben, because if Gray couldn't find Stone he would use any means possible to flush him out, including kidnapping his friends.

Stone said calmly, "The big man we thought was gone isn't. Is your phone listed in your name?" Stone thought he knew the answer because he knew Reuben very well.

"Nope, I'm actually piggybacking on a friend of mine's service," Reuben said evasively.

"Luckily you just recently moved and don't have an official address. Otherwise I would've already had you relocate."

"I got *evicted* from the other place, Oliver. Left in the middle of the night because I wanted to avoid a certain rental dispute."

"Now everyone needs to lay low because friends of mine are valuable to him. I'll check in later."

He needed information from the inside and he needed it now. There was only one man who was in a position to give it to him. Stone hadn't seen the fellow in thirty years, but figured now was a good time to get reacquainted. Indeed, he wondered now why he hadn't made the visit decades ago. Perhaps he'd been afraid of the answer. Now he was no longer scared.

He had focused on the Rayfield Solomon case because, in his long career, it had been the one Stone felt the most regret for. After he'd been assigned to kill the man, Stone researched his background. He hardly seemed like a traitor, though that was not Stone's case to make. He'd heard of Solomon's personal link to the legendary spy Lesya. And if she'd survived and was still out there, the woman might be exacting her revenge on the people who'd killed Solomon. An innocent man.

63

Max Himmerling closed his book, yawned and stretched. Ever since his wife, Kitty, had died of cancer two years ago, his routine rarely varied. He worked, he came home, he ate a simple meal, he read a chapter in a book and he went to bed. It was an unexciting life, but his life at work was exciting enough. He had grown bald and fat in the service of his country. A nearly forty-year veteran of the CIA—he'd started there right out of college—his job was totally unique. Blessed with the most orderly of minds, he was like a central clearinghouse for the most diverse sort of matters. How would a coup in Bolivia or Venezuela orchestrated by the U.S. impact on the West's interests in the Middle East or China? Or if oil dropped another buck a barrel, would it behoove the Pentagon to open a forward military base in such-and-such country? In a time of supercomputers and servers filled with trillions of bytes of data and spy satellites that stole your secrets from outer space, it made Max feel good that there was still a strong human element in the work of his agency.

He was unknown outside the corridors of Langley, was considered only a low-level bureaucratic grunt within it, and would receive neither wealth nor honors. Yet to the people who mattered, Max Himmerling was an indispensable asset to the world's most elite intelligence-gathering agency. And that was enough for him. Indeed, after his wife's passing, it was all he had left. His importance to his agency was represented by the two armed men who guarded the exterior of his house when he was home. Himmerling would retire in two years and dreamed of traveling to some of the places he'd analyzed all these decades. He was worried, though, that his money would run out before his life did. The government provided a good package and first-rate health care, but he hadn't saved much on his own, and to continue living in this area, which he very much wanted to do, was expensive. He supposed he would cross that bridge when he came to it.

He lifted his tired, fleshy body from his easy chair and started up the stairs to his bedroom. He never made it.

The figure came from nowhere. The shock of the man standing in his living room nearly gave Max a heart attack. That was nothing compared to the shock he received when the intruder spoke.

"It's been a long time, Max."

Max put a hand against the wall to steady himself. He said in a shaky voice, "Who are you? How'd you get past the guards?"

Stone stepped into the small wash of light from a table lamp. "You remember the Triple Sixes, don't you, Max? How about John Carr? That name ring any bells for you? If it does, even after all these years, you can pretty much figure out how I got past the two idiots lying unconscious outside that you call *guards*."

Max stared up fearfully into the face of the tall, lean man standing across the room from him. "John Carr? It can't be. You're dead."

Stone stepped closer to him. "You know everything that goes on at CIA. So you knew John Carr wasn't in that grave they dug up."

Max slumped back down in his chair and looked pitifully at Stone. "What the hell are you doing here?"

"You're the great brain. You always figured out the best logistics for our missions. They almost always went off without a hitch. And when they didn't you were always thousands of miles away. So what the hell did you care? It was our asses on the line, not yours. So tell me, great brain, why am I here? And don't disappoint me. You know how I hate to be disappointed."

Max drew in a sharp breath. "You want information."

Stone glided forward and put a vise grip on Max's arm. "I want the truth."

Max grimaced from the pressure on his arm, but there was absolutely nothing he could do about it. His strength was mental, not physical. "About what?"

"Rayfield Solomon. Carter Gray. And anyone else you know who had his finger in that debacle."

Max had shuddered at the mention of Rayfield Solomon. "Gray's dead," he said quickly.

Stone's long fingers tightened on the man's arm until a bead of sweat broke over Max's forehead. "That's not what I meant by being truthful."

"His home was blown up, damn it!"

"But he wasn't in it. Now he's out there, plotting and planning, just like he always did. Only I'm the target. Again. And I don't like it, Max. Once was enough." Stone squeezed harder.

"Look, you can crush my arm if you want, but I can't tell you things I don't know about."

"I'm not going to crush your *arm.*" Stone let go and slid a knife out from his coat sleeve.

Max wailed, "John, you're not a killer anymore. You got out. You were always different. We all knew that."

"That didn't seem to help me back then. My wanting to get out almost cost me my life."

"Things were different back then."

"So people keep telling me. But once a killer, always a killer. I did it very recently, in fact. In self-defense. But I still killed a man. Slit his throat from ten feet away. And he was a former Triple Six. I guess they're not making 'em like they used to."

"But I'm defenseless," Max pleaded.

"I *will* kill you, Max. And it *will* be in self-defense.

Because if you don't help me, I'm a dead man. But I'm not going alone." He placed the edge of the blade against Max's quivering carotid artery.

"For God's sake, John, think what you're doing. And I lost my wife recently. I lost Kitty."

"I lost my wife too. I didn't have her nearly as long as you had your Kitty. But then you probably were the one who worked the logistics of the hit on me out on your nice, neat paper."

"I had nothing to do with that. I only learned about it after the fact."

"But you didn't go running to the authorities about it, did you?"

"What the hell did you expect me to do? They would have killed me too."

Stone pressed the blade harder against the man's flesh. "For a genius you sometimes say stupid things. Tell me about Rayfield Solomon before I lose my patience. Because this is all about Solomon, isn't it?"

"He was a traitor and you killed him, on orders."

"We did kill him, as ordered. Roger Simpson said it came right from the top. But there's obviously more to it. A lot more. Was Solomon innocent? And if he was, why were we ordered to kill him?"

"Damn it, John, just let it go! The past is dead."

Stone's knife cut into Max's skin a millimeter beside the artery, and a drop of blood appeared. "Was Solomon innocent?" Himmerling said nothing. He just sat there with his eyes closed, his chest heaving.

"Max, if I sever this artery, you will bleed to death in less than five minutes. And I will stand here and watch while you do."

Himmerling finally opened his eyes. "I've kept secrets for nearly forty years, and I'm not going to start talking now."

Stone swung his gaze around the room and stopped at the pictures on the mantel. A young boy and girl.

"Grandkids?" he asked with an edge to his voice. "Must be nice."

A trembling Max followed the man's gaze. "You . . . you wouldn't dare!"

"You people killed everyone I loved. Why should you get any better treatment? I'll kill you first." He pointed at the pictures. "And them next. And it won't be painless."

"You bastard!"

"That's right. I am a bastard. CIA-built, owned and operated. You know that as well as anyone, don't you?" Stone looked once more at the photos. "Your last chance, Max. I won't ask again."

And so for the first time in four decades, Max Himmerling let a secret slip out. "Solomon wasn't a traitor. He knew some things, but he didn't know all of it. People were afraid if he found out the truth, he'd talk."

"People like who? Gray? Simpson?"

"I don't know."

Stone made another nick on Himmerling's skin. "Max, I'm losing my patience."

"It was Gray *or* Simpson. I never knew which."

"And the secret?"

"Not even I knew that. It involved a mission Solomon and the Russian Lesya handled against the Soviet Union. The whole thing's on the front burner now. I don't know why."

"One more question. Should be an easy one. Who ordered the hit on me?"

"John, please—"

Stone violently seized the man around the throat. "Who?"

"All I can say is you have the same choice as with the last answer," Himmerling gasped.

So Gray or Simpson. Not that he was surprised.

Stone put the knife away and said, "If you try and tell anyone I've been here, you know what will happen. Gray will find out and he'll suspect you told me things. And you can't lie to him. He knows ways to get the truth out of the toughest people, much less someone like you. And when he finds out what you told me, guess what, Max?" Stone placed an imaginary pistol against the man's head and pantomimed pulling the trigger. "Enjoy the rest of your evening."

"Would you have really killed my grandkids?" Himmerling asked in a quavering voice.

"Just be glad they don't have to find out."

64

After Stone left, Max Himmerling breathed a sigh of relief; it caught in his throat. *The guards. They'll know someone came. They'll contact* . . . He ran to pack a bag. He had long ago worked out a doomsday scenario of having to flee. Ten minutes later he was on his way out the door, boarding pass printed out, fake ID in his pocket. The ringing phone made him stop. Should he answer it? Something told him to. He picked it up. The voice on the other end was very familiar to him.

"Hello, Max. What did you tell him?"

"I don't know what you're talking about."

"Max, you're a brilliant man, but a very bad liar. I don't blame you. I'm sure he threatened you, and we both know what a dangerous man he is. So what did you tell him?"

Once more Himmerling spilled his guts.

"Thank you, Max, you did the right thing." The line went dead.

Himmerling dropped the phone as the back door opened.

"Please," he said. "Please."

The silenced gun fired and the bullet hit him in the forehead. The body was placed into a black bag. In a minute the truck had carried it away. Officially Himmerling would be reassigned to a foreign post on short notice. When the next American chopper went down anywhere in the world, it would be recorded that Max Himmerling had been on it, his body burned beyond recognition. Thus would end the man's near forty years of service to his country.

At least he would no longer have to worry about outliving his pension.

In his bunker Carter Gray smacked his fist into his palm. The loss of Himmerling was a heavy if unavoidable one. Gray knew he should have anticipated it, but he hadn't.

He looked back at the computer screen in front of him. He had received the birth records from hospitals in major Canadian cities for the year in question. Even electronically they were voluminous. He had to separate the wheat from the chaff. Fortunately, he had known Rayfield Solomon well. They had been good friends, and friendly rivals. Indeed, it could be said that Solomon was the only man of his generation who could match Carter Gray in ability. Gray had to concede that in the field, Solomon might well have been his superior. So uncovering the man's tracks wouldn't be easy, but he did have the advantage of knowing him intimately.

He had focused his efforts on the name of the father listed in the birth records. Lesya would not have used her own name, of course. The name of the son would not help either, since Gray was sure that it would be different today. So it came down to the father. Rayfield Solomon was very proud of his Jewish heritage. Though the demands of his work did not allow him to practice his religion in a traditional fashion—critical missions could not be interrupted even for the exercise of his faith—Solomon had been an ardent scholar of his religion. He and Gray had had numerous discussions about theology. Gray's wife had been a devout Catholic. Gray had not been particularly religious until his wife and daughter had been killed on 9/11. Solomon had often told him, "Find something to believe in, Carter, other than your work. Because when you leave this life, you leave work behind. If that's all you have, then you have nothing. And eternity is a long time for nothing."

Wise words the man had uttered, though Gray had not necessarily believed them back then.

His fingers skimmed over the computer keys, trying this and that search combination. The list of names was further and further reduced. He continued to scan the names until he came to rest on one proud father.

David P. Jedidiah, II.

He smiled. *You blundered there, Ray. You let personal trump professional.* Over the years since his family's death Gray had also become a keen reader of the Bible, so the name of *this* father had particular relevance for him.

Solomon was the *second* son of David, his first legitimate child with Bathsheba. Jedidiah was the name that Nathan, the future King Solomon's teacher, called him. And in Hebrew Solomon means "Peace," hence the middle initial, *P.* Rayfield Solomon had used the name David P. Jedidiah, II, in the birth records. Carter Gray looked at the mother's name, and then at the son's. He picked up the phone and relayed this information. "Trace the son," he ordered.

He put the phone down and said aloud, "So where are you now, son of Solomon?"

65

It was morning, with a chill in the air. Harry Finn stood by himself, hands in pockets, and stared at it: the empty hole in the ground at Arlington National Cemetery, where John Carr was supposed to be resting, for all eternity. That had been a lie. And why was Finn surprised? The government always lied about the most important things.

Even though he previously believed the man was dead, Finn had researched John Carr's background. As a Navy SEAL he had done joint intelligence work with the CIA. Using the same skills that he made his living with today, he had slowly unearthed much of the history of his father's last days, and also the pasts of the men who'd been involved in killing him.

Judd Bingham's, Bob Cole's and Lou Cincetti's histories were pretty much the same. They had worked for the CIA, seemed to relish their duties in fact, until they'd retired to a life of comfort and leisure. Retirements that Finn had abruptly ended.

Only Carr was different. Officially, he had been killed while a member of an army unit, in the type of skirmish that popped up from time to time around the world and to which the United States was morally if not technically required to respond. Before becoming a member of the CIA's Triple Six Division, John Carr had been one of the most decorated veterans of the Vietnam War, including four Purple Hearts, and none of them for hangnails. There was even talk of his receiving the Congressional Medal of Honor, the highest military award of all. Every soldier who earned it had instantly attained a place of immortality in the eyes of professional warriors, though many had been awarded the honor posthumously. This had led some to dub it "The medal you'll never get to see."

Carr had certainly seemed an ideal man for the military equivalent of an Olympic gold medal. Finn had read the official report with both thrill and horror. Carr had single-handedly saved his ambushed platoon of soldiers in a murderous firefight with a far larger mass of North Vietnamese backed by artillery support. Sergeant John Carr had personally carried four wounded men to safety on his back, repeatedly going back into harm's way to do so. He had been hit twice by enemy fire and still somehow managed to kill a dozen Viet Cong, three of them in hand-to-hand fighting, while shooting several more out of trees with a marksman's skill that the report described as nothing short of supernatural.

Finally, manning a machine-gun post, Carr had repelled repeated attacks, survived multiple mortar rounds exploding all around his position and still managed to call in an airstrike that had driven the enemy back, allowing his men to safely retreat. He had walked off the field of battle under his own power despite his uniform being soaked in his blood. Finn could not help feeling a certain level of respect for the man. He had always considered himself to be a soldier of the highest level, but he was thinking that John Carr had perhaps surpassed him on the ability scorecard that all professional military people kept in their heads.

Yet Carr had not been given the medal. Finn didn't know that it had to do with politics rather than heroics on the battlefield. He didn't know that John Carr's growing ambivalence about the war had turned his superiors against him. His CO had not even recommended him for the medal until others had stepped in. Yet somewhere along the line, folks even higher up the command chain prevented a deserving soldier from receiving the military's highest honor.

Instead Carr had disappeared from the ranks of the army until resurfacing years later, only to die in that minor skirmish and supposedly be buried at Arlington. Finn knew what Carr had been doing in the interim. He'd been killing, on orders from his government. Yet he was a man who had been on the receiving end of death too.

It had taken two years of foraging on databases he was not supposed to have access to, but Finn had learned that Carr's wife had died one night when their house was supposedly burgled. The couple had had a daughter, but she had simply disappeared too. Finn was smart enough to read between the lines. The "burglary" had CIA hit written all over it. Carr must've angered his superiors somehow. Finn had been glad initially to learn that John Carr was dead. He had no interest in killing war heroes who had never gotten their just rewards, nor a man with the courage to buck the most powerful spy agency in the world.

But now perhaps Carr wasn't dead. And if he wasn't Finn knew what he had to do. What his mother expected him to do. Whether he liked it or not. And regardless of what sort of man John Carr was, he'd killed Finn's father. For nothing.

Finn left the graveyard. He had work to do.

For now, John Carr would have to wait.

66

It was a nontraditional penetration so Finn had grabbed a couple of guys from his office who normally sat behind a desk analyzing the data that he and his team of specialists routinely gathered. However, the client on this case had wanted low-level people headed up by someone who knew what he was doing—namely Finn. This was because the facility that manufactured vaccines for several man-made biological germ agents was not considered a high-priority target for terrorists. Still, they wanted to see how it measured up. Enter Finn and company.

They had no trouble scaling the unguarded fence at the rear of the facility, though one of the office boys, a hefty fellow named Sam, had a bit of trouble hoisting his bulk over. Finally, with Finn's help, he managed.

They were able to enter the facility from the rear through an unlocked door. A door being unlocked in a building housing valuable vaccine was something that sounded impossible but that nevertheless happened every day in countries all over the world. Why, indeed, would someone take home a laptop with the personal data of millions of military veterans only to see it stolen during a burglary? It's what kept bad guys in business and the good guys on antidepressant drips.

Inside, they spread out, their cover stories having been worked out in advance. Finn had donned a white lab coat he'd carried in a duffel bag. An ID was on a lanyard he put around his neck. He also carried an electronic pad for inputting notes. Thus outfitted, he worked his way to the front entrance area. To the guard stationed there he mentioned the name of a scientist who worked in the building. Finn had gotten the name off the Internet, knowing full well that the chap was on vacation. He'd obtained this bit of intelligence by going through the man's garbage one night and seeing a copy of the detailed travel itinerary for him and his family that the "genius" had cavalierly thrown away. When he was informed that the scientist was away, he said, "That's right. Bill told me he was taking the family to Florida." He then mentioned another name he'd pulled off the building directory. He had pulled this maneuver with the guard to both gain credibility and put the security person at ease. Both of these things were usually accomplished by concocting a personal connection with someone who worked at the place he was targeting.

"I can just pop up and see him for a few minutes," he told the private security guard. "I know the way. I have some test results to go over for the A/B run they did last week on the two new microbe trial vaccines. You in the loop on that?"

The guard, a kid barely out of his teens who proudly wore the standard-issue sidearm, said, "No, I'm not in the loop on that," and went back to his coffee and computer screen on which Finn caught sight of an online dating service's latest offerings.

Finn waited patiently inside the elevator car until someone came along. He held up a plastic card he had just taken out of the slot. "Damn RFID's malfunctioning again," he said, referring to the encrypted smart card that was needed to access the elevator. "Third time this month. And every time they said they fixed it. Yeah, right."

"I know the feeling," the other man said as he swiped his card through the slot and the doors closed. "What floor you want?" he asked.

"Fifth," Finn replied, as he put his son's plastic library card back into his pocket.

He got off on the fifth floor and found the door he wanted right next to the elevator bank. It also required a smart card for entry. He slipped inside a nearby bathroom and dabbed some water on his pants leg. When he heard the elevator ding, he opened the door to the bathroom, pretending to be rubbing his wet hands dry as the doors to the elevator slid open. The woman stepped off and swiped her card in the secure door as Finn stood behind her, his library card in hand.

The woman glanced at him and smiled. "Looks like I beat you to it."

Finn put his card away. "Hasn't been a great morning. I spilled coffee on my pants leg on the drive over." He pointed to the wet stain.

The woman smiled again. "Bet that woke you up."

"Oh, yeah," said Finn as he followed her in.

"You here to see anyone in particular?" she asked.

Finn shook his head and held up his phony but genuine-looking ID tag that had the imprint of Homeland Security. "Just a random drop-in. Feds need to see how the tax dollars are being spent."

"Don't I know it. Have a good one," she added as she walked off.

Finn strolled around the lab, surreptitiously taking pictures with his buttonhole camera and nodding to people as he walked along jotting down notes on his electronic tablet with his stylus. It really did amaze him. If you looked like you belonged, people never challenged you. He even had several people give him helpful details on certain vaccines' potencies. He left and made his way back down to the main entrance, courtesy of the help of another clueless Good Samaritan. When he exited onto the main lobby, however, he froze.

Sam, the fat kid from his office, was up against the wall and the security guard was doing a very unprofessional pat-down. Any person who knew what he was doing could have taken the guard's gun in a second with no trouble.

"What's going on here," Finn called out as he headed over.

"Spy!" the guard said. "Caught him red-handed. I'm calling the cops."

Finn had no choice now but to pull his credentialing letter and alert their contact inside the building that they'd been uncovered. He didn't like to have to make that call, but when you brought rookies with you, it sometimes happened. At least Finn had penetrated to where he needed to go. That's how it would have finished if Sam hadn't done something incredibly stupid. Panicked at the sight of the gun, he pushed the guard away and started to run.

The guard pointed his pistol at Sam's broad back and shouted, "Stop!"

"Don't," Finn screamed as he hurtled forward. The guard fired his weapon just as Finn collided with him. In an instant Finn had the gun away from the man and pushed his credentialing letter in his face. "Call John Rivers in security, he knows all about—" He broke off what he was saying and stared down the hall. Sam was lying on the floor, blood pouring out of a wound on his back.

"Son of a bitch!" Finn jumped up and raced to Sam.

67

The ambulance pulled away thirty minutes later. After reaching Sam, Finn had stanched the bleeding and then performed CPR on his colleague when Sam had ceased breathing and his heart had stopped, perhaps from shock. The EMTs had arrived and taken over from there. Sam would live, but his rehab would take a while because it looked like the bullet had done some nasty damage to a few of his organs.

Finn watched the red rack lights until they disappeared. Standing next to him was John Rivers, the head of security, who had apologized profusely for the guard's shooting Sam in the back when he was not being threatened.

"Thank God you were there, Harry," Rivers said. "Otherwise he'd be dead."

"Yeah, well, he wouldn't have gotten shot if I hadn't dragged him here."

"They give us no money or time to train our guards," Rivers complained. "They spend billions on the facility and security *technology*, but then they put a gun in the hands of a punk who's earning ten bucks an hour. It makes no sense."

Finn wasn't really listening. He had never had anything like this happen before. Sam was a good man but strictly a desk jockey. Finn had never liked taking inexperienced folks with him on these outings, and had voiced that opinion several times. Maybe now they would listen to him.

He drove home and later took Patrick to baseball practice, silently watching his athletic middle child field all balls hit his way and later mercilessly pound the automated pitches in the batting cage. Finn didn't say much on the way home, letting an animated Patrick talk about his day at school. Over dinner that night, Susie recited her lines from the upcoming play—although it didn't appear that trees were given much to say, a fact her two older brothers ribbed her about. She took the kidding well before finally telling them both, "Stuff it, dorks." That comment drew a warning from Mandy, who'd had her hands full lately with the three because Finn had been so buried at work.

David said, "Hey, Pop, you coming to the soccer match on Friday afternoon? Coach is gonna let me play goalie."

Finn said absently, "I'll try, son. I might be tied up." He had to go visit his mother. His wife would not be happy about that.

Mandy gave David some pocket money for when

his class went downtown on their field trip the next morning. She took a small bite of food and looked over at her husband, who was obviously not mentally with them.

"Harry, you okay?"

He stirred. "Just some stuff at work." There had been no news coverage of the incident, even though the police had been called, because Homeland Security had stepped in to put the kibosh on it. Having Finn exposed in the press would put a severe crimp in the red cell contract work that his company did for Homeland Security, work that was critically important to national security. With DHS in Finn's corner, the local cops had quickly rolled over. The young security guard had not been charged with anything other than being stupid and undertrained, and his gun had been taken away. He had been reassigned to a desk job and told that if he said anything to anyone about what had happened he would regret it for the rest of his life.

After dinner he drove to the hospital to see Sam. He was in the ICU after surgery, but his condition had stabilized. He was on heavy meds and didn't even know Finn was there. His parents had been flown in from New York that afternoon and were in the ICU waiting area. Finn sat with them for an hour, explaining the situation and downplaying Sam's complicity in getting shot by stupidly running away from a nervous kid with a big gun.

He left the hospital and drove around for a while with the all-news radio station on. He finally turned it off after bad news became awful news and then moved on directly to terrible. What a world they were leaving for the next generation.

He headed downtown, because he didn't want to go home to the Virginia suburbs just yet. He could tell from the expression on Mandy's face at dinner that she wanted to talk about things, but he really didn't want to. He didn't know how he was going to break the news of having to visit his mother again. With the kids' busy schedule, his being gone really left his wife scrambling. And yet he had to do it, particularly after the John Carr revelation.

He crossed over the Theodore Roosevelt Bridge, passing the island named after the very same president. He kept straight and headed down Constitution Avenue, arguably the capital's second most famous street behind the one named Pennsylvania. Hooking left, he headed up toward the White House before turning right onto F Street and working his way through a congested shopping and business district that was crawling with renewed nightlife. To his right stood the concrete-and-steel skeleton of an uncompleted building whose developer had gone bankrupt. As Finn waited at a red light he stared up at the new residential condo building on his left. His gaze went up seven stories, drifted to the corner unit of the luxury high-rise, and that's when he stiffened slightly. He had not come here by accident. The drive-by was completely intentional; he did it often.

The lights were on and as he watched a tall figure passed by one of the windows.

Senator Roger Simpson from the great state of Alabama was home.

68

Annabelle stood next to Paddy who was slumped in a chair in her hotel room. Daughter nodded at father and on cue he picked up the phone.

Before he punched in the number, she put a hand on Paddy's shoulder.

"You sure you're ready for this?" she asked.

"I've been ready for this for years," he gamely replied, his voice cracking a bit.

He didn't look ready, she thought. The man seemed tired and scared.

"Good luck," Annabelle said.

As soon as the number was placed, Annabelle picked up another phone and listened in.

"Hello, Jerry," Paddy said. "It's Paddy Conroy. Long time no kill. But then again, maybe that's not entirely accurate. Hear you've been busy on that score."

Annabelle stared at her father. Paddy's entire manner had changed. His smile was wide, and his voice was confident. He was sitting up big and fearless in the chair.

Bagger was not a man easily shocked. But when he heard that name, he felt his knees slightly buckle. The next emotion he had was far more familiar. He nearly crushed the phone in his hand and screamed, "How the hell did you know how to reach me, you bastard?"

"I just looked in the phone book under A for assholes."

On that remark, Annabelle had to stifle a laugh.

"Seen that bitch of a daughter of yours lately?"

"Heard she ripped you for plenty. Enough to get the wind up at the Jersey Control Commission. I must've taught her good."

"Yeah, maybe you're behind the whole thing. And if you are, all I can promise you is a skin peel that takes about two days."

"Stop talking dirty, Jerry, you're getting me horny."

"What do you want!"

"I want to help you out."

"I don't need help from a two-bit, washed-up con."

"Don't be so quick on the draw, Jer. The definition of help is when I have something you want. And I do."

"Like what?"

"Care to guess?"

"Care to have me rip your balls off?"

"I have Annabelle. You still want her or you gotten

over her making you look like the world's biggest idiot?"

"You'd turn over your own daughter to me, knowing what I'm going to do to her?"

"Not going deaf on me, are you? That's what I said."

"And you're doing this out of what, the goodness of your heart?"

"You know me better than that, Jerry."

"So how much do you want for your little girl?"

"Not a dime."

"Excuse me?" Bagger said in disbelief.

"I don't need any more money."

"So what then?"

"You have to promise me that if I give Annabelle to you, you'll never come after me again. I got a little time left on this planet and I don't want to spend it looking over my shoulder for the likes of you."

"Let me get this straight. You'll give me Annabelle so long as I leave you alone?"

"That's right. I know you've been on the lookout for me ever since I ripped you off for that lousy ten grand. And I'm getting tired of it."

Bagger screamed into the phone, "*You're* getting tired of it?"

"Is it a deal? And I want your word. Because I know you're a lot of things, but you've never gone back on your word. You get Annabelle and you leave me alone, forever."

Bagger stared down at the floor, the veins throbbing in his neck.

"I want to hear you say it, Jerry. I *have* to hear you say it."

"I'll pay you millions for her."

"Yeah, sure. Say it, Jerry. Say it or no deal."

Paddy stared over at Annabelle, who was holding her breath as she clutched the phone.

"Why do you hate her so much?" Bagger finally said.

"Because she's blamed me all these years for what happened to her mum. You killed the woman but I've paid the price. Ain't been one bloke in the whole con world who'd give me the time of day since. She ruined my life. It's payback time. *My* payback time." Paddy glanced over at Annabelle and smiled weakly.

"How are you going to set her up? She's not stupid. So I know she doesn't trust you."

"Leave that to me."

"I haven't agreed to nothing."

"But you will. You're too smart not to."

"I can just catch her myself. I came close the other night. And maybe you too if I get real lucky."

"Then go for it. And two weeks from now when you realize she's long gone, you can't say old Paddy didn't tell you the truth. Because the longer you wait, the more time she has to hide, and we both know the girl is good at what she does. Take your time, think about it. I'll call you back."

"When?"

"When I want to."

In one motion, Paddy and Annabelle put down their phones.

She gripped his shoulder. "You did great. You baited him just right."

He put his hand on top of hers. "We'll give him a little time to stew on that. That'll give your friend some time to get his end in gear. I have to say, I was surprised he agreed to help us, no questions asked."

"Like I told you, he's not your typical fed. One thing." She paused, worried. *Was her father really not up to this?* "You didn't poke around about where Jerry might be staying."

He looked at her, a smile playing across his lips. "I'm not losing my touch, Annie, if that's what you're thinking. You don't push too hard on the first go-round. Old pro like Jerry will sniff that out every time. Next call, I'll let him make the slip. Then I'll hit it."

"Sorry, I didn't mean you didn't know what you were doing."

"Ninety percent of the con is preparation. The other ten percent is seat of the pants, being able to adapt on the fly."

"But without the ten the ninety is worth shit."

"Exactly."

"That stuff you said to Bagger. About my ruining your life?"

"I ruined my own life, Annie. All I'm doing now is trying to get a little piece of it back."

He gripped his daughter's hand tightly. He now looked old, sick and scared; his body collapsed into the chair again. "You really think we can pull this off?"

"Yes," she lied.

69

Dressed in the outfit of a Capitol Grounds maintenance crewman, Harry Finn stood outside the Hart Senate Office Building with the remote detonator in his hand. He stared up the façade of the building until his gaze came to Simpson's office. In his other hand was a small device that looked like an iPod. Actually, it was the receiving unit for the wireless pin video camera he'd hidden in Simpson's office. The images on the small screen were razor-sharp. Simpson was meeting with several of his staff, no doubt reporting back on his vital "fact-finding" mission to the Caribbean.

Finn was waiting until Simpson was alone in his office, for only Simpson was going to die today. He tensed as the staff people rose and left. He then watched as Simpson checked his hair and face in the mirror on one wall, adjusted his tie, walked to his desk and sat down.

The end had finally come. Finn's finger was poised over his BlackBerry. He would send the e-mail first. He would be able to tell from Simpson's reaction on the screen that he had seen the photo of Rayfield Solomon, right before he died.

Finn's thumb descended on the BlackBerry key. *Good-bye, Roger.*

"Hey, Dad!"

Finn glanced up, recognizing the voice. "Damn it," he breathed.

David Finn came running up to him, smiling. "What are you doing here?"

Finn quickly slipped the devices into the duffel slung over his shoulder.

"Hey, Dave, what are *you* doing here?"

His son rolled his eyes. "You going senile on me, Pop? The school visit to the Capitol? You signed the permission slip? Mom gave me the money last night at dinner?"

Finn's face paled. *Oh shit.* "Sorry, just a lot going on, son."

David noticed his dad's clothes. "What's with the uniform?"

"I'm working," he said quietly.

David's face brightened. "Cool, you mean you're undercover?"

"I really can't talk about it, son. In fact, you better get going. It's not really great that you're here actually." Finn's heart was beating so hard it was a miracle his son didn't seem to hear it.

David looked disappointed. "Hey, sure. I get it. Secret stuff."

"Sorry, Dave. Sometimes I wish I had a normal job."

"Yeah, me too." He jogged back to his friends.

When Finn looked back at the screen, Simpson had left his office.

He stared over at David and his friends. His son glanced over at his father once and then looked away. The group of students marched down the sidewalk toward the Capitol.

Finn walked off in the opposite direction. He would have to try another day. Now he had to see his mother. He'd been hoping to report to her the news of Simpson's death. So intent was he on what he was doing that he never saw the man emerge from behind a nearby tree and start following him.

After what Max Himmerling had told him the night before, Oliver Stone had come here to check out the office of Roger Simpson too, at least from a distance. Either Gray or Simpson had ordered Solomon's death and the hit on Stone. Since he couldn't get to Gray, Simpson was the next best thing. Now, however, there had come a detour. Stone had heard and seen enough of Finn to make him more than a little curious. Finn was good, to Stone's experienced eye. Others around the area, even the police officers, would have noticed nothing suspicious about the man. But Stone was not like other people. He had run down many leads that led to nothing. His instinct told him this would not be one of them.

When Finn hopped on the subway at Capitol

South, Stone did the same. The men rode it to National Airport. Stone followed Finn in. The latter went into a bathroom and came out dressed in street clothes, the duffel still over his shoulder. Now Stone believed that his hunch had just struck gold.

Finn bought a round-trip ticket for a short flight to upstate New York. Standing within earshot, Stone later did the same, using the fake ID and money Annabelle had given him. He went through security, his heartbeat ratcheting up a bit as TSA agents scrutinized his picture on the ID. They let him through and he allowed Finn to pass from his line of sight. He knew which gate the man was going to, after all.

Stone bought some coffee and a magazine. The flight was called. Finn was in the front of the full plane, Stone the rear. Forty minutes later they were wheels up. Less than an hour later, they touched down. Now it got dicey. The airport was small and the patrons few. Finn seemed preoccupied, but Stone couldn't be certain. If he was the man running around murdering highly skilled killers in their own right, Stone could not underestimate him.

Stone was debating what to do when Finn surprised him. He bypassed the small rental car counter, ignored the taxi stand out front and walked down the road away from the airport.

Keeping an eye on him, Stone stepped over to a taxi and leaned in the window. "Got a layover. Anything within walking distance of here?"

"Some residences, some shops, a nursing home," the driver said as he idly read his newspaper.

"Nursing home?"

"Yeah, you want to go there for a little R and R during your layover?" He chuckled.

Stone slid in the backseat. "Just drive for now, *slow*."

The driver shrugged, put down his paper and the taxi pulled off.

70

Herb Daschle was a veteran employee of the CIA. He'd done years of fieldwork, seen the world, ridden a desk for the last decade and then accepted his current position. It was not all that exciting, and the public was totally unaware of it, but it was vital to the security of the CIA and thus the nation. Or so said the Agency's internal manual.

For two months Daschle had been coming to this nursing home three times a week and sitting in a chair in the private room of a man who was lying unconscious in the bed. The man was very high up in the CIA and his head was filled with secrets that could never be revealed to the public. Unfortunately, he'd had an aneurysm and was not quite himself. He could say things without knowing, disclosing vital national secrets unintentionally.

That could not be allowed, so men like Daschle came out and stayed with incapacitated Agency employees possessing such sensitive knowledge. There had been a man in the operating room when the surgery was done to relieve the pressure on the brain. There had been an agent stationed in the post-op, and there was 24/7 surveillance here at the nursing home, where it was hoped the man would eventually recover. Even the man's own family was never allowed to be left alone with him. This had come as quite a shock, because the family was not aware that this husband, father and grandfather even worked for the CIA.

Twelve o'clock came and Daschle rose from his seat as a fellow agent, his replacement for the next shift, sat down. The two men exchanged pleasantries and Daschle mentioned a few items from his watch, nothing of importance. He left the room, dying for a cigarette, and wandered down the hall toward the snack room to buy a can of soda and some crackers before he left. The voices coming out of one room that he passed stopped him. It seemed to be Russian. Daschle knew that language well, having been stationed in Moscow for nearly nine years. Although if what he was hearing was Russian, it was a particularly mangled version. It actually sounded like an amalgam of several Slavic languages. He'd also been stationed in Poland and Bulgaria for a time. He edged closer to the door of the room, which was open just a crack, and listened a bit more. Then he heard enough to make him hustle out of the building. And it wasn't for a cigarette.

As soon as he was gone, Oliver Stone stepped from

around the corner where he too had been listening. He watched the fleeing man.

Damn.

Inside the room Lesya was speaking while Finn sat quietly in his chair.

"So now John Carr rises from the dead like the Phoenix," she said in her tortured Cyrillic mishmash.

"It seems so," Finn said. "But I can't be sure."

"And the senator still lives."

"Not for long."

"What about Carr?"

"I'm working on it. I told you that. But I have no idea where he is or even if he's really alive. They just dug up his grave. That's all anyone knows."

She coughed hard. "Time grows short."

For you or me? Finn wondered. He was still thinking about the encounter with his son. *So close. Too close.*

"But you will find out. I will help you find out."

"Let me handle it."

"I can tell you what I know about the man."

"I know a lot about him already." He paused. "I don't think he's like the others."

She looked at him sharply. "What do you mean by that?"

"I think the Agency tried to kill him. I think they killed his wife. And perhaps his daughter. I believe he's suffered a lot. And he was a war hero too."

"He is *just* like the others. An evil man. A murderer!"

"Why, because he followed orders and killed my father and your husband?"

"You have no idea what you're saying, Harry. No idea."

"You know, I was just about to kill Simpson this morning, when David showed up. He almost caught me."

"David your son?" Finn nodded and his mother clamped a hand to her mouth. "Good, God. Did he suspect?"

"No, but I promised myself that I would never let this part of my life impact on that part of my life. And now it has!"

Lesya sat down next to him, grasped his hand with her bony one. It felt slightly repulsive to him now.

"Harry, my son, my loving son, it will soon be over."

"You can't possibly know that. And it might end with me dead."

She slowly withdrew her hand from his. "So what now?"

"Simpson and then Carr."

"You will do this. You swear?"

Finn nodded.

His mother scrutinized him a bit longer and then shuffled over, opened her drawer and removed a photo. She handed it to him. "For Carr," she said bitterly as she spat on the floor. Then she lay back on her bed. "Let me tell you a story, Harry."

He sat back, but for the first time ever he wasn't listening.

When the door to the room opened, they both turned to look.

"What do you want?" Lesya said angrily in English. "I have a visitor."

When the man started speaking in Russian, the breath caught in her throat.

"Who are you?" Finn asked in English.

"They used to call me John Carr," said Oliver Stone. He looked at Finn. "You're right. I'm not like the others. And you both need to get out of here, just as fast as you can."

71

When Paddy called back, Bagger answered after the second ring.

"Yeah?" Bagger said.

"Have you had time to decide that I'm right?" Paddy began politely.

"Do you know how many times I've killed you in my mind since we talked?"

"It's nice to be popular. But I need to hear your answer."

"How do you want to do this?" Bagger said bluntly.

"We don't do nothing until I hear from you what I need to hear."

"Come over to my hotel and I'll tell you in person. I know she's in D.C., so you must be too."

Paddy smiled and said, "What, after you've put a bullet in my brain? Don't think so. Besides, I don't go into the shitty parts of town, Jerry. You casino dicks always trend to the scum side."

"Yeah? I make more money in one second than you've made in your whole life."

"Money ain't everything, Jerry. It can't buy class. I

don't care if you're staying at the bloody White House, though I doubt they'd let the likes of you in the door."

"Well money is everything if you want a *view* of the White House like I got. That costs a grand a night."

Paddy smiled and pointed at Annabelle, who gave him a thumbs-up sign.

"You going to give me your word or do I hang up? 'Cause once this line goes dead, I won't be calling back."

Bagger swore under his breath and then said very slowly, "If you get me Annabelle, I give you my word that I will never come after you again."

"And that you and your people will never cause me any harm. And you give me your word."

"Okay."

"I need you to say it, Jerry."

"Why?"

"Because I know once those words come off your tongue I'm really safe."

"And that me and my people will never cause you any harm. I give you my word." This last part was so painful for Bagger that he slammed his fist down on the table next to him.

"Thank you."

"You still haven't explained how I get her."

"She's going to walk right into your arms, Jerry. I'll see to it."

Paddy hung up and stared at Annabelle, a smile creeping across his face.

"Grand a night with nice views of the White House. Can't be many of those."

"Can't be," Annabelle agreed.

72

"Can you get me a list of the hotels in D.C. that have views of the White House and cost a grand a night?" Annabelle asked Alex as they sat in the same coffee shop as their previous meeting.

"Why?"

"It's all part of those details I talked to you about."

"I'll get the list. You need any help?"

Annabelle started to say no and then stopped. "How good are you on your feet?"

"Excuse me?"

"Are you quick on your feet?"

"I'm a Secret Service agent. That's what we do."

"Then you can help me."

Later that day Annabelle walked into the second hotel from the list provided by Alex. She approached the front desk and discreetly flashed her phony FBI credentials to the clerk there.

"What is this about?" he said nervously.

"Potentially a big problem for your hotel, but we

might be able to work around that if you cooperate. I've got a strike team standing by outside."

The astonished clerk immediately looked over Annabelle's shoulder.

"You can't see them," she said. "That would sort of give it away, wouldn't it?"

"I think I should get my supervisor," the clerk said nervously.

"No, I think you should stand right here and answer my questions, William," she said quietly, eyeing his nametag.

"What sort of questions?"

"Do you have a guest staying here named Jerry Bagger?"

"I can't possibly give out that sort of information. It's confidential."

"All right, I guess we'll have to do this the hard way." Annabelle took a small walkie-talkie from her pocket that she'd purchased from a sporting goods store. "Bravo One to X-Ray strike team. Are you in position to crash all entry points? Affirmative. Squad leader, rules of engagement, no gunfire unless absolutely necessary. Repeat, unless absolutely necessary. There's potential collateral damage throughout the lobby."

"What is this, some sort of joke?" the clerk snapped.

On a cue from Annabelle, Alex, who'd been standing behind a pillar in the lobby, walked over. The tall agent looked down at the clerk.

He held out his Secret Service creds and showed the badge and gun on his belt. "Is there a problem?"

The clerk pointed at Annabelle. "She said she's with the FBI and she's looking for some guy and they're going to send a strike something-or-other."

Alex leaned down close in to the shorter man. "It's not a strike something-or-other. It's called a strike *team*. And I'm heading it up. We're part of a joint antiterrorist unit. I've got twenty-five agents in heavy Kevlar body armor with MP-5 submachine guns ready to bust into this place because this 'some guy' is number two on our most wanted list right behind Osama. I've been after this 'some guy' for two years of my life, and I'm not about to let a little prick like you screw it up. So you either get on your computer and tell us if he's here, or your ass will be the first one I arrest for obstruction."

"Holy shit!" the clerk exclaimed. "You can do that?"

"With a smile on my face."

Alex turned to Annabelle and he nodded. "Proceed, Agent Hunter."

Annabelle took a sheaf of papers from her pocket. "We have a search and arrest warrant for Mr. Bagger and his associates." She eyed the clerk sternly. "We don't like putting innocent people in harm's way, William, but this Bagger is a killer, into drugs, arms dealing, every bad thing you can think of. But if you cooperate we can put a tail on him and take the bastard *outside* the hotel. I think your supervisor would probably approve of that."

William stared at her for a few moments and then started clicking on his computer. "We don't have a Bagger listed," he said in a shaky voice.

"I would be astonished if he used his real name." Annabelle described Bagger to him in detail. "He'd always come and go with a bunch of muscle."

Alex added, "I would think a guy like that would tend to stick out here, am I right?"

William nodded. "He *is* staying here, under the name Frank Walters. He has the best suite in the hotel. Wonderful views of the White House."

"I'm sure. Okay, thanks for the assist, William. But don't say a word to anyone. You understand me?"

"Absolutely, best of luck, Officer," he said weakly.

Alex nodded, gave him a hard slap on the arm and left with Annabelle.

Outside Alex called in a team to cover the hotel. Now where Bagger went, so would they.

As they were leaving in Alex's car Annabelle said, "You *are* quick on your feet. That was great in there."

"Coming from you that's a real compliment. So now what?"

"So now we pull the trigger."

73

Finn, Lesya and Stone just stared at each other for a long time. Then Lesya uttered a curse and slowly rose from her chair. She gripped a small wooden box on her nightstand and looked ready to hurl it at Stone's head. "John Carr," she spat out. "You? Here? You murderer."

Stone turned to Finn. "A man was eavesdropping on you both. From his expression he understood some or all of what he heard. He ran out of here. I saw the room he originally came out of. I 'accidentally' looked in that room. There was another man in there keeping watch over a patient."

Finn hadn't moved a muscle. "Who is the man?"

"At the CIA we used to call them crypt keepers. An agent with a serious brain injury who might reveal secrets is watched over by other agents until the person either dies or recovers. I believe that's what's going on here."

"The CIA here?" Lesya hissed, an incredulous expression on her face.

"And the other man was also a crypt keeper presumably going off duty. He overheard us and he understood what we were saying?" Finn said slowly.

"The language you were speaking provides a good cover. Almost no one would understand any of it."

"But you did?" Finn said.

Stone nodded. "Language skills came with the territory. And that's why we have to leave. Now."

Finn glanced at his mother, who was still staring at Stone with loathing. "And why should we trust you? You could be leading us right into a trap."

"That's right," Lesya said. "A trap. Just like they did to your father."

"If that were my intent I would simply have waited until *you* left here," Stone said, indicating Finn. "And shot you on your way back to the airport. There's a stretch of woods in between that's particularly convenient. As for your mother here, this place is not well guarded. An unlocked door, a pillow, a brief struggle." He shrugged. "And if I worked with the CIA I wouldn't have come here and warned you. I would've just let them take you."

"How did you know to even come here?" Finn said.

"I followed you from Washington. I saw you outside Senator Simpson's office building this morning. You seemed a bit suspicious-looking."

"I didn't think I was that obvious."

"You weren't. I've just been trained how to look."

"And why were you at Simpson's office?"

"Because a man told me, against his will, that the matter of Rayfield Solomon had become a priority for the CIA again."

"And why is that?" Finn said warily.

Stone sized him up. And came away with a clear impression. *He reminds me of me, all those years ago.* "If you kill for revenge, you want the victim to know why. So you either send them something ahead of time or give it to them right before you pull the trigger. I think that was done with Cincetti, Bingham and Cole. And it was also done with Carter Gray. And he knew that it was tied to Rayfield Solomon. But of course Gray didn't die."

"What!" Lesya screamed and then looked accusingly at her son.

Finn didn't even blink. "Carter Gray is alive?" he said.

Stone nodded. "And no doubt the man who ran out of here is—"

"Going to get the message to Gray," Finn finished for him. He grabbed his mother's bag from under the bed and stuffed her few belongings in it.

"What are you doing?" his mother said.

Finn grabbed her arm. "Let's go."

"Where?"

"Out of here," Stone said.

Finn glanced at him. "Plane?"

Stone shook his head. "No doubt covered by now. They don't know about me, at least not yet. I'll rent a car from the airport. That stretch of woods I mentioned? I'll pick you up there in twenty minutes."

"You can't trust him, Harry! He is a killer. He killed your father." Lesya said this in pure Russian.

Stone answered her in Russian. "Everything you say is true. I led the team that killed your husband. Now I know that he was innocent. I lost *my* wife and daughter violently because of what I used to do for my country. I have spent the last thirty years of my life trying to make amends. I doubt I have enough years left to settle my debt. I know you have no reason to trust me. But I swear to you that I will sacrifice my life to save both of you."

"Why? Why would you do this?" Lesya said, though her voice was calmer and now she spoke in English.

"Because I simply followed orders without question. Because I took the life of another human being and I had no right to do it. And because you've suffered enough."

Five minutes later, they left the nursing home by a back entrance. Even with her walker, Lesya managed to keep up a brisk pace. She was not as immobile as she had led people to believe.

Stone left them hidden in the woods, hustled to the airport and rented a car using the credit card Annabelle had given him. He could already see subtle activity all around him that did not bode well for their escape. He drove off with the car, picked the pair up, and with Finn reading a map and guiding, they made their way through a series of back roads to the interstate.

"Where to now?" Finn asked.

"Washington," Stone answered.

74

Jerry had nearly paced a trench through the rug in his hotel room.

When the phone rang he jumped for it and then immediately calmed. He was Jerry Bagger and the Conroys were shit. Yet he would have to settle for the daughter, because Paddy was off-limits now. The thought made Bagger want to tear his own heart out. He would just take it out on Annabelle, giving her enough pain for two.

"Hello, Jerry," Paddy said. "You ready to dance with the princess?"

Bagger said, "You got her? Prove it."

"You'll see for yourself soon enough."

"Put her on the phone."

"Well, she's a wee bit tied up right now. And duct-taped."

"Then un-duct-tape her," Bagger said firmly. "I wanta hear her voice."

A minute later she said into the phone, in a beaten voice, "I guess you win, Jerry. First Tony, now me."

Jerry smiled and sat down. "Annabelle, don't even

mention yourself in the same sentence with that screw-up. But I wanted to let you know that I'm really looking forward to seeing you."

"Go to hell, you prick!"

"Still kicking to the end. It's a shame, it really is. We could've been a great team."

"No we couldn't, Jerry. You killed my mother."

"And you ripped me off for forty million, bitch!" he shouted. "You cost me respect. You cost me everything I've worked my whole life for."

"And it still wasn't enough for me. All I want is your fat, ugly head on a stick."

With an immense effort Jerry calmed. "I tell you what. I'll let that remark slide. People close to death, they say stuff. And I'll tell you something else. I was going to make you feel pain like you never felt before. But instead I'll do you fast, not slow. *After* you tell me where my money is. You know why I'm doing that? Out of respect. For your talent. Your *wasted* talent. If you'd learned that little concept of respect you might've lived longer."

"Tell me something. How much did you pay my old man to set me up?"

"That's the best of all. Didn't cost me a dime. You're one cheap date."

"Good-bye, Jerry."

"No, not good-bye, baby. This is just hello."

Paddy came back on the phone. "Okay, Jerry,

you've exchanged your pleasantries. Now it's time for business."

"Where and when? And don't say in front of the White House or the Washington Monument or some Hollywood bullshit like that or the deal's off. For me agreeing to leave your ass alone I want privacy."

Paddy said, "They're building a new ballpark in town near the Anacostia River."

"So I heard. What's that got to do with anything?"

"They're tearing down a bunch of buildings and neighborhoods around there. Lot of abandoned places. At eleven o'clock tonight I'll call with the address of an old parking garage. There'll be a white van parked on level two. Inside that van will be Annabelle tucked neatly in a roll of carpet. The keys will be in the van."

Bagger hung up and looked at his men.

Mike Manson said, "This could be a setup of some kind, boss."

"Gee, Mike, you think so? Not that I believe for one minute that Paddy Conroy is working for anybody other than Paddy Conroy, but I'm not stupid. He may have a big beef with his daughter about Mom getting killed. And that may be why he's willing to hand her over to me so I'll leave him alone. But nothing's for sure with that son of a bitch."

"So how do we do it?"

"We wait for the address. Then you guys are going to do the pickup at midnight. Bring her to a place where I'll be waiting. A place that's a lot more private than an abandoned parking garage."

"And we just drive off with her? What if they tail us?"

Bagger smiled and picked up his newspaper. "Says in here there's a World Bank conference today downtown and then fancy dinners and speeches all over the city. Big muckety-mucks flying in from all over the globe."

"So?" Mike said.

"So I say that's some great timing if you got the right exit strategy."

75

Carter Gray had risen from his bunker once more and wondered if his beloved Agency had grown so weak and incompetent that he was going to have to pull the damn trigger himself on Lesya and her son. After a fruitless nationwide search they'd had a wonderful, absolutely golden opportunity at the nursing home in upstate New York of all places, and it had come to naught. The room was empty, mother and son gone. And a third person had been seen with them. Something told Carter Gray that John Carr had gotten in his way once again after losing Gray's men and getting to Himmerling. And Gray now had to change his original plan to bag all three.

The description of the old woman left no doubt in Gray's mind that it was Lesya Solomon. Age had not been kind to her; she was no longer the beautiful, enticing Soviet spy. But it was Lesya, Gray just knew it.

Yet what would John Carr have been doing with the very people who wanted to kill him? Had he lied about his identity? Had he taken them by force? Had they teamed up? *That might actually make my job easier.*

Gray looked out the window of the chopper as it soared over the Virginia countryside on its way to Langley. With the overpowering force of the president's authorization burning a hole in his pocket, he would take command of the search. No questions would be asked. Still, the mission required delicacy, stealth and, when the target was sighted and then fixed, an unstoppable show of force. He would one-up the military on what shock and awe really meant.

He studied the topography below. Carr, Lesya and her child were down there somewhere. Only three people marshaled against him, one of them a woman in her seventies. Gray had unlimited people, assets and money. It would only be a matter of time. David P. Jedidiah's son was now being sought with the combined might of America's intelligence empire. And there was another way to speed up the process. As soon as the chopper landed at CIA, Gray started implementing his attack.

With Finn driving they crossed into Maryland that evening. Lesya sat in the backseat looking tired and frightened. Stone heard her keep muttering in Russian, "They will kill us all."

He glanced over at Finn, who was staring ahead,

but Stone noted that his eyes kept checking the rearview mirror.

"You have a family?" Stone asked.

Finn hesitated and then said, "Let's stay focused on the task at hand."

Lesya leaned over the front seat. "And what is that? What are we focusing on now? You tell me."

"Staying alive," Stone answered. "And with Carter Gray after us, that's not going to be easy."

"They dug up your grave," Finn said as they traveled around the Capital Beltway.

"Gray's doing, to flush me out."

"He knew you were alive?"

"Yes. We reached an understanding of late. He left me alone and I left him alone."

Lesya pointed an accusatory finger at Stone. "You see, you see? They are allies, son. They are working together. We are in the hands of the enemy."

Stone turned around in his seat to stare at the woman. "Lesya, you were one of the greatest spies the Soviet Union ever had. It was said that you turned more foreign agents than anyone ever had."

"I am Russian. I worked for my country. As you did yours, John Carr. And you're right, I was the best."

He was silent as he saw the pride creep into her hollow features. He allowed her to feel it for only a few seconds before he snapped. "Then start *acting* like it. Stop with the hysterical and stupid comments, because we're going to need all the help you can give us if we're going to survive this. Or are you just going to sit there and let your son die?" he finished bluntly.

She stared coldly at him, the sudden anger narrowing her eyes. And then her expression cleared. She looked at Finn and then back at Stone. "You are right," she said matter-of-factly. "I am being stupid." She sat back. "We need to formulate a plan, keeping in mind that Carter Gray has enormous resources at his disposal. Only sometimes, enormous resources cannot move with agility, while we can. They may find that we have a trick or two they didn't anticipate."

Finn stared at his mother in the mirror. He had never heard this tone of voice, seen this calm confidence before. Her Russian accent was completely gone. It was as though she had taken thirty years off her life. She was even sitting up straighter!

Lesya continued, "They may not know of my son's involvement, at least not yet, but they will before very long."

"How?" Finn asked.

"They will check the flights into the airport today. Match descriptions. It is a small place, it won't take long."

"I didn't use my real name. I had a fake ID."

"Video surveillance at the airport," Stone said. "They'll match your face to some database. I assume it's in at least one." Finn nodded. "Then your family may be compromised."

"Call them, now!" Lesya urged.

Stone could see the enormous pressure the younger man was under as he gripped the phone.

In a shaky voice Finn spoke into the phone. "Please, honey, no questions now. Just get the kids and take them to a motel. There's a cell phone in my desk drawer. Use that to call me. No one can trace it. Get cash out of the ATM. Don't use your credit card or your real name at the motel. Stay there. No school, no baseball games, soccer or swimming, nothing. And don't tell anyone. Please. I'll explain later."

Stone and Lesya could hear the woman's frantic responses.

A bead of sweat slid down Finn's forehead. His voice dropped still lower and finally his wife calmed. "I love you, sweetie. I will make this all right. I swear it."

He clicked off and slumped back. Lesya slid a hand on his shoulder and squeezed.

"I'm sorry, Harry. I'm sorry for doing this to you. I . . . I . . ." Her voice trailed off. She removed her hand and eyed Stone.

"You say Gray knows you're alive, Carr? He flushed you out of the grave, as it were. Do you have anyone he can use to get to *you?* To flush you out again? Because as I said, undoubtedly someone at the nursing home saw us leave and will already have given a description. He will know you are with us. He will know the easiest way to get to us is to get to you. So tell me, is there?"

"I do have people he can exploit, but I already warned them, *before* I went to the hospital."

She shook her head. "A warning is meaningless unless it's acted on with skill. They are capable people who can take care of themselves, follow orders, these friends?" she asked as she scrutinized him. "Don't color the truth. We need to know exactly how it stands."

"One of them is and he's with another friend of mine. But there's a third friend . . ." *Caleb, please don't do anything stupid.*

"So that is the flank Gray will exploit. Tell me, how close do you value this friend?"

"Very!"

"Then I am sorry for you and your friend."

Stone leaned back against the seat and felt the smacks of his heart. He hated what the woman was saying and yet he knew she was absolutely right.

She added, "And if it comes down to it, will you trade us for your friend?" Stone turned around to find her looking at him. He had never seen a more piercing stare than the one Lesya was giving him now. No, he was wrong about that. He had seen a gaze like that once before: on Rayfield Solomon, right before Stone killed him.

"No," he said. "I won't."

"Then let's work to ensure it doesn't come down to that, John Carr. And maybe you *can* redeem yourself for killing my husband."

She glanced out the window and said, "And I *was* the best agent the Soviet Union ever had. But Rayfield was even better."

"Why?" Stone asked.

"Because I fell in love with him. And he turned *me*."

"What?" Stone blurted out.

"Didn't you know? I was working for the Americans when you murdered him."

76

Jerry Bagger had been working the phones ever since he'd talked to Paddy Conroy. The casino chief had been thinking a lot in the last few hours and he'd arrived at a decision. Normally, in any confrontation, Bagger's instinct was to trade blow for blow until he or the other guy fell down. He wasn't going to do that this time, for a lot of reasons. Chief among them was the fact that he'd seen Annabelle in action. He knew how good, how convincing she could be. And there was a little tickle in the back of his brain that reminded him that a jab-jab-jab was a great setup for a left hook, a haymaker that had put many an opponent down permanently. He didn't intend to be on the receiving end of one of those.

Yet he couldn't bring himself to *not* go through with the whole thing, because the opportunity of getting his hands on Annabelle—in the event Paddy was playing straight with him—was too good to let pass. If he had a shot at getting the lady, he had to go for it. But you always had to have a backup plan, because the first plan almost never went perfectly.

And sometimes it went so badly you weren't sure if you were going to wake up the next day. Annabelle had taught him a valuable lesson by ripping him off. Unpredictability was a powerful thing.

He first called his money guy, instructing him to park a ton of cash in a safe place offshore with instant access for Bagger, and untraceable by anyone else. With money you could do anything. He had his jet fly back to Atlantic City to pick up some things for him, including his passport, and land back at a private airstrip in Maryland.

Next, he phoned another associate of his, a very trusted colleague who had one unique talent. He could make anything go boom. Bagger told him what he wanted and the man said he could have it ready in two hours, delivered. Bagger offered to pay his asking price and added a five grand bonus on top of it.

"You must need it bad," the colleague said.

It was true, Bagger really did need the boom bad. Ironically, such devices almost always killed people, lots of people. Yet in this case, it might just let one person live.

Me.

"Okay," Annabelle said to Alex and her father. "We need to get me to that van."

Paddy stood and shook his head. "Afraid not, Annie."

"What?" she said quickly with a sharp glance at Alex. He seemed as puzzled as she was.

"You're not going to be in that van. *I* am," Paddy said.

"That's not part of the plan. Jerry wants me, not you."

"I'll tell him you got the better of me. He'll buy that. He damn well knows how smart you are."

"Paddy, I'm not letting Jerry near you."

"You've got your whole life ahead of you, Annie. If something goes wrong and I'm the one who buys it, so what?"

"Why didn't you tell me this part before?"

"Because I knew you wouldn't go along with it, that's why. Now we've gone too far to turn back."

"Alex, talk to him."

"Well, what he's saying makes sense, Annabelle."

"You'll put me in the van," Paddy continued. "I'll buy some time with Jerry telling him how you outsmarted me, but I can still get to you if he lets me have another chance."

"Paddy, he'll kill you as soon as he sees you."

"I've known Jerry a lot longer than you have. I know how to play the fella, you just have to trust me on that one."

"I'm not going to let you do—"

"I have to do this. For a lot of reasons."

She looked from her father to Alex and back to Paddy. "What if something goes wrong?"

"Then it goes wrong," replied Paddy. "Now let's get this show on the road. I'm not getting any younger." He pointed a finger at Alex. "But one thing. No cavalry until the bastard admits to killing Tammy."

The call came at eleven o'clock with the address. At midnight Bagger's men went into the parking garage and found the white van on the second level. In the back, neatly hidden in a roll of carpet, was a person.

"Shit!" Mike Manson said as he shone his light on the person's head. "It's some geezer."

They unrolled the carpet and there was Paddy Conroy. He was apparently so weak from being bound up that they had to help him stand.

Manson shoved a gun in his sweating face. "What the hell is going on? Who the hell are you?"

"What's going on is that my damn daughter screwed me."

A smile eased across Manson's face. "You're Paddy Conroy?"

"No, I'm the king of Ireland, you dumb-shit."

Manson shoved him across the van and Paddy hit the sidewall and slumped down. Manson got on the phone and relayed the news to Bagger.

The casino boss was delighted at getting ahold of his old nemesis, but he also didn't like this abrupt change in the plan. No, he didn't like it at all, because that meant Annabelle was out there somewhere.

"Bring him," he instructed Mike.

Manson clicked off. "Now we go for a little ride. But first."

The two men expertly searched Paddy for any surveillance devices.

A minute later the white van roared out of the garage, hit a hard left, sailed down an alleyway, turned right and slid to a stop behind three black SUVs parked there in a column.

Paddy was hustled by Mike Manson into the middle one. All three trucks fired up and sped out of the alley. One turned left, one right and the third went straight.

The vehicles reached main roads and Bagger's plan quickly became evident. Everywhere there were motorcades of black SUVs carrying World Bank conference attendees to or from important events. Bagger's three SUVs were readily absorbed into this crush of dignitaries and bureaucrats.

At ten-thirty that evening Bagger left his hotel with his men. They drove to a disused warehouse that Bagger's men had located in a run-down industrial area in Virginia. There they waited until the black SUV with Paddy Conroy and Mike Manson pulled into the warehouse.

As soon as Bagger saw Paddy he walked over to him and belted him right in the mouth. Paddy fell back against the vehicle and then tried to get to Bagger, but Bagger's men held him back.

"That was for the ten grand you stole from me. Been waiting a long time to pay you back on that one."

Paddy spat blood out of his mouth. "Best ten grand I ever took."

"Yeah, we'll see how you feel about that in a few minutes. You got no idea how good I feel. You see, no Annabelle means my agreement not to go after your ass is *null and void*, as the prick lawyers say."

He studied Paddy's gray, gaunt features and his threadbare clothes.

"Looks like life's been treating you real well. You sick, poor or both?"

"What's it to you?"

"I'm insulted. I mean even you at the top of your game might not be good enough. You think it was smart coming after me wearing rags and looking like you're knocking on the grave?"

Paddy looked around at the armed men surrounding him. "Right this minute, not particularly smart, no."

Bagger sat down on a packing crate, his gaze never leaving Paddy's face. "So Annabelle outsmarted you? How'd she manage that, Paddy?"

"Like I said before, I guess I taught her too good."

"You sure about that?"

"What's that supposed to mean?"

"Maybe father and daughter got together to screw me. How about that theory?"

"My daughter hates my guts."

"So you say."

"So I *know*. But if you believed otherwise, why do the deal at all?"

"You know why. But now here you are and no Annabelle. So where is she?"

"No clue, Jerry."

Bagger stood slowly. "I think you can do better than that. So you and me are gonna have a little chat."

"I'm not in the chatting mood."

Bagger took a serrated knife out of his jacket pocket and slipped on a plastic glove. "Oh, I can be pretty damn persuasive." He looked at his men and nodded. A minute later, Paddy's pants and underwear were off and Bagger was sizing up the man's privates for cutting.

"I used this technique on a little asshole named Tony Wallace in Portugal after I *chatted* with the people he'd hired to run his mansion with my *money*. And let me tell you something, he talked and talked right before we beat his brains out. In fact, that was the way I was able to track down Annabelle. And now you're gonna do the same thing for me, old man. You know where Annabelle is and now you're gonna tell me. And when you do I kill you fast, no pain. If you don't talk? Well, you just don't wanta go there, trust me. "

Paddy struggled against his captors, but they were too strong. As the knife came closer and closer to a spot no man would want a sharp instrument to be, Paddy cried out, "For Chrissakes, don't! Just put a bullet in my brain."

"Tell me where Annabelle is, and I promise I'll kill you fast. That's the only deal you're getting now. And if you really hate your daughter, you should have no problem telling me where she is, right?"

"If I did know do you think I'd be here, you idiot?"

Bagger slapped him across the face. "You show some respect."

"Here's my respect." Paddy spat in his face. "That's for Tammy."

"Right, your old lady you left behind for me."

"I was in jail on the night you murdered her, you bastard. Otherwise you'd have had to go through me to get to her. She was the only thing I ever loved in my whole life. And I swear to God above, before this was all over, I was planning on putting a bullet right into *your* brain just like you did her."

"Was that before or after I killed your daughter?"

"Any price I had to pay to get you, I was willing to do it," Paddy screamed at him.

"But Annabelle screwed that all up, didn't she? Didn't she, old man?"

"Can't blame her for turning the tables on me."

"Since you were planning to whack me for killing your wife, why don't I fill you in on her last minutes of life? Would you like that?"

"I'll find some way to kill you, Jerry. I swear it."

"I'll take that as a yes. We crashed her house, and she recognized me right away. And you know what she said? She said, 'Why are you doing this, Jerry? Why are you going to kill me? I didn't do nothing to you.' And you know what I told her? I said, because your chickenshit husband ripped me off and left you holding the bag. That's how much he loved you, you dumb broad. And then I pumped a round right into her brain. Now, anything else you want to know about it before I start carving you up?"

"No, that's about it," a woman's voice said.

They all turned as Annabelle and Alex walked out from behind a stack of crates. Alex had his gun pointed right at Bagger, while eight guns held by Bagger's men pointed back at him and Annabelle.

Bagger said, "How the hell did you get here?"

"I came with the FBI," Annabelle said.

"Nobody could've followed my boys."

"We didn't tail them. We followed *you*. The place is surrounded, Jerry. You've got no way out."

"Yeah? Working for the FBI now? Look, baby, you con me once, shame on you, con me twice, shit on me." The man's voice was confident, but his look was something less than that.

"She's telling the truth, jerk-off," Alex yelled. "So just lay your weapons down before you don't have a choice in the matter."

"Kill 'em," Bagger said.

A split second later doors on all sides of the warehouse burst open and two dozen men in body armor came barreling in, sub-machine guns in hand.

"FBI, put down your weapons. Now!"

Bagger dropped the knife and his men quickly put down their guns in the face of the overpowering show of federal force.

Bagger's gaze went from Annabelle to Paddy. "Two con artists working with the feds?"

"You do what you got to do, Jerry," Paddy said as he hastily pulled his clothes back on.

Bagger looked at one of the FBI agents and immediately regained his swagger. "That bitch ripped me off for forty million. She bother mentioning that to you while she was playing snitch?"

"That's not my concern."

"Oh yeah, so what exactly am I being charged with?"

"Aside from kidnapping and assault, you're being charged with the murders of Tammy Conroy, three people in Portugal and Tony Wallace, who died yesterday."

Bagger snorted. "I got a dozen eyewitnesses who'll testify I wasn't around when any of those people got killed."

Annabelle held up a video recording device. "We've got your whole confession right here, Jerry. I have to hand it to you, you speak very clearly." She gave the device to the lead agent.

Bagger looked at the FBI men, Paddy, Alex, and then his gaze came to rest on Annabelle.

"Well, I guess this is it, then," he said. His hand slipped to his pocket.

"Hold it," an FBI agent said. "Take that hand out very slowly."

Bagger did so. His hand was cupped around something. He said, "This is a detonator, folks. My thumb comes off this thing, I got a chunk of C4 in the SUV right behind me that'll blow everything and everyone within a hundred yards sky-high." He nodded at the lead agent. "See for yourself if you don't believe me."

The lead agent nodded to one of his men. The man looked in the back of the vehicle. His glance back at his commander said it all.

Bagger said, "Now here's what we're going to do." With his free hand he pointed at Paddy and Annabelle. "They're coming with me."

"We're not letting you leave this building," the commander said.

"Then I'm going to blow us all to kingdom come."

"I don't believe that," the FBI agent said.

"Best I can hope for is lethal injection, right? Well, I ain't going alone. So if you don't think I'll do it, you don't know Jerry Bagger." He glanced at twin snipers who had placed red dots on his forehead. "And your boys shoot me, hot-shit FBI man, this thumb is coming off whether you like it or not."

The commander gazed uneasily at Alex and then Annabelle.

She stepped forward. "Okay, Jerry, you win. Let's go."

Alex stepped forward too. "I'm going too."

"No you're not, Alex," she snapped.

Bagger smiled maliciously. "Alex? Alex, is it? You sound like you finally found a friend, Annabelle. And I don't want to take your friends from you." He looked at Alex. "Congratulations, *jerk-off*, you get to go too."

Bagger eyed the commander. "Just so you know, I'm a fair guy, so you can keep a few of my boys to make you look good." He pointed to Mike. "Including Mike there."

"Mr. Bagger!" Mike started to protest.

"Shut up," Bagger snapped before turning to Annabelle and the others. "Get in the SUV." Several of his men retrieved their weapons and everyone climbed in.

Alex, Annabelle and Paddy slid into the middle seat. Bagger and one of his men got in the front seat, three others in the rear.

Bagger rolled down the window. "I see one car or hear one chopper following us, I start popping people, understand?" He waved to the FBI agents as the vehicle sailed out of the warehouse.

"Where to, Mr. Bagger?" the driver asked.

"Private airport in western Maryland where I had them park the jet. I thought I might need to get away on short notice. I'm calling ahead right now to tell them to warm it up." He glanced at Annabelle. "I'm sorry to say you three *won't* be joining us."

77

Carter Gray was a remarkable fisherman. Only he had not caught the fish he most prized, and that was because he could not find the right bait. He had burned thousands of man-hours and looked at a mountain of digital files until his eyeballs were ready to fall out. And yet for all that trouble he only had one name to show for it: Harry Jedidiah, son of Lesya and Rayfield Solomon, a.k.a. David P. Jedidiah the second.

He had tried to find Oliver Stone's ragtag band of freaks: the big man and ex-military Reuben Rhodes that Gray remembered from Murder Mountain; the mousy librarian Caleb Shaw who had not been to his home or job at the Library of Congress in recent days; and Milton Farb, the cherubic genius with OCD. Gray had a dossier on each man, and yet they had simply vanished. Farb and Shaw hadn't used their cell phones and Rhodes didn't have one registered in his name. And Rhodes had recently moved and left no forwarding address. Nor was wherever he was living listed on any real estate records, because Gray's men had checked. Still, with Carter Gray's resources no one should be able to simply vanish. No wonder these terrorist sleeper cells were proving nearly impossible to uncover. America was too damn big and too damn *free*. In some ways the Soviets had had it right: *Spy on everybody because you never know when a friend might turn into an enemy.*

He now turned his attention to locating Lesya's son. And he had focused on one aspect in particular as the point of least resistance. He rose from his chair in his bunker and flipped on the TV. Then the intelligence chief hit a button on the remote he was holding.

The scene he was looking at was from the Hart Senate Office Building. Roger Simpson clearly would be a target of Lesya's son. If so he could hit the senator either at his home or at his office. Gray had already checked the surveillance cameras at Simpson's condo building and found nothing helpful. Now he had turned to the office.

He watched hour after hour of people coming and going into the building. There were many and their numbers tended to dilute everyone down to useless silhouettes. Then Gray thought of a second angle. He put in another DVD, sat back and started watching the hallway outside Simpson's office. He spent three hours doing this, methodically checking out each person coming into frame.

Finally. He sat up and viewed it again. The man working on the door to Simpson's office. He zoomed in on the man's face. Penetrating disguises was something Gray had been long trained in. In the cheekbone was that a touch of Solomon? The chin, the eyes, that of Lesya? Contrary to what he'd told the president, he knew the woman well.

He made numerous calls, and the story came into focus quickly. No one from Simpson's office had called for a government repairman for the door. Simpson's receptionist, though, reported that that's what the man had said—that he'd been told to come. Yet he hadn't gone in the office in the footage Gray had, and a review of the other surveillance discs turned up no such penetration. A bomb-sniffing dog was brought in but found nothing at which to bark. No one bothered to check for bugs, because a bug couldn't kill a man.

The next step was to take the picture of the door repairman, pare it down to its essentials and run it through every database the government had. They were doing the same with the video feed from the airport and the descriptions that had been received from the nursing home. Even though the computer age had infinitely speeded this process up, it would still take a little time, something Gray did not have an abundance of. Allowing Lesya to be taken by the authorities was not an option. She had far too much she could tell. It was certain that she had passed this knowledge on to her son. And if Carr was with them, none of them could be allowed to live. It would be cataclysmic for the country, for the world. And for Carter Gray.

78

Bagger ordered his man to take a route through the city instead of getting on the Beltway to Maryland. They stopped once and switched out the license plate on the SUV in case the FBI had it. Then they drove on, blending in with dozens of other similar vehicles on the road.

Bagger sat back with a contented look as he clicked a button on the detonator, disarming it.

Paddy sat very still in his seat, his gaze on Bagger. Annabelle kept her eyes forward. Like Paddy, Alex was watching Bagger, or more precisely, the man's thumb.

Annabelle said, "A bomb, Jerry? And it doesn't seem your style to run like this."

He smiled. "You taught me that lesson. Unpredictable. Sometimes you learn more from getting your ass kicked than you do from winning. You came right at me with the long con instead of targeting the casino. So I gave you some of your con stuff right back at you. Jerry Bagger never backs down, always stays and fights. Well, not this time, baby. And how sweet it feels."

"Glad I could be such an example for you," she said dryly.

"So what's the plan?" Alex said. "Dump us in the woods on the way to the plane?"

"What the hell does it matter to you? You'll be dead."

"But once you get rid of us, you've got no more hostages. You think they're going to let you just fly away?"

"They got no idea I have my jet here or where it is. I'll be outta the feds' jurisdiction in a couple of hours."

"We have extradition with just about everybody."

"I know the gaps there, trust me."

"And the Pompeii goes down the tubes."

Bagger turned around to grin at him. "You think a guy like me doesn't have plenty stashed away somewhere?"

"I'm sure you do. But you're still not going to get away."

"Yeah, right. Who says?"

"I do."

"You're in a real good position for that." Bagger glanced at Annabelle and tapped his temple. "You really should've gotten some class-A talent, Annabelle. I mean, first Tony Wallace and now this whack job."

"Would you like to know why you're not going to get away, Jerry?" Alex said.

"Yeah, tell me, I'm just dying to know."

Alex looked out the window. They were crossing over the Potomac. "Because the FBI knows exactly where you're going."

"Really? How? They telepathic now?"

Alex and Paddy exchanged a glance and the Irishman's body tensed.

Alex undid a few buttons on his shirt and opened it. Underneath was revealed a wire. "You ever think about searching your hostages for bugs, *moron*?"

"Shit!" Bagger screamed, right as Alex shot forward and slammed the casino boss into the driver, in turn whipping the man's head into the door glass. Paddy lunged forward and wrenched the detonator from Bagger's hand. The driver fell limp across the wheel, his foot pushing forward on the gas. The SUV careened out of control and flew across a lane of oncoming traffic.

In the same motion, Alex kicked the passenger door open, grabbed Annabelle and jumped. Annabelle reached out for her father's hand and clutched it. A second later she was falling out of the truck as her father, with a strength that had stunned his daughter, pulled his hand free.

The last thing Annabelle saw before hitting the street was her father with the detonator in hand looking at her.

The next instant she and Alex hit the pavement, with her landing on top of him. A second later the

SUV slammed into the side of the concrete bridge, broke through and went airborne.

Alex and Annabelle jerked up as the explosion rocked the air. The SUV was blown apart as it sailed toward the river below.

Alex covered Annabelle with his body as parts of the truck rained down around them. Thirty seconds later they rose, bruised and bleeding, on shaky legs, staggered to the side of the damaged bridge and gazed over. What was left of the SUV and the men inside was already disappearing into the Potomac.

As the last part of the vehicle slid beneath the water, Annabelle turned and walked slowly down the road. She seemed shell-shocked.

People stopped their cars on the bridge and raced to the side to gawk. Others rushed at Alex and Annabelle.

One man said, "Are you hurt, mister?"

Another, an old gent, exclaimed, "What the hell happened, lady?"

Alex flashed his badge at these folks. "Secret Service. Get back in your cars and drive on. Now!" Then he hustled forward, put a protective arm around Annabelle, flashed his badge at another group of onlookers to back them off and the pair walked quickly off into the night.

79

The three were in a cellar of a building that hadn't been occupied in over a decade. It was a rat-infested, malodorous place, but right now it was the only location where they felt safe. The light was from a battery-powered lantern, the only chairs mounds of junk. It was the place of last resort for Oliver Stone. He only came here when he had nowhere left to go.

Stone leaned against a dank brick wall and stared at Lesya, who sat on a pile of old carpet, obviously lost in thought. Finn hovered by the door, every sense on alert. Stone turned his gaze to the younger man. "You killed Cincetti, Bingham and Cole, and you tried to kill Carter Gray by blowing up his house with an incendiary bullet after filling the place with gas. You climbed up the cliffs to get to his house and then jumped off the cliffs to make your getaway."

"Don't answer him," Lesya said sharply, shooting Stone a suspicious glance. "I agreed to work with this man to keep us alive, but that doesn't mean we have to trust him."

"I wasn't expecting an answer," Stone said. "I was

just expressing my admiration. It's not easy to take out killers like that."

"So do you think you deserve to die then?" Lesya said sharply. "You were a killer too."

"Frankly, I've been dead for a long time."

"They murdered your wife, didn't they?" Finn said.

"Because I wanted to get out. And they almost killed me. To make matters even worse, Roger Simpson adopted my baby daughter. She never knew I was her father."

"Simpson!" Lesya spat on the floor. "That is what I think of Roger Simpson."

"You said you were working for us all those years ago," Stone said. "But we were told that you had turned Solomon and that you both were working for the Soviets. That's why he was targeted for termination, because he was a traitor."

"They lied to you," Lesya said simply.

"I know that now. But if you both were working for us, why would they want to kill you? Or him?"

"Because of a highly dangerous and confidential mission which Rayfield and I were given. We carried it out successfully with a group of Russians loyal to me."

"What was this mission?"

"I haven't told anyone all these years, not even my son."

"Why?"

"I was a spy. We do not give up our secrets easily."

"If I'm going to help you, I need to know the truth."

"You, the killer of my husband, you make demands of me?"

"We can't outresource Carter Gray. Yet together we might be able to outthink him. But before I help you I need to know the *whole* truth."

Lesya did not look convinced.

Finn stepped in front of his mother. "I've already scared my family to death. I have no idea if they're really safe. If I try to go to them, I could be leading Gray right to their door."

"I told you there would be risks, many of them."

"Like there was ever a question that I would turn my back on you," Finn said angrily. "My whole life you've prepared me to do this. That it was my duty to make it right. That I was the only one who could do it."

"Every man has a choice," Lesya said. She pointed at Stone. "Like this man. He chose to follow rather than question orders and he killed an innocent man."

"He was a soldier. He was *trained* to follow orders."

"So were Bingham, Cole and Cincetti," his mother pointed out. "Why is he different?"

"Because he came to warn us. But for him you and I would be dead now. That's the difference. I think he's earned our trust. *Your* trust."

"I've never trusted anyone in my life, other than your father."

"And me," Finn said.

"And you," she conceded.

"Well, if you really trust me, listen to me! You can't go through your whole life thinking everyone is against you."

"That philosophy served me well for many long years."

"And if you hadn't trusted Rayfield Solomon?"

Lesya fell silent, studying her son closely. Then she slowly turned her attention to Stone. "How well do you know your Soviet history?"

"I was there a lot if that means anything."

"Do you know the two heads of the Communist Party before Gorbachev came to power?"

Stone nodded. "Yuri Andropov and Konstantin Chernenko. Why?"

"Soviet leaders were generally known for their longevity. Yet Andropov lasted barely thirteen months, Chernenko roughly the same."

"They were old men in ill health," Stone replied. "They were filler after Brezhnev died. No one expected either of them to last long."

Lesya clapped her hands together. "Precisely. No one expected them to last long, so when they died, no one was surprised."

"You mean they were killed?" Stone said.

"It is not that difficult to kill old, sick men. Even when they're Soviet premiers."

"On whose orders were they killed?"

"Your government's."

Finn stared at her in amazement. "That's impossible. Under U.S. law it's illegal to assassinate a head of state."

She scoffed. "What does that mean when you're trying to prevent a nuclear war that will wipe out the planet? Andropov and Chernenko were old men, yes, but they were hard-line Communists. They were in the way. No real change would occur under them. And the Soviet Union was crumbling. Its back was against the wall. There was growing talk of very desperate measures that the Communist Party leadership was considering taking to restore its place as a superpower. That could not be allowed to happen. Gorbachev had to be given a clear field. Because even though early on Gorbachev seemed to be the same as the other party leaders, *we* knew he was very different. We knew things would change under him. He was still a Communist and we knew he would not dissolve the Soviet Union, but we also knew that the threat of war would go down considerably with him in power. Then Yeltsin came along after Gorbachev. No one could have predicted that, but it was under Yeltsin that the Soviet Union was dismantled.

"But we had to get rid of the old Communist Party leaders. We had to! And we told the Americans our beliefs about this. They agreed with us. And Rayfield thought the same. He knew as much about the inner workings of the Soviet Union as any American alive. But we did not come up with the assassination plot. That was the Americans." She eyed Stone. "You believe it's true, don't you?"

"Heads of state have been assassinated before," Stone admitted. "But are you saying Gorbachev knew of the plot?"

"Of course not. Only a very few of us did."

"How did your orders come on this?" Stone asked.

"From our contact on the American side."

"Who was that?"

"Does it not seem obvious? Roger Simpson."

"And you and your team killed Andropov and Chernenko?"

"Let us say we helped them to their graves prematurely, yes."

"And Rayfield Solomon was involved?"

"Deeply. The Soviets thought he was working for them."

"How do you know this was approved by the U.S. government?"

"I just told you. We received the instructions from Simpson. He was our case manager. And he reported directly to Carter Gray. And Gray to the head of CIA."

"So you just followed orders, without question."

"Yes."

"And killed Andropov and Chernenko, two innocent men?"

Lesya and Stone exchanged a long look. "Yes," she said slowly.

Finn said, "Why would the Americans kill my father and try to kill you if you completed your assignment successfully? Why would they try to paint you as traitors?"

Stone answered. "Because the American government *didn't* order the assassinations. Possibly it was the CIA, or Simpson and Gray could have done it on their own. And once the deed was done they had to discredit and then get rid of anyone who knew about the murders." He looked at Lesya. "Isn't that right?"

"Yes," said Lesya. "And what do you think they would do to prevent *that* truth from coming out now? It could cause war between Russia and the United States. What do you think they would do?" she asked again.

Finn answered. "They'd kill anyone they had to."

"And unfortunately we are David and they are Goliath," Lesya added bitterly. "The Americans are always Goliath."

"But David beat Goliath. And so can we if we get to them first," Stone replied.

"Just the three of us?" Lesya said skeptically.

"We're not alone," Stone said. "I have friends."

If they're still alive.

80

Alex had hailed a cab and he and Annabelle had driven off. He had decided not to wait for the other feds to show up. The charred truck and the floating corpses that awaited them would be self-explanatory in any event. He did call the FBI lead commander and let him know what had happened and that he and Annabelle were the only survivors. "If you need us, we'll be at my house," he told the man. "I'm in the book."

The commander protested but Alex cut him off. "We've had enough for one day. Go and clean up the pieces and talk to us later. It's not like you have to take Bagger to trial. He gets to go before a higher judge now."

The cab dropped them off at Alex's house in Manassas, a one-story rancher with a single-car garage, set off by itself down a gravel drive. Inside the garage was Alex's fully restored '69 fire red Corvette, the only extravagance the Secret Service agent had ever allowed himself. His fed cruiser was parked out front.

"You hungry?" he asked Annabelle, but she merely shook her head.

"I guess asking if you're okay would be pretty stupid right now."

"I'll get through this."

"I'm sorry, Annabelle."

She sat down in a chair. "All these years I've hated my father because I thought he just let my mother die. Then I find out he didn't . . ." Her voice trailed off.

"And now you lose him too," Alex finished for her. "But at least you found out before he died, Annabelle. And he knew that you knew."

"He could've gotten out of that truck. He could be alive right now."

"For six months of the cancer eating him away?"

She stared up at him. "For six months of being with me. I would've taken care of him. I guess he thought blowing himself up was a better alternative."

"No, maybe he wanted to get Bagger even worse than you did. Maybe he was willing to die to avenge his wife and your mother. At the very least you have to admire the guy's courage."

"I do," she finally said. "But I still wish he hadn't done it."

"And he gave you that scar. He wasn't the world's greatest father."

"But he was my father," she said quietly.

"And a criminal."

"Alex, *I'm* a criminal."

"Not to me, you're not." There was an awkward pause before Alex added, "You said you weren't hungry, but I'm going to make some coffee. And when you're ready to talk, we'll talk. How does that sound?"

"Can I take a shower first? I feel really, really dirty."

He showed her to the bathroom that was off his bedroom, and then he went into the kitchen, washed up, put on a pot of coffee and cleaned himself up. By the time he was done, she was out of the shower. She walked into the kitchen wrapped in one of his bathrobes.

"Hope you don't mind," she said.

Her hair was wet and hung down straight.

"Shower make you feel better?"

"Not even close."

They drank the coffee mostly in silence. Then Alex built a fire in the living room fireplace, and Annabelle sat on the floor in front of it, holding her hands out to the flames.

She said in a low voice, "I guess the FBI will have a bunch of questions for me."

"Some. But I can help you field them, if you want."

"Thanks for helping me."

"You put your life on the line too."

She gazed up at him. "Can you sit with me? Just for a little while?"

Alex got down on the floor and they sat quietly in front of the fire as the flames slowly died.

Carter Gray was brooding. None of Carr's people had been located. Then another possibility occurred to him: the Secret Service agent, Alex Ford. He and Stone were tight. They had been at Murder Mountain together. He knew as much of the truth about what Gray had done as did Stone. If he got Ford, used him as bait? It would be a little tricky. The man was a federal agent. He couldn't just kidnap him. Or maybe he could if he somehow discredited him first. This was a favorite tactic of Gray's. Destroy the reputation of the victim first—indeed, make him appear to be a criminal—and then seize him at his most vulnerable. It was far easier to do than most people would have thought. And by the time it was all figured out, it wouldn't matter. Gray made a couple of calls and put the operation into motion.

He quickly received a call back from a mole of his at the FBI. The man there had some interesting news. He told Gray the details of what had happened that night with Ford and Jerry Bagger. And also that Ford had a woman with him, a woman apparently of questionable past. They had walked away from a fiery explosion in Washington. Ford had told the FBI that he would talk to them tomorrow. He had presumably gone home with the woman.

Gray thanked his spy and hung up.

This new intelligence changed things remarkably.

Alex Ford's career was just about to take a nasty turn for the worse.

81

After Annabelle went to bed, Alex sat up in the kitchen drinking another cup of coffee. He glanced every now and then in the direction of the bedroom as he thought things over. But what really was there to think over? The case was done, the bad guys vanquished. This was where the movie ended, the credits rolled and maybe some outtakes played. In the real world, of course, it wasn't quite that simple. There would be enough paperwork to fill out to clear-cut a small forest. And then an internal investigation to ensure that nothing Alex had done had improperly led to a bunch of men getting blown up over the Potomac. Explanations would be made and corroborated and Alex was confident that relatively soon, many months from now, it would all be over.

Yet he didn't want it to end. Not really. Because that scenario would mean that Annabelle would be on her way. He sighed. She would probably be on her way regardless. And maybe that was a good thing, at least officially. After all, she was a con, and he was a cop, and if that wasn't human oil and water, he didn't know what was.

He glanced in the direction of the bedroom once more. *No, it just isn't that simple, is it?*

When she woke up what could he do? Ask her to please stay? He could invent some lie. *You have to stay until the official inquiry is complete.* That sounded totally bogus even to him. Annabelle would see right through it.

The next second he stopped thinking about that issue. They were just about to receive visitors, unwelcome ones from the looks of things.

Alex bent low, slipped to the window and looked out. Down the gravel drive, nearly out of sight, was a vehicle that he didn't recognize. It was a nondescript black van. Alex hated nondescript black vans. They often carried nondescript men with large guns and bad attitudes. This fear was confirmed when he grabbed a pair of night binoculars from a shelf and used them to take a closer look. There was a small satellite receiver pod on the roof of the van. And if he'd still had lingering doubts, the movement in the bushes next to his house erased them. People in the bushes, satellite vans, maybe the glint of rifle optics in the moonlight—none of it was making Alex feel too good right now. And he'd thought nearly losing his life once already tonight was enough.

Yet this was a tad different from the encounter with Jerry Bagger. This had government strike team written all over it. And why would the government be bothering with one of its own? Alex nearly instantly answered his own question.

Carter Gray couldn't find Oliver Stone so he'd decided to cast his net wider. Whether this was actually true or not, Alex wasn't going to wait to find out. He had already had one near-death face-off with Carter Gray at Murder Mountain; he had no desire to go for a second round.

He grabbed a set of keys off the hook over the kitchen phone and raced to the bedroom. Clamping a hand over Annabelle's mouth in case she screamed at being awoken from a dead sleep, he whispered, "Someone's outside. Get dressed. Fast. We have to roll."

Annabelle had barely thrown on her clothes and grabbed her bag when two men came through the front door and another pair through the rear. They had body armor and MP-5s and Alex's pistol would be no match for them. So he opted for going out the door off the kitchen leading to the garage.

"Stop!" one of the armored men called out to them from the hall.

Alex had no intention of doing anything other than running like hell. He only bothered to open the garage door enough to let his Corvette scoot underneath, clearing it by about an inch. He grabbed another gear and they shot down the gravel road past the van right as the front door of his house burst open.

As the Corvette spat rocks in all directions, bursts of machine-gun fire zipped over their heads. Annabelle ducked down in her seat.

"Damn it!" Alex cried out.

"Are you hit?" Annabelle said anxiously, as she sat back up.

"No, but I think one of the shots hit the car."

He screeched onto the main road, keeping his foot mashed to the floor. He looked in the mirror and breathed a sigh of relief. There was no one back there.

"Alex, what's happening?"

"I wish I knew, Annabelle."

"Where are we going?"

"I wish I knew that too. Hold on."

He speed-dialed one of his buddies at the Service's WFO, or Washington Field Office, where he was stationed.

"Bobby, it's Alex. Something really weird is going on, man."

"Like what?"

Alex filled him in. "I don't know who those guys were, but they were carrying some serious hardware. Find out anything on your end and then call me back."

He hung up and looked at Annabelle. "Bobby's good, he'll be able to dig up something to help us."

"Why don't you just go to your headquarters or whatever you call it? We should be safe there."

"I would except for one little tiny problem."

"What's that?"

"I've seen the jumpsuits those guys were in before."

"Where?"

"At a joint exercise the Service did down at Camp Peary."

"Is it that bad?" she said, looking at him uneasily.

"It's one of the CIA's main training facilities, known as the Farm."

"The CIA!"

"Their paramilitary units wear that sort of gear."

"The CIA has paramilitary units?"

"Yeah, is that a secret outside the Beltway?"

"So you're saying our own government might be after us?"

"That's right."

"We got rid of a psychopath casino owner, my father just blew himself up and now the CIA's on our ass?"

"That sums it up pretty accurately."

"I have to say you're taking it very calmly."

"If nothing else, the Service teaches its agents to remain cool. But I have to admit, it's getting more difficult by the minute."

"It's nice to know you're human. What now?"

"As much as I hate to do it, we have to ditch my Corvette and find a place to hole up. Then we wait to hear back from Bobby and hope it's good news. But I sort of doubt it will be."

82

They jettisoned Alex's Corvette, grabbed a cab to Old Town Alexandria and then walked to a nearby motel. Annabelle checked in paying cash and using her fake ID while Alex hid outside. They went to their room and bolted the door.

An hour later Bobby called back. That he was whispering told Alex all he needed to know.

"The official story we just got in is you opened fire on federal agents who were attempting to make an arrest at your house. And that you're harboring an unnamed fugitive, a woman. None of us believe it, Alex, but the director's going nuts. Word is he and the CIA director just had a dustup on the phone."

"Those *federal agents* were either trying to kill or kidnap *me*, Bobby! And the only thing I'm harboring is a strong desire to kick somebody's ass to get some answers."

"Hey, I'm on your side. You didn't walk out of the office today and become a felon. But you still better come in and give your side of things." He paused. "Alex, *do* you have someone with you?"

Alex stared over at Annabelle, who looked anxiously back at him. "Thanks, Bobby. I'll be in touch."

He clicked off and threw the phone down on the bed in disgust. "Okay, we've obviously been teleported to an alternate universe where all the good guys are screwed."

Annabelle sat down on the bed next to him. "Thank you."

"Look, sarcasm I can do without right now."

"I'm not being sarcastic. I'm thanking you for saving my life tonight. *Twice!*"

"I'm sorry, Annabelle. I just didn't see this twist coming until it was too late."

"But why would the CIA target us?"

"The only thing I can think of is that I have a connection to Oliver."

"But why come after Oliver now?"

"A while back when the president was kidnapped and the U.S. was on the verge of a nuclear strike—"

"Oliver was involved in that!"

"We both were. And not by choice. But when that happened, Carter Gray was also involved. And not in a good way. Oliver's the reason the guy ended up resigning."

"So Oliver had something on Carter Gray and used that to make him quit his job?"

"You got it."

"But Gray's dead."

"They never found his body."

"So maybe the man's plotting from beyond the grave."

"That's what it looks like. And we're trapped right in the middle of it all."

"We have to find Oliver."

"Won't be that easy. If the CIA is involved you can bet they've put the hammer down on the other agencies either to cooperate or stand down."

"But we just helped the FBI," Annabelle countered.

"Doesn't matter. National security trumps everything else. So that means our movements will really be restricted. And unlike in TV shows and the movies, it's almost impossible to run from the cops. You have millions of eyes watching and somebody will see something and then that's it. And they sure know what I look like."

Annabelle held up her bag. "I can do something about that. Step into the changing room." She had Alex sit on the commode in the bathroom while she pulled out a small box from the bag and readied some items. It took an hour, but at the end of sixty minutes Alex Ford no longer looked like Alex Ford.

He gazed at himself in the mirror. "You're good at this stuff."

"Comes in handy. Tomorrow morning we can find a wig shop and get a few other clothes and things to improve the disguise. Give me a little more time with you and I doubt Mrs. Ford would recognize her husband."

"That wouldn't be hard since there isn't a Mrs. Ford."

She packed the kit back up. "I suddenly realized I'm starving."

"I saw a McDonald's down the street."

"Super-size me," Annabelle said.

As Alex was walking to McDonald's he got a call from Stone. "Bagger's history but Gray almost nailed us," he told Stone. "Paddy's dead. Annabelle's taking it kind of hard."

"I'm truly sorry to hear that, but I'm afraid I need your help, again."

Alex listened for a few minutes and then told Stone that he and Annabelle would meet him two nights from now, allowing things to settle down a bit.

He clicked off and hoofed it to the McDonald's, where he super-sized them both. On his way back, his arms full of artery-busting food, he wondered if this might be one of his last meals.

83

For one of the few times in his career, Carter Gray screamed in uncontrolled fury after being told that Alex Ford had escaped.

With a disgusted look he dismissed the stone-faced men standing in front of him. They'd missed Carr, Lesya and her son, and now this! Such incompetence never would have happened in the old days, he told himself. When he had men like John Carr . . .

Three deep breaths later and Gray was all business again. It was a setback, but only a setback. He had gotten another intelligence breakthrough barely thirty minutes ago. He'd discovered over the years that they tended to come in bushels.

They had matched the man's face to a database. The gentleman with Carr and Lesya was named Harry Finn, a former Navy SEAL who now performed consulting work with the Department of Homeland Security as a member of a red cell team. Or he *did* such work. Gray couldn't envision the man's career continuing, because he was undoubtedly Lesya Solomon's son. And that meant he was a murderer. And he had to die before he ever came to court.

Gray had already dispatched a team to Finn's home. He lived in a cozy place in the suburbs; had a lovely wife and three darling children. He coached soccer in his spare time and from all accounts was a model citizen. And Gray was sure that when his men got to the house it would be empty. A phone call he received ten minutes later confirmed this.

However, his team didn't come away entirely empty-handed. In a safe in the garage they discovered some interesting details. They also found some paperwork about a storage unit. When they got there, they hit the treasure trove. It was filled with the histories of Bingham, Cole and Cincetti. And Carter Gray and Roger Simpson. And finally John Carr. Though nary a scrap of information could be found about Rayfield and Lesya, Harry Finn was undoubtedly their man. Only where was he now? And where were his wife and children? In hiding, of course. And it was up to Carter Gray to flush them out. He only hoped he would have better luck.

Yet he sensed that he would. It was completely counterintuitive for them to do it, but for some reason Gray felt as though Stone, Lesya and Harry Finn were very close by. And if they were, they would succumb to a mistake at some point. It would not necessarily be *their* mistake. There was another factor to be put into the equation: Finn's very ordinary family.

He lifted his phone. "Put a trace on every credit and debit card and every cell and hard-line phone registered to the Finn family. You know where he works, so put surveillance on all his co-workers and his office. Watch the kids' schools and Mom's book club group. If they show themselves, take them. Move heaven and earth, but get them."

84

They had passed another day sitting in the cellar and now the darkness was settling in. Stone, Finn and Lesya had spent the time developing a plan of action. The next night Stone's team would assemble and they could execute that plan.

Finn, who'd been pacing in increasing agitation suddenly said, "I have to see my family. Now."

Lesya started to protest but Stone asked, "Where are they?" Finn told him.

Stone turned to Lesya. "You stay here. I'll go with him."

"You're going to leave me here, alone?" the old woman said.

"Just for a little while," Stone added. "You'll be safe."

The two men left the cellar.

"How bad is your wife?" Stone asked once they were outside.

"Bad! And who the hell can blame her?"

"We can get to them on the Metro and then it's a bit of a walk."

"You were Army Special Forces in Nam," Finn said. "I looked it up."

"And you?"

"How do you know I was anything?"

"I can just tell."

"SEAL. Look, we need weapons. They'll have searched my house by now. I have a storage unit with some stuff in it, but they'll have found that too."

"I have a place with guns," Stone replied.

Thirty minutes later, Stone waited outside while Finn entered the motel room in a run-down area of south Alexandria.

His children immediately flew to him, nearly crushing him against the wall. Even George the Labradoodle got in the act, barking and jumping on his master. As Finn hugged his kids tightly, all their tears mixing together, he saw his wife through a tiny crevice between David and Susie. Mandy was sobbing too but made no move toward him.

After a few minutes of hugs and cries, Finn managed to get his kids to sit down on a bed. Susie clutched the bear her grandmother had given her, tears trickling down her plump cheeks. Patrick nervously chewed on his bloody, bitten-down nails. He did that before every test and every ball game, Finn knew. And it pained him that his son was now doing it because of something his father had done.

David eyed his dad nervously. "Pop? What's going on?"

Finn took a deep breath. He could no more tell them the truth than he could jump to the moon. On the way over he had thought of the lie he would use, but it didn't seem so plausible now. He could never say, "I'm a killer, kids, and the cops are after me." No he could never say that, because these were his children. They and Mandy were all he had. Mere justice didn't constitute an adequate defense of what he'd done.

"Something happened at work, Dave," he began as Mandy looked on. In her eyes was stark fear, but also something else that devastated Finn: distrust. He put his hand out to her, but she drew back a little.

He decided to abandon his cover story. He rose and leaned against the wall. When he was finally ready to speak he looked directly at them.

"Everything you know about your grandparents, my mother and father, is a lie. Your grandfather didn't come from Ireland and die in a car accident a long time ago. Your grandmother wasn't from Canada. And she's not in a nursing home because she belongs there." He took another deep breath, trying not to focus on his family's collective astonishment.

And he told them. Their grandfather's real name was Rayfield Solomon. He'd been a spy for the Americans. Their grandmother's name was Lesya, a Russian, who'd been a spy for her country until coming over to the American side with Solomon and also marrying him.

"They were framed by some people at the CIA," he said. "Rayfield Solomon's picture hangs on the wall at Langley, the 'Wall of Shame' they call it. But he doesn't deserve to be there. He was killed by these same people so the truth would never come out. Your grandmother survived but has been in hiding ever since."

To their credit and Finn's relief, his children seemed to readily accept his explanation, even be excited by the revelations. "But what is the truth?" David asked. "What were they framed for doing?"

Finn shook his head. "I can't tell you, son. I wish I could, but I can't. I only found out a short time ago."

"Where's Grandma?" Patrick asked.

"I'm going back to her after I leave you."

Susie flung herself around Finn's leg. "Daddy, you can't leave. You can't leave us," she wailed. The sounds were cracking Finn's heart in half. He could barely breathe as the tears streamed down his daughter's face. He lifted her up and held her. "I'm sorry, baby, but I promise you one thing. Are you listening? Can you listen to Daddy for just a minute? Please, baby, please?"

Susie finally stopped crying. She and her brothers stared at their father. They were so still, it didn't seem like any of them were actually breathing.

"I promise you this: that Daddy will fix everything. And then I'm going to come and get all of you and we're going to go back home and everything will be like it was. I promise you. I swear to you that it will."

"How?"

Everyone looked at Mandy, who now moved toward her husband.

"How?" she said again, her voice rising. "How will you fix it all? How will you make everything like it was? How can you possibly fix this . . . nightmare?"

"Mandy, please?" Finn glanced at the kids.

"No, Harry. No! You've been deceiving me, the kids, for how long? How long, Harry?"

"Too long," he said quietly. He added, "I'm sorry. If you just knew—"

"No, we don't want to know." She took a struggling Susie from his arms. "I called Doris, our next-door neighbor. She said men came to our house today and searched it. When she tried to ask them what was going on, they said they were looking for you, Harry. They said that you were a criminal."

"No! NO!" Susie screamed. "Daddy is not a criminal. He's not, he's not!" She started hitting her mother. Finn grabbed Susie away and clutched her tightly. "Susie, you never do that, you never hit your mother. She loves you more than anyone in the whole world. You never do that. Promise me."

A tearful Susie said, "But you're not a bad man, are you?"

Finn looked desperately at Mandy and then at his

sons, who stared at him, their faces pale, their eyes wide in fear.

"No, he's not, Susie. Your father is not a bad man."

They all turned to look at Oliver Stone, who had just come quietly in the door. George the dog hadn't made a peep. He just sat next to Stone looking up at him.

"Who are you?" Mandy demanded fearfully.

"I'm working with your husband to try to right some wrongs. He's a good man."

"I told you, Mommy," Susie said.

"What's your name?" Mandy asked.

"That's not important. What is important is that Harry has told you the truth, or as much of it as he can and still keep you safe. It was incredibly dangerous for him to come here tonight, but he insisted. He even left his mother, who is old and frail, to come and see you, because he was so worried. He had to see you." He looked at Mandy. "He had to." Mandy's gaze went from Stone to her husband. Finn slowly put out his hand. She slowly took it. Their fingers instantly gripped like steel.

"Can you right these wrongs?" Mandy asked, looking at Stone anxiously.

"We're going to try our best," he said. "That's all we can do."

"And you can't go to the police," she said.

"I wish we could, but we can't. Not yet."

Finn put Susie down and picked up the bear she'd dropped. "I told Grandma how much you love your bear." Susie clutched it with one hand and her father's leg with the other.

After twenty minutes, Stone told Finn they had to leave. At the door Mandy slid her arms around her husband and they hugged while Stone and the children kept a respectful silence.

"I love you, Mandy, more than anything in the world," Finn said into her ear.

"Just make things right, Harry. Make things right and come back to us. Please."

After they left, Finn turned to Stone. "Thanks for what you did in there."

"Families are the most important things there are."

"You sound like you speak from experience."

"I wish I did, Harry, I wish I did. But I don't."

85

David Finn was very upset about the events of the night before and he welcomed the opportunity to get out of the motel room and go to the grocery store. The room they were staying in had a kitchenette and their mother had been fixing their meals there.

When he was in the checkout line he realized that he didn't have enough cash, so he pulled out the debit card his mother had given him for safekeeping but then told him not to use. But what could it really hurt, he thought.

A lot, as it turned out.

As soon as the card was swiped through the receiver, an alert signal was received electronically in a room two thousand miles away. It was then relayed to CIA headquarters and nearly instantly thereafter to Carter Gray. Within two minutes' time four men had been dispatched to the location where the card had been swiped.

David was barely halfway back to the motel when the car pulled over and two men got out. The tall boy was swallowed up between their bulk, thrown in the car and it was rolling, all in less than five seconds. Thirty minutes later he was twenty miles away in a dark room secured to a chair. His heart was pounding so fast he could barely breathe. He said in a low voice, "Dad, please come and help me. Please."

The voice came out of the darkness. "Dad's not coming, David. Dad's not coming ever again."

Stone, Finn, Lesya, the rest of the Camel Club and Alex and Annabelle were congregated in the cellar. Standing in the center of the room, Stone made introductions, and then told them the entire story. They sat back, an enraptured audience. Several of them occasionally glanced over at Lesya or Finn.

"My team and I killed Rayfield Solomon," Stone concluded. "We killed an innocent man."

"You didn't know that, Oliver," Milton protested, a response that Reuben and Caleb echoed.

Stone had noted gratefully that his fellow Camel Club members had taken his frank admission of being a former government assassin attached to the Triple Six Division of the CIA without much surprise.

As Caleb had pointed out, "We knew you weren't a retired librarian, Oliver. I can sniff those folks out pretty easily."

Lesya said, "Why do they call you Oliver? Your name is John Carr."

Milton, Reuben and Caleb all exchanged curious

glances. Stone looked at Lesya and said, "Have you kept your real name all these years?" Lesya shook her head. "Well, neither have I. For obvious reasons."

Stone next looked over at Alex Ford. "Alex, you're the only lawman here. And since what I'm proposing isn't exactly lawful, you can bail out now."

Alex shrugged. "I care about the truth as much as the next person." He shot Lesya a glance. "But to play devil's advocate for a minute, how do we know her story is true? We only have her word for it that all this happened. What if Solomon really was a spy? What if she didn't come over to the American side? I mean, I've heard of Rayfield Solomon. And it seems like the gent was guilty as charged."

All eyes turned to Lesya.

Stone said, "I have my own reasons for believing her, including someone at the CIA who would know."

"Granted," Alex said. "But we're all going to be risking pretty much everything here. So I'd like to know it's for the right cause. I mean, if she was this terrific spy she must be a pretty damn good liar."

Stone started to say something else, but Lesya put up a hand and rose. "I will defend myself if you don't mind. I'm actually surprised the question is only coming up now." She gripped her walker, flipped it upside down, took off the foam booty and unscrewed the covering on the metal tube. Out came two rolled-up pieces of paper.

"These are the written orders we received from the

CIA. We insisted on it because of the magnitude of what we were being asked to do."

They all read through them. They were each on CIA letterhead, addressed to Lesya and Rayfield Solomon. The first instructed them to carry out the assassination of Yuri Andropov; the second, that of Andropov's successor, Konstantin Chernenko. Each had Roger Simpson's signature at the bottom. Everyone looked stunned.

"I take it you didn't trust Simpson," Stone said.

"We only trusted each other," she replied.

"That's Simpson's original signature," Stone said. "I know it well."

"There's no countersignature from the president?" Alex said incredulously. "Are you telling me you killed *two* heads of the Soviet Union on the orders of, what, a low-level case manager?"

"Do you think the president of the United States would actually put his signature down on such an order?" Lesya said with equal incredulity. "Our chain of command was what we worked with. If it came down that chain we had to rely on it being approved from the top. If we couldn't rely on that, we couldn't do our jobs."

"She's right about that," Stone said. "Triple Six operated the same way."

He was examining the letter against the lightbulb. He glanced at Lesya. "There's a code line next to the watermark."

She nodded. "That special encoded paper was only available from at least one level above Simpson."

"Carter Gray?"

"Yes. We knew the orders had really come through Gray. And it was our experience that if they came through Gray, they had come from the top. We didn't trust Simpson that much. He was a loose cannon."

"But Gray might have played you for the fall guy too," Stone pointed out. "The president might not have authorized the killings."

She shrugged. "There is always that possibility. I am sorry but I did not have the opportunity to go to your White House and ask the president personally if he wanted me to kill two Soviet leaders," she added in a bristling tone.

"Why didn't you take this letter to the authorities back then?" Alex said.

"I had no reason to even think of doing so until Rayfield was killed. Even then I didn't know he'd been murdered by the Americans until much later. Then an attempt was made on my life when Harry was still a child. At that point I knew we had been betrayed. We had to go into hiding. I spent decades finding out the truth, the people responsible. But even so, how could I use this evidence? I was a Russian spy. It was only Rayfield, Simpson and Carter Gray who knew I was a double agent. If I had come in from the cold even with this evidence no one would have believed me. They would have just killed me."

She paused and looked at each of them as they stared back at her in some disbelief. "You think your people would hold back from doing something like that?" She glanced at Stone. "Ask him."

"I believe you, Lesya," Stone said. "I know it could have happened exactly *that* way."

"Rayfield and I were married in the Soviet Union. I was already carrying Harry. We couldn't tell anyone we were married, either Soviet or American. We assumed double lives, new names, eventually settled in America. Rayfield spent as much time with us as he could. When Harry was still small Rayfield severed almost all ties with us. Someone was after him. He knew this. His fear was confirmed in São Paulo. He was still working for the Americans, his own country. And they killed him."

"Wasn't there an investigation?" Alex added.

"What did I care for investigations that went nowhere? I didn't want the truth covered up. I just wanted revenge." She took Finn's hand. "We both did."

Alex said, "Oliver, can't we just take this evidence to the authorities now?"

"That's what I was thinking," Annabelle added.

Stone shook his head. "We don't know that the CIA and the president at the time didn't order those assassinations. If they did, others, who are still in the government, may know too."

"And we go waltzing in with it," Alex said slowly.

"And are never seen again," Lesya said. "Look what happened to my poor husband."

"And making this public now may start World War Three," Stone said. "With the state of Russia right now and the tarnished global image of the U.S., I doubt the Russians would take kindly to us having killed two of their leaders even if it did lead to the fall of the Soviet Union."

"So what's your plan?" Alex asked.

"We have to get to Carter Gray," he said. "And I think I know how to do it."

Stone had just started to lay out his plan when Finn's phone buzzed. He listened, clicked off and looked at the others. His face had gone very pale. "That was Mandy. David didn't come back from the store."

Lesya said quietly, "Carter Gray has taken him. As bait."

Finn stood. "Then it's over. I'll trade myself for my son."

"The only result of that will be *both* of you will die," Stone said. "Gray never allows for leaving witnesses if he can help it."

"I have to get my son back," Finn snapped.

"We will get him back, Harry. I promise," Stone said.

"How?" Lesya exclaimed. "How will you do this if Gray has him? You just said the man does not allow for survivors."

"We need someone else to trade David for other than you and Harry."

"Who would that be?" Reuben asked.

"Someone Gray can't afford to lose."

Lesya said instantly, "Roger Simpson."

Finn whirled around to stare at Stone. "And I know just how to get the son of a bitch."

86

Roger Simpson was sitting at his desk in his office at the Hart Building working when his computer screen went blank. A second later a picture appeared on it.

Simpson gasped. It was the image of Rayfield Solomon materializing across his screen. *How can that be?*

Typed letters next appeared on the bottom of the screen. "I hope you recognize your old friend."

"What the?" Simpson said, looking around. "What the hell is this?"

"What the hell is this?" a voice said, sending Simpson nearly out of his chair. It was coming from the wireless unit Finn had hidden there when he'd broken into the senator's office.

"Who are you? *Where* are you?" Simpson said fearfully.

"What's important is that there's a bomb hidden inside your computer."

"What!" Simpson exclaimed, half rising from his chair.

"And if you try to leave the room it will detonate."

Simpson immediately sank back down. "But they swept my office for bombs."

"Unscrew the back of your computer. There's a screwdriver in your desk drawer, I checked when I was in here."

"But I—"

"Do it!"

Hands shaking, Simpson retrieved the screwdriver, undid the back cover and stared at the device Finn had put there.

"It's designed to use the chemical and electronic components in the CPU to cause a chain reaction and then a big boom. By the way, I can also see everything you're doing, so if you try to disarm the bomb I'll blow you up. Understood?"

Simpson slowly nodded.

"Don't just nod, I want to hear you say it. Do you understand?"

"I understand. For God sakes, I understand."

"A man will come to your office shortly. You will go with him without resistance. If you try to warn anyone I will detonate the bomb and your whole office disappears. Once out of your office, if you try anything, say anything to anyone to try and get away, your wife is dead. Do you understand that?"

"You have Donna?"

"The former Miss Alabama is doing very well right now. That status could change, depending on your level of cooperation. Do you understand?"

"Yes," Simpson said in a defeated tone.

"Good. Now compose yourself and wait for him to come. I'll be listening and watching until he does. He'll explain that he's taking you to an emergency meeting at Langley to cover a crisis that just came up, one that the chairman of the Intelligence Committee needs to be in on. You will confirm to your staff that this is true. Understood?"

"Yes."

A few minutes later there was a knock at Simpson's office door. Shortly after that the pale but composed senator was escorted down the elevator by Stone dressed in a black suit; he was also wearing sunglasses. They got into a car driven by Reuben. As the car pulled away Stone took off his sunglasses and stared at Simpson.

"Hello, Roger, it's been a long time."

"Do I know y—?" Simpson's breath caught in his throat as Stone's gaze bore into him.

"I guess I haven't changed as much as I thought," Stone said. "Actually, I think I did all my aging while working for you and Gray."

Simpson stammered, "John, please, you have to believe me, I had nothing to do with what happened to you or your wife." He added quickly, "And we took care of Jackie. We loved her very much."

Stone elbowed the man hard in the ribs. "*My* daughter's name was *Elizabeth*, not Jackie."

"Gray gave her to us. He didn't tell us she was your daughter. He only told me the truth recently."

"So who did order the hit on me?"

"I have my suspicions," Simpson said.

"Gray?"

Simpson said slowly, "Could have been. He said you wanted to leave Triple Six. He didn't like that one bit. That's the truth."

"Apparently neither did a lot of people. You ordered the hits on Andropov and Chernenko, didn't you?"

Simpson almost choked on his own breath. "Who told you that?"

"Did you?"

"That's in the past. But if I did anything of that magnitude, which I'm not admitting that I did, it would have been duly authorized from the highest possible level."

"I'm sure you covered your ass. I talked to Max Himmerling before he died."

A tic started at Simpson's left temple. "Himmerling?"

"Yeah. I'm assuming Gray had him killed because he knew he'd tell me everything. And Max knew where all the skeletons were buried."

"What all did he tell you?" Simpson asked nervously.

"Everything I needed to know," Stone said quietly.

"Like it was either you or Gray who ordered the hit on me."

Simpson could barely speak now. "Are you going to kill me?"

"That depends on you, doesn't it?" Stone put on his sunglasses and sat back. "*And* how much Carter Gray values your *friendship*? If he doesn't take the bait, you're of no value to me."

"I could well be the next president of this country!" Simpson snapped.

"Like I said, no value to me at all."

87

Simpson spoke slowly into the phone. His words had been scripted. If the man had any desire to deviate from that script, Stone was holding a gun against his head to dissuade him.

"They want to meet, Carter," he said in a strained voice.

"I have no idea what you're talking about," Gray said. "*Who* are you talking about?"

"You know who!"

"Well, tell them, whoever they are, that if they're recording this conversation, I wish them luck in trying to use it against anyone."

"Carter, dammit, they've kidnapped me!"

"I can call 911 if you'd like. Any idea where they might be holding you?"

"They have something you want."

"Really?"

"They know about David."

"Again, I don't know what you're talking about."

"They have the orders I signed, you know the ones."

"No, I really don't."

Simpson said angrily, "You authorized that order, Carter."

"Again, without possibly knowing what you're really talking about I can try to make a trade."

"Me for the boy."

"No, for the orders."

"What about me!"

"What about you, Roger?"

"They'll kill me."

"I'm very sorry to hear that. But you've lived a fairly long and full life. Where do they want to do the exchange?"

"You son of a bitch!"

Stone took the phone. "We'll call you back with the place and time. And we'll throw in Simpson for no extra charge. I have no desire to keep him."

"John, nice to hear your voice. Do you know how difficult you've made things for me?"

"It seems to be the only thing I live for anymore."

"And of course you won't be lying in wait to ambush me."

"You'll have to take your chances, just like I will."

"And what if I don't show up?"

"Then the orders for Andropov and Chernenko's assassinations get sent to five people in D.C., none of whom you'd call a friend. And then we can let the distinguished senator sell you out to save himself. I think he'd make a great witness."

"After all these years you think anyone will really care?"

"Fine, if you don't think it matters, why bother coming? We'll just messenger them out and let the chips fall. Take care, Carter."

"Wait!"

A few moments of silence passed.

Stone said, "I don't hear anything."

"Where did you get these orders? Lesya?"

"You don't need to know. Roger has seen them. And judging by the paleness of his skin I'd say he thinks it matters a lot."

"He was always a bit excitable. Not like you and me. All right, John, but if you really want to do a deal, you'll have to sweeten the pot. I want the original recording you took at Murder Mountain."

"That's not negotiable."

"Oh, but it is. You cost me my career. I want it back. And don't try to run and make copies. We have technology now that shows that."

"And if I don't?"

"I don't have to tell you the consequences, do I?"

Stone looked at Finn. "All right. I'll call you back with the time and place. And you have to be there in person or it's no deal."

"Then I'd prefer to pick the location."

"I know, that's why *I'm* doing it. One more thing. Anything happens to David Finn, you won't walk away alive."

"You're not what you once were, John. I have fifty men as good as you ever were."

"Make that forty-nine. I ran into one of your *best* about a month ago, an ex–Triple Six turned spy."

Gray put down the phone and wiped a trickle of sweat from his face.

88

Mandy and the rest of the Finn family were moved to other quarters by Reuben, Caleb and Alex that night, after taking great precautions to make sure they weren't followed. They also brought Lesya to stay with them. Caleb was left on guard with strict instructions to phone immediately if anything seemed suspicious. Then Reuben and Alex left to help the others with the preparations for the exchange of Simpson and David Finn.

Back at the cellar Stone quickly made it clear that only he and Finn would be directly involved in the exchange.

"Oliver," Alex said. "You have no idea how many people Gray's going to be bringing. If you remember Murder Mountain, it was a lot of guys with submachine guns."

Stone said, "This time we'll have the advantage." He looked at Annabelle. "However, we need someone to lead David out. For a number of reasons, you fit the bill. Are you game?"

Alex stepped between them. "Wait a minute. If

anyone's going in there with you, it's going to be me, not Annabelle."

"She will only be involved in getting David out of the building. We have a way to do that that doesn't involve confrontation with Gray and his men." He looked at Annabelle again. "I know you have a great deal of nerve. But I wouldn't ask you to do this if I could think of any other way." He added quietly, "And you have no reason to help me. I certainly abandoned you in your time of need."

She looked at Stone and then over at Alex. "Well, your handpicked replacement did a pretty good job. So I am game. Where is this all going to go down?"

Finn answered, "The Capitol Visitor Center."

"It's not finished yet," Milton said.

"Which is exactly why we're using it," Stone answered.

Finn explained. "The company I work for has been targeting the visitor center for a penetration. We do that under contract to Homeland Security as a way to evaluate the security of a particular facility. We do penetrations on airports, shipping ports, nuclear reactor facilities; highly sensitive and strategic operations like that."

"But the visitor center isn't even open, like Milton said," Reuben added. "Why would Homeland Security want you to test its defenses now?"

"Because that's exactly what a terrorist might think. Hit it now before it's fully up and running. But the more important reason is that the visitor center is connected by tunnel to both the Capitol building and to the Library of Congress. Terrorists might use that to attack either of those buildings from below ground. I've already done extensive reconnoiters of the visitor center. I have a way to gain access and also a way to get my son out."

"When is all this going to happen?" Annabelle asked.

"Tomorrow night," Stone answered.

Alex said, "But that's the night of the mock terrorist attack on Capitol Hill. We got that notice a while back. The place will be total chaos, Oliver. Ambulances, police, fire trucks, casualties, total bedlam."

"Chaos always makes it easier to escape," Stone noted.

"*If* you escape," Annabelle said. "The two of you are basically going into an unfinished building with limited exits to meet a heavily armed force of government killers led by a guy who sounds about as brilliant and ruthless as they come."

"You've summed it up nicely," Stone said.

"How do you know Gray won't just kill Simpson? He might be pretending to agree to do an exchange and then his men will just kill all of you." They all turned to stare at Milton as he finished speaking. "When you've been around Oliver long enough you do tend to get a bit paranoid."

Stone smiled before answering. "Milton, you're

absolutely right. In fact, I don't think Gray would have any trouble killing Simpson and then blaming it on us. But I do have something he really wants. And I knew he'd ask for it."

"The evidence you used to make him resign," Alex said.

"That's really the only reason he's coming. The orders we have only tie Simpson to the assassinations of Andropov and Chernenko."

"So Gray comes with a lot of firepower and the exchange is made. Once he has what he wants, how are you going to get David and yourselves out of there safely?" Annabelle wanted to know.

"There is a way," Stone said. "And we're going to need help from all of you to do it."

89

Finn's red cell team had prepped a tractor-trailer rig for use on its planned penetration of the visitor center. Those plans had been put on the back burner due to the incident involving Sam. Yet the truck was ready to go and when Finn told Stone about the rig's capabilities, the ex–Triple Six had bluntly replied, "Go get it."

And Finn had, with very little trouble actually since he had the keys to the tractor and access to the secure storage facility where it was housed.

He was now driving the rig through the middle of the capital. As he pulled into the entrance to the visitor center he could see preparations for the mock terrorist attack unfolding all around him.

He brought his truck to a stop in the loading dock alley and hopped out. He wore the requisite uniform and had the proper ID and shipping orders, all phony but good enough to fool a very bored government gunslinger. He showed the manifest to the guard and then popped the back door of the truck. The guard inspected the cargo, even pulling the tops off some of the boxes and peering in before closing them back up.

Finn had arrived here at half past six because he knew the construction workers were scheduled to go off duty promptly at six because of the mock terrorist attack. The next shift came on the following morning. The exchange with Gray would be set for midnight as soon as the call was made two hours from now by Stone. This would give them an opportunity to put their exit plan in place and give Gray very little time to make his own preparations.

Down the street Milton was sitting in a parked car with a cell phone in hand. He was the failsafe. If everything seemed to be going to hell, he was to call the police, the FBI, the fire department and anyone else they could think of. Since they would all be in close proximity, their response time should be very fast, although it still might not be fast enough. Caleb was back at the hiding place keeping watch over Lesya and the rest of the Finn family. Reuben and Alex were nearby, waiting for word from Stone.

"This is going to take some time," Finn told the guard. "I not only have to offload the equipment, but I have to unpack it too. And my helper called in sick."

"How long is long?" the guard asked.

"Probably after midnight before it's all done."

"You better get to it, then," the guard said, walking away without bothering to offer to help.

Finn used a power-driven hand truck to offload the

boxes of HVAC equipment and take it inside the visitor center. Four of the cargo boxes had compartments cleverly concealed in the bottom. Out from one box popped Stone, and from another, Annabelle. From another box they pulled a gagged and bound Simpson. From the fourth box Stone and Finn retrieved their weapons, including sniper rifles that Stone had used when he worked as a Triple Six. Finn looked at them doubtfully.

"They still work just fine," Stone assured him. "Despite their, uh, vintage."

"No night-vision equipment?"

"No."

"Gray's men will have them, state of the art," Finn said slowly.

"I'm actually counting on that."

"And body armor, latest generation."

"I always aim for the head."

They put the bound Simpson behind a crate of ceiling tiles and Finn showed Stone and Annabelle the interior rooms, most of which were unfinished.

Stone stopped at one room and looked up. "Balcony?"

Finn nodded. "This is the Great Hall. It looks down on the main visitors' area. There's also the atrium, the congressional auditorium, exhibition gallery, theaters and dining area."

"I like this room," Stone said firmly as he stared at

the waist-high concrete wall along the balcony. "High ground is always good ground. Now show me where the closest power supply is."

After that was done, Finn led them through a series of doors that ended in a long hall that was closed off. "That's the underground corridor leading to the Capitol. It's totally blocked off for now."

"So how do I get David out of here?" Annabelle asked.

Finn nodded and pointed overhead. "The ventilation ducts. That was going to be the focal point of our penetration. That duct there will carry you directly into the Capitol. I've drawn up a map." He handed it to her and went over various points, including how the duct ended in a small storage room.

"You only have to walk down a short hall and there's an exit door there. It's not guarded and you can open it from the inside. I had an associate go through it when we made an initial penetration. It was a tight fit for him, but he was bigger than you and David. You two should have no problem; you're both very lean."

Stone looked at Annabelle. "That's why you fit the bill. There's no way Reuben or Alex could have fit in there. Caleb and Milton are small enough, but—"

"I know," Annabelle said. "If we run into any problems I can try and talk my way out."

"Alex and Reuben will be stationed near the exit you'll be using. If need be, Alex can use his Secret

Service credentials to get you past any security checkpoints."

"So where do you want me to be, Oliver?" Annabelle said.

"Right here next to the entrance to the ductwork. We'll bring David to you."

She looked at the tall and broad-shouldered Finn and Stone. "But I don't understand. Harry and you obviously can't fit in the ductwork, so how are you two going to get out?"

"Let us worry about that, Annabelle," Stone said.

90

For the next two hours, Stone and Finn choreographed what would happen later that night. Finn was highly experienced when it came to work like this, but he finally had to admit to himself that when it came to killing other people while putting oneself in the best possible position to survive, Oliver Stone was his clear superior.

And then they were as ready as they were going to be. Stone made the call to Gray and then they both took up their positions and waited. Stone knew that Gray would send in an advance guard to recon the place. Sure enough, two hours later, men came sniffing and poking around, with the security guards out front no doubt either tied up or suitably intimidated by the men's badges.

Then the man himself appeared. Carter Gray was looking chunkier than usual. From his sniper's post Stone instantly discerned why: body armor. That didn't bother Stone in the slightest since, as he'd told Finn, he always aimed for the head. People couldn't survive without a brain. Although it did seem that more than a few people in Washington managed to do so quite nicely.

Next to Gray was a man pushing a hand truck with a bag on it. He unzipped the bag and helped the boy out. David Finn was blindfolded and had sound mufflers over his ears. Wobbling, he stood next to Gray, who looked around the vast interior of the uncompleted Great Hall.

"Well," Gray said to the emptiness. "We're here."

Harry Finn walked out into the room, a gagged Simpson in hand. "Give me the boy."

Gray looked mildly annoyed at being talked to in such a manner. "Harry Finn, Lesya and Rayfield's son. You take after your mother more than your father."

"Let me have my son!"

"Where are the orders? And where is my recording?"

Finn pulled a set of papers and a cell phone from his jacket pocket. He held them up. "I want David next to me."

Finn pushed Simpson toward Gray. The senator jogged the last few steps. When he reached Gray the intelligence chief immediately had the gag and hand bindings removed.

The guard pushed David toward his father. Finn hugged his son. "It's okay, Davey, I've got you." He took off the blindfold and sound mufflers.

"Dad!" David said in a trembling voice as he squeezed his father tightly.

Gray held out his hand. "Give them to me. Now!"

Finn tossed the items to him. Gray looked at the orders. "It's hard to believe these have survived all these years."

"Lots of things have survived all these years, including my mother," Finn said as he edged David behind him. He could sense everyone's fingers edging toward triggers.

Gray listened to the recording on the cell phone, then handed it to a man next to him, who placed it in a small electronic device and played it again. He read off the result displayed on an LED screen on the side of the device. "It's the original, copied once."

Stone had given one copy to Gray previously.

Gray smiled, pocketed the cell phone and looked at Finn. "And how is your mother?"

"A widow, thanks to you."

Gray looked around. "John, I know you're out there. Perhaps you have your little ragtag regiment with you. But just so you understand the playing field, I have this place surrounded and sealed shut. And it has been placed off-limits to the police, FBI, Secret Service and anyone else you might be counting on. I'm sure you know there is a mock terrorist attack going on outside right now. That's probably why you selected this place tonight. You no doubt hoped it would help you to escape. But what it does, instead, is ensure that if there is any shooting in here, no one outside will hear it, or if they do, they won't bother to investigate."

As they listened, the sounds of staged sirens, gunfire and bombs exploding, all part of the drill, reached them.

Gray glanced back at Finn. "And you might want to thank this young man, John. He killed Bingham, Cincetti and Cole. You have no way of knowing this, but it was your three former colleagues who were part of the team sent to kill you. They missed, of course, but they did get your wife. Cole claimed he was the one who killed her, but Bingham disputed that. They actually volunteered for the job. I guess you weren't too popular with them."

Only silence greeted this verbal right cross from Gray.

Gray waited a moment and then added, "You also might want to see who else I stumbled on while I was on my way here."

91

Finn's heart sank as he saw Milton being marched in between two of Gray's men.

From behind the concrete parapet on the balcony Stone's finger eased near the trigger of his rifle. He could take both men out before they could harm Milton. The only problem was he didn't know where the rest of Gray's strike team was. He needed to flush them out.

Finn said quietly, "I think that concludes the exchange."

Gray shook his head. "Actually, Harry, it's just starting."

He nodded to his men as he backed out with Simpson. When they reached safety, Simpson called out, "By the way, John, I was the one who ordered the hit on you. No one leaves Triple Six voluntarily. My only regret was we didn't get you then. But good things come to those who wait."

From the balcony Stone stared down at the spot where Simpson was speaking from. The senator was smart enough to have put a thick wall between them.

For an instant Stone's mind went blank, then everything clicked back on. He had a job to do and nothing Simpson could say would interfere with that. He raced over to a large powered winch they'd set up earlier.

On cue, Finn grabbed his son and flung him down, pulling a gun from his waistband and shielding David with his body. The next instant a large object dropped from the rafters. It was a heavy Jersey wall they'd hoisted up earlier. Stone had just let it go and hustled back to his shooting position.

The barrier hit its mark perfectly, landing a foot in front of Finn and his son. The impact nearly broke it in half but they immediately took cover behind it.

Gray's two men took aim at Milton, the easiest target. Before their fingers could squeeze the triggers, two rounds from Stone's weapon fired a second apart killed them.

Next to Stone was a long electrical cord attached to a power strip. He hit a button and the entire room went black.

Stone raced down from the balcony. He had memorized the number of steps and turns, so the darkness didn't slow him much. He dropped on top of a flat roller that they'd found in a storage room, the kind that mechanics use to glide under cars. He slid across the floor of the Great Hall, heading toward Milton. The original plan had been to get Finn and his son out this way. But Milton was in the most immediate danger.

He called out, "Finn! Cover!"

Finn immediately started laying down fire.

As he rolled along, Stone blinked rapidly, making his eyes adjust to the absence of light. He hit one dead body, his fingers snagging the NV goggles off the dead man's belt. As he put them on he said, "Milton!"

"Over here," Milton answered weakly.

Stone powered on the goggles and looked to his right. Milton was lying there, his hands over his head. The other dead man had fallen on top of him.

Stone asked, "Are you hurt?"

"No."

Stone pulled the body off his friend and, "double-decking" on the roller, they slid across the room toward the stairs to the balcony while Finn emptied two clips from his pistol to cover their escape.

Stone said to Milton, "I'm taking you to Annabelle. She, you and David will get out via a duct that leads to the Capitol. It'll be a tight fit, but you can make it."

"Oliver, I can't go out that way."

"Why not?"

"I've got claustrophobia."

Stone sighed. "All right, then you can leave with me."

"No tight places," Milton said nervously.

"It's all tight places in here, Milton," Stone snapped. "Did you see how many men Gray brought with him?"

"A dozen."

"Then he has ten left."

Stone knew that the next part of their escape involved running through quite a bit of open space. Gray's men were certainly watching for any sign of them through their NV goggles. Stone was actually counting on that. The goggles were wonderful tools, but they had one Achilles' heel.

Stone pulled off his goggles, tensed and then hit the button on the power strip again. Lights blazed on all over. He heard voices calling out in pain. Gray's men. When bright lights came on and you were caught wearing your NV goggles, the result was you wouldn't be seeing anything except hot stars for at least a minute.

He and Milton ran for it.

No sooner had they gotten behind cover than Gray's men recovered and opened up with overwhelming firepower. Stone left Milton and raced off again. Finn and his son were still behind the barrier, pinned down by fire. Stone grabbed the motorized hand truck full of commercial HVAC equipment and made his way to Finn and David. The bullets fired by Gray's men bounced off the heavy metal.

With this shield they made their way back to relative safety and collected Milton. They sprinted down the hall and through a series of doors, handing a terrified David off to Annabelle.

Annabelle saw Milton and said, "My God, what are you doing here?"

"Long story and no time to tell it," Stone said.

"You and David can get out through the ducts. Milton will come with us."

Finn hugged his crying son, who kept his arms tightly around his father.

Finally Finn eased the boy off and told David he had to go with Annabelle. "You have to help your mom," he said. "I'll be there as soon as I can."

"Dad, they're going to kill you. They're going to."

"I've been in tougher spots than this, believe me," Finn said, managing a smile.

Annabelle looked at Stone, took his hand and squeezed it. "Don't die, Oliver. Please don't die."

They helped her and David into the duct. Finn led Stone and Milton to another tunnel paralleling the one they had been in. It had been put in in case construction workers had to evacuate the place and they couldn't get out for some reason through the visitor center's exit.

They came to a stop at a secured door. Stone shot the lock off, and Finn opened the door, revealing a long passageway.

"That'll take us to the Jefferson Building," Finn said.

Stone nodded. "Caleb told me how to get out of the Jefferson without anyone seeing us. Harry, you go first, Milton in the middle and I'll bring up the rear."

Milton peered down the long, dark corridor. "Are you sure it's safe?"

"As safe as—"

Stone never knew where the shot came from. He

barely heard it. He never saw Finn raise his gun and fire. He never saw the sniper fall.

All he saw was the look on Milton's face. The eyes widened slightly, as though he was only mildly surprised. Then he dropped to his knees, still looking up at Stone. The blood started dripping from his mouth. He only said one word: "Oliver?"

Then Milton Farb dropped face-first to the hard floor, his body twitched once and he lay still, the large hole dead center of his back oozing red.

Stone had seen many wounds just like that one, all of them fatal.

Milton was dead.

Finn stared down at the body. "My God."

Stone knelt down, lifted his friend's body up, carried it over to a corner and placed him gently down. He closed the blank eyes and put the small, slender hands over the still chest. Then he rose, clenched his weapon and walked past Finn without a word. He wasn't heading toward safety. He was heading back to the visitor center.

Harry Finn eyed the door to the Jefferson Building and freedom. His son was safe. He could join him in a short time if he left now. This wasn't his fight anymore. John Carr had killed his father. What did he owe the man?

Everything. He saved me, my mother and my son. I owe him everything.

He gripped his gun and raced after Oliver Stone.

92

It wasn't mild-mannered, middle-aged cemetery caretaker Oliver Stone who strode out into battle that night. It was a killing machine called John Carr, thirty years younger, with all the skills and ferocity of a lifetime spent ending other people's lives in ways unimaginable to most people. He used every one of those skills that night. And yet there seemed a greater power at work. Bullets that should have ended his life numerous times missed by less than an inch. Disaster that should have struck never did. Maybe it was finally his time for justice. He only thought about that later. Tonight, he just killed. And the unfinished visitor center ran red with blood. Finn had killed only one more man. Stone had finished off the other six, two with shots that Finn had never seen anyone make before. He still couldn't fathom how Stone had done it. It seemed the man had simply willed the bullets to find their marks.

To Stone, there was another explanation as to how he had survived. Undoubtedly, Gray's men were younger, stronger, faster, superbly trained. These days they always had overpowering force before they attacked. They had killed thousands of times—in practice.

It was altogether different when one did it for real. And counting Vietnam, Stone had probably killed more people than all of Gray's men combined. And he had never had overpowering force. He had often only had himself. That just made you better than the other guy.

When the last man had dropped, Finn and Stone left via the emergency exit, reaching the Jefferson Building and leaving from there as Caleb had told them. An anguished Stone carried Milton's body over his shoulder. While he waited behind some bushes with the body, Finn managed to sneak out and snare a spare EMT uniform from a body recovery truck stationed near the epicenter of the mock terrorist attack. Next he spotted an ambulance that was parked near the library with the keys still in the ignition. A few minutes later Milton's body was loaded into the ambulance by Stone and Finn on a gurney, a sheet placed over his face. With all the chaos going on everywhere around them, no one could tell a fake corpse from a real one. With Stone riding in the back, Finn drove away, the ambulance lights flashing.

Finn glanced in the rearview mirror. Stone was sitting next to his friend, his head hanging down. He had not escaped the battle unscathed. A bullet had sliced through his right arm, leaving a bloody gash.

Another had left a crease on the left side of his head. The man took no notice of them. Finn had had to bandage them up using gauze and tape from the ambulance's supplies while Stone had just stared down at his dead friend.

Stone lifted the sheet, took Milton's still warm hand in his and squeezed it. He started mouthing words that Finn could not hear clearly, but he instinctively knew what the man was saying.

"I'm sorry, Milton. I am so sorry."

A tear trickled down from Stone's weathered face and dropped onto the sheet.

Finn didn't want to break into this very private moment but he had no choice. "Where do you want to take Milton?"

"Home. We're taking him home, Harry."

Leaving the ambulance about three blocks from the house, they carried Milton's body through the woods at the rear of his neighborhood. Stone placed him gently in his bed and turned to Finn.

"Give me a minute."

Finn nodded and respectfully withdrew from the room.

Stone was a man who had suffered more heartbreak in life than any human being should have to. He had done so stoically, trying to look ahead rather than focusing on the past. Yet as he gazed down at his friend's body, every memory of every personal tragedy in his life came charging at him from the darkness.

And for one of the very few times in his life, Oliver Stone sobbed without restraint. He cried so hard his knees buckled and he ended up on the floor, his body curled tight like a child in distress, suffering the anguish of a million nightmares that had collected inside him all these decades, nightmares that had suddenly been released, like the crush of water over a collapsed dam.

Thirty minutes later he had no more tears left to shed. Stone rose and touched his friend's face with his hand. "Good-bye, Milton."

93

After the exchange, Gray and Simpson had left the Capitol area quickly.

Simpson said, "How soon will you know when Carr and Lesya's son are dead?"

"Anytime now. You know, it was quite ballsy of you to confess to Carr that you were the one who ordered his execution."

"I didn't want him to die without knowing. It would have left me unfulfilled."

"Still, I wouldn't have done it," Gray said.

Simpson took the old orders from Gray and studied them. "The world is better off because of what we did."

"I agree. Two dead Soviet leaders. We cleared the way for peace."

"We never got the credit we deserved, though."

Gray said, "That's because it wasn't authorized. We took matters into our own hands."

"Patriots have to do what they have to do. So what now?"

"The orders and this cell phone will be destroyed." He took the papers back from Simpson.

"What's on the cell phone? I couldn't hear."

"Be glad you couldn't, Roger. Otherwise, I would've had to kill you too."

Simpson stared at him with an incredulous expression. "You're joking."

"Of course I am," Gray lied.

At four o'clock in the morning, Carter Gray received the news. His men had been wiped out. Carr and Finn had escaped. Carr, the killing machine, obviously hadn't lost his touch. He immediately called Simpson.

"Well?" Simpson asked.

"Just like we planned, Roger. Carr and Finn are dead. There'll be nothing in the news. We'll cover it all up."

"Excellent. Now we can finally put this behind us."

Gray hung up. *Right.*

He met with the president later that day after he had taken care of sanitizing the visitor center.

The commander in chief was not particularly happy about these events. "What the hell happened there last night? I was told they found blood in there and evidence of a gun battle."

"Sir, we were able to track down John Carr and Lesya's son at the visitor center."

"My God, in the middle of the Capitol!"

"I have no idea how they got in there, but they

did. We received a tip, went down there with a detachment of paramilitary and had a very intense shoot-out."

"And what the hell happened?"

"The appropriate people were terminated," Gray said vaguely.

"Did we take any casualties?"

"Yes, unfortunately. Families are being notified."

"Where are the bodies?"

"We're having them flown overseas for discreet disposal. We have to keep this hush-hush, sir. The press would have a field day with all this."

"Look, Carter, I am the president. I want to know what all *this* is. And I want to know right now."

Gray sat back. He had of course been expecting this. He pulled the orders from his pocket. He'd destroyed the cell phone, but these orders were too valuable. Valuable principally because they didn't have his name on them.

The president read through the documents. "Roger Simpson?"

Gray nodded. "Let me tell you the entire story, sir." It was mostly fabrication, but Gray delivered it with such authority and assurance that when the president sat back, it was clear he accepted all of it as truth.

"And Lesya and Rayfield Solomon's involvement?" the president asked. "Solomon has been labeled a traitor to this country. Was he? If not, we have to make this right, somehow."

Gray hesitated. "I cannot say with assurance that he was a traitor, sir."

"But you said he was terminated. You said he was a traitor."

"Back then it seemed clear that he was. Now, perhaps less so. I have to investigate further."

"You do that, Carter. You do that. And if the truth is that this man was innocent, we will make it right, do you understand?"

"I'd have it no other way. Ray Solomon was my friend."

"My God, two Soviet leaders assassinated by this country. I can't believe it."

"Not many of us could, sir."

"You're saying you didn't know?" the president asked sharply.

Gray chose his words carefully. "Things operated differently back then. We had evidence of Soviet plots to kill U.S. presidents from time to time, but we took measures to counter them. The truth couldn't come out because it might have led to nuclear war. They were never official plots of the Soviet leadership, you have to understand, but the Cold War was played for all it was worth."

"So who the hell ordered the assassinations of Andropov and Chernenko?"

"The orders didn't come through me."

"Are you telling me that Roger Simpson, who if I recall was merely a case agent, did this on his own?"

"No, not at all. He never would have done something like that by himself. He must have received authorization from higher channels."

"Channels that circumvented you? Why? You were his superior, were you not?"

"Not for all matters, sir. And my feelings on assassinations of foreign leaders was clear. There was an executive order making it illegal, and that was where I drew the line."

"Well, perhaps I should talk to Roger about this directly."

"I'm not sure that's wise, sir. He's going to make his own run for the White House. He's a fellow party member of yours. You start making inquiries, then there're leaks to the press and eventually everything comes out. As you know it's much harder these days to keep secrets."

"Damn whistleblowers; yes, I know."

"And what would Senator Simpson say? His signatures are on these orders. He will claim that higher-ups ordered the killings. He might even say I knew about it. You can hardly blame him for trying to cover his tracks. But the matter is over. Two men were killed. Illegally? Probably. Did the result justify the means? I think humanity would judge that it did.

I say we let sleeping dogs lie, Mr. President. Just let sleeping dogs lie."

"I'll think about it, Carter. But keep me informed of further developments."

"One more thing, sir."

"Yes."

"I'd like to come back to work. As the intelligence chief. I want to serve my country again."

"Well, as you know, that slot is presently unfilled. So it's yours if you really want it. I doubt the Senate will have any problem confirming a Medal of Freedom winner."

"I really want it, Mr. President."

He shook Gray's hand. "I appreciate your frankness today, Carter. You're a true patriot. Wish we had more like you."

"I'm only doing my job, sir." Actually, Gray was thinking that with Carr still out there, he wanted to be surrounded by as many heavily armed men as possible.

"You know, I believe you'd make a good president."

Gray laughed. "Thank you, sir, but I don't think I have the right qualifications." What Gray left unsaid was he believed he was *overqualified* for the job. Plus, he wanted a position with *real* power. All a president could really do was start wars, and those came along all too infrequently. Other than that, the office was fairly impotent, Gray felt.

He left the White House and climbed into his chopper. As it rose into the air, he knew he should feel good, victorious. Yet he didn't. In fact, he had rarely felt this depressed in his life.

94

Oliver Stone didn't attend Milton's funeral, though most of the others were present and grief-stricken. Caleb was so distraught at his friend's death that Alex and Annabelle had to hold him upright. Harry Finn had wanted to come but he was still in hiding with his family.

Alex had checked in with his supervisor and had found that all of his problems had gone away. "I don't know what the hell it was all about," the supervisor said, "and I don't think I want to know."

They all gathered a week later at Caleb's condo to honor Milton's memory. This time Finn came with Lesya.

"I can't believe Oliver missed Milton's funeral," Reuben said, staring down into his beer. "Can't believe it," he said again, his eyes red.

Annabelle looked at Alex. "No word from him at all?"

Alex shook his head. "Harry, you were the last one to see him. Did he say anything about where he was going? What he was going to do?"

Finn shook his head. "I know he blames himself for Milton's death."

Caleb said angrily, "And I read in the paper where Carter Gray is going to be the head of the intelligence community again. Isn't that just wonderful? We all know what he's done. We know, but we have no proof." He slumped down in a chair and stared at a photo of Milton that he'd placed on a shelf for all to see. Tears slid down his fat cheeks.

Finn said, "My family and I will have to leave the country, somehow. Gray won't stop until he gets us."

"I think not. It is time to end this foolishness."

All eyes swung around to Lesya, who sat in one corner.

From her bag she pulled an item, a very unusual object for an elderly woman to be carrying around. It was a bear.

"My granddaughter's beloved bear. My beautiful Susie's bear that I gave her when she was very little."

Everyone simply stared at her, no doubt wondering if she had at that very instant lost her mind.

"It is with Susie's permission that I do this." She took a small penknife from her purse and cut the stitching holding the bear together. She parted the seam, reached in and pulled out a small box.

"I had a craftsman in Russia make it for me." She took out a key, unlocked the box and took out a thumb-size electronic device with a USB port. "Does anyone here have a computer?"

The scene on the computer screen was a small sparsely furnished room. Four people were seated around a wooden table. A younger Lesya and Rayfield Solomon were on one side. Across from them was Roger Simpson as a young man. And next to Simpson was another man who hadn't really changed all that much.

"Carter Gray," Alex said.

Lesya nodded. "It was Rayfield's idea to secretly film this. The mission was so monumental, you see."

As they watched the four discussed the assassination. It seemed that Andropov had already been killed, and they were now focusing on Konstantin Chernenko as the only man standing in the way of Gorbachev's rise to power.

"You did wonderfully the first time, Ray and Lesya," Gray was saying. "There wasn't the slightest doubt that Andropov died from natural causes."

"There are certain poisons that leave no trace," Lesya commented. "And there are those high up in the Soviet Union who were not sad to see poor Yuri go."

"Perhaps it will be the same with Chernenko," Simpson said, "now that he's been named the general secretary."

Gray cut in. “But wait a bit. At least a year. It will allow us time to arrange things on our end and cut down on suspicion. All roads now point to Gorbachev taking power after Chernenko dies.”

“If we wait, Konstantin may accommodate us without poison. He is not a well man,” Solomon pointed out.

“So we give it a year,” Gray said again. “Then if he’s still alive, you and Lesya can make sure he isn’t living much longer.”

“And the director and the president are on board with this too?” Solomon asked.

Simpson answered, “Absolutely. They see it as critical to world peace and the destruction of the Soviet Union. As you know, there are many on the Soviet side who want this too.”

Gray was beaming. “You’ll both be heroes,” he said. He turned to Lesya. “Your coming over to our side has made all the difference. If there is peace between the U.S. and what’s left of the Soviet Union, it will be in large measure because of you. And though it can never be made public, you will have earned the eternal gratitude of your adopted nation. You and Ray have risked your lives countless times on behalf of this country and I bring a message directly from the president that he expresses his heartfelt gratitude for all that you’ve done for America.”

The film ran for a few more minutes and then stopped. Lesya said, “I have never seen any human beings who could lie as well as your Carter Gray and Roger Simpson. Next to them, I was but a rank amateur."

"Why the hell didn't you show us this before?" Alex demanded.

"When you gave us the written orders?" Finn added.

"Only fools give up all they have on the first go-round. You keep something back always. I had the film saved and put on this device before I placed it inside the bear and gave it to Susie."

"My God, people died, Milton died," Caleb said in a hushed tone.

"I could do nothing about that," she said simply. "If we had given them this too, where would we be? People would still be dead. Your friend would still be dead. And we would have nothing."

"But what do we do with this?" Alex said.

"I want to meet with Carter Gray."

"What!" Finn exclaimed.

"Gray and I must sit down face-to-face."

"What if he won't?" Alex said.

Lesya smiled. "Let me talk to him on the phone. Then he will see me."

95

"It's been a long time, Lesya," Gray said as the two sat across from each other. They were in a motel room in Fredericksburg, Virginia. "You've changed quite a bit," he added politely.

"Given recent events it is clear that you haven't changed at all."

"You said on the phone that you had something I needed to see?"

"I know you have men outside. You always have men outside, Carter."

"Yes, in my line of work one has to take precautions. The thing you wanted to show me? I don't have a lot of time."

Lesya opened the laptop computer she'd brought with her. Gray sat watching it until the screen went dark. He looked over at her.

"Was the film Rayfield's idea?"

"Yes."

"If he suspected the truth, why did he carry out the plan?"

"He was loyal. You were not. But he really did it

to protect me. He knew how vulnerable I would be. He at least had the cover of the Americans. I had nothing."

"What happened to you and Rayfield was something that I've always deeply regretted, Lesya. In many ways he was the best friend I ever had."

"He trusted you, Carter. I did not, but he did. It was Simpson he was always wary of."

"He was a good judge of character." Gray sat forward, seeming eager to finally tell the truth. "Lesya, I did not order his death. That was Roger's doing. I never would have done that to Ray. Never. I was furious when I found out, but there was nothing I could do. And I tried with all my might to have Ray's name removed from the Wall of Shame at CIA. But Roger had fixed that up too neatly. He had built a very convincing story of Ray's treason. And with Ray dead, and unable to defend himself, there was nothing I could do."

"I don't want your explanations, Carter. What's done is done. Nothing can bring my husband back."

"But the right result was achieved. You of all people understand what that meant for the world. Ray would have understood that."

"Oh yes, he would. But my husband died. And his name is now synonymous with traitor in the country of his birth. He died for his country and they call him a traitor. This I cannot live with."

"If there had been anything I could do about that,

I would have. But my hands were tied. If I exposed Roger, I would have exposed myself. He knew that. He may be dishonorable, but he's not stupid."

"So you would not expose yourself to save the reputation of *your* 'best' friend? You would not give up your career to do that? Rayfield might have been your best friend, but you were clearly not *his* friend."

"I admit that I was weak and selfish not to give myself up for Ray."

"Yes, you were," she said bluntly. "So the assassinations were not authorized by your government? It was you and Simpson and a few others. None in political leadership positions. I know you won't answer my question, but it is the truth. I've had many decades to think about it." She sat back and studied him. Gray's normally confident demeanor had faded markedly.

He said, "Roger was afraid that if Ray found out the plan wasn't authorized he would have exposed him. And the truth is Ray would have. Regardless of the damage it would have done to him personally."

"That is exactly right. My husband was an honorable man. And yet he was murdered and Roger Simpson has a fine career as a senator of this country."

"Lesya, you know how things were back then."

With a wave of her hand, she cut him off. "Things back then were exactly the same as they are today. Nothing has changed except the people. And the people who play these games are all the same. They talk of doing good, of making the world a better place. That is all bullshit. It is about power and about protecting their interests. That is all it is ever about. Always!"

Gray sat back. "So what do you want? I'm sure you've thought about that too over all these decades."

"Oh yes, I have thought about it. And I know exactly what I want. And I have been waiting to tell you for thirty years, you son of a bitch. And you're going to sit there and listen. And then you're going to do *exactly* as I say."

When she had finished, Gray rose to go. "Can I expect to have the original of that film and all copies in return for doing what you've asked?"

"No, you cannot. You only have my word that I will take it to my grave. And you and Simpson should consider yourselves fortunate. I could destroy you both. Nothing would make me happier. But I am a person who actually thinks of things besides my own happiness. And that is the only thing that has saved you and the miserable Simpson. Now leave me. I do not want to see you again. Oh, but you can tell the good senator something for me."

"What's that?"

"I've heard he wants to be president."

"Yes, he intends on running."

"Well, you can tell him to rethink his plans. Unless

he wants to explain the contents of that film to the American people. You will tell him that."

"I will. Good-bye, Lesya. And for what it's worth, I'm sorry."

With another wave of her hand she dismissed a man who would shortly be running America's intelligence empire once more.

Rayfield Solomon's picture was taken down from the Wall of Shame at CIA. A bogus reason was given for his revised history. It was hidden under the rubric, "New evidence coming to light." And then the CIA classified the evidence. Scholars might get a shot at it in a hundred years or so. Solomon was then posthumously given the CIA's highest award for fieldwork. Never again would his name be spoken in the same sentence as traitor.

Lesya Solomon was awarded the Medal of Freedom, the first time it had been given to a former Russian spy. Again the reasons for this were classified, but it still made the national news. She even gave an interview praising the progress in American-Russian relations. She finished by saying that she wished her heroic husband, who did so much to end the Cold War, could have lived to see it. She refused all other interviews and once more disappeared.

Not surprisingly, Gray's nomination to be the intelligence chief sailed through the Senate. A chopper flew him from his highly secure Maryland retreat to his office in Virginia every day. His life was once again filled with clandestine activities, hard decisions that influenced the entire world. One word from Carter Gray and nations trembled, it was said. The man was in his element once more.

But for those who knew him well, he had changed. The overpowering personality, the absolute intolerance for the smallest mistake, the stunning confidence front and center all these years had diminished. He was seen sitting in his office from time to time staring at the wall, an old photo in his hands. No one had ever seen what that picture was, because he kept it locked in a safe.

In the photo Lesya, Rayfield Solomon and Carter Gray were decades younger and looked happy and full of life. They were doing exciting work, risking their lives so that billions could live in peace. In those countenances one could see the friendship, even the love that had formed among them. Sitting there staring at that photo, Carter Gray would occasionally cry.

96

Six months passed and no one had heard a word from Oliver Stone. Caleb returned to work at the library, but the old books that had given him so much pleasure now seemed just like, well, old books. Reuben went back to work at the loading dock and then came home and sat on his couch, beer in hand, and yet he never drank any of it. He would pour it down the sink and go to bed.

With one member dead and its leader having disappeared, the Camel Club seemed officially disbanded.

Harry Finn rejoined his red cell team and started doing work for Homeland Security again. Because of Lesya's demand and the evidence she held, it was certain that Carter Gray would make no move against him or his family ever again. And it was also certain that Finn would never stand trial for killing three men and attempting to kill Carter Gray.

Yet Finn did not have the soul of a killer, and what he had done haunted him. He finally took a six-month leave of absence. He spent all his time with his family, shuttling his kids to school and sports, and holding his wife as she slept. He kept in contact with his mother, but she refused his pleas for her to come and live with them. He wanted to come to know her in a way that didn't involve secrets and plotting violent deaths, but his mother apparently didn't want this. If this wounded Finn, he did not show it.

Annabelle could have left D.C. and spent the rest of her life living on the millions she'd conned from Bagger, but she didn't. After she and Alex finished explaining things to the FBI about Bagger and Paddy Conroy, an explanation that left out any details of Annabelle's multimillion-dollar rip-off of Bagger, the lady worked another con. The target this time was the church that owned Stone's cottage. She convinced them that she was Stone's daughter and she volunteered to move in and keep the cemetery in decent shape until her father returned from what she described as a much-needed vacation.

She had the place fixed up, brought new furniture in, all while carefully preserving Stone's things. Then she started taking care of the grounds. Alex came by to help her often. They would sit on the porch in the evening.

"Amazing stuff you've done to this place," Alex said.

"It had good bones to start with," Annabelle said.

"Most cemeteries do." Alex gave her a sideways grin. "So you think you might hang around here for a while?"

"I've never really been able to call a place home before. I used to kid Oliver about living in a cemetery but I sort of like it here."

"I can show you around town. If you want."

"Save me, now date me? You're quite the full-service cop."

"All in the line of duty."

"Right. I'm the con, remember? That's my line."

"Let's make that 'retired' con, okay?"

"Absolutely." For once she didn't sound that convincing.

They sat back in their chairs and looked out over the tombstones. "Do you think he's still alive?" she asked.

"I don't know. I hope so, but I just don't know."

"Will he come back, Alex?"

He said nothing, because only Oliver Stone could make that decision. He had to want to come back. And with each passing day Alex was growing more certain that he would never see his old friend again.

97

When Carter Gray had informed Roger Simpson of Lesya's demand, the senator's initial response had been predictable.

"There must be something we can do," Simpson had wailed. "I've worked my whole life to make this run for the White House." He eyed Gray hopefully.

"I don't see what can be done," Gray replied.

"You know where she is? If we can—"

"No, Roger. Lesya has suffered enough. This is about more than you or me. She gets to live out what's left of her life in peace."

It was clear from Simpson's expression that he was not in agreement with this. Gray gave him one more warning to leave it alone and then left.

Months passed and still Simpson brooded. Solomon's name cleared. Lesya given a medal! Gray was back in power. It was all so unjust. This all gnawed at the man, making him even more morose and insufferable than usual. Indeed, his wife started spending more time in Alabama; friends and colleagues avoided him.

In the predawn hours one morning Simpson sat moodily in his bathrobe, which he typically did, after retrieving the newspaper from outside the front door of his condo. His wife was visiting friends in Birmingham. That had been another thing that had infuriated him. No one had kidnapped his wife. That simply had been a bluff that Finn and Carr had used to get him to go quietly. Once out of his office and away from the bomb he could have had Carr arrested immediately. Only he had been too afraid. This just made him angrier.

Well, he'd really had the last laugh. Both Finn and John Carr were dead. Simpson had not bothered to check up on Finn, and Carr *had* vanished. Yet it was also true that he would now only be a senator, his shot at the Oval Office gone. The destruction of his lifelong dream made Simpson throw his cup of coffee against the wall.

He slumped down at the kitchen table and stared out the window into the darkness; the sun was still hours away from making its creep up the wall of the eastern seaboard.

"There must be a way, there must be," he told himself. He could not let a former Russian spy, who by all rights should be dead, deny him the highest office in the land, an office he felt he was predestined to hold.

He sighed, opened his paper and froze.

Staring back at him was a photo that had been

taped inside the front page of the newspaper he was holding.

As he stared at the picture of the woman, it suddenly occurred to him who she was.

Then her head disappeared. Left in its place was a large hole. Simpson gasped and then looked down at his chest. Blood was pouring out of it from where the bullet had entered after passing through the newspaper and neatly obliterating the identity of the woman. By any standard, it was a hell of a shot.

His eyes started to flutter as he stared out the window where the glass had been cracked by the bullet. He looked at the shell of the building across the street, the one that had never been finished. As he pitched forward, dead, onto his kitchen table, the thought did occur to Simpson of who had just killed him.

98

In quickly rebuilding Carter Gray's cliffside house overlooking the Chesapeake Bay, great pains had been taken in ensuring that the intelligence chief would be safe and secure. This goal, obviously, included preventing someone from blowing up the place a second time. With that in mind, and taking into account some of Oliver Stone's observations, the windows were all now made from bulletproof glass and the gas regulator was no longer accessible from the outside. The guards still slept in the cottage near the main house and the underground chamber and escape tunnel had been rebuilt as well.

Gray rose early and went to bed late every day. He put many miles on his personal chopper that landed in the rear grounds at all hours. He had a private jet at his disposal that carried him to hot spots all over the world. He knew that he would retire in a few years with his reputation intact as one of his country's greatest public servants, and that meant a lot to the man.

The storm was fast approaching from the bay; the rumbles of thunder reached Gray's ears as he dressed in his bedroom. He checked his watch; it was six o'clock in the morning. He would have to hurry a bit. There would be no chopper ride today; the winds were too strong and unpredictable and lightning was already starting to flash across the sky.

He climbed into a three-SUV motorcade; his vehicle was in the middle. A driver and guard were in his Escalade; the other two SUVs carried six armed men in total.

As the cars pulled out of the estate and onto the road, the rain began to sprinkle lightly. Gray studied a briefing book open on his lap in preparation for his first meeting this morning, but his thoughts truly were elsewhere.

John Carr was still out there.

The motorcade slowed to round a curve and that's when Gray saw it. He rolled down the window to get a better look.

Set into the grass next to the road was a tombstone with a small American flag stuck into the ground in front of the white grave marker. They were exactly like the ones used at Arlington National Cemetery.

An instant later, Gray realized what he had just done. Before he could even scream, the round from the long-range rifle slammed into the side of his head, ending his life.

The armed men exploded out of the truck, guns drawn and swinging in all directions. Yet there was nothing to see, no shooter to kill.

As several guards sprinted in the direction of where the shot probably had come from, another one opened the passenger-side door and a bloodied Carter Gray slumped out, still encased in his seat belt.

"Son of a bitch," muttered the guard, before punching in a number on his cell phone.

99

Oliver Stone had shot Gray from such a long distance away that he did not need to sprint away from the man's bodyguards. In truth, he had made even more difficult shots in his career, but none that meant more to him. He made his way slowly back through the woods to the dead man's home. As he walked along the rain started coming down harder, and the flashes of lightning and accompanying cracks of thunder picked up their pace.

He'd killed Simpson from the unfinished building across the street, his sniper rifle perched on an oil drum. The photo Stone had taped inside the newspaper was of his wife, Claire. He wanted Simpson to know. He'd placed the photo at a precise spot on the page, gauged his shot accordingly, leaving behind no evidence of who was in the picture.

Stone had driven here right after the shooting because he had to kill Gray before Simpson's murder was discovered and Gray went deep into hiding. He'd checked the forecast the night before. The approaching storm front from offshore was critical. Choppers didn't take off in such weather. That limited Gray to his motorcade. Stone had set the tombstone and flag by the side of the road, certain that even a cautious man like Gray would roll down the window to get a good look at it. That few seconds was all Stone had needed. With his scope and trusty rifle, and killing skills that one never really lost no matter how many years passed, it was a near certainty that he would get his man. And he had.

He skirted the edge of Gray's property, his gait steady but unhurried. He knew Gray's men would be coming soon, but in many ways he'd waited his entire adult life for this moment. He did not intend to rush it.

He reached the edge of the cliff and looked down at the dark water far below. Racing through his mind was the image of a young man very much in love, holding his wife in one arm, his baby girl in the other. The world seemed to be theirs. Their potential seemed unlimited. And yet how very limited it had all become. Because the next mental image was one of John Carr killing as he ran from one brutal murder to the next over a span of a decade.

He had built his life on lies, deception and swift, violent death with "government authorization" as his sole justification. In the end it had cost him everything.

He had lied to Harry Finn that day in the nursing home. He'd told Finn that he, John Carr, was different from the likes of Bingham, Cincetti and Cole. Yet he really wasn't. In many ways, he was *just* like them.

He turned and walked away from the edge. Then John Carr whipped around and ran straight toward the edge and over it. He sailed out into space with his arms spread wide, his legs splayed. It was thirty years ago and he had just killed another man. It was a successful hit, only there were dozens of men intent on killing him. He had run like the wind; no one could catch him. Faster than a deer he was. He had run straight to the edge of a cliff three times as high as this one and without a second thought had jumped into nothing but air. He had plummeted down, bullets raining all around him. He'd hit the water cleanly, come up and lived to kill another day.

As the water rushed toward him, Carr's arms and legs came together in perfect form. Some things you just never forgot. Your brain didn't need to send a message; your body just knew what to do. And for most of his life, John Carr had known just what needed to be done.

An instant before he hit the water, Oliver Stone smiled, and then John Carr disappeared beneath the waves.

AUTHOR'S NOTE

DON'T READ THIS UNTIL YOU'VE FINISHED THE BOOK

Hope you enjoyed *Stone Cold.* One note so people won't e-mail telling me I made a glaring mistake: I've played with the time-line, putting Yuri Andropov and Konstantin Chernenko in office as heads of the Soviet Union so it would match Oliver Stone's career as a government assassin. As a fiction writer, I have full latitude to do so. It's an entitlement actually granted to me by the Novelist's Bill of Rights, under the subsection "Why Bother with the Truth When You Can Just Make It Up?" It was duly enacted by Congress, an august body that has enviable experience in same.

ACKNOWLEDGMENTS

To Michelle, the ride continues, and there's no one else I could ever do it with.

To Mitch Hoffman, here's to the first of many.

To Aaron Priest, Lucy Childs, Lisa Erbach Vance and Nicole Kenealy, who let me focus on writing. And for always giving it to me straight.

To David Young, Jamie Raab, Emi Battaglia, Jennifer Romanello, Martha Otis and all the wonderful folks at Grand Central Publishing, for being with me every step of the way. New name, same great people.

To David North, Maria Rejt and Katie James at Pan Macmillan, for leading me to the top across "the Pond."

To Grace McQuade and Lynn Goldberg, on a great new partnership. Thanks for all your hard work. It really paid off.

To Shane Drennan, for all your expert advice. I hope I did it justice.

I owe the craps table scene to Alli and Anshu Guleria and Bob and Marilyn Schule. Thanks, guys. See you in Vegas.

Stone Cold

To Deborah and Lynette, the stellar Starship *Enterprise* crew.

And to the millions of Camel Club fans for seeing light when others only saw the darkness.